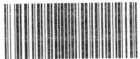

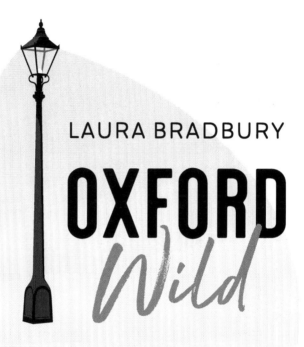

LAURA BRADBURY

OXFORD *Wild*

BOOKS BY LAURA BRADBURY

GRAPE SERIES

My Grape Year

My Grape Québec

My Grape Christmas

My Grape Paris

My Grape Wedding

My Grape Escape

My Grape Village

My Grape Cellar

THE COOKBOOK BASED ON THE GRAPE SERIES MEMOIRS THAT READERS HAVE BEEN ASKING FOR!

Bisous & Brioche: Classic French Recipes and Family Favorites from a Life in France

by Laura Bradbury and Rebecca Wellman

THE WINEMAKERS TRILOGY

A Vineyard for Two

Love in the Vineyards

Return to the Vineyards

Published by Grape Books

Paperback ISBN: 978-1-989784-20-4

eBook ISBN: 978-1-989784-21-1

Visit: www.laurabradbury.com

Oxford Wild is for anyone brave enough to leap out of their comfort zone.

Bravo.

OXFORD
Wild

I decided to apply to read English at the University of Oxford because it was the most impossible thing I could do.

Jeanette Winterson

NOTES TO READER

» In *Oxford Wild* the royal family is fictional, with a King who has three sons.

» The terms at Oxford University are divided into eight weeks. Each week begins on a Sunday.

» The week before the beginning of term is referred to as **Nought Week**.

NOUGHT WEEK

OXFORD UNIVERSITY, BEAUFORT COLLEGE
MICHAELMAS TERM

CHAPTER ONE

Alfie

I whistled as I strolled down Holywell Street on my way to the Bod to do a few hours of research. Whistling was *not* something I was prone to do, but the satisfaction expanding under my sternum had to escape somehow.

My hard work and self-discipline had finally paid off. The head of the literature department of Beaufort College—the admirably strait-laced Professor Edwin Harris—had stopped by my table in Hall as I ate a chicken pot pie for lunch. He asked me if I was interested in taking on the role of an apprentice thesis advisor for the incoming group of MPhil Medieval Literature students.

What a question! Of course I was. It was my dream to become a senior fellow. I was so lucky to have Professor Harris as my mentor. I modeled myself after him—his self-discipline and rigid adherence to propriety. They had taken him far, as I knew they would for me if I stuck the course.

For the first time in a long time, all was right with my world. The early October sky seemed bluer, and the robins chirped an even more lyrical song than usual. Despite what my father always told me, following the rules *had* taken me somewhere, exactly where I wanted to be.

I popped into the newsagent on Broad Street to grab a copy of The Guardian. My happiness flash froze when I caught sight of my father's familiar figure on the cover of the Daily Mirror.

The photo was blurry—no doubt taken with a telephoto lens—but I'd recognize that careless, defiant line of his shoulders anywhere. Beside him was a red-haired woman who was easy to identify as one of the three, very much married, royal princesses. My father's arm was slung around her shoulders, and he appeared to be whispering something in her ear. It didn't take much imagination to presume it was something lewd.

My eyes scanned the other tabloids—The Sun, Daily Mail, The Express—different versions of the same intimate photo of my father and the princess meeting up in Scotland graced all their covers.

The Sun had also included a small, inset photo of the princess's husband—second in line to the throne after his older brother. He was in Patagonia on an expedition to a glacier or some such thing, surrounded by a knot of beefy-looking men.

Acid filled my stomach and left a bitter taste on my tongue. My father's sense of timing was, as always, cruel. He hadn't even called ahead to warn me that the backlash to this would no doubt soon fall on my head.

They were having an affair. I knew my father, so while the tabloids could only speculate, that truth landed in my stomach with absolute certainty. The man had been born without a moral compass—guilt was no impediment to taking what he wanted.

Would Professor Harris see this? My sense of achievement had dried up to become a shriveled, gray thing now. What would he think of me? I knew deep down that he, like all of Oxford, was just waiting for me to make a misstep and show I was truly my profligate father's son.

Perhaps I could call him? No, that would achieve nothing. He would dismiss my concerns with laughter and accuse me, yet again, of being a crashing bore. That familiar ache of being alone with all of this radiated out from my center to the tips of my fingers.

"You going to buy that, sonny?" the newsagent demanded in a rusty hinge of a voice.

I dropped the copy of The Sun I'd been holding like it was on fire. "No. Thank you."

"You're missing out." He chuckled deep in his throat. "That Duke of Invernay is a right rogue, and he'll have the princess's skirts around her ears in a jiff. No disrespect to the royalty, of course."

I barked out a bitter laugh. Did this newsagent truly think he'd eliminated the disrespectful thing he'd said about the princess's skirts by adding "no disrespect" as an afterthought? "I think I'd rather not have that image lodged in my head," I said, even though it was already there.

He let out another crack of laughter. "Mark my words, there will be plenty of rutting going on behind those gates in Scotland, and not the kind that has anything to do with deer if you catch my drift."

Subtlety was clearly not one of this man's strengths, but then to be fair, I remembered with a sharp pain between my ribs, it was not something my father ever chose to indulge in either.

I mumbled good day and, after shutting the newsagent's door firmly behind me, I stood on the pavement. That familiar sensation of being contaminated by my father's grubby behavior made my forehead prickle with shame, while at the same time my insides felt encased in ice. There was no way I could concentrate on my doctoral research now. I turned on my heel towards the Bridge of Sighs, and that little alley underneath that led to my favorite pub, The Turf Tavern.

The Bodleian Library could wait. It had been there since 1602—it was hardly going anywhere. What I needed was a pint and then maybe another to warm me up and make me forget, even for a moment, about the price I always had to pay for my father's disregard for the rules.

CHAPTER TWO

Cedar

Grizzlies I could handle. Same with cougars and stitching up my own leg that time I impaled it on a pointy fir branch. This grumpy man in the weird black hat at the reception area of the college was proving to be a different ball of wax altogether.

I was so thoroughly turned around by the endless travel and the sheer noise of life outside the forest that this surly welcome made my stomach clench with doubt—maybe my father had been right about the outside world not being worth the effort.

"I should be on your list of new students," I insisted.

"Another American," the man grunted under his breath.

"I'm Canadian," I said, louder than necessary. I had nothing against Americans, but I was one hundred percent Canuck. Where I came from, right on the border with Alaska, that meant something.

"What's the difference?" He rolled his dark eyes.

"A lot," I said. "Trust me, Americans would object to that generalization as much as I do."

But instead of admitting his mistake, he lectured me for five minutes about how, if I ever lost my room key, I would basically end up tarred and feathered on Oxford's town square. But did Oxford even have a town square? I'd come here to taste a life that was radically different from what I'd grown up with, but I'd never expected this spinning in my head and adrenaline shooting through my veins like that time I fell through the ice on a frozen lake.

Tears pricked at the corners of my eyes, but I would *not* let this bully of a man see me cry.

I didn't understand any of his instructions about where my room was located, but I had the number, and there was no way in hell I was going to ask him to repeat himself.

When I went outside the Lodge and into the college itself, I felt like I was in a forest of stone. All these buildings and staircases and rock walls ... how was I ever going to find Room Three on Staircase G? Unlike the trees I was used to, the buildings seemed to press down on me with all their weight, making my breath come in ragged jags.

No. I was so close. I couldn't chicken out now.

Up the fourth staircase I tried—it was dark and the letters of the staircases were very hard to see in the dim yellow light cast by the occasional lamp—I finally found my bedroom door.

As I slid my key in the lock, I tried to slow my breathing. Oxford would seem less like a Picasso painting in his cubist phase after some food and a good night of sleep.

I opened up the door into the tiny, dark space, flicked on the light, kicked my brand-new suitcase across the floor on its wheels, and sat down on the edge of my unmade bed. Thank God I'd brought my sleeping bag.

My head felt like it was going to roll off my neck. I dropped it forward into my hands. If only it would stop spinning ... I didn't need first aid. I had shelter. Water couldn't be far away. Food. That was it, I needed food. I hadn't eaten since ... was it the breakfast on the plane before it landed in London? I could barely remember.

I had no idea where to go, but the gnawing of my stomach and the way I still felt like I was on the airplane, tilting to one side and then the other even when I was sitting still, were unarguable signs that sustenance was a priority.

That meant I'd have to face the grumpy man again who worked in that reception area ... what did they call that place again on the Beaufort College map they'd mailed me? *The Lodge.*

The Lodge was described in my student guide as the hub of my life as a Master's student at Beaufort College, Oxford, founded in 1325. However, there had been no mention of a surly man in a weird hat behind the reception desk. Still, I'd built a log cabin by myself, and hunted moose for the family. I could handle him ... surely?

I dragged myself off my bed and tried to swallow around the lump in my throat as I made my way back down to the Lodge.

***

I took a deep breath and straightened my shoulders when I saw he was still there behind his little booth thingy.

It hit me then. I'd handle him like an ornery bear. My parents were world-renowned bear researchers, which is one of the reasons—but far from the only one—why they chose to live amongst *Ursus arctos horribilis* (grizzly bears) and *Ursus americanus* (black bears). The animals had been a constant fixture in my life, and I had learned the hard way that when they got aggressive, boldness was the name of the game.

"You!" I said to the man. His head jerked back a bit, and he arched his left brow.

"What did you just say?" he asked, more confused than belligerent.

Excellent. I'd caught him off guard.

"I need to go find something to eat. Where's the nearest place I can find food?" I demanded, hating the strident inflection of my question, but determined not to show even the smallest sign of weakness.

The man's indignation made him grow at least three inches in height. "You might be a student at Oxford," he said. "But that does not, under any circumstances, give you the right to speak to me in that tone of voice. Whatever some of you students might think, I am not your servant."

Dammit. So that backfired. I'd meant to intimidate him, not insult him. It seemed the laws of the wild didn't cross over to Oxford as well as I'd hoped. The problem was I didn't know any other way, but I was currently in no state to learn. My adaptation skills were completely tapped out after a day of navigating a million times more people that I'd ever seen in my life. My life in our cabin back home consisted of myself, my parents, and a lot of trees.

"I'm sorry," I backtracked, treacherously close to tears. "I just ... I just don't know how to deal with you. I've traveled from so far away and I'm so, so hungry."

He shrunk back down to his normal height. "Well ... don't let it happen again," he said, in a softer tone, looking more closely at my face now.

"I won't," I muttered, my head bowed. I thought I was escaping that gnawing loneliness I could never seem to shake by moving here and being around people, but its sharp teeth sunk into my heart more painfully than ever.

"The Turf Tavern," he said, his voice gruff.

He took a map from underneath his desk, circled something with a red pen, and handed it to me. "Have a pint and a Ploughman's or something." He checked his watch. "Hurry though. Almost last call." He shooed me out the college door and on to the cobblestone street ... or was it a lane? Outside.

Noise came at me again from all directions—honking cars, music coming from somewhere, shrieks and guffaws. I shook my head, missing the whisper of the wind in cedar boughs.

I started to walk in the general direction of the Bridge of Sighs the taxi had driven underneath on the way from the train station to the college. I had read about that landmark in my guide too and was eager to get a better look.

Groups of students staggered along the sidewalk, clinging on to each other and hooting with raucous laughter as they splashed through the puddles made by the steady drizzle. Some were wearing black capes that billowed out behind them like the outstretched wings of a raven.

I dug deep for some optimism. I was going to eat soon, in a real British pub! I'd read about them in the Inspector Morse books and, of course, the Tabard in Canterbury Tales. How many times had I fantasized about this moment? There was so much time to daydream in the woods. I couldn't be put off by the fact my limbs felt like they'd been filled with concrete and the buildings on either side of the street hunched over me.

I peered at the map in my hand. The alley that accessed the pub had to be around here somewhere.

I looked up and saw the iconic Bridge of Sighs spanning the

lane. My breath caught at its beauty. It was even more magical than the pictures, despite the fact it was night. Its faceted panes of leaded windows glittered like diamonds in the yellow light of the streetlamps. A tiny spark of wonder flared under my breastbone. *There.* It hadn't been extinguished completely. I walked a bit farther and stared up at it from the other side.

A wave of shouting filled the street, echoing off the stone walls of the buildings. It was a bunch of people—men—running past me towards a small gap between two buildings that I'd just passed. That had to be the alley to The Turf I'd been searching for, but ... what were they doing?

All at once, I was blinded by flashes of the brightest white light I'd ever seen. Once most of the spots in front of my vision cleared, I saw these men were all carrying cameras with massive flashes attached. They were snapping photos in the same way a commando would fire a machine gun.

Their attention was focused on a man half lying, half crouching on the slick cobblestones.

He was trying to say something, but his words came out garbled—or maybe that was just a weird type of British accent?

One of the photographers bellowed, "What do you think about the news of your father accompanying the princess to Scotland?"

"Go away!" The crouched man's voice was slurred. The poor guy was hammered.

"Are they having an affair?" another photographer yelled. I could see his spittle in the light of the flashes, and my adrenaline kicked in, just the same as when I sensed a threat in the forest.

"Bugger off," the man on the ground spluttered. Where were his friends? Why was he all alone, not to mention drunk, and having to deal with these awful camera people with no help? My parents had told me my whole life that the only person I could depend on was myself, but deep down, I didn't want that to be true.

A few students had stopped, but instead of helping the man on the ground, they were filming him with their phones. They were leaving him to the mercy of this pack of braying animals—wait, I was too. Not understanding what was going on was no excuse for my inaction.

I darted forward. When I reached the man's side, I pulled him up off the ground. *Oof.* Whoever he was, there was a lot of him. He leaned heavily against me.

The photographers began heckling us almost instantly. "Is this your girlfriend?" they demanded. "Is she *saving* you?"

But the stranger wasn't paying attention to them now. He blinked at me through the rain and the strobe light of the flashes. "Who are you?" he asked loudly, tilting his head. *Jesus Murphy.* The malted scent of beer wafted from every one of his pores.

Where could I take him? The only place I knew was back within the doors of my college.

The pack of photographers started shouting louder. "Look at you, young Lord Invernay! Saved by the woman like a damsel in distress. Is that what your father is doing with the princess? Is she saving him?"

"Shut up," the man said, but the photographers paid no attention. "Bunch of twats," he breathed in my ear. He was so close now I caught a whiff of expensive things—oiled leather, wet wool, and pipe tobacco—underneath the prevailing fumes of alcohol.

"Set the record straight—are your father and the princess having an affair?" another one yelled.

I had no idea what the photographers were talking about. A princess? I must have heard that wrong. Sure it was England, but I didn't think the royalty made a habit of hanging around Oxford when they had castles and all that other stuff.

"Come on." I began to drag him down the street towards the huge, curved oak door of Beaufort College. "Let's get you out of here." On closer inspection, he looked close to my age, even though he was easily a head taller than me.

The pack broke up briefly and then reformed under the Bridge of Sighs between me and my escape route. Blood pounded in my ears. I was not used to people, definitely not people who moved in one fluid mass like a pack of attacking wolves. I ran through my options. Maybe the bear aggression technique hadn't worked with the man at the Lodge, but here was a perfect opportunity to test it again.

The trick was to make myself as big and loud and threatening as possible. Some so-called experts instructed people to play dead during bear attacks, but all of us who coexisted with the animals knew that advice was more likely to get you killed, then probably eaten.

I was short, but I knew I needed to make myself as big as possible. I looked wildly around me for a big stick or a branch—those always helped. Nope. Nothing but cobblestones, and not even any loose ones. I'd have to work with what I had.

"Follow my lead," I hissed at the man, but he just stared at me with wild, bewildered eyes. A flash caught us then, lighting his irises. They were the translucent blue-green of a glacier lake. "Make yourself big," I instructed.

"Whasssat?" He squinted at my face, as though trying to bring me into focus.

I gritted my teeth. In any other circumstances, he would seem like quite an amusing drunk, but his charm was no help now.

"Look," I said in the most penetrating voice possible. "It's clear you're hosed, but—"

"Hosed?" He blinked. "What is that word? What's its etymology?"

Amazing. He couldn't pronounce *what's that* but he could perfectly enunciate the word *etymology*. I had indeed arrived in Oxford.

"It means drunk," I said.

"Does it really?" he whispered back at me. "Fascinating."

"Yes, but beside the point. You need to listen to me."

"Listening," he intoned, frowning in concentration, still swaying on his feet.

"I need you to make yourself as big as possible. Copy me. Wave your arms, bare your teeth, growl, yell."

He nodded but kept blinking at me in a way that had me wondering if any of my instructions had penetrated.

"OK, let's do it." I made my free arm as big as possible and stood as high as I could on my toes, deeply regretting my lack of inches. I took the deepest breath of air I could and bellowed, "GET OUT OF MY WAY!"

The photographers between us and the college door didn't do more than scuffle around a bit. I nudged the stranger to join in, but he just stood there, staring at me with his mouth partially open.

Awesome. My plan was going spectacularly well.

I let out my most impressive stream of curse words in the loudest roar I could manage, silently thanking the trappers and fishermen I'd crossed paths with over the years. They'd taught me to swear so proficiently it could incinerate a person's ears.

The mass of photographers fell silent. *Ha! It was working!*

I used their moment of collective shock to hustle the man towards the college door. We were only about twenty feet away when, belatedly, the stranger seemed to pick up on my technique and began swearing at the top of his lungs, albeit in what sounded to my ears like the King of England—a lot of 'bloody this' and 'bugger that'. My swearing was *way* better.

The photographers were jerked back to the present by this, because they began moving in a mass between us and the oak door.

The whir of their flashes firing up overwhelmed the whispers of the crowd.

The man I was trying to get to safety growled and snapped his teeth at them. *Yowza.* He was getting into the spirit of things. The cabal parted like the Red Sea, but clicks, flashes, and shouts dogged us. I could hardly blame them—now the man had picked up my gauntlet he was putting on quite a show.

I dragged him to the door and grabbed the key from my pocket. The growling and swearing seemed to have steadied him. He still wasn't moving quickly, but he stuck close to me and was no longer lurching around.

I pulled him inside the college and slammed the door shut behind us. I rested my back against the solid wood to catch my breath. Well ... I'd come to Oxford to experience something different. That certainly qualified.

The man leaned against the door like me. "Bastards," he groaned.

I could see him better now in the light of the college entrance. He looked like the quintessential Oxford student—the kind that was plastered all over the website and the brochures they'd sent me.

He was tall, broad-shouldered, and wore a navy wool pea coat with a plaid scarf wrapped negligently around his neck. His brown hair was short, although if it grew any longer it looked to me as though it would curl at the ends. His jaw was chiseled, but the saving grace from him looking too perfect was a certain unevenness of his features. Finally, somebody *new*.

Those startling eyes of his studied me. “I was confused,” he said, never taking his eyes off my face. “And a bit lost. Nobody came ... then you did.” His voice cracked on his last word, and my heart thumped oddly.

“I couldn’t leave you like that.” I shook my head. “I wouldn’t leave *anyone* like that. Why were those men taking photos of you?”

He waved his hand and stumbled forward a bit. *Ah*. Still fairly drunk then.

“Swines,” he said, not answering my question, but after a while he turned an angelic smile to me. “But not you. You’re lovely.”

“Um ... thank you?” After who knew how many hours of travel, I felt encased in a coating of grime. “Given the amount of beer you’ve had tonight, I won’t hold you to that.” I had been into Stewart—the small town closest to our cabin in the forest—enough times to know about beer goggles.

He didn’t protest as I steered him towards the Lodge. Despite the grumpy black-hat man, I had to find out where this stranger belonged. Maybe I would even still have time to find food afterwards.

CHAPTER THREE

Cedar

The man in the hat met us at the door to the Lodge with a thunderous expression in his black eyes. I wasn't going to back down this time, even though everything had taken on that surreal quality of extreme fatigue. No matter what he might accuse me about bringing this stranger into the college, I could not leave another human being lying on the street. I braced myself for him to shout at me again.

Instead, he grabbed the stranger's arm, dragged him into the Lodge, and sat him down on the chair behind the glass partition.

"Robbie!" the stranger exclaimed with a sweet smile. "Hullo there." He hiccupped.

Robbie? Was that the black-hat man's name? How did the stranger know him?

"Blast it," the man-who-might-be-named-Robbie said. "Alfie! I mean, Lord Invernay. Did that pack of rabid dogs find you again?"

The stranger-apparently-named-Alfie nodded.

"You know him?" I asked Robbie.

Robbie turned and narrowed his eyes at me. "You don't?"

I snorted. "Not likely. I flew in today from Northern Canada."

"Well, I'll be ..." He turned to Alfie. "Did this girl help you?"

Girl? I was twenty-two.

Alfie shook his head. I gasped with betrayal. Not only was that grossly unfair of him, but it was too much for his addled brain because he listed sideways and both Robbie and I had to grab him before he fell out of the chair.

Before I could defend myself, Alfie continued, "She didn't help me," he said. "She *saved* me. We roared like animals! Like lions!"

Robbie turned to me. "What on God's green earth is he on about? *Lions*?"

I was far too woozy to explain. "Long story."

Robbie fingered his chin. "Well, I don't know what to make of that, but it seems you helped him. I apologize if I was a bit stroppy with you earlier. It's just with all these incoming students—" He didn't finish, but he stuck out his hand. This was not *at all* how I saw this going.

I shook it. "I'm sorry if I was aggressive earlier. I didn't know what else to do."

"You have a funny name, don't you?" He arched an eyebrow.

"My name is Cedar," I said. "I never thought of it as particularly hilarious."

Robbie took his hat off, threw it on the counter behind him, and examined me more closely. "It's different all right," he declared. "But it suits you. My name is Robert, but you can call me Robbie, like Alfred here does."

I smiled. "Nice to meet you, Robbie, but how do you know—"

"Robbie!" Alfie interrupted in a penetrating voice. "Can you please be kind enough to tell me who she is?" He pointed at me.

"Now, now, Lord Invernay," Robbie said. "Where are your manners? You can ask her directly, you know. Her name is Cedar."

What was all this Lord Invernay business? Did that have something to do with the princess questions the photographers had been lobbing at Alfie?

Alfie's head jerked back. "Cedar? What sort of name is that?" he demanded, sounding like the King of England again. "It's most irregular." If he was a Lord, maybe that wasn't too far off.

Robbie slanted a pair of sharp eyes to me and shook his head, aggrieved. "You'll have to excuse Lord Invernay's behavior. When he's not full of ale, he's got impeccable manners. He's just been under so much stress, you know, with his father ..."

I was completely in the dark. "Like I said before, I *don't* know. Is his father sick? Or dead?"

Robbie's eyes widened again. "Right. You really don't know, I suppose."

"No clue whatsoever. Is he really a Lord?"

"Yes," Robbie said, shooting me a speculative look. "Have you never met a Lord?"

"Nope."

"You'll be tripping over them here at Oxford. No need to be intimidated."

There was no danger of that. "I'm not. He seems to hold his liquor no better than any other mortal." I looked down at Alfie, who at that moment was examining his left pinky finger. "Maybe less so."

Robbie let out a bark of delighted laughter. "Just so. Well ... you see, Cedar, Alfie's father—"

"Don't tell her!" Lord Invernay, which was quite a mouthful, shouted. His eyes were frantic. "Please."

Robbie clicked his tongue and put a reassuring hand on Alfie's shoulder. "Ah, you poor sod. You have had a hard time of it, haven't you?" He turned to me. "I doubt he'll remember any of this in the morning."

"Alfie. Alfred. Lord Invernay," I repeated. "What's his actual name?"

"His Christian name is Alfred, but people who know him well call him Alfie. We like our nicknames here in England, as you'll quickly find out, although I'll admit to you I would have no idea what to do with Cedar. His title, which I should use without fail because I'm just a lowly porter, is Lord Invernay. His father is a Duke, and the family seat is up in Scotland—very close to Balmoral. They say Laird instead of Lord up there, but Oxford is firmly in England, so Lord Invernay it is."

Now my head was spinning for an entirely new reason. "I'm never going to remember all that. I'm far too tired. So his father *isn't* dead?"

Robbie grimaced. "Sometimes I think Alfie would be better off if he were, but no. He's very much alive and causing scandals that make Alfie's life a hundred times more difficult than it should be."

"I'm going to be sick," Alfie announced in a regal manner. I had to give credit where credit was due.

"Bugger," Robbie muttered and grabbed a nearby garbage can. The man was quick on his feet.

Alfie proceeded to be heartily, although tidily, sick in it.

Robbie clucked and winced but took care of business with a pragmatism that left me equally impressed. "You're a resourceful man, Robbie," I said. "That's an important personality trait where I'm from."

He cast me a rueful look. "You've no idea, lass." He put the garbage can back behind his desk, hopefully to clean out later.

"Am I right in thinking Alfie is a student at Beaufort College too?" I asked.

Robbie nodded. "He just got a promotion today, to Junior Fellow. Did his undergraduate here too. We know each other well."

Alfie grabbed my arm with a vice-like grip. His hands were hot and so strong my fingers started to tingle from lack of blood. "Whatever you do, don't tell Professor Harris," he pleaded. "He mustn't know. Not ever."

Robbie cleared his throat and pulled Alfie's hand off my arm.

"You must be exhausted," Robbie said to me. "Why don't you head to bed, and I'll deal with our young Lordship here. You can trust me with him."

Funnily enough, I did trust him, but an ache in my stomach reminded me that wasn't the problem. "Sure, but I'm going to head out for some food before I turn in. I hadn't made it to the pub yet when I found Alfie on the street."

Robbie frowned. "We can't have that. All right then, can you deal with him for just five minutes, keep him propped up and the garbage can on hand?"

"No problem."

"I'm just going to nip out. Be right back."

I watched him go as he ducked out the college door, hoping with every fiber of my being that he was scrounging up some food. When I turned back to Alfie, he was staring up at me with an intensity I didn't know what to do with. I wasn't used to people noticing me.

"What?" I asked finally. "Do I have something on my face?"

"No," Alfie answered. "You're beautiful."

My heart stuttered for a weak moment, before it hit me that I couldn't take him seriously. "Not that again. Call me beautiful when you're sober, then I'll believe you."

He frowned. "I will, but in the meantime, thank you. I felt like the world was against me when I started drinking, but now ..."

I could so easily sink into those eyes. *Wait. What*? That was ridiculous.

"It's better now," he said.

What was he talking about? "Now what?"

He smiled then—a spontaneous, joyful smile that made my breath catch in my throat. I'd never been the recipient of a smile like that before. "Now you're here."

Something in the simplicity of that created what felt like a tether connecting the two of us. I'd been feeling isolated, then there he was, all alone on the ground. Maybe I wasn't as solitary as I'd believed an hour ago.

"Can we be friends?" he asked, and my heart did something weird. How had he known that was one of my wildest daydreams—to have real, in-the-flesh friends?

"I'd like that."

"Can we kiss on it?" His eyes assumed the expression of a begging dog.

"No."

"Is it because I sicked up?"

The sincerity of his question made laughter bubble up in me. "That definitely doesn't help your case." I bit back my amusement. "But also friends don't kiss where I'm from."

"Shame."

"Not really. It's clearer that way." The few other men I'd been with had all been strapping, outdoorsy types—two trappers and a fisherman—basically the complete opposite of Alfie. I couldn't even begin to imagine what anything beyond friendship with someone as—well, as different from me as him—would be like. A *Lord* to boot. Give me a break.

Robbie came back in the door, holding something that looked

like two lumps of aluminum foil in his hand. "How's our boy?" he asked.

Our boy? "Better," I said. "No more barfing."

"Capital." He passed one of the foil packages to me, along with a plastic fork he plucked from the pocket of his black suit jacket.

"What's this?" I asked, not because I was picky—my diet back home regularly featured moose heart—but because I was curious.

"Jacket potato," he said as he carefully unwrapped the other and placed it in Alfie's hand. "Got it from the kebab van on Holywell Street. Can't have you starving, good Samaritan that you are, and it will do Alfie some good to get something in his stomach to absorb all the ale."

Unease made my stomach squirm. "Can I pay you back?" I was brought up to be beholden to nobody.

He waved my suggestion away. "My treat. Eat."

My empty stomach dissuaded me from protesting further. The warmth of the package soaked into my palms and when I opened up the foil on top, the warm, earthy scent of hot potato made my mouth water. It was split open and stuffed with melting shredded cheese and rich baked beans.

"This looks *amazing*," I breathed.

"I got you the works." He winked at me. "I just got cheese for Alfie, as I don't imagine anyone wants to revisit the baked beans if they don't settle well."

"Wise move," I said through bites of food. The melted cheese and the ketchup-flavored beans and the hot potato mixed in such a comforting way that I sagged against the counter I was leaning on. "This hits the spot," I groaned.

Robbie was still helping Alfie, but he grinned up at me. "Thought it might."

I devoured it, and afterwards crushed my foil wrapper into a ball. Alfie was working ponderously through his potato. Even worse for wear, he still ate incredibly neatly.

"I can help you get him back to his room," I said to Robbie. "It might be easier with two people. He's pretty heavy."

"He's a rugby player. Wing of course, given his build and his speed. Earned a blue for it." He smiled down at Alfie with an air of paternal pride. "But I'll manage. You need to get to bed now you've eaten."

I had no idea what "a blue" meant, but the floor of the Lodge kept tilting up towards me, so I didn't ask. Still, I hated to abandon Robbie. "Honestly. I can help—"

"I'm not saying you're not capable," Robbie said. "But I know Alfie. He's a private person—keeps himself to himself, if you understand what I mean. He'll be embarrassed about tonight."

I waved that away. "Nobody's perfect."

Robbie shook his head. "Perhaps not, but Alfie has convinced himself he needs to be. Almost nobody sees him ..." He made a helpless gesture with his hand. "Well ... like this."

"She's enchanting, isn't she?" Alfie, who'd been studying me again, said to Robbie. "A tad terrifying, the way she growls, but there's something about her face ... I can't stop looking at it. Why can't I stop looking at her face, Robbie?"

Robbie winced. "You see what I mean? He'll be mortified when he sobers up. Off with you now, and don't miss Hall in the morning."

He must have clocked my blank expression because he clarified. "For breakfast." He took out a college map and circled a square on it. "Be there at eight o'clock sharp. Now, off to Bedfordshire with you."

"Bedfordshire?"

"Bed."

"Ah ... Bedfordshire ... *bed* ... I get it. That's funny!" I leaned over to Alfie and squeezed his hand. "I hope you feel better." I enunciated clearly, as though talking to an animal or a young child. "Make sure you sleep on your side so you don't choke if you yack again."

Alfie stared up at me with astonishingly clear eyes. "That's excellent advice," he said. "Thank you. I'll see you tomorrow, new friend."

"I look forward to it." I cracked a yawn, and with that, I left for Bedfordshire.

CHAPTER FOUR

Alfie

I woke up to a throbbing head and Norris, my contraband rescue dog, licking my ear with contented snorts.

The bitter aftertaste of bile in my mouth made me gag. I was curled up on my side, which was rather odd as ever since I was a child I'd slept on my back. On the floor beside my bed was a strategically placed rubblish bin. *Good Lord. What had I done?*

Disjointed memories flickered like a horror movie against the insides of my eyelids when my door slammed open. I lifted my head and an explosion detonated in my skull. All I could do was groan some more and clutch at my head.

Annabelle, my Scout, barged into the room. She clucked her tongue as she took in the sight of me and, I was quite sure, the smell. Mortification prickled along my hairline.

"My apologies, Annabelle." My voice came out reedy, as it was rather difficult to talk with my tongue sticking to the roof of my mouth.

She laughed, chipper as always. "It's not as though I haven't seen my share of soused students, m'Lord." *Ugh. M'Lord.* She insisted on calling me that. I hated it. It made me feel as though I was masquerading as Darcy in Pride and Prejudice or something equally pretentious.

She moved towards the bed to get a closer look at me. "Heavens above—you do look worse for wear. It's not out-of-character for some, but for you ... you are always so *correct*."

Scouts were an integral part of Oxford student life, but there were mornings like this one when I would happily opt-out of the tradition.

Still, Annabelle was more precious than rubies. I knew I could trust her about Norris, and I could count the number of people in my life I could trust on one hand. This late fiftyish woman who considered herself the de facto mother of all the students on her stairwells studied me now.

Pets were banned in Beaufort College, but Annabelle was an animal lover, and kept the secret of Norris safe. I never stopped being grateful for that, or for her.

"Were the press after you again, my poor lamb?" she clucked, wiping her hands on the white cleaning apron she always wore over her house dresses.

As much as I appreciated her concern, everything about this was undignified. My chest was bare. I had no idea how I got into bed the night before. I stunk of beer. I sniffed the air. Yes, the unmistakable odor of vomit too.

Annabelle was quite a different style to the discreet and distant servants I'd grown up with—they would never ask me such a personal question.

I never knew quite how to act with this garrulous woman who was not exactly a maid but not exactly an acquaintance either. People who didn't fit into categories unnerved me—they made it difficult to know how to act. I was determined to be someone who lived by the rules—my contraband dog was the sole exception, and I blamed that one on Robbie.

"I'll be fine, thank you," I answered, regretting the starch in my voice. I had no intention of sounding rude, but it had come out that way regardless. Was it too much to hope that Annabelle would suspect it stemmed from the mortification that made my skin feel clammy? "However, I could use a glass of water. Would you mind? There's a glass on the sink in the bathroom. Oh, could you also check that Norris's stairs are pushed up to the toilet?"

Secrecy had obliged me to toilet train my dog and build him a set of stairs so he could climb up to the toilet. Yes, I was aware of my ridiculousness.

"In a jiffy, luv." She bustled in there, bless her.

I tried to sit up, pulling my duvet around me. I swallowed again to test that the remnants of the night before stayed down.

The flashes of photographers came back to me. *Bullocks.*

I remembered the feel of slick cobblestones under my knees. It started to come back in a rush—the headlines about my father spending two "intimate" weeks with the princess at her and the prince's private family estate in Scotland. Trying to drown out that feeling of guilt by association in pint after pint at The Turf.

It often went like this. Whenever the press couldn't figure out a way of getting to my father and his scandal of the moment, they would hunt me instead. It wasn't as if I was difficult to find. I'd wager anything that he hadn't spared a moment's thought about how it tarnished my reputation at Oxford and, more importantly, with Professor Harris.

I dropped my head in my hands. *What had I given the paps?* Instead of my usual "no comment" response, I'd served them up a fresh scandal—the Dastardly Duke's son follows in his lead, lying drunk on the cobblestones of New College Lane. *Disaster*. I had let my father's life leech into mine. I could lose my junior fellowship over this. It was the kind of impropriety that Professor Harris could not abide.

Annabelle came out of the bathroom and passed me the glass of water.

"Thank you," I said. "You're so kind."

She placed two paracetamol on my bedside table, took my rubbish bin—thank goodness it didn't look as though I'd been sick in it—and blew me a kiss as she left me alone again.

The vague memory of leaning against someone who was yelling like a wild animal kept circling back. Wait... had it been a girl? No, that couldn't be right. No female in my acquaintance would ever do that. Certainly not my ex-girlfriend Imogen.

Moving gingerly, I headed towards the bathroom to brush my teeth, the prospect of what I wasn't able to remember filling me with the cold prickle of dread.

***

I dashed across the Withert's Quad (well, not across, walking on the pathways, as walking on the grass was strictly forbidden) with my black master's cape flying out behind me. The sledgehammer still pounded against my skull, despite Annabelle's paracetamol.

My skin burned like I was breaking out in a rash. I was late—I hated being late.

I took the worn stone stairs leading to the third floor of the Fitzjames building two at a time. Professor Harris's study was on the third floor in this golden, gothic pile that was front and center on Beaufort's website.

I'd worked so hard to achieve this junior fellowship, but I still had everything to prove. Being late for my very first tutorial as an advisor was beyond the pale. There were stringent rules for success at Oxford, and I had to follow them to the letter if I had any hope of escaping the infamy of my father.

My heart skipped when I saw Professor Harris standing in front of the door to his study, checking his watch.

"Professor!" I gasped, but I would have been better not to speak at all. I sounded frantic, out-of-breath—the complete opposite of my mentor.

He raised his eyebrows at me. Like everything about him, they were straight and neat. He never had a speck of lint on his academic robes or a scuff on his polished dress shoes.

"I thought I would come on your first day to let you in," he said, the censure clear in his voice. "I certainly wasn't expecting you to be so tardy."

My stomach ached at the idea he thought my diligence was slipping. I couldn't disappoint him.

"I had to assist a lost fresher in the quad," I fibbed.

He studied me for a moment, his critical brown eyes narrowing a bit. "Fine," he said finally. "But don't let it happen again."

"I won't." I couldn't.

He nodded once, dismissing the matter, and slid his key into the lock. I remembered the first time I had been ushered into his study. It was October of my first term up at Oxford, and he was the professor for my Medieval Literature course.

I'd just come off a tortuous summer hidden away in Scotland while my father conducted a torrid and very public affair with the Chancellor of Germany's wife. My mother had all but moved to St. Barts.

I knew I didn't want to follow in my father's sordid footsteps or emulate my mother's habit of vanishing when things became difficult (thanks to my father, they always were). The problem was I'd never been shown any alternatives.

I'd heard about Professor Harris's reputation before my first tutorial with him—he had skyrocketed through the ranks of Beaufort College at a vertiginous speed. He was a full professor at only thirty years old.

The moment I walked into Professor Harris's study and saw him, trim and self-possessed under his gown, a photo of his blonde, sweet looking wife on his desk, I wanted what he had—desperately. He was the example I'd been longing for.

Now, the door swung open and Professor Harris's waved me into his study, where I would be running my first official tutorial, with a ceremonious sweep of his hand. "After you."

Goosebumps rose on the back of my neck. "Thank you."

I admired the neat rows of books lining the walls, as I always did. Calmness settled over me. There was something so steadying about this place, so *orderly*.

Professor Harris picked up a folder from his desk. "You will have three master's students to advise this year. As usual, the administration is tardy in providing more information, but that should follow if they ever manage to get their act together," he sniffed.

"Doubtful," I quipped.

He tilted his head in agreement. He relished sharing his dissatisfaction with things and people that did not perform up to par, and I was blatantly using that knowledge to make him forget my late arrival.

"I suppose you'll have to do a round of introductions. Painful, but necessary."

"Yes," I agreed, matching his level of disdain. "Still ... torture all the same."

He cracked a smile. *Victory.* I was determined to make a life for myself here at Beaufort College—a calm, safe life like Professor Harris had. I relished the structure inside the college's medieval walls and the steady, ordered way things had been run for centuries. Oxford was my refuge, and I couldn't afford to make a false step.

"Right then." He placed the manila folder back on his polished oak desk. "I'll turn it over to you. Don't let me down, Alfred."

My thoughts flew back to flashes of cameras, unyielding cobblestones ... but it all felt so vague that I couldn't be sure what had actually happened and what I had dreamed. In any case, I couldn't think of that now. A spark of hope kept me going. Maybe if I acted like nothing had happened, Professor Harris wouldn't find out?

"I won't," I promised.

He left and I sat down on the chair behind his desk. My knees were definitely not working properly. I finally let out the sigh I'd been holding.

Another unwelcome memory came to me—I'd been sitting on a chair in the Lodge with Robbie and a girl that I'd never seen before was conferring with him while casting me speculative looks.

Had she been real? I'd been physically incapable of *not* staring at her. She must have been. Please Lord let me never cross paths with her again.

***

Somebody knocked on the door. Should I walk over and open it up? On second thought, Professor Harris acted like he was above all that. "Come in," I called out instead.

The door opened slowly, and in lumbered a mountain of a

young man. He towered over me by several inches, and I was six foot two. His burly shoulders were hunched over, and his black hair was so overgrown that I could barely make out his face. It was as though he was trying to attract as little notice as possible—not an easy feat for someone his size.

He was off-putting, but maybe he was hiding a formidable brain in that bulk. I stretched out my hand. "Pleasure to meet you. I'm Alfred Invernay, your junior advisor. Your name is?"

"Raphael," he said in a low rumble of a voice. "Raphael Coates."

He suited Jack or Hugo, not an ethereal name like Raphael. There was nothing remotely ethereal about this student. Still, socially awkward yet brilliant students were not exactly a novelty at Oxford, and mentally I placed him in that category.

"Please." I gestured to the leather couch across the opposite wall. "Have a seat."

My next student lounged in the door wearing his academic gown over a pair of purple pajama bottoms, flip-flops, and an old Duran Duran concert T-shirt—worn ironically, I imagined.

"Welcome," I said, and repeated the same introduction. The cocky toss of his head confirmed what I suspected—he was one of those students whose hobby was scorning authority.

I gave him a hard look, but he just smirked. He didn't appear in the least bit intimidated by me or the fact he was late for his first tutorial. He stuck out his hand in the manner of someone whose welcome in any room was a forgone conclusion.

"Shaun," he said. "Shaun Webb."

That explained it. He was the son of the flamboyant—and famous—entrepreneur who owned everything from airlines to trains to TV streaming services. His father was a self-made multi-billionaire who also did amazing work countering the racism that, as a black man, he'd experienced growing up in London, all while making an indelible mark in the business world. I'd heard some vague chattering about his son being accepted at Beaufort.

Shaun was going to be tricky. His father was incredibly respected, but the son had clearly strayed far from this good example. It would never have crossed my mind to show up to a tutorial in pajamas. I hated the lack of respect it showed, but at the same time I wasn't certain if it was actually against the rules. I made a mental note to check.

My stomach did something odd again and I regretted every pint of ale and the few glasses of Scotch I'd had the night before, but it wasn't just my hangover. It was nerves too. I had to make a success of this tutorial. Failure—not to mention disappointing Professor Harris—was unthinkable. He was my chosen role model, and his approval was everything.

I stood up from the desk chair and walked around to perch on the edge of the desk. My stomach felt slightly less vile when I wasn't sitting down. "We'll just wait for the final student. There will be three of you in this master's group."

Time clicked by on the ornate clock sitting on the marble fireplace mantel. I checked my watch. Definitely tardy. No matter who this proved to be, it was an inauspicious start—even worse than Shaun's.

"Do you think they're coming?" Shaun asked, settling back deeper in the couch and crossing one pajama-clad leg over the other. Somehow he had the gift, like his father every time I saw him on the telly, of making his movements always appear unrushed and elegant.

"To be perfectly honest, I'm not sure," I admitted. "I wasn't given much information about the three of you."

"Maybe they're dead," Raphael said in his ominous rumble of

a voice.

"Pardon me?" I asked, unsure I'd heard correctly. Why would any sane person jump to that conclusion, of all things?

"Aren't you a right ray of sunshine?" Shaun looked at Raphael in disbelief.

Raphael hunched his shoulders over even more and stared down at his very large knees. "Didn't realize I said that out loud."

Shaun let out a crack of laughter. "Well, you did. How delightfully bizarre."

Somebody opened the door without knocking and crashed into the study. At first, all I could make out was a blur of wavy brown hair and a heaving chest. A girl, and clearly one who'd been running.

She bent over and placed her hands on her knees. "Sorry!" She held up her hand after a few seconds, gesturing for us to give her a moment while she caught her breath. After a minute or so of this, she stood up again, and the first thing I registered was the constellation of freckles across the bridge of her nose.

I froze. I remembered wanting to reach out and trace those exact freckles with my fingertip. It felt like an anvil had been dropped square on my chest. The girl from the night before was real. Worse yet, she was my third student.

CHAPTER FIVE

Cedar

It was him! My only friend here in this weird new place. I was still trying to catch my breath, but my entire body exhaled when I recognized him.

"It's *you*," I laughed. He was studying Medieval Literature too? How great to have already become friends with a student in my program. Thank God the professor hadn't arrived yet so we could chat.

My morning had not started well. I'd slept through my alarm—jetlag was real, despite what I'd previously believed, and gotten lost on the way here. It made no sense. I had an amazing sense of direction—how could I be so much more disoriented in buildings than in the forest?

"How are you feeling?" I inspected Alfie's face. "You still look a bit green, to be honest, but that's not much of a shocker, eh?"

Alfie sent me a look I couldn't interpret. It was sort of *beseeching*.

"I'm fine, thank you," he answered. His tone was formal,

whereas last night he'd been so friendly—over-friendly at times. His breath was coming fast. What was going on with him? Maybe just a truly nasty hangover? That could throw anyone off kilter.

"I'm so sorry all those people were taking photos of you last night," I said, eager to let him know I was on his side. "They were awful."

He opened his mouth, but nothing came out.

"Wait." A boy wearing pajamas and flip-flops on the couch held up his hand. "Your accent ... where are you from?"

"Canada." I turned to him. I'd been so excited to see the one fellow student I knew that I'd failed to look closely at the two guys on the couch. The other one was hunched over and wouldn't meet my eyes.

"Well, that explains your bizarre clothes," the pajama guy said. "My name's Shaun." He jerked his thumb over at his couch mate. "This is Raphael."

What was wrong with my clothes? I looked down at my worn jeans, leather boots, and dark-green fleece. They were no odder than Shaun's. "Look who's talking, or don't you own a mirror?"

Alfie's mouth dropped open. Shaun—far less shocked than Alfie—laughed. "I think I like you."

Were Oxford students always so outwardly outspoken about their opinions? I hated I had no way of knowing if this was normal or not. I shrugged and used an expression I'd learned from the Québécois mushroom-pickers who based themselves around Stewart during chanterelle season. "*Je m'en calisse.*"

Shaun tilted his head. "I speak perfect Parisian French, but I've never heard that."

"It's Québécois."

"Huh," said Shaun, nodding. "You can teach me stuff. More importantly though, how do you and Lord Invernay know each other?"

Alfie frowned at him, but Shaun took no notice. I searched my brain for why Alfie was acting so cold towards me that hoar frost was starting to grow on my insides. Sure, Robbie had warned me that Alfie would be embarrassed about being drunk, but that was hardly an uncommon experience for university students from what I'd read.

"We met last night," I said.

"I need more details." Shaun polished his knuckles on his T-shirt. "I have a bit of a knack for sensing where there's a good story."

Both Alfie and I cast him dirty looks, but he stared back at us, undeterred. Alfie launched himself from where he'd been leaning against the desk and waved me to the couch. I sat down. "Where is your gown?" he demanded in an autocratic tone that punctured my delight at finding him again.

Wait. Was *he* the teacher? I vaguely remembered something Robbie had said about a Junior Fellowship. I sat down beside Raphael and Shaun on the couch.

"My gown?" I looked over at the others—I was the only one not wearing one. Luckily, there was a perfectly reasonable explanation for that. Alfie walked over to close the study door, then sat in the chair behind the desk. Crap. Definitely the teacher. Still, that didn't explain his complete personality transplant. "That's easy to explain."

He arched a haughty brow. "Oh?"

He didn't fool me acting so high and mighty—I'd watched him chund in a garbage can not that many hours ago. "Don't you remember? Like I told you last night, I arrived less than an hour before I found you. That's why I slept in—I guess I do owe you an apology about that. The thing is the time difference between

England and the West Coast of Canada is nine hours, you know, and it's the first time I've ever had jetlag. Usually, I wake up with the sun, but—"

"I didn't ask for an exegesis," he said, with such a sharp edge to his voice that I jerked back against the leather. "It's the rule that students have to wear their academic gown to all of their tutorials."

My cheeks went cold as the blood drained from my face. How dare he act so horribly to me after I'd helped him? I'd come here to prove my parents wrong about humanity. They had preached my entire life that people were uniformly disappointing and not worth the effort. Alfie's rude, ungrateful behavior was proving them right.

"Surely there's an exception when students have literally had no time to buy one," I pointed out through a clenched jaw.

He steepled his hands on the desk in front of him. "Not that I know of."

I gasped. He'd been *nothing* like this last night. Robbie had neglected to warn me that sober Alfie was a jerk. A toxic mix of disappointment and anger made my arms feel like concrete blocks. "Common sense trumps rules," I said.

Shaun chuckled. "It's clear you haven't been here at Oxford for long."

"Today is just a meet and greet," Raphael pointed out shyly. "Don't be too hard on her."

I cast him a smile of gratitude.

"The rule applies any time a student meets with their tutors," Alfie insisted.

That familiar hollow loneliness made me feel like getting up and running from the room, but there was no way I was going to back down in the face of such unfairness.

"That's just idiotic," I said. "If you are in fact here in the role of our teacher—"

Alfie cleared his throat. "I'm your Junior Thesis Advisor."

I let a puff of air out of my nostrils. "Whatever. Acting like a tyrant is a bad way to start."

"How dare you—" Alfie began, but Shaun flapped his hands to shush us both. "Shhh. We're getting sidetracked here. We need to know how Lord Invernay and ..." He turned his head to me. "What's your name?"

"Cedar," I said. "Cedar Wild."

Shaun dissolved into gusts of merriment. "You are *shitting* me," he gasped finally, wiping his eyes. "That cannot possibly be your actual name?"

"Why not?" I demanded, baffled by how things were going. Surely in-class school wasn't like this ... or was it? I had taken online school in my cabin, so I was sorely lacking any point of reference. "First name Cedar, family name Wild."

"Cedar Wild," he repeated, his voice ripe with disbelief. "From Canada." He slapped his knee in delight. "That's priceless. I think I've quite lost my heart to you. Where in Canada are you from?"

Alfie's head was pinging back and forth between me and Shaun. Why wasn't Alfie telling Shaun it was none of his business to interrogate me like this ... unless ... the look in Alfie's eyes was intent and centered on me. Was Alfie curious too?

"British Columbia," I said, with an arch of my brow at Alfie. *Ha.* Two could play that game. "Actually, that's not quite accurate. I grew up in a log cabin about forty kilometers from the town of Stewart, in the forest of ... well, I guess you wouldn't know it. We lived off-grid. My parents are bear researchers, so we lived where the bears lived. They still do."

Three pairs of eyes stared at me in stupefaction, as if I'd just announced I'd been teleported to Oxford directly from Jupiter.

"Oh my Lord." Shaun threw his hands up. "I think it's sinking in for all of us that your extraordinary name might be one of the least interesting things about you."

Interesting? Me? That couldn't be right. My parents had always found the bears they studied far more worthy of their attention than me.

"I honestly don't even know where to begin with my questions," Shaun said. "Is that why you didn't knock on the door?"

I met Alfie's eyes. His were clear and questioning now, more like last night. "Was I supposed to?" I asked.

"Yes," Alfie said.

"Then I apologize for that. I'm not used to having neighbors."

"You'll know for next time," he said, far more gently. "For now, we must begin. I'd like you all to briefly tell me what drew you to medieval literature. Shaun, you can go first."

Finally. This was more what I'd been expecting. I adored medieval literature, particularly the legend of Tristan and Iseult, both the British and French versions. I was hoping to do my thesis on some comparison between the two. One of the main reasons I'd come to Oxford was to geek out with others who also shared the same weird obsession. I'd never even met anyone who studied medieval literature before.

"Are you joking?" Shaun said. "Cedar is *fascinating*. Chaucer and Chretien de Troyes can wait."

I glared at Shaun.

"No, they cannot," Alfie said in a stern tone. "One might also wonder, Shaun, why the son of England's most famous philanthropist billionaires is working towards an Oxford MPhil. Especially as from what I've witnessed so far, his primary goals seem to be hijacking tutorials and wasting all of our time."

Shaun's mouth clamped shut for the first time since I'd met him. A spurt of gratitude made me thaw a tiny bit—like a smidgen—towards Alfie.

"We have the next two years to get acquainted with one another," Alfie continued. "Now is the time to turn our thoughts to your specific areas of interest and initial ideas for your eventual thesis. What are your particular areas of study, Raphael?" he asked.

Even though I was still confounded and annoyed by Alfie's behavior, I sank into my first academic conversation at Oxford with a sigh of relief.

CHAPTER SIX

Alfie

Lachlan wiped his broad brow with one of the towels provided as we collapsed on the bench at the side of the rugby pitch after our practice. "Out with it," he said, after we'd caught our breath.

"What do you mean?" My limbs were heavy with exhaustion, but in a good way. If only the rugby had done the same for my mind.

"Don't try that, Alfie," he chided. "Now that you've stopped playing with the Blues the only time you come out and run around with us is when something has gone wrong in your plan to become a dusty Oxford Don or some fresh scandal your father has brewed up. I heard about the princess business. You have to give credit where credit is due—he never takes a holiday from being conspicuous, your father."

Why did I even try to bother hiding anything from Lachlan? He was such an unlikely friend for me—a huge Scot with a propensity for colorful swearing, downing pints, and enjoying the ladies. Still, as the son of our gamekeeper in Scotland, we'd been friends since we were children. I could keep no secrets from him, even if I wanted to. Some part of me had known that when I agreed to join him for a friendly game of rugby that afternoon at Oxford's Iffley Road complex.

I sighed. "Everything has gone sideways." I told him about my new fellowship, the photographs of my father and the princess, my overindulgence at The Turf, the girl named Cedar who helped me, and then my disaster of a first tutorial that morning.

His eyes grew wider. "Och Alfie. That's a lot."

I nodded glumly, the tangle of it all pushing up against my throat. "Professor Harris will probably take away my—"

Lachlan made a guttural noise of disgust. "That prig. I still dinnae ken why you admire him so much."

This was a point on which we were never going to see eye to eye. The two of them were polar opposites—how could they possibly understand one another? As much as I valued Lachlan, I was aware that if we hadn't known each other forever, we probably wouldn't be friends at all.

"This girl though. This Cedar," he continued. "I want to know more about her."

The flash of pain in her brown eyes when I'd spoken to her so coldly had been playing on a loop in my mind since the tutorial. "I don't want to talk about her."

"That's a shame then, because I do. You were harsh with her. You act aloof and untouchable most of the time, but harsh … that's not like you, Alfie."

I threw up my hands, the frustration I'd felt in the tutorial rushing back. "What was I supposed to do?" I demanded. "I had to get her to stop talking. She immediately started referring to how we met in front of my new students, on my very first day in this role that is everything I've worked for. How could she not know how to conduct herself? It wouldn't have been difficult to just do the proper thing and not mention the unpleasantness."

"Aye, that would have been easier for you," Lachlan admitted.

"Exactly! I tried telegraphing her with my eyes to *stop talking*, but she wasn't picking up on any of the social cues. How hard would it have been for her to just pretend we'd never met?"

There was an unspoken agreement amongst British people that unpleasantness was hardly ever mentioned. If it was, it was addressed only in the most oblique, dismissive way, as in, "heard your wife left you, old boy. Bad luck, but have you heard about George's new polo pony?"

"But she's not British," Lachlan reminded me in that way he had, gently pointing out my mistakes.

"No, she's Canadian," I said. I didn't add that she was also—if that incredible tale she told was true—from a small cabin in the middle of the woods. That would just drive home Lachlan's point.

If my heart hadn't been pounding with panic and if I hadn't also been using every available brain cell to try and not sick up on Professor Harris's immaculate Turkish carpet, I would have taken this into account.

"You don't realize it, Alfie," he said. "But you can be very intimidating when you don that Lord of Invernay persona."

I let out a gulp of laughter. This, from my six foot six, eighteen stone rugby prop of a friend. I thought back to the expression on Cedar's face. She'd been confused for sure, and hurt—that knowledge lodged under my ribs like an arrow point—but daunted? No.

"She wasn't scared of me." I thought back to the way her dark, definite brows had drawn together over her luminous eyes, and how that sharp chin of hers had become even more stubborn. "Not for a second."

Lachlan tilted his head and narrowed his eyes at me. "Wait.

That sounds interesting. Certainly a vast improvement on ... what was her name? That pale, lifeless lass you deigned to be with for a time?"

"Imogen," I said, with some asperity. "And we parted on perfectly good terms. She is truly a sweet, cultured girl. I won't hear you bad mouth her."

"She was a bore," he said. "This Cedar sounds far more interesting."

Lachlan didn't know the half of it—where she came from, the way she'd roared like a bear to get the paps out of our way. Had I told her she was *beautiful*?" It was all rushing back now, every excruciating detail.

I groaned and dropped my head in my hands.

"What?"

"It just came back to me. I threw up in a rubbish bin in front of her."

Lachlan looked at me for a stunned moment then bent over, guffawing with laughter.

"It's terrible," I said, after a while.

He wiped the tears from his eyes. "Terrible? It's pure dead brilliant."

I whipped my towel at his leg, and it snapped in a most satisfactory way. I was always better than him at towel snapping when we were children.

He clutched his calf. "Och! Careful there. This is still the body of an Oxford Blue, unlike you now. Precious stuff."

"Pretentious prat," I said, comfortable in our well-worn banter.

"I'm not the Lord, and I didn't bully a brand-new student."

I sighed. Lachlan didn't fully understand the context like Professor Harris would, but still, he was partially right. "I'll apologize to her." I knew Lachlan wouldn't be satisfied unless I said it out loud.

"Of course you will," he said.

I nodded. The robins were chirping overhead. For October it was a remarkably sunny day and the warmth of summer still clung to the sunlight. Lachlan and I sat like that for a bit, resting on the bench with the clubhouse wall at our backs, our faces turned up to the sun like we'd done on fields and hills in Scotland when we were boys. There weren't many people I could be quiet like this with—that I didn't feel like I needed to be projecting some kind of image for.

Eventually my thoughts snagged back to the strobe lights of the pap's flashes in New College Lane. "There were so many photographers there Lachlan," I said. "I'm scared of what is going to show up in the tabloids tomorrow. It was too late at night for anything to show up today."

Lachlan, with his thick neck, turned his massive head towards. "Is it possible it might not be as bad as you think?"

I grimaced, that familiar sensation of the ground falling out from underneath me, making my sweat go clammy on my skin. "I think it could be worse."

Lachlan clapped one of his hands on my shoulder. "You deserved a better father."

But there was nothing I could do about that, was there? Since my mother lived full time in the Caribbean now, it was just my father and me. It hit me like a punch that the only approval I truly desired and needed for advancement—Professor Harris's—might be lost forever over this.

"Once he sees the photos, Professor Harris is going to take my fellowship away," I said. "And I won't blame him."

Instead of disparaging my mentor as he usually did, Lachlan squeezed my shoulder. "Look Alfie," he said. "I think maybe I know better than anyone else what that father of yours has made you endure, and how your mother just left you alone with all of it. That's a lot for any person."

I shook my head. "People deal with worse, and with far less privilege, every day. All over Britain."

"Maybe so, but that hasn't made what you have had to struggle with any less painful. I wonder if that's why you've attached yourself to someone like Professor Harris—"

"Lachlan," I said, my voice almost pleading with him to try to understand. "I'm desperate for a life like his, can't you see that? Calm. Ordered. Predictable. I'm done with chaos. I need to carve out my own space where I'm not constantly having these crises lobbed at me."

Lachlan frowned at me but didn't argue.

"I'll shower back at College," I said, standing up. "I could probably use a sleep too."

Lachlan got up as well. "Och, you could. You're looking in ribbons from last night, even after the rugby. You know I'm here when you need me."

I nodded. "I do." I picked up my cleats and headed home, already dreading the future apology to Cedar.

FIRST WEEK

CHAPTER SEVEN

Alfie

I woke up the next morning with another heavy head—not from a hangover this time, but from the thought of photos of me appearing front and center at the newsagent. It was grim that it fell on a Sunday, when all the papers produced huge editions packed with extra content. I flexed my fingers. They always went numb when I was anxious. What I would give to experience anonymity—nobodies had no idea how fortunate they were.

I heaved myself out of bed. Sundays meant no Annabelle, which was a good thing considering I was in no way fit for early morning conversation.

As I brushed my teeth and Norris used the toilet beside me, I stared at myself in the mirror. I would have to find Cedar and apologize to her as well. Might as well pack everything terrible into the same twenty-four hours.

I had gone over what I should say to her roughly one thousand times in my head, but I still hadn't settled on the perfect formula. How would she react? She was so completely foreign to me and my world that I couldn't assume anything.

I got dressed and threw on my robe. I would try to intercept Cedar in the Hall at lunch. Until then, I would get some research done at the Bod and, more importantly, hide for a bit. Even if there were a few paps hanging around when I left college, surely they realized I would be acting circumspectly.

I fed Norris and tried to scratch him under his chin like he usually loved, but while he ate greedily, he continued to give me a cold shoulder like he'd been doing since I'd come back from rugby with Lachlan.

Could he sense that I'd been unkind? No, that was ridiculous. Still ... this was so unlike him. Maybe he was upset because I'd slept through our usual night walk the night before.

He growled at me. I stared down at him in disbelief. I remembered an article in The Guardian about the canine ability to sense the energy of the people around them. I hadn't believed it then, but now I wondered. Had my rescue dog picked up on my guilt?

As I unlocked my door to leave, he ran across the room and grabbed on to the edge of my academic robe with the few teeth he had left.

"Let go, Norris," I muttered at him. I had to keep him quiet. Now was not the time for him to be discovered, not to mention the fact that if anyone heard him, they would make me give him up and ... well ... even though he'd been foisted on me by Robbie very much against my will, he'd grown on me. "You're going to rip it." Norris eased his grip. "That's it. Be a good boy. I'll be back soon."

Just as I turned to step out into the hallway, he bit it again and pulled with all his might. My robe ripped straight up one side and he stood there in the entrance of my room, shaking the black strip of fabric in his jowls and prancing around gleefully.

"Dammit!" Now I'd have to go to Ede & Ravenscroft and get a

new robe before the day started. I could hardly go around without one after I'd berated Cedar for it. "That was very, very naughty." I shook my finger at Norris, but he just stood there, wagging his tail at me, satisfaction evident in his proud shoulders and cocked, lopsided ears.

"I suppose you think I deserved that?" I asked him.

If I didn't know better, I could have sworn he winked at me. "You're not entirely wrong," I sighed, and shut my door behind me.

***

My chest squeezed with foreboding as I approached the Lodge to check my pidge and find out just how disastrous the photos were. I knew Robbie's schedule—he'd be working. He'd show me the tabloids. It was better to get it over with and as horrible as it was going to be, I'd rather do it in Robbie's bossy, supportive presence than anywhere else.

Robbie was bollocking two freshers for losing their room keys. The pounding of my heart and my constricted lungs prevented me from appreciating this unexpected entertainment as I sorted through the invitations to black-tie dinners and lectures that were jamming up my mail slot. Really, I was just biding time until Robbie and I were alone.

The freshers almost fell over themselves rushing out when Robbie finished. A familiar sensation of falling took hold of me. I would do anything—use any kind of distraction to snap myself out of the sickening certainty that everything around me wasn't real. There was nothing solid to anchor myself to. *Small talk.* That was it. I had to act like today was just any normal day.

"You shouldn't be so hard on the newbies, you know," I said to Robbie. My voice was strained, but perhaps he wouldn't notice.

"They're terrified of you."

"That's the way I like it." Robbie sniffed. "Anyway, they're not all terrified by me."

This was good. Keep the banter light and inconsequential. Pretend like everything was fine and maybe, magically, it would be. Hope flashed through me. The light had been bad—perhaps there were no usable photos, after all.

"I find that hard to believe," I said. "You frightened me out of my wits when I was a fresher."

"What do you expect? You kept locking yourself out of college, you pillock."

"True." Still no mention of the photos. Hope started to push aside the dread.

Robbie made an exasperated noise. "Cedar is new, and she wasn't the least bit scared of me, or of those bloody paparazzi for that matter." Robbie rubbed his chin—a sign I knew meant she'd impressed him. "I sincerely doubt that chit fears anything."

My shoulders dropped. It was going to be okay. I'd built it all up to be worse than it was.

"I have something you need to see." Robbie's voice had turned gruff.

Oh God. Spots floated across my eyes and my windpipe shrunk to the size of a straw. I grabbed on to the porter's desk for support.

"I'm glad you popped in, because I was just about to come and find you." He looked at me, his eyes full of sympathy. My heart beat sluggishly in my chest.

I joined him behind his plexiglass partition, and he slipped a copy of The Mail on Sunday across his desk towards me. I didn't want to look at it—all I wanted to do was shove it in the bin, or better yet, set it on fire. At the same time, I couldn't look away.

There, in full color, was a small photo of two blurry figures I recognized as the princess and my father walking side by side in what looked to be the Highlands. Thank God they hadn't been so careless as to be holding hands ... or worse. My father was capable of far worse.

Still, there wasn't much to the photo—nothing the paps could prove. Even if they could prove the identities, which was far from certain, my father wasn't doing anything blatantly incriminating for once. This was the reason, encapsulated in one blurry image, why the paps had come for me.

The larger photo at the bottom of the page was, sadly, far clearer. It captured the moment when Cedar was helping me up off the street. For a few seconds, I couldn't look at anything beyond her eyes. There was a fierceness there I didn't understand. No one else had helped me, but she had, and I'd rewarded her with rudeness.

When I finally looked beyond her, I saw that in the photo my eyes were half-shut and my mouth was twisted in a grimace. I'd disgraced myself. I knew with absolute certainty that my father wouldn't be bothered a whit by that. What would upset him was that I got the cover shot and his photo only appeared like a footnote.

"I'm never going to live this down." My voice came out strangled.

Robbie patted my shoulder. "Now, now, lad. It'll blow over. Remember when Professor Whitshaw was bucked into the Cherwell by his horse? Everyone talked about it for a week, but then that student had a bad spell and tried to scale the Radcliffe Camera starkers. Nobody talked about Whitshaw after that. The gossip mill keeps churning. That's the way it's always been, and you'll be no different."

Robbie was wrong. It was different. Because of my father, I was on a much shorter leash than my peers. Everyone in college was waiting for me to show the first signs of being like him.

I had tried to get my father to understand how much I hated the notoriety of being his only son and heir, but he quite simply couldn't understand. He lived for being in the public eye and hopscotched from scandal to scandal to stay there.

"I'm going to lose my fellowship over this," I said. I was going to have the only path in life I'd ever felt steady on snatched out from underneath me. My stomach heaved at the thought of being rudderless again ... of having nothing solid to hold on to.

"I shouldn't think so," Robbie said, frowning down at the tabloid on his desk. "What college members don't go on the lash from time to time? It's all part of the Oxford experience. You're not responsible for what your father does either. Anyone who knows you would understand why you needed to let off some steam when the news of your father and the princess broke."

Robbie's kindness was well-meaning, but naïve. I shook my head. "How could I have let myself be so weak?"

Robbie rolled his eyes. "For goodness' sake, Alfie, you're a man, not a saint. Stop being so hard on yourself."

I forced myself to look back at the photo on the tabloid again. Maybe if I wallowed in its poison long enough, it would inoculate me against any future carelessness. "If only everyone saw it the same way as you, Robbie."

"I'm sure many people do, even if they don't say it," Robbie said, reassuringly. "Cedar, for example, had no idea who you were or who your father was. Probably still doesn't."

I couldn't bear to tell Robbie about my behavior towards her at the meet and greet. He was one of the last remaining people, besides Lachlan, who still gave me the benefit of the doubt. My throat thickened at the idea of losing that. Maybe she'd already told him?

"Have you seen Cedar again?" I asked.

"Not today." He shook his head. "I like her. Quite a fierce lass, to be sure, but there is something vulnerable about her. She strikes me as being a little lonely, perhaps."

I'd let her fill Robbie in on her incongruous background. He probably wouldn't believe me anyway. "Maybe she's just used to being alone, rather than lonely."

But as soon as I said it, I knew I was just making excuses. That relief in her eyes when they landed on me after she'd burst in the room, then the subsequent betrayal there ... those were emotions I recognized. Loneliness bracketed my life too.

Robbie shook his head. "She needs someone to help her get settled. You know, orient her around town."

As much as I regretted my unkindness, if Robbie thought I was going to volunteer for the position he was dead wrong. My plan was to find Cedar, apologize for my behavior, request her discretion, and then to put as much distance between her and myself as possible. Something about her felt dangerous—the complete opposite of the order and calm I was striving for. She was too unpredictable for me to be comfortable ... rather in the same manner as an unexploded bomb. I couldn't blame the chaos of the past thirty-six hours on her, but she wasn't completely separate from it either.

"She strikes me as independent," I said, rather lamely.

"I worry about her," Robbie said, reminding me how unlikely he was to give up easily once he had the bit between his teeth. "She would be better off if someone who knows the ropes here backwards and forwards—you, for example—took her under their wing."

"It would be inappropriate for me to take on that role, Robbie." I tried to sound responsible, instead of just unnerved. "I'm her junior thesis advisor. It would be a conflict of interest. Besides, I'm already deep enough in it with Professor Harris as it is."

This gave Robbie pause. "You may be right."

"What do you think I should do?" I tapped the wretched front page photo of Cedar and me. "Confess to him or—"

Robbie shook his head. "Are you mad? Pretend like nothing happened and chances are it will all blow over. He's such a priggish sort though ...". Robbie looked sharply at me as his words died off. I knew he was not friendly with Professor Harris, but this was the first time he'd actively expressed disliking him. My heart sunk. Lachlan had made his views on Professor Harris abundantly clear, but now Robbie too? I also knew that Robbie could be easily fired for talking disparagingly about a member of the college.

"Let me know if you see anything else," I said to him.

He nodded briskly. "As always. Where is your robe?"

I grimaced. "I have to go get a new one before I do anything else. That dog of yours ripped a huge chunk of it off as I tried to leave my room this morning. I'm blaming you, just for the record."

Robbie chuckled. "Aw, don't say so. You and Norris were made for each other. I did you a favor the day I gave him to you."

I snorted. "I believe you've got that backwards—I was doing you the favor."

Robbie grinned. "Call it what you will, but you're good for one another."

A professor walked in just then to get a replacement key to his study. Robbie wasn't allowed to shout at senior members like he did at the students, even though they appeared to give him ample opportunity.

I waved at him. "Thank you as always, Robbie. I'll be off."

As I neared the door to the college, I realized I'd forgotten to ask Robbie if anyone had reported paps lurking about. Surely, he would have told me if there had been.

Somehow, spending time with Robbie—while it didn't solve any of my major problems—gave me enough strength to think that maybe I could somehow survive the day.

CHAPTER EIGHT

Cedar

Please let the Hall serve pancakes for breakfast. I sniffed the air as I made my way up the massive stone staircase. I'd missed my first Beaufort breakfast because of jetlag, and I was counting it as progress that I'd only gone the wrong direction three times before finding my way to Beaufort College's dining hall.

I'd seen photos of the Hall at Beaufort on the internet and all over the information packet they'd sent me. It dated back to the founding of the college in 1325 and much of the original medieval structure had been painstakingly preserved.

Goosebumps prickled my skin. I reached the door, which was propped open, and stood there for a long time, taking in the vaulted stone ceilings, the intricately carved, dark-wood panels on the walls, the long, polished tables, and the oil portraits of dour men lining the walls. The appetizing smells of bacon and eggs and coffee filled the air, with an underlying scent of wood polish.

Nothing held a candle to the real thing. My lungs expanded as a prickle of awe raced up my spine. In the forest, I suspected

I could never be satisfied without experiencing life first-hand. I was right.

Thank God Alfie's dismissive treatment of me hadn't extinguished my sense of wonder at being in Oxford. Come to think of it, Alfie had looked just like those sullen men in the portraits when I arrived late to the tutorial without a cape ... or gown ... or whatever he'd called it. Why did that still bother me so much?

I lifted my chin. Yesterday had been a bit of a bust, but today was a new day. I would make new and better friends.

I followed the flow of students streaming into an adjacent room. Simple. I could do this. The sheer amount of food options on the other side of the serving counter were daunting, but my father always said hunger was the best ingredient, and even though we didn't see eye to eye on much, I had to agree with him there. My stomach grumbled loudly.

I took scrambled eggs, toast, sausages, bacon, and what looked like fried tomatoes plus a large side of baked beans. There was no room for regretting pancakes.

I followed the students going to sit at the tables. How had they met each other already? Sure, some were returning students, but I also knew there were plenty of new students like me. A spurt of annoyance reminded me how much I hated not knowing how things worked.

Near a group of students eating and talking animatedly, I sat down on one of the long benches and dug in. The eggs were silky and piping hot, the bacon nicely crisp. Once the edge to my hunger was satisfied, I began to look around the room. How did one go about making a friend? I'd never had to do that before, certainly not in a setting like this where nobody else seemed to be affected by the overwhelming cacophony of so many voices talking at the same time.

The students on the other end of the table spoke of camping in Italy, surfing in Cornwall, staying in some sort of cave hotel in Greece, and doing a summer term of university in California. The world they talked about was head-spinningly bigger and more stimulating than my existence back home. I'd experienced so little compared to them ... almost nothing beyond the trees and the occasional study excursion with my parents in other areas of Northern BC. I had so much catching up to do.

I longed to establish connections to not just trees, my dogs, the clouds in the sky, and the fish in the lake in front of our cabin—but to actual sentient human beings. Hopefully, they weren't all going to be as much of a letdown as Alfie.

My solitary life had been one hundred percent due to being the only child of two people who had turned their backs on the world and were obsessed with each other and their research to the exclusion of all else.

William—who was the reason I was here at Oxford in the first place—had been the closest thing to a friend I'd ever had, and he was a globe-trotting billionaire from England with a penchant for dangerous adventures in remote places. He was not exactly the sort of friend I saw on a daily basis once he'd left our cabin, arranged to send me here to Oxford, and was off to his next adventure.

Surrounding myself with people seemed the obvious solution to my loneliness, but now a new, fearful thought had me in its jaws—*was I going to be alone here in Oxford too, even though I was surrounded by people?* Alfie had been so kind and amusing, then so cold and harsh. How could someone change so completely? More importantly, why would they? My throat thickened. I put down my fork and swallowed hard against the lump that had formed there.

Shaun wasn't much better. He'd treated me like a freak—a zebra in a zoo.

A tray banged into mine. I looked up. Sitting down on the bench across the table from me was a girl with fuchsia, closely shorn hair. She tapped the edge of my tray with her fork. "That's a lot of food. I'm intrigued."

I looked down at my tray and then over at everyone else's. She was right. I'd taken three full plates of food—the other platters only had one.

"This is my first time eating in here," I admitted. "Where I'm from, when there's an abundance of food, we eat our fill."

She eyed me with curiosity. She was giving me that zoo-animal look like Shaun, but beggars couldn't be choosers. "Is that so? How fascinating. My name's Binita. It means 'modest' in Hindi."

This set her off into gales of laughter and I couldn't help but join her despite chewing on a mouthful of sausages. "You're not modest?" I asked.

"Definitely not, much to my parents' eternal disappointment. Poor them. It wasn't from lack of trying."

Huh. The idea that parents would put in the effort to try and shape a child was something I had never known.

"My name's Cedar," I said, then thought of Shaun's reaction to my name and figured it might need some sort of explanation. "Like the tree."

"How odd."

Maybe I should just accept that I was an anomaly at Beaufort College. "There are a lot of trees where I'm from. Most likely my parents just named me after the first thing they saw out the window after I was born." I shrugged. "I never thought to ask but I was an accident, and they were pragmatic that way."

She peered at me with intelligent eyes. "Where are you from?"

"From northern British Columbia, on the west coast of Canada. There's a lot of forest up there."

"Exotic. I'm from Manchester, decidedly less so."

"Trust me," I said. "Manchester sounds very exotic to me. It's up north, right? I remember reading how it was originally a town that was known for its manufacturing during the Industrial Revolution." Maybe I could make up for my lack of experience by being well read.

She waved a beautifully manicured hand, adorned with purple nail polish that glittered under the yellowish hall lights that sat on the tables every few feet. "I'm sure, but I don't want to talk about Manchester. So how much forest are you talking about?"

I thought about this for a second. "Occasionally small aircraft go down in our section of the Province, and if the pilots aren't killed in the crash, they usually die from starvation or dehydration before they find a way out of the bush, or they're eaten by a bear," I added. "That happens too."

She breathed deeply, her eyes shining. "Bears? Brilliant."

Bears had always been such a huge part of my life that I had never formed any sort of opinion about them. Something about Binita's forthright manner reminded me of the way people talked back home and made the muscles across my shoulders unknot a bit. In stark contrast to the last time I'd seen Alfie, I had the impression of knowing exactly what was going on in Binita's head.

"I'm glad you came over," I admitted. "I just arrived, and I was feeling a bit alone."

She nodded. "It's surprisingly easy to feel alone at Oxford. What are you studying?"

"I'm doing a Masters—"

"You mean an MPhil," she corrected me. "I don't mean to nitpick but the earlier you get a hang of these Oxford-isms, the easier things will be for you."

"Right," I said, grim. I had naively thought that speaking English was enough to figure out things at Oxford, but apparently not. "OK, I'll say it right. I'm doing an MPhil in Medieval Literature. You?"

"I'm doing a DPhil—that's a doctorate everywhere else in the world—in mathematics, particularly how stars and satellites communicate in terms of chaos theory."

My eyes widened at how she just tossed out that piece of information like a crumpled piece of scrap paper. "Holy cow," I said, with complete sincerity.

"Before you ask, yes. I'm a genius." She tilted her head in acknowledgement of this fact. "But that's hardly a novelty around here."

"Really?" I sent silent thanks to Willy for getting me here. Was Alfie a genius too? That reminded me ... "I have a question that's probably an insult to your intelligence, but I need to know the answer anyway."

"I'm listening."

"I need to get an academic robe ... gown ... you know, a black cape-y thing. My tutor was extremely rude about me not having one yet."

Binita narrowed her eyes at me. "Which tutor? We have some world-class tutors here, and some complete prats."

I thought of Alfie's haughty expression when I'd arrived in the already intimidating tutorial room. It had hit me like that time I'd been deep in the forest on a new trapline, and the iron-rich rock nearby threw off my compass readings. I still felt disoriented by it.

"Alfie," I said. "I mean Alfred, Lord Invernay."

Her eyes went wide. "I know of him, although he rarely has

much to do with us plebes. He's a stupidly wealthy and clever lord and always acts like he's above the rest of us. Still, I'm surprised he got stroppy with you. He's not known for that sort of thing."

I didn't need any further prompting and poured out the entire story from finding Alfie on the cobblestones to his aloof demeanor in the tutorial. After, I felt so much lighter.

"You call him Alfie?" Bonita blinked at me.

I shrugged. "He was fine with it the night we first met."

"You'd better call him *sir* to be on the safe side."

"Sir?" I had never in my life called anyone sir, or by any sort of formal label. My parents had always insisted I call them by their first names. "That's impossible. He's barely older than me." Not to mention he hit on me when he was under the influence.

"How old *are* you?"

"Twenty-two," I said. "I did an undergraduate degree online. My parents aren't big on the world outside the woods."

"Were they upset about you leaving?"

"Very." They'd given me the silent treatment for the two months leading up to my departure. They said it was because I was going against their beliefs about the evils of society, but I suspected it was because for years I had taken over most of the hunting and foraging so they had more time for their research.

"Excellent! We're both colossal disappointments to our parents. Now, back to Lord Invernay. Most Junior Advisors let their students call them by their first names. Usually that whole relationship is rather casual, but I don't imagine anything is casual with him. He's always struck me as quite … daunting."

I thought back to him listing slightly in Robbie's chair in the Lodge, telling me I was beautiful, and how I'd laughed at him. How could he ever be daunting to me after that? "He's not. Not really."

"From what I've seen he keeps very much to himself besides

the occasional dull as dishwater, socially acceptable girlfriend inevitably wearing a velvet Alice band."

What on earth was an Alice band? No, that would steer us too far off course. "I just can't wrap my mind around it," I said. "It's like he's two different people, and I don't know which one is real."

She winced. "I would have to bet the sober one is the real one. Sorry."

My heart weighed heavy in my chest. My head told me she was right, but still something in me didn't want that to be true. "I guess."

"How did you end up here, anyway?" she asked. "I mean, people ask me that question all the time, but that's just racism, pure and simple. For you ... well, your skin's pale enough, but it sounds like where you come from couldn't possibly be further away from Oxford."

I appreciated her directness. "You're right, it's a leap for me. The short answer is I'm here because of William Cavendish-Percy. Have you heard of him? He liked to drone on and on to me about how famous he is in England."

Binita's head jerked back. "You mean that aristocrat who loves living in huts in the middle of nowhere?"

"That's the one. As it turned out, one of those huts was our cabin. He came and stayed with us for a few months last winter. There was a lot of time for conversation, so we got talking about my undergraduate degree in literature I did online, and my own independent work."

"Unbelievable," she murmured.

"He took the idea in his head that he had to get me here to his old alma mater in Oxford, so he concocted some scheme to strengthen the ties of the Commonwealth by sending students—namely me—from remote corners of the Commonwealth—namely my forest—to Beaufort College to study. He even managed to sell the idea to the King."

"Blimey."

"I know, eh?" I appreciated the opportunity Willy had given me with every fiber of my being. I could not let some snotty tutor taint that. "I'm the first student sent by the program, but I won't be the last. From his travels in Canada alone, I think Willy has already picked out three other students."

Binita shook her head. "Sorry … sorry … I just can't get over this. William Cavendish-Percy *lived* with you?"

"And my parents, and my dogs, yes. I taught him how to hunt and butcher up animals and run a trap line. He was quite a quick learner. Not squeamish, thank God."

Binita pulled out her phone, which was covered in a furry fuchsia phone-case that matched her hair. "Bother. I could talk to you forever, but I have to go to a tutorial. I would play truant but, alas, I'm teaching it. What's your phone number? I'll enter it into my contacts, and—"

"Willy's apparently sending me a phone, but I don't have it yet. A phone wasn't any use to me in the woods. No reception beyond our solar generator."

"Well, let me know when you get it. In the meantime, we can look out for each other here in Hall."

"Yes, but before you go, we got distracted from the question I asked you about where to buy a gown."

"Ah yes, us geniuses do tend to get sidetracked. You'll definitely need a gown with matriculation coming up."

Matriculation … I remembered reading something about that in the notes Willy had printed up for me. I'd have to go back to my room and check again.

She checked her watch again. "Go to the Lodge and ask the

porter for directions to a shop called Ede & Ravenscroft."

"Will they know where it is?"

She chuckled. "Without a doubt. It's an institution in Oxford—just a short trot."

"Awesome. Thank you."

She dashed off to do her genius things, and before taking my tray back I sat there for a moment, basking in the thrill of a new friend. Alfie may have been a false start, but Binita was pink-haired confirmation that some people were worth spending time with.

CHAPTER NINE

Alfie

I stepped over the threshold of the college and took a few steps, furtively glancing around. No flashes or cameras from what I could see. Maybe Robbie was right. Maybe this would all blow over. Hope jumped in my heart.

My breathing had nearly gone back to normal by the time I neared the bend in the lane. A penetrating voice called out, "Lord Invernay! Are you upset about the princess becoming your new mother?"

I froze. There were at least twenty of them. They'd been lying in wait, just out of sight. The pack split into two and half of them ran behind me, cutting off my escape.

"Do you think you should check into a treatment center for alcoholism?"

"What were you crying about?"

For a brief moment of insanity, I missed Cedar by my side. I shook that thought out of my brain. She was the last thing I needed.

"How does your father feel about you supplanting him as the

most scandalous Invernay?"

My head swiveled at that, and I felt like growling and gnashing my teeth, like Cedar had taught me to do. It had been bizarrely satisfying. The paps and their questions were so absurd that it had been a joy to shock them for once. But no. I couldn't have them saying I was scandalous. I would lose my place at the University for certain, not to mention Professor Harris's approval.

"Who was the girl who helped you? Is she your girlfriend? What's her name?"

Lord, if the paps ever got hold of Cedar's identity and back story ... *disaster*. They'd have a bloody field day with her. She was far too interesting.

I kept walking, my head bowed, even though I wanted to yell at them to sod off. They were unusually persistent, closing around me, jostling me. My breath was coming in short staccato bursts and my head spun. I was gulping for air when a shrill honk made them scatter.

Thank God for Lachlan in his Mini Cooper, painted with the blue and white Scottish flag over the roof. He leaned on the horn and beckoned me over through the windshield. Relief washed over me.

The paparazzi tried to block my route to the passenger door, but they backed up when Lachlan and his rugby prop body emerged from his side of the car. It looked as though he could pick up his Mini in his fist and squash it.

"Away with ya bunch a bawbags!" Lachlan shouted at them, reminding me of Cedar and her roaring like a bear. I made a final push through the crowd, leapt in, and slammed the car door behind me. That was the thing with us rugby wingers—we were fast.

"How did you know?" I turned and asked Lachlan as he revved his engine.

"Saw the papers, didn't I?"

I groaned. "Right."

Lachlan started driving through the crowd of paps.

"You're going to kill one of them," I said, but in a resigned voice.

"Nae danger there. They'll get out of me way. Sure, they want a photo of you, but you're not worth dying for."

He was right. Once they realized Lachlan was ready to plow them down with zero compunction, they scattered like dandelion fluff. How freeing it would be to be like Lachlan and Cedar and do whatever you wanted. Nobody paid attention to them, but because of who my father was, I had to be on guard every second of every day.

"Now, where are you off to?" Lachlan asked me when we'd lost them.

"I need a new gown," I said. "Ede & Ravenscroft."

"Right-o. I know you probably need a shoulder to cry on about that tabloid nonsense. I would take you out for a pint, but I have to get to practice. I was just stopping by to check in on you."

"Perfect timing then. The photo is ... well, you've seen it." I waved my hand hopelessly.

He nodded his head, grim. Lachlan wasn't one for sugar-coating reality. "So was that Cedar—that girl you mentioned—in the photo?" He quirked a shaggy brow at me.

"You're missing the point, Lachlan." I rolled my eyes. "This is even worse than I predicted. It's an unmitigated disaster."

"It's not good," he admitted. "But Cedar looks like a lovely lass. Maybe a bright spot in this whole mess?"

"*No!*"

He shrugged. "Don't get in a lather. I just thought it was kind of her to help you—not many people seem to do that sort of thing these days. Have you apologized to her yet?"

"I haven't seen her, but I intend to find her today and do just that."

"Good."

"Stop acting like my nanny, Lachlan."

He shook his head. "I could never be that. I don't have nearly enough facial hair to pass for Nanny MacLeod."

I snorted with laughter. She had had a definite problem in that area. The poor woman. Lachlan and I had made her life far more stressful than it needed to be with our antics.

Lachlan screeched over to the side of the road in front of the venerable boutique. It's bow windows, and "Ede & Ravenscroft Est 1689" written in gold type over a green background on the sign was a mainstay on the High Street.

"There you go m'Lord." Lachlan gave me a roguish grin.

"Shut up," I said, but he had somehow managed to make me smile—something I would have thought impossible ten minutes before.

"I'm around if you need to talk."

"I know." I climbed out of the car. "I appreciate it, believe me. There's not many people in my corner."

"There's more than you think, Alfie."

I shut the door behind me. He zoomed off with a long honk and a cloud of exhaust. Feeling slightly less alone, I went into one of my favorite Oxford shops.

***

The tiny gold bell jangled over the door as I stepped inside.

For a few moments, I just stood on the plush red carpet and soaked in the calm hush of tradition. I needed more of this in my life, and less of screaming paparazzi and students who didn't know the first thing about social conventions.

A conversation from the rear of the store filtered over me.

"You don't need a fresher's robe," the salesperson said to his customer in a patronizing tone. "You need a post-graduate gown. It reaches the knee, and the streamers are longer."

"Oh. Okay."

Wait ... that voice.

"Tee one of those up for me then."

The salesman sniffed. "I will go and find your size."

"Great."

It was Cedar. It had to be. I wanted to apologize to her, but in a place of my choosing. Not here in the middle of one of the shops in Oxford where I was known.

I took a step backwards but just before I could sneak out the door, a floorboard under the carpet creaked and the salesman who had been helping Cedar caught sight of me.

"Lord Invernay!" he cried. "What a pleasure. What can I help you with today?"

Cedar's eyes caught mine. From her shrewd gaze, I knew she had seen me trying to back out of the store, and I also suspected she had picked up on the gushing tone the salesman had used to welcome me compared to his condescension towards her.

Had I been as snooty to Cedar in the meet and greet? Yes. I had. The shame of it burned my skin.

She straightened her spine. I might as well get this over with, but certainly not here with an audience.

"Yes, I require a new gown," I said to the man. "Mine was ripped in an unfortunate mishap."

"Right away, Lord Invernay." He clasped his hands together.

I nodded towards Cedar, who stood there, her indignation made clear by the crease between her brows. "I can wait. I believe you were helping another customer already?"

The salesman grimaced. "Yes. I won't be but a moment though." He dashed to the back.

I could hardly blame Cedar for being disgusted. Still, this was Oxford. What did she expect?

I walked over to her, my mind filling with what felt like static on an old telly. She was not at all the sort of woman to catch my interest, but I couldn't tear my gaze away from those freckles across her nose and her wild hair and snapping eyes. She was a live wire, and her chaotic energy blocked my most basic skills. How did I talk again? And walk? And breathe?

"Hello Cedar," I finally managed. I gave an awkward nod that I immediately regretted.

She crossed her arms across her torso and lifted a brow that made me feel incredibly rude and guilty. How did she *do* that? I stood by my assessment—dangerous.

"I see you're getting your academic gown," I managed.

"Bravo." She lifted her chin. "You just proved you're not blind. How perceptive you are, Lord Invernay."

The salesman had come back just then, a robe in each hand. He froze, his face rigid with shock. "You know each other?" he spluttered.

I took a deep breath. "I'm her tutor."

"Junior Advisor," Cedar corrected me.

The salesman's eyes widened. He was waiting for me to reprimand her for disrespect, but I wouldn't, not this time. A little part of me even thought that perhaps I deserved her contempt, even if it went against every unspoken rule of hierarchy here at Oxford. The salesman seemed to have completely forgotten he was carrying our gowns.

"Are those ours?" I asked.

With no further sharp words, but with a great deal of unspoken acrimony, Cedar and I purchased our gowns and left the store. I scanned the High Street for photographers but couldn't see any. Once I'd left with Lachlan, they'd likely lost my tracks.

Cedar turned and began to walk away. My brain was still not working well enough to formulate words, so I reached out and grabbed her arm. She spun around, her eyes flashing. A shot of white-hot electricity coursed through my fingertips and up to my shoulder. *Jesus*. What was that?

"Can I take you out for a pint?" I managed.

Her eyes narrowed. "Why?"

"It's about your academic program." The lie landed like a bad kebab in my stomach, but I had to get her somewhere private before I could offer my apology.

"Where do you have in mind?" she asked, looking far from convinced.

"Follow me."

She didn't move. "I will not be following you anywhere. I'm not a sheep and this whole thing feels wrong. You can't act like an asshat to me one day and then invite me out for a pint the next like nothing happened."

I winced. "Fair enough." I couldn't blame her for that. "I was thinking of a pub called The Bear. It's not far from here. It's extremely historic. I think you might like it." It was also dimly lit with lots of little corner tables.

"It's about my academic program?" she demanded again.

"Yes," I fibbed.

She shook her arm free of my grasp and splayed her fingers over where I had been holding on. Was her skin feeling that live wire shock too?

CHAPTER TEN

Cedar

Alfie led me down a narrow side street off the High Street and into a little pub that was white with its name "The Bear" in gold lettering on a black wooden panel above the black door. He had to duck to get through the low doorframe.

I wouldn't admit this to him, but I was grateful to get off that street. My lungs were closing off against the fumes of the cars, and the constant racket of squealing wheels, shouting people, and engines revving made my ears ring. I'd also gotten lost several times on the way to finding Ede & Ravenscroft, so following someone—even him—felt like a reprieve.

Still, what was this about? Every one of my instincts was on alert. I hoped he knew he didn't have the power to expel me from the college or my program. I was confident that William, who had put me here in the first place, had far more power than a Junior Fellow—even one who happened to be a Lord.

The light was dim inside the pub, so much so that I had to watch where I was putting my feet and wait until my eyes adjusted.

When they did, I saw Alfie was leading me to a table tucked into the far corner. Something above me caught my eye. *Look at that.* The bizarrely low ceiling was covered with cut-off ties. Same with the walls. Each one individually labeled—Lincoln College Goblin Club, Royal Scottish Pipes Society, Hong Kong Police Force, Hertford College Pints & Snooker Association ...

Alfie pulled out my chair. He made a gallant gesture for me to sit down. How absurd. Why bother being polite to me now when he was so rude to me in my first tutorial? I sat, mainly because it was too small and crowded for me to make a point of standing.

The whole place was impregnated with the smell of spilled beer, but I found it comforting rather than off-putting. It reminded me of The Nugget Bar back in Stewart. The wooden floor stuck to the soles of my boots and, despite the fact I was here with Alfie, my whole body exhaled the tiniest bit. There was something approachable and unpretentious about this spot that reminded me of the first version of him I'd met.

I was in a real British pub, finally. Alfie murmured something about 'getting the pints in', whatever that meant, but I was craning back my head to make out all the different ties on the ceiling.

"What do you think of this place?" he said when he came back. He placed a pint in front of me and took his seat again. "I thought you might like it."

Amazement ran through me at the idea he'd thought about me at all, especially after the other day. "You did?"

"Yes. It dates back to 1240 or some such thing. I can't remember which year."

"Really?" There was no way I could keep the wonder out of my voice. Damn him, I *did* like it. Loved it, actually. "This is my first time in a pub, you know." It just slipped out.

"Truly?" he asked, that cloak of formality he'd been holding so tightly around him loosening.

I nodded. "I was on my way to The Turf when I found you on the street. I think you remember enough to know why I didn't end up making it to a pub that time."

The tips of his ears went pink, and he rubbed his nose. It was not a perfect nose—uneven at the bridge, and maybe slightly too long at the tip. His features were a bit off kilter, although honesty forced me to admit that made them no less striking. "About that," he said. "I cannot begin to explain my mortification—"

"I've read about British pubs in books for so many years and I've always wanted to have a drink in one." I didn't want to hear his regrets of that night. Despite everything that had happened since, helping him remained a good memory for me. I didn't want him to taint that like he had everything else. I took a sip of beer. "This is not at all how I planned my first pub visit, but here I am."

He lifted his pint glass and clinked it gently against mine. "Here *we* are," he said. "And for that night ... I truly apologize."

How could he not realize he was apologizing for completely the wrong thing? I shook my head. "There's nothing to apologize for about the night we met."

He frowned down into his pint. "I beg to differ."

Was he always so serious about everything? "I guess the throwing up in the garbage can wasn't exactly a fun thing to watch, but better an empty house than a bad tenant, right?"

Alfie's eyes lit up and he laughed—a natural, spontaneous laugh that completely transformed his face, and made all of his features work together to create something greater than their parts. He *was* hiding in there—the other Alfie—my sort-of-friend. Warmth rushed through me.

"Let's agree to disagree about that night," he said. "But sharing your first pint with you during your first pub visit ... I'm honored."

He put his hand on his heart. "Truly."

The most amazing thing was I believed him. How could two such completely different men reside in the same body? I took another sip of the yeasty, slightly bitter, nut-brown pint. Whatever it was, it was delicious. "Now," I rested my elbows on the table. It was as sticky as the floor. "What about my academic program did you need to talk to me about?"

Alfie cleared his throat. "I lied about that." At least he looked sheepish.

"I thought so."

"You did? How?"

I shrugged. "Instinct. Anyway, I'm listening."

Hope fluttered under my breastbone. The only apology and explanation I wanted was about the tutorial.

He took a steadying breath. "As I was saying, I owe you my gratitude for helping me and sincerely apologize for the state I was in the night we met."

We'd already covered this.

"As you probably realize by now, I couldn't exactly thank you in the tutorial yesterday morning. It was all very ... awkward. Do you understand?"

No, I didn't, and he hadn't offered a genuine apology either. Instead of answering, I just watched him, waiting for more.

He flexed his fingers, then a minute or two later took another sip of his beer. *He was hopeless.*

"No, I don't understand," I said, at last. "Why couldn't you just thank me in the tutorial, like a normal person?"

"Like a normal person? It was you who didn't know the basic—" His breath came out in a frustrated little puff. He straightened his shoulders and clamped his lips together. I wished he didn't try so hard to tame his emotions. I'd far rather have the unvarnished version of Alfie. "I had to maintain my authority as a teacher. Letting the other students know you lifted me up from the cobblestones and dragged me back to college to save me from a pack of paparazzi would have greatly undermined that."

I studied him as I considered this. I'd never had an actual in-person teacher before, but I still felt Alfie was overestimating his need to establish authority over a bunch of students who were practically his age.

"I don't see it that way," I said. "I would think it would make you more relatable to your students."

"But I don't *want* to be more relatable," he said, his brows drawn together in consternation.

"Why not?"

He opened his mouth like he was going to say something, then snapped it shut again. *Damn.* I wanted to hear the reason he'd almost blurted out, rather than the one which I could tell from his veiled eyes he was currently concocting. "At Oxford it would be highly irregular for a junior fellow in my position to encourage familiarity." He clutched his pint so tight his knuckles were turning white. "I'm not quite sure how to phrase it, but how can you not know?"

I considered the possibility that maybe I hadn't read the situation correctly. In any case, it felt like a frank question that merited an honest answer. "I haven't had enough contact with people to know what's normal, especially at Oxford."

Alfie leaned forward over his pint towards me. I caught another whiff of that expensive cologne and pen ink. It was a surprisingly pleasant combination.

"You truly grew up that isolated?" His eyes softened.

"Oh yeah."

"Didn't your parents teach you these things?"

I snorted. "They paid far more attention to the bears' behavior than mine. I was encouraged to figure things out for myself, and social skills were not a top priority in the forest."

"What was their area of study?"

So far, nobody had asked this question, yet I could explain it in my sleep. My parents talked about almost nothing else. "They have a hypothesis they're trying to prove that links different grizzly bear populations—there are three distinct ones based on their DNA samples—to similarly distinct indigenous language families. It's a combination of etymology and genetics that, if they're right, will completely transform currently held beliefs about the links and relationships between grizzlies and indigenous populations in Northern British Columbia."

Alfie's glacier-turquoise eyes widened. "Gosh."

"Yeah." I nodded. "They're both considered brilliant."

"And you? You're not interested in doing what they do?"

The mere idea made my skin prickle, like that one time I'd broken out in a rash from taking a shortcut through a field of stinging nettles. I respected my parents' research, but I had plenty of reasons to hate it too. "No. It's their thing."

"But medieval literature ...." Alfie shook his head. "It's such a complete departure from that."

"Exactly." I couldn't quite keep the bitterness out of my voice.

"Oh," Alfie said, understanding in his eyes.

My parents found my studies unworthy of their interest, but that hadn't come as a surprise. "I had my fill of bears and DNA, although I was drawn to the etymology part. I use that in Medieval Lit through studying Tristan and Iseult in both old French, old English, then all the subsequent variations. I love drawing comparisons between them. In fact, I was thinking of centering my thesis around that."

Alfie's eyes sparkled. "Impressive. What do you think of the hypothetical 'Ur-Tristan' poem that Joseph Bédier argued for?"

I had never tried drugs before, but this must be what feeling high was like—the rush of talking to someone who had extensive knowledge in my field jump-started every cell in my body. "I think he makes a solid argument. I've actually been trying to teach myself some old Breton to see if I can study some of the original texts."

"Truly? That's impressive. You'll be amazed at how many originals they have in the Bodleian. The medieval archives we have access to as Oxford students are second to none."

My head spun with the possibilities of having all these sources so close to me. "I cannot wait."

Alfie nodded, biting his lip as he mulled over something. "Were you lonely in the forest?" He shook his head. "Sorry. I shouldn't have asked that—it's too personal a question. Forget it. We'd better stick with Thomas of Brittany."

"It's fine." Now that I'd rediscovered the first Alfie I'd met, it dawned on me I was willing to make significant efforts not to lose him again. "There was no valid reason for me to be lonely, at least that's what my parents told me. My friends were books and the animals in the forest, trees, and lake we lived on."

"Cedar." He softly clinked his pint glass against mine. "You didn't say you *weren't* lonely, just that you didn't feel justified for feeling that way."

I sighed. "I don't know if I would call it loneliness." I had never really bothered to give it a name—that low, deep ache in my soul that was my constant companion. "On second thought, that's probably what it was. I guess I always had this sense of wanting *more*. That was something my parents never understood."

He nodded, his eyes focused on mine. "My father," he said.

"He's the reason I have to be so circumspect. He makes a point of being scandalous, so I have to counteract his reputation by making mine just as spotless as his is tarnished."

"So that's what those photographers were hassling you about?"

"Yes. The night we met was a major lapse in that regard. I am so sorry to have to tell you this, but there is a photo of you helping me off the street in the tabloids today. It's splashed all over the front page. I'm so very sorry."

A photo of me? I chuckled at the idea I had somehow stumbled into being front page news. Only as a prop though, I reminded myself, not as an actual source of interest.

"You're not horrified?" he demanded.

"No. I think it's hilarious." A few more giggles escaped.

"You think it's *funny*?" His eyes went wide, incredulous.

"God, yes." I waved at the air above my pint. "Anyway, I'm not interesting enough for them to care about in the long run."

"You will be, if they find out who you are." He was still deadly earnest, miles away from seeing any humor in the situation.

I shook my head. No. I couldn't believe that.

"I broke all the rules I made for myself that night." He began to shred the paper coaster he'd placed under his beer. "I didn't want anyone else to know about it but now that it's in the paper, of course, everyone does."

"So that's why you were so unfriendly in the tutorial? You were trying to keep it a secret?"

"Yes. I'm sorry."

Ah, here it was. It wasn't so much the apology that was satisfying, but the way he was talking to me so openly. "You asked me to be your friend that night," I confessed. Did he remember that at all?

"I'm sure I did, but Cedar ... I was not in my right mind."

"What's wrong with us being friends?"

"I don't think we *can*." Was that regret darkening his eyes? Whatever it was, it made fire flash up my spine—of anger or something else I couldn't figure out. "Cedar, I hate to break this to you, but you just don't understand how things work here at Oxford. You're going to have to learn."

Maybe he was right, but if something didn't make sense to me, I wasn't going to pretend it did. "I still don't see the problem."

"It's inappropriate for a student and teacher to be friends."

I couldn't help but roll my eyes. "How old are you?"

"Twenty-four."

"I'm twenty-two," I said. "It feels completely insane to me to not be friendly when we're almost the same age. Also, you're just the junior thesis advisor. Yesterday, I finally read enough of the information left for me to know that as far as *actual* power over my studies here, you have approximately zero. Your role is to help me, but that's the end of it."

"Believe what I'm telling you," he said. "Things work differently here."

I thought of the strange names for the Masters and Doctorate degrees. Oxford was definitely quirky, but could it be that absurd?

"I'd very much appreciate it if you didn't mention the incident to anyone," he added. "The quicker people forget about it—if that's even possible—the better it will be for both of us."

"I mentioned it to Binita, but I can ask her not to say anything."

He blinked at this, but eventually recovered. "Yes, please do ... but that isn't exactly who I meant."

Did he think I was about to go to the press or something? My stomach hardened. I would never do that, even if I knew how to go about it, which I didn't. All I wanted from Alfie was a bit of camaraderie, but he'd made it clear he didn't want that.

"Sure," I said, my vision blurring for a few moments. I blinked to clear it. I shouldn't care about him not wanting to be my ally. My body just needed to catch up.

He sat back heavily in his chair and snapped his coaster into two with a muffled crack. "You're agreeing to keep quiet about it, just like that?"

I didn't understand the question. "Why wouldn't I?"

"You want nothing in return?"

I frowned. What had people done to him, that he would think such a thing? "Where I'm from, we help each other out. End of story."

His eyes darted around my face, flustered. Whatever he'd been expecting from me, it hadn't been that answer. "That's generous of you."

I cocked my head, trying, but failing, to understand his surprise. Had he thought I was going to blackmail him or something? "It's just what any normal person would do."

"Thank you. You're sure you won't say anything to anyone, even in error?"

I bore my eyes into his, so he knew just how insulted I was. "You may think I'm an uncouth hick, but I know the difference between right and wrong."

SECOND WEEK

CHAPTER ELEVEN

Alfie

It wasn't until three days after my poor excuse for an apology to Cedar, which had no doubt left her even more disgusted with me, that Professor Harris summoned me to his study.

Waiting for word from him had been a special kind of torture. At first, I had tried to delude myself that Professor Harris wouldn't stoop to reading tabloids, but Robbie informed me everyone at college, and indeed, the United Kingdom, had seen them.

Fellow students and even the dons tried to catch my eye, but I followed Robbie's advice and laid low. I worked in hidden corners of the Bodleian, had a few pints and a moan with Lachlan in a pub that locals only frequented in the dodgiest outskirts of town, and snuck Norris out for his walks even later than usual.

So far, I'd avoided being photographed again by the paparazzi—either that or they'd lost interest. Sometimes it was hard to tell. They moved together like a chattering of starlings, always unpredictable.

I knocked quietly on Professor Harris's door, my heart in my throat. Was he going to take away my fellowship? The thought of disappointing him made me feel like an absolute failure—unable to cure myself of my father's DNA coursing through my veins.

"Enter," he said.

He sat behind his desk, his brown hair cut so short it almost looked military, his neat navy blazer over a perfectly tied Windsor knot. He studied me with a neutral expression. What I would have given at that moment for him to be more like Robbie, and to take the entire ordeal with a grain of salt. That wasn't Professor Harris's way.

He waved me towards the leather couch where my students had sat. "Please," he said. "Sit."

I remembered the day of my first tutorial with him. I'd been so disgusted with my father and the uproar he'd been creating with the German Chancellor's wife while I'd spent the summer months stuck up in Scotland, alone. Lachlan had been invited to a prestigious rugby camp in France.

I had asked my mother if I could stay with her on St. Barts, but she tutted and said although she would adore that, it wasn't the right time. She'd already accepted an invitation to spend several weeks on a friend's yacht.

I'd tried to convince my father to hide with his lover *du jour* instead of bringing me up to Oxford, so I could arrive at college alone, and like a normal student. I already had Lord attached to my name, and in my mind that was plenty conspicuous enough.

He refused, ignoring my pleas. When we arrived at the entrance to Beaufort College, a storm of paparazzi waited for us. My father spent twenty minutes by the front door of the college, posing for the photographers with his sunglasses perched jauntily on his nose and his fedora tipped just so.

He answered their questions as provokingly as possible to

stoke rather than stifle their interest. Meanwhile, I had to stand beside him, with my suitcases and my trunk, burning with embarrassment as the other new students and their parents filed by, staring at my father, then me, and whispering to each other.

Anywhere near my father's orbit felt hazardous—a land constantly threatened by earthquakes, tsunamis, and hurricanes. How I yearned for solid ground under my feet.

Then I arrived for my first tutorial with Professor Harris, and there, right in front of me—trim, polite, and calmly detached—was the solution to my problems.

Professor Harris struck me as the kind of person that nothing could throw off-balance. I wanted a carbon copy of what he had with every desperate ounce of my soul: including his studies, a blonde, sweet wife, two children—a boy and a girl—and a pristine white house in Banbury. Every time I was around him, I felt like he nudged me back on the right track and made the murky path in front of me crystal clear.

I sat down on the couch. Due to my lack of self-control, his mentorship might be ending here and now.

"I imagine you know why I've summoned you here?" he asked with a perfectly calibrated arch of his eyebrow. He was never one for self-indulgent expressions of emotion.

I sucked in a deep breath of air, suspecting I would need it. "The photos," I said, and it wasn't a question.

He steepled his hands in front of him. "Yes. I've considered it, and I concluded perhaps it would be best if I give you an opportunity to explain what led to those." His lips pinched together.

In halting sentences, I explained my shock at seeing my father's photos, and how I'd gone to The Turf and indulged more than usual. I reassured him I'd had no notion the paparazzi were going to pounce and tried to paint it as a regretful confluence of events.

"It was my fault that I drank too many pints that evening," I admitted. "But if the paparazzi weren't there, nothing much would have come of it."

Professor Harris frowned at me. Shame made my stomach lurch. "Come now, Alfred. The photos show you were in a disgraceful state. That is never acceptable. Yes, it is commonly done here at Oxford. If you were a fresher, that's one thing, but you're not. You're a junior fellow, Alfred. You have a certain stature to uphold. I understand that learning about your father's latest peccadillo must have been displeasing, but as we've discussed before, his behavior is all the more reason for you to act in a way that is even more circumspect."

His words landed like iron weights in my gut. He was right, and I knew it.

"It was a momentary lapse," I said. "I can promise you it will never happen again."

He narrowed his eyes at me. "No," he said. "It will not. I seriously contemplated reversing my decision on your junior fellowship, Alfred. It was truly unacceptable behavior and for it to be broadcast all over the country ... well, it is most unsavory. It reflects badly on Oxford, on Beaufort, and on me as your mentor."

I hung my head. "I realize that, and I am sincerely sorry for it." This was every one of my worst nightmares being thrust at me by the one person I hoped to emulate and impress.

"I've decided to give you one last chance," he said. My heart skipped a beat. "However, if an incident like this happens again—"

"It won't."

"I'm glad to hear it." He nodded. "When I said the best students at Oxford work hard and play hard, I meant on the rugby field, not at The Turf Tavern." I knew this play on words was his attempt to lighten the mood a bit, but it sounded stilted. Professor Harris was many things, but a natural comedian was not one of them.

I laughed a forced laugh, but it rang hollow. Nothing about this was funny. I didn't think I would ever laugh about how badly I'd let him down. "Thank you for giving me another chance."

"Make sure you don't disgrace me again. Now, let's discuss more pleasant things. How have your tutorials been going with the MPhil group?"

"Fine," I said, still trying to catch up with this abrupt dismissal of my disgrace. "They are a very ... diverse lot."

"So I've learned," he said drily. "The administration office sent me their files at long last. Quite the mix you have. How is Shaun Webb?"

I gathered my wits about me. "Cocky, needs a very short leash, but far from stupid. However, as to his work ethic ... I have my doubts."

"Keep reporting back to me about him. The college has their eye on his father for the refurbishment of the chapel. You have the unenviable job of making him do his work, yet not offending him or his father."

That all sounded a tad unethical but, if Professor Harris was saying it, surely it fell more on the side of being merely pragmatic.

"Raphael Coates?" he asked.

"Big hulk of a man," I said. "Socially awkward, but again I don't believe he's lacking in intelligence. He won't be a problem."

Professor Harris nodded again. "That brings us to this dreadful girl from some cabin in the middle of nowhere they have saddled you with."

Was he talking about Cedar? Something inside me revolted, but I tamped it down. After all, Professor Harris's opinion was no different from what mine had been at first but, without me realizing it, things had slowly begun to shift in my mind. Our conversation in the pub made me understand she was far from uneducated; she was quick-witted too, and different. Not my type of female at all—that went without saying. Still, if only I hadn't offended her so badly in the end.

"Cedar Wild," I said, as neutrally as possible.

"Yes, that's her. I cannot believe the Warden has gone along with William Cavendish-Percy's ridiculous Commonwealth Scheme or whatever such nonsense it is. Our students at Oxford are hot-house flowers, they have been carefully cultivated their whole lives to come and learn here." He snorted. "The idea that one of the spots which should have gone to a worthy student has been given to a heathen from the Canadian wilds sets my teeth on edge. There is no way that she, or indeed any of the students William Cavendish-Percy intends to foist on us, are Oxford material."

I was hardly in a position to argue after my latest mishap. Yet, I couldn't let Professor Harris go on thinking of Cedar in such a negative light.

My previous girlfriend, Imogen, had been clear about wanting nothing more in life than a man to look after and provide for her, so she could stay at home and look after the house, just like Professor Harris's wife did. Yet, despite Imogen being exactly the sort of girl I needed, she'd struck no desire in me to protect her or look after her.

Why did Cedar—she of the wild bears and dense forests who was one thousand times tougher and more capable than Imogen—spark my protective instincts? It was unacceptable for Professor Harris to mistakenly think she was stupid or incapable, even though that was exactly what I'd believed not that long ago.

"You'll be happy to know she is very intelligent," I said. "The breadth and depth of her personal research, particularly on Tristan and Iseult, is admirable. She has taught herself medieval

French so she can use it to study Chrétien de Troyes and other comparative texts."

His head jerked back at this, but rather than relief on his face, his nostrils flared. "That doesn't mean she knows how to conduct herself or write a proper essay."

He had a point—she didn't know how to conduct herself, and I was becoming increasingly doubtful that she was willing to learn. Still, Professor Harris didn't know how determined she was, or how interesting. "I'll do my best with her," I said.

"I know you will, but we know each other well enough that we don't need to lie to one another. Let me reassure you, Alfred, that I am doing my best behind the scenes to have her removed from Beaufort and to have this silly Commonwealth Scheme abandoned." His lips turned up in the corners with a not-very-kind smile. "Would you like to wager how fast I can do it? How about one hundred quid?"

"I beg your pardon?" I asked, truly confused. Professor Harris was going to bet on a student? That was ... very surprising.

"Are you not one for laying odds?" He tapped his fountain pen against the blotter on his desk.

I'd honestly never thought about it before. "No ... I suppose not."

"Pity. In any case, this Commonwealth Scheme is bad for the college, and I have much more influence among the other dons than you realize, Alfred."

"That doesn't surprise me," I said. He would have to be an expert at politicking to advance so quickly in college.

He looked pleased by this. "I hate to end this, but I have a group of students arriving," he said. "None as promising as you were at that age, I regret to say."

This bone of approval made me judge his words in a different light. After all, how could I blame him for forming the same assumptions regarding Cedar that I had held myself so recently?

CHAPTER TWELVE

Cedar

I couldn't say I had adjusted yet to the noise and lack of trees that came with living in Oxford, but at least I didn't get lost several times a day—only once or twice now.

The worn stone steps of the stairs to Hall dipped in the middle to fit my foot—surely from centuries of students running up and down them, just like I was doing on my way to breakfast.

I caught a flash of pink hurtling down towards me.

"Binita!" I cried. I hadn't seen her since we'd had lunch together several days previously, and it warmed me up to recognize an ally, maybe even a friend?

"Cedar!" She wrapped me in a hug. I jerked in surprise—my parents had never been physically affectionate, but then warm familiarity made me hug her back. It felt strange but nice.

"What have you been up to?" I asked when we released each other. "You disappeared."

"I had to go back up to Manchester. My cousin got married."

"Did you have fun?"

"Hindu weddings are *always* fun." She smiled. "They're elaborate, multi-day parties with more delicious food than you could possibly eat. They make me feel sorry for other cultures."

How I would love to experience that myself. Weddings were not something that featured in my life at all. I didn't even know how or where my parents had tied the knot. Probably in a canoe or city hall or something. Knowing them, it was an afterthought—after all, it had nothing to do with bears.

Binita grabbed my arm and pulled me over to the stone banister so we could chat without being knocked over by the stream of students going in both directions.

"Gorgeous day, eh?" The air was crisp and the leaves on the oak trees had taken on an orange tinge.

She raised her eyebrows. "Is it? I pay scant attention to the weather."

"Too much thinking to do?" I couldn't imagine not paying attention to the weather. It predicted so many of my days back home.

"Of course. I can't believe I just missed you at breakfast. We really must plan better."

"I know."

"How is it going?" she asked. "Getting settled and all that?"

Now that school term had officially begun, I was always busy going to lectures or tutorials or researching my thesis. I devoted a lot of my energy to just trying to get the hang of the logistics of life at Oxford. None of this left much time for contemplation, unlike back home in my forest. "It's a work in progress," I said.

"How about the daunting Lord Invernay? I expect you've had another tutorial with him."

I'd had more than that, I'd thought, thinking back to The Bear pub. Since I'd agreed to secrecy, the few times I'd seen him around campus he'd been icily civil.

"I did." In our last tutorial he'd barely even looked at me.

The real Alfie I'd had back for a brief moment at the pub had vanished again, perhaps for good. I hated that I found myself mulling over him when I was supposed to be listening to a lecture about a new interpretation of the original Welsh texts of Geoffrey de Monmouth, or researching Margery Kempe in the college library.

"So ...?" She gestured with her hands. She did that a lot, I noticed, and her movements were always fluid and fascinating.

"He's being professional."

"Ugh. I told you he's the imperious sort." She flicked the air with disgust. "Thinks he's better than the rest of us, I suppose."

I nodded, annoyed that his coldness still had the power to make me feel glum. The distance he'd put between us left me stinging with rejection, and heavy with a sadness I didn't understand. He had shown himself to be an idiot, so why did I care? I clearly didn't matter to him, so why should how he act matter to me?

She reached out and patted me on the shoulder with her long fingers, sympathy in her perceptive eyes. "I'm teaching a tutorial, but let's meet in Hall tonight for dinner? Six-thirty? We can talk more about it then."

"I don't think I want to talk more about it," I said.

She rested her chin on her long fingers and contemplated me. "Right," she said, unconvinced. "That's your prerogative, of course."

I waved goodbye, then went to eat my *bangers* as Shaun had taught me to call sausages.

***

My stomach swooped in awe as I stepped into the library. I couldn't wrap my head around the fact that I was inside one of the oldest continuously operating academic libraries in the world—dating back to 1325—the same year the college was built.

Students sat at the huge oak tables, some scrolling on their phones, nonchalant. How could anyone ever be blasé about such a magical place? Awe froze me in place as I contemplated the medieval murals painted on the upper part of the stone walls, or the ornate wooden bookshelves, and the sliding ladders.

In my cabin back home, I had a difficult time comprehending that such a place existed. I finally stepped forward, following the signs to the manuscript room.

I opened its heavy wooden door and closed it reverently behind me.

In our tutorial, Alfie had recommended Shaun, Raphael, and I take full advantage of Beaufort's rare collection of medieval manuscripts. He'd avoided my eyes while saying it, of course. He'd managed not to meet them for the entire ninety-minute duration. Quite a feat given as there were only four of us in the small study.

My breath came slower. The scent of old pages and oiled leather and polished wood was pushing away my frustration.

After slipping my hands into my white gloves, as per the instruction sign tacked to the wall, I carefully removed the Summa de Accidentibus Mundi from its archival box and placed it on the reading table. I ran my hands as lightly as possible over the cover. To think, John Ashendon had written this text in the 1300s, making connections to celestial events and earthly events like plagues and floods—he'd lived through the 1348 plague himself, so he knew the subject first-hand. I'd read about this text and here I was ... actually touching it.

I opened it up, and lost myself in the thickness of the old pages against my fingertips, the vivid colors of the ink, the sheer beauty of the artistry. Nothing could have prepared me for this all-encompassing wonder that saturated every cell with gratitude. This was night and day compared to studying this text online.

Alfie was probably the type to stride into a historical building like this, not noticing any of the incredible details around him—nearly as bad as the students staring at their phone screens instead of reveling in this privilege.

Forget Alfie.

Maybe I'd just imagined that connection running between us. I would probably never know whether the real Alfie was that man of unguarded words and smiles, or the judgmental prig who found it so impossible to accept my word at face value. Probably the latter, as Binita had predicted.

The door to the manuscript room slammed opened, and Shaun rushed in.

My gloved hands froze as I turned the page.

"There you are!" he gasped. "Raphael and I have been looking all over for you. I *told* him I'd find you here."

What was this all about? "Here I am."

He jerked his head towards the door. "Well then, chop, chop! You're already late, and you're not even in sub-fusc."

Shaun was wearing a tailored dark suit with a white bow tie under his academic robe. He held a square black mortarboard in his hand.

"What are you talking about?" I carefully closed the manuscript and set it softly back in the archival box. "Late for what?"

"It's our matriculation! Didn't you read the notice in your pidge?"

Oops. I hadn't quite gotten into the habit of doing that. I was used to a float plane landing on the lake in front of our cabin twice a year and bringing our mail and the bigger supplies we couldn't get in Stewart. "I guess not," I said. No point getting into details.

I slid the manuscript box back onto its shelf and folded the gloves. He tugged on my arm. "Come *on*," he urged. He dragged me out of the library and by the time we were going down the stone steps to the main quad, we were both running.

"Do you have a robe?" he demanded over his shoulder.

"Yes." I'd taken care of that, at least.

"How about your mortarboard and your black tie?"

Sweat broke out behind my neck. I remembered the shopkeeper droning on about those things at Ede & Ravenscroft but it hadn't truly registered, and then Alfie had come in and ... "No," I answered. Just when I thought I was finally getting the hang of things, the scandalized look on Shaun's features told me that my oversight was no minor problem.

He groaned as we continued to run towards the Lodge along the leaf-strewn path around the quad. There were signs everywhere saying we were not allowed on the grass. It was being kept for ornamental appearances only, which always made me chuckle to myself. It was just so *bizarre*.

"This is going to be Mission Impossible," he burst out. "You also need a black skirt, you know, for *sub-fusc*, and a white blouse and dress shoes. Do you have *any* of those things?" Shaun scanned my clothes—my usual outfit of boots, jeans, and a fleece—his nostrils flaring. "Don't bother answering that," Shaun said. "I'm sure you don't. Now we are well and truly buggered."

Binita's pink hair appeared like a beacon emerging from her staircase in the far corner of the quad. I was about to shout out for her help, but Shaun beat me to it. "A savior, perchance?" he quipped and called out her name as he sprinted over to her.

He was fast, but I kept up.

Binita stopped walking and goggled at both of us. "What is it?"

Shaun gave a succinct summary of my predicament and, without hesitation, Binita grabbed my hand. "Cedar, give your room key to Shaun. Shaun, you fetch Cedar's gown from there. In the meantime, I'll go to my room and get her kitted out with the rest of it. She squeezed my hand. "We'll get you out of this jam, don't fret. Come on." For once, I did what I was told.

***

Binita's room was up two flights of the narrow, stone stairs. The floor was covered in books and brightly colored saris and scarves—their sequins and encrusted jewels sparkled even in the dim light.

"I'd tell you it's usually not this messy," Binita said, as she rushed over to her wooden armoire in the corner and began rummaging. "But I'd be lying."

She chucked me something from her closet—a white, long-sleeved top. I yanked my fleece and T-shirt over my head and pulled on Binita's blouse and buttoned it up with shaking fingers—must be the adrenaline. *I should have checked my damn pidge*. I hated that this proved Alfie right. That maybe I truly didn't know how things worked at Oxford, and that my ignorance was a problem.

She threw me over a small black ball.

"Stockings," she answered my unspoken question. "Put them on. No time to lose with modesty."

I'd never worn stockings in my life. I sat down on the edge of Binita's bed. I tried to find the foot part, but the silky material kept slipping out of my fingers. I was breathing hard and my forehead had started to sweat. When I tried to pull them up they just twisted around my leg. How did women do this? More to the point, *why* did they do this?

Binita had something else in her hand now and my struggling must have caught her eye.

"You're never going to manage like that!" She came over and kneeled in front of me. "Have you never put on a pair of stockings before?"

"Nope."

"Lucky," she said with a frown. "They're dead wretched, but one must suffer to be beautiful."

I'd certainly never heard that take before. What a load of garbage.

"Cedar, listen to me. I need you to sit still and go loose like a puppet. Just do what I tell you and we'll have these on in a jiff." She gripped her bottom lip in her teeth and put those dexterous fingers to good use.

My insides squirmed with this new and extremely unwelcome sensation of being helpless, but at the same time Binita's hands flew around my legs like stocking ninjas. Within thirty seconds, she yanked them up around my waist.

The fine mesh compressed my flesh. It was the weirdest sensation, like my legs were being strangled. "Ugh. These feel like straightjackets for my legs."

She passed me the other black item. "Agreed. Being female sucks sometimes. Now put this skirt on while I find you a pair of shoes."

I slipped it on and zipped it up the back. It was so narrow. "How do you walk in this?" I tried to swing one leg forward, but the fabric stopped it after a few inches.

Binita threw me a sympathetic glance. "You just sort of teeter forward, but you'll look fabulous while doing it."

I would have gladly traded fabulousness for mobility, but she was helping me out of a bind of my own doing. "Thank you," I began. "I don't know—"

She held up a hand. "Shut it. There's no time for that." She chucked a pair of shoes at me. "Now, for my mortarboard and that godforsaken ribbon. That thing is so small and slippery I can never put my hands on it. Maybe I could make one by cutting my black sari?" she muttered to herself. "I don't think they'd mind the sequins, at least not much."

"Ah!" She threw her mortarboard at me with a dexterous flick of her wrist, making it spin through the air like a frisbee. I caught it. Thank God, because in this skirt there was no way in hell I would have been able to bend down and pick it up off Binita's floor if I'd missed.

Shaun flew into her room just as Binita extracted a thin, black silk ribbon from the drawer of her desk. As she tied it around my neck, she shook her head. "I can't believe I actually found the ribbon—I can never find it."

"Nice work," Shaun said, as he threw my black robe over my shoulders. I had been trained for action in the forest, not standing stock still being dressed like a doll, yet ... *gratitude*, I reminded myself.

The ribbon tied, Binita pulled back a bit, stared at my hair, and frowned. "You need to look a bit more coiffed. Matriculation is a big deal." She twisted my hair up and anchored it at the back with a hair clip.

She stepped back and did one final check. "My work here is done. Shaun, she's all yours. There'll be a party organized for you afterwards by the college, so dinner won't work tonight, but let's eat together in Hall tomorrow, shall we?" She spun me around and gave me a push out her door. "You look divine," she said, as

Shaun grabbed my arm. "Now leg it back to the Lodge as fast as you can."

"Yes, we need to crack on." Shaun pulled me, but as I tried to take a step, my ankle turned on Binita's towering stilettos I'd slipped on. When I finally managed to straighten it, my leg hit the fabric of the skirt. By the time Shaun and I reached the bottom of the stairs, tears of frustration were pooling in the corners of my eyes.

"You have no idea how to walk in heels, do you?" Shaun looked down at me, exasperated. "Come on," he urged, giving me his arm. "You'll have to teeter faster than that."

I tried, but as much as I wanted to hurry, I was moving like a newborn fawn, my legs trapped in a skirt prison. The only saving grace was Binita's room happened to be very close to the Lodge.

I could see a crowd of students dressed like us milling around under the vaulted stone arch ahead of us, chattering excitedly. They began to flow out the door at a brisk pace.

"Run ahead and tell them I'm coming as fast as I can!" I gasped at Shaun.

He shot me a questioning look, but then nodded. "You're right. You're hopeless. It's our best option." He sounded like a wartime surgeon triaging patients. Normally I would find the whole ridiculous situation hilarious, but I wouldn't be in the mood to laugh at myself until I caught up. If I could ever catch up.

Shaun dashed forward, his black-suited legs stretching out into a gallop. Even then, he didn't take the obvious shortcut across the grassy middle section of the quad. *Wow*. That "No Walking on the Grass" rule was really treated like gospel.

He rushed up to a figure I could see in the distance, holding the college door open for the students flowing out. I tried to teeter faster, as Shaun had urged, but my ankle twisted the wrong way again. Pain shot up my calf. *Please don't let him shut the door on me!*

As I passed the Lodge, my left heel caught on the rim of the doorway out to New College Lane. I tried to stretch my opposite leg forward to stabilize myself, but the tight black fabric made that impossible. The cobblestones rushed up at me as I flew, sprawling through the open door into the street.

CHAPTER THIRTEEN

Cedar

A dagger of pain lanced my elbow. The crack of my kneecap echoed against the stone, then a blow like a sledgehammer there. My lungs forgot how to breathe.

I swore under my breath—an odd, hissing sound. There was a collective gasp above me, then a few chuckles.

I didn't care. The sickening throb of my elbow and knee consumed all my attention. How was I going to get up? Was that even humanly possible in these heels and skirt? Nobody was rushing forward to help me, or even check if I was OK.

Was this what it had been like for Alfie? How awful and alienating. Worse, the people surrounding him had been taking photos and videos. Did Alfie hate the feeling of being abandoned as much as I did? The way he'd been acting towards me, I'd probably never know.

A reassuring hand touched my back and I managed to gasp in a lungful of air. There was something overwhelmingly kind about the touch, but being sprawled on my stomach, I couldn't see who it belonged to.

Binita's hair clip had been knocked out of my hair and lay on the cobblestones about a foot or so away.

I tried to flip myself over, but my elbow and knee screamed in protest. How was I ever going to get to Matriculation now?

"Are you hurt?" The voice wasn't Shaun's. Wait ... it was Alfie's. The burn of embarrassment mingled with relief. Of all the ironies, it was Alfie who had come to help me. There was definitely something weird with us and this lane.

I tried to use my good arm to prop myself up. Jesus Murphy. Even that hurt. Please let it be the good Alfie, not the cold, distrustful one.

Alfie's face appeared in front of me. "I know I was an idiot at The Bear," he said. "But please ... let me help you."

I met his eyes, searching them for mockery, or at least an unspoken I-told-you-so. Instead I found compassion.

"Do you think you've broken anything?" he asked, his voice low—not for the crowd—just for me.

"I don't think so. No."

Sure, my kneecap felt like it had been jammed to the wrong place in my leg and my arm throbbed, but I'd dealt with worse. I thought of the scars on my torso and my thighs.

His fingers brushed my arm and I shivered. I turned to look at what he was doing and saw crimson blood—my blood—seeping through the white sleeve of Binita's blouse. I'd torn a big hole in it.

"Shit." Who would have thought that life outside the forest would be so riddled with hazards?

"You *are* hurt," he said with sympathetic reproach. His touch and words were so gentle and so clearly just for me that my breath hitched. Those tears still threatened, but for different reasons now.

"Binita's going to kill me," I said. "She lent me this top." My stomach lurched. Would she still want to be my friend when she'd seen what I'd done? I was screwing everything up.

Alfie cleared his throat. "Please head down to the Sheldonian," he said, in a clear, commanding tone to the crowd of matriculating students I hadn't realized were clustered around us. At least if they were snapping photos of me, they were doing it discreetly. "I'll assist here, and we'll catch up. Wait for me just in front. We have to enter the theater as a group. Cedar and I won't be long."

I heard the rustle of them leaving, but I couldn't quite meet Alfie's eyes. Was he going to tell me this was the result of me willfully ignoring all those unspoken rules of Oxford life, like us not being able to be friends? Yet here and now he felt like a friend.

"You should go ahead," I said, even though it was the opposite of how I felt. "I'll manage. I'm used to it."

"What do you mean?" His left brow quirked up. "When you say, 'I'm used to it'?"

I struggled to get my legs behind me so I could attempt standing up. "It means I've had plenty of practice. When I was fifteen, I sliced my hand with a butchering knife. I asked my parents to help me—hands bleed a lot—but they were busy pouring over their latest DNA statistics, so they gave me their medical textbook, opened it to the page how to stitch up a wound, and left me to it."

Alfie made a strange little noise of indignation. "But that's dreadful."

I shook my head. "They told me I would be glad for the skill if I found myself injured in the wilderness. They were right."

"I beg to differ." His voice was laced with steel. "Now, if I help you, do you think you can stand up?"

"I really don't want to make you and everyone late." The mere thought was mortifying. "I'll be fine. You go on."

He sighed. "Don't be stubborn, Cedar. You helped me. Honestly, I'm relieved to have the opportunity to return the favor."

It was clear he had no intention of abandoning me, which left me with a little bonfire kindling in my chest that I couldn't quite explain.

He anchored his arm under mine and, with his support, I managed to get somewhat vertical. My knee was definitely off-kilter and screamed in pain—maybe I'd cracked my kneecap?

"There," Alfie said. "How does that feel? Do you think you'll be able to walk?"

"Of course," I scoffed, but as we began to shuffle slowly towards the Bridge of Sighs and the Sheldonian, I realized I'd momentarily forgotten about the skirt and heels. I let out a little moan of frustration.

"Are you in unbearable pain?" His words were tight with concern.

"In pain, yes. Unbearable, no. I'm bearing it. That wasn't why I made that noise."

His arm slid around my waist, strong and supportive. Yes, that helped. I leaned heavily on him, a mirror image of the night we first met. "Why, then?"

It struck me that I didn't want to explain about not being able to walk in dressy clothes. He already thought I was little better than a feral animal. "You," I said instead. "You're very confusing."

Our eyes met, and in his blue-green ones there wasn't a trace of the reserve. There it was again, that invisible current between us I'd felt until he'd shunned me. That was what I'd been so sad about losing. I hadn't imagined it.

"I'm not," he protested, as we made it underneath the Bridge of

Sighs. There was something reassuring about the way it loomed, graceful and unperturbed above us, just like the enormous trees back home.

"I beg to differ," I said. "You act cold and disapproving with me one minute, and then kind the next. Honestly, I'd prefer if you just picked one and stuck to it. I'm baffled enough these days."

He remained silent for a moment. "If I've come across that way, I'm sorry. I thought we'd discussed this at The Bear. It's just that with my father ... my life ... Professor Harris ... I have to be guarded."

I examined his face. I wasn't sure if his overzealous rule-following was truly necessary, but I could tell from the distress on his features that *he* thought it was necessary.

By the time we left the Bridge of Sighs behind us I realized that, even with our best combined efforts, we were moving at a snail's pace. In the far distance, I could make out the crowd of black-gowned students milling around the theatre. Most of them were disappearing inside the icing cake of a building, except one group. I didn't need to guess who that was—the Beaufort College group, because of me.

"We're never going to make it there in time," I said. "Honestly, you go ahead and take care of the group."

He shook his head. "Not a chance. I heard the sound when your knee hit the cobblestones. I'm not leaving you. Besides, I will not allow you to miss Matriculation."

Hell, I was going to have to fess up. "It's Binita's skirt and heels," I confessed, frowning down at them. "I don't know how to move in them. It's hopeless. Leave me here." To alleviate some of the embarrassment of my predicament, I added a bit of levity. "Save yourself."

He stopped and turned to face me. "I will do no such thing."

He flashed a sudden grin, clearly catching on to my battlefield tone. Something appeared in his eyes then—a hint of mischief I'd never expected to see. I never imagined Alfie could be *fun*. "Turn around," he instructed like a drill sergeant.

I did what he asked. There was a first time for everything.

He kneeled down and his hand wrapped firmly around my ankle. My leg jerked with the tingly warmth of his touch. Why did it feel as though his fingers plugged my body directly into a live circuit? He held on tight, anchoring me.

Heat flowed up from his fingers to areas of my body I hadn't associated with Alfie until that very moment. Now I couldn't stop feeling them. His palm shifted slightly, smooth over the silky stockings, and my legs wobbled. My legs *never* wobbled. There was a tug at the back of Binita's skirt, then the sound of tearing fabric echoed off the stone walls on either side of us.

What the heck? I twisted around to see Alfie standing back up again, brushing his hands together, the satisfaction of a job well done on his face. He'd ripped open the back seam of Binita's skirt by about a foot. A protest hovered on the tip of my tongue, but I took a test step, then another. My knees were sore, but free! I could walk. A grin spread over my face.

"Better?"

I lunged forward with one foot and then the other to demonstrate. "This is amazing," I laughed. "I'll never wear another tight skirt again."

He watched me, his eyes glowing.

"Uh oh," I remembered. "We've just trashed Binita's skirt."

He waved that concern away. "I'll buy her a new one. This was an emergency. Come on, we still have to hurry." That gleam in his eyes grew even more inviting.

I took a few fast steps forward but within the first few feet, the heel of one of the stilettos I was wearing lodged between the crack of two uneven cobblestones.

"Give me those heels." He held out his hand. "Nobody could walk in those."

I knew Binita could, but there was no time for arguing that point. I shucked them off and passed them to him.

He took them both in one hand and jerked his head towards the Sheldonian. "Now, can you run with your knee?"

My stomach somersaulted. With the relief of a convict sprung from prison, I ignored the pain and sped down New College Lane in my stocking feet, Alfie in fast pursuit.

Robbie was right—Alfie *was* athletic underneath that fancy exterior. He passed me just before screeching to a stop underneath one of the huge, sculpted heads which adorned the stone pillars surrounding the Sheldonian.

"Wait!" he held out his arm to steady me as I skidded to a halt beside him. He took Binita's hair clip out of his pocket. "I picked it up off the street after you fell. Turn around," he instructed. That crease low on his right cheek was proof I wasn't the only one enjoying myself.

"I'll do it." I reached for the clip. I couldn't really, at least not as skillfully as Binita had pinned my hair up, but the phrase was hard-wired into my brain after years of living with my parents.

"Cedar, I told you to turn around," Alfie growled in such an unexpected way that my heart skipped a few beats.

I turned around.

Oh God. His fingers were even more ... more *everything* ... on the nape of my neck than around my ankle. He gathered my hair, and a shiver that had nothing to do with the brisk wind vibrated through me as he twisted up my hair.

"Who are these bearded stone dudes anyway?" I couldn't let

Alfie know the effect he was having on me—hadn't I been humiliated enough for one day? I pointed to the stone heads adorning the pillars enclosing the Sheldonian.

"Nobody knows for sure." There was something unsteady in his voice. "But there's thirteen of them, and they're known collectively as "The Emperors." He secured the clip, and then his fingers were gone and all I could think of was how I wanted them back.

"There," he murmured. He took a step back to examine his handiwork. "I don't really know what I'm doing, but I think it looks passable."

"I'm sure it's fine," I said. "I'm not picky." I turned to face him again and our eyes met. Neither of us said anything for a few seconds. Was he feeling that ... what was it, even? ... *thing* between us?

He finally jerked, as if waking up after a trance. "Bollocks," he said. "Matriculation."

"Yes." For a second there I'd forgotten everything except that intent expression on his face. "We're very late."

He passed me my heels and watched me as I slipped them on.

"Thanks," I said. "I owe you one."

He shook his head. "You owe me nothing." He gave me a crooked smile that was miles away from the tight, pained smiles he'd been giving me around college. "It was my pleasure, Cedar."

We rushed up the stairs and I heard him giving instructions to the Beaufort contingent of students as I teetered up on my heels, joining the group from the rear. I could only half concentrate on the instructions Alfie was giving out, his spine straight and the tilt of his head regal and commanding.

The kind Alfie was the true Alfie. Now I had proof.

CHAPTER FOURTEEN

Alfie

On my way to meet Lachlan at our favorite kebab van, my head bowed against the chill in the air, I could not exorcise one specific memory from my head—the warm, silky feel of Cedar's skin when I brushed my fingers against it as I attempted to clip up her hair. I could have spent hours just staring at the nape of her neck. This was a problem. Cedar was the last woman on earth I should be attracted to.

Once we bought our kebabs filled with the usual spicy, indeterminate meat and hot sauce, Lachlan and I headed down to Christ Church Meadow to walk along the Thames. The golden towers of Merton shimmered in the distance like a mirage. The fog hadn't burned off like it normally did and hugged the grass on the fields.

Lachlan, as was his habit, had bought two kebabs. He rolled up the paper from his first one and threw it in one of the green metal bins along the river footpath before he tore into his second one.

"Out with it, Alfie," he said gruffly.

I'd been trying to figure out how to even begin talking about it ever since we'd paid for our kebabs, but I had no idea where to begin. Important things first. "I didn't lose my fellowship, but I'm on some kind of probation according to Professor Harris."

Lachlan turned his blue eyes to me, anger in them. "Put there by the college or by him?"

I shrugged. "By him, I suppose, but he has a lot of influence. It's basically the same thing."

He made a guttural noise of disagreement then studied me for a few moments. "That's not why you're upset."

It should be why I was upset, but he was right. "No."

"So?"

The pea gravel crunched under our feet. "Cedar. The Canadian girl."

I gave Lachlan a run-down of the events of Matriculation and how I'd helped her, without going into specifics about how those events made me feel. Lachlan had a lively sense of humor and roared with laughter at me ripping her skirt. "I knew you still had it in you."

"That's the problem."

He stopped and stared at me. It was an annoying habit of his and never failed to make me squirm like he was pressing me under his thumb. I feigned interest in two ducks swimming down the river.

"The ducks aren't the solution," he said, finally getting a chuckle out of me.

"Maybe they are," I mused, as we started walking again. "They seem so serene, which is how I try to come across, and how Professor Harris *does* come across, but are they all paddling as madly under the water as me?"

"Don't think you're distracting me with this duck rubbish. I think the problem is less about the fact you helped this lass than how she makes you feel."

Damn. Lachlan knew me all too well.

"Maybe," I admitted.

"It's not a tragedy ya' daft bawbag. How *does* she make you feel?"

As much as we were like brothers, I could hardly tell Lachlan how I ached with the need to pull Cedar against me and kiss those scattered freckles on the bridge of her nose, and its upturned tip, and that stubborn chin and those full lips. I longed to see what it would do to those luminous tortoiseshell eyes of hers. She made me feel so *alive*, so much so that merely touching her ankle had made me go hard in the middle of New College Lane. Who *was* I anymore?

The reasonable part of my brain sounded an alarm. Professor Harris didn't approve of her and as far as I knew, he was actively trying to get rid of her. Hadn't I learned anything from my father's scandals? Cedar had "danger" written all over her. Why would I choose to go towards that?

I cleared my throat, homing in on the crux of it. "Being around Cedar makes me forget all the decisions I've made about how I want to conduct my life."

Lachlan frowned at me and shook his head. "Alfie, please listen to me. You don't need to be a complete prig to not be like your father. There's middle ground, ken?"

But Lachlan didn't ... couldn't know how wrong he was. He didn't know how my wilder impulses beat inside me like a drum all the time, and how squashing them down took sustained effort and discipline, every minute of every day.

"Lachlan," I said. "I ripped her skirt, I took off her heels, I held her hand as we ran down the street together. What would have happened if a pap or even any bloke with a smart phone had snapped a photo? I would be banished from Beaufort. How could I be so careless?"

"Alfie," he said. "Maybe it's time—"

"She makes me careless," I cut him off. "She's all wrong for me ... I can't even understand it."

He threw his second kebab wrapper in the bin and turned to me. "I have one question for you. Does she make you feel good?"

Good? That was too feeble a word. She made a fever, like I'd never known before with any other woman, flare instantly in my blood. "She terrifies me. I try not to make eye contact with her in tutorials, but I can't continue on like that forever."

"What is it about being around her that scares you?"

I threw away the rest of my kebab in the river for the ducks. My appetite had vanished. "At Matriculation, when I saw her fall, I would have done anything to help her, just to make her smile again. I didn't think for a moment of the consequences."

"Have you ever considered that maybe you need that in your life?"

I wasn't really listening to him anymore. "Worse, she's someone who doesn't follow rules. Bloody hell, she doesn't even *know* the rules."

Lachlan chewed his fingernail, deep in thought. "You know what I think?" he said, at last.

"No," I said. "And I'm suspecting maybe I don't want to."

He lifted one of his massive shoulders. "You'd be right about that, but here it is anyway. I think she sounds perfect for you."

***

I stalked back to college, fueled by indignation. *Perfect* for me? Ha. Fat chance. Cedar was everything that was wrong and destructive for me. I had chosen a path—a good, peaceful path—for my life and she didn't fit in any way, shape or form.

How could I put academic ambitions aside when they were what I was building my whole life and future around? That was insane. The only intelligent way forward was to act friendly but distant with her and hope that my reaction to her would fade with time. This was just lust, that's all. I refused to be like my father and give in to my baser desires.

Robbie had the day off. I always felt the emptiness of his absence when he did, but the poor fellow deserved a break from time to time. One of his co-workers—I think his name was Dan—was manning the porter booth.

"Lord Invernay," he said, as I was sorting through my mail. "I was just coming to fetch you."

I froze. In my experience, that was rarely good, and more often than not had something to do with my father.

"The Warden would like you to go to her lodgings. Immediately."

Ice filled my veins. I had been beginning to think my drunken paparazzi incident in Nought Week had been shrugged off by the College. Foolishly, I'd stopped waiting for the hammer to drop. When would I learn I could never take a break—no matter how short—from being vigilant of my reputation?

I had to act unconcerned for appearance's sake. The college staff had a well-known rapacity for gossip. Even if Professor Harris had put me on probation that didn't mean the Warden necessarily agreed. She may want to give me the boot altogether, and I could hardly blame her.

The thought she had seen those photos too ... dread had my stomach in its grip. How many times would I be made to suffer the consequences of that blunder? It wasn't over, apparently.

"I'm on my way," I said, managing to sound unconcerned. Robbie would never have bought it, but no other porter was perceptive like him.

I skirted the medieval wall that ran alongside the main quad and continued towards the Warden's lodgings, still wary for sightings of Cedar.

I tried to pay attention to my surroundings to combat the iron band squeezing my lungs. The leaves on the trees that dotted the Warden's garden had turned crimson. What did the trees in Cedar's forest look like in the autumn? No. I couldn't think about her—not ever, and especially not now.

CHAPTER FIFTEEN

Alfie

I was met at the door of the medieval stone Warden's lodgings by an old-school butler in an actual butler's uniform. He escorted me to the Warden's study with great ceremony. I imagined his services came with residence in the lodgings.

Our present Warden was the first female in the history of Beaufort College to be voted into the role. Despite her being a formidable scholar whose list of publications would put most of the other dons to shame, her appointment created an uproar and even now, two years later, resulted in many disparaging whispers at High Table where she presided.

From what I could tell, she was a vast improvement to the bumbling, lazy excuses for male wardens in the past. She had a reputation of being clever and sharp-tongued though, which didn't bode well for me.

I crossed the plushly carpeted threshold into her regal study; all stone walls with priceless paintings by British painters and a roaring fireplace. I was quite certain those were portraits of dour men by Henry Gibbs and William Dobson adorning the walls. We had some by them in Scotland.

The Warden stood up and held out her hand to me. "Lord Invernay, thank you for joining us."

At first glance, one would think she was frail with her white hair and bird-like bones, but that assessment was quickly revised when she pinned you down with her sharp blue eyes.

Even though her hand was delicate as I shook it, she radiated an unbendable strength that I wasn't about to underestimate. Her expression was inscrutable. *Wait.* Had she said 'us'?

I looked over to one of the three overstuffed wingback chairs clustered in front of the fire. A lanky figure stood up.

I recognized him immediately from the same magazines and tabloids my father frequently graced. William Cavendish-Percy—the man responsible for Cedar's presence at Oxford. We hadn't crossed paths in person before. Surprising, as we ran in the same privileged circles.

On the other hand, I didn't think he stayed in England for much longer than brief visits. In the articles about him in newspapers and magazines, he made it clear that his preference was exploring the farthest corners of the Earth. To think, in one of those corners he'd found Cedar Wild. My heart did something odd that I didn't want to analyze too closely.

I knew his father was an Earl and one of the King's cronies. His mother had been a Singaporean socialite—their marriage had been quite a scandal at the time, but it was amazing how the mind-boggling wealth his mother brought to the family coffers smoothed things over in short order, even with the highest sticklers.

William was tall and handsome—something the paparazzi loved, I imagined. He was far younger looking than I expected, probably only five or so years older than me. Spots flashed in front of my eyes. What had happened exactly between him and Cedar? *No Alfie! You are not going to be jealous.*

"Pleasure to meet you," he said. "I'm William Cavendish-Percy." He eschewed using the "Lord" title that, like in my case, was rightfully his. His choice made me feel suddenly pretentious in using mine.

Cavendish-Percy's grip was strong and self-assured when we shook hands. What was he doing here? Professor Harris hadn't managed to have Cedar rusticated so quickly, had he?

The mere idea of her leaving before ... before what? I didn't quite know, but even though her departure would be the best possible thing for me, the prospect felt like I'd been stabbed in the chest.

The Warden waved me to the remaining wingback chair. "So Alfred," she began, reverting to my Christian name, which felt like a relief. "I requested this visit because I wanted you two to meet."

Cavendish-Percy had sat back down in his chair and nodded towards me. His skin looked baked by the elements to a hard polish, so that his high cheekbones had an unearthly sheen to them.

"Pleasure." I sat down, remembering my manners instead of blurting out that he couldn't take Cedar away, not now. "I followed your dogsled expedition to the North Pole."

"Didn't every Brit with a television?" the Warden said, gracious as always.

Cavendish-Percy had an engaging smile, his teeth straight and white against his weathered face. "Indeed! That was a popular one. It was far from the most outrageous of my adventures, yet it caught public opinion more than the others."

"It certainly did," I said, the manners my nanny had drilled into me since forever were something I could trot out on automatic pilot.

"The Warden has informed me you've met my first protegé?"

I touched the soft skin on the back of her neck, and it almost undid me. I blinked to clear that thought out of my head. "Cedar? Yes. She happens to be one of the MPhil students I'm advising."

He tilted his head, studying me. I had the unsettling sensation he could see deeper than I wanted him to. "An extraordinary person, isn't she?"

Unarguably, though I had to think of anything but Cedar to halt this telltale flush creeping up my throat. *Mushy peas. The whiskers that sprouted from my Nanny's chin. Haggis.* Ah. Better. "She's surprising," I said. "Oxford strikes me as an unconventional place for her."

"That's where you come in." The Warden smiled at me, beatific.

Relief that it didn't seem as though Cedar was being sent away ... at least not yet ... warred with encroaching dread. If she stayed, I needed to exercise even more restraint. I liked to think my willpower was an inexhaustible commodity but suspected perhaps it wasn't.

"I'm not sure what you mean." I schooled my face into a bland expression.

"As you may know," William said. "This Remote Commonwealth Student scheme was something I concocted with the King to strengthen the ties of the Commonwealth countries to Britain. Those ties have been loosening more than we would like over the years."

The redolent scent of pipe in the study could have easily lulled me into the sort of self-satisfied discussions common amongst the British aristocracy—the kind that generally veered into what was best for other people. For some inexplicable reason, today I just couldn't.

Take Cedar, for example. What could the King and his wayward offspring, including his son who was currently being cuckolded by my own father, mean to her inside her log cabin in the woods? Nothing. *Dammit.* I was thinking of Cedar again.

"Alfred?" the Warden prompted.

I wanted to say *well, can you bloody blame the commonwealth countries for wanting their independence*? But that would go against the unspoken rules of Oxford social etiquette when talking with the Warden and her guest. "I suppose from a uniquely British perspective that makes sense."

William laughed. Maybe he *could* see through me. "You don't think that, but I don't either. However, that is the approach I use when talking to the King. My real motivation was to give these remarkable young people a chance to study here and, more importantly, for Oxford to benefit from individuals like Cedar. You know, I lived with her and her parents for three months."

I leaned forward in my chair, unable to curb my curiosity. "What was it like?"

"Far more arduous than my trek to the North Pole, I can tell you that." Cavendish-Percy laughed.

"I find that hard to believe," the Warden said, but her eyes sparkled with interest all the same.

"Believe it. The nearest town, Stewart—and keep in mind Stewart is a small frontier town of four hundred people with only the simplest medical facilities, not to mention a treacherous and often unpassable road to get out—is forty kilometers away from her cabin. The trek to get from Cedar's cabin from there was harder than most sections of my North Pole Trek."

Surely, he was exaggerating. "How can that be?"

"The forest is denser than you could possibly imagine. The mountains are gigantic and clogged with ice and glaciers in the winter. Most importantly, though, the area is teeming with bears. It's why her parents settled there, after all. It's one of the highest concentrations of bears—both grizzly and black—in the world."

The indomitable Warden shrunk back in her chair.

"That's how Cedar and I met," Cavendish-Percy continued, his eyes glowing. "I was nursing a beer in Stewart's only bar, called the Nugget because of the gold mining history in town, when Cedar came in for a drink and a chat with the bartender. Apparently, she always popped in to get the news when she came to town for supplies.

"We got to chatting and she was showing me where her family lived on a map on the wall when the back door of the café slammed open and in walked a grizzly bear—"

The Warden gasped, every bit as spellbound as me.

"Everyone looked to Cedar, who just sighed, clapped her hands together like a teacher with an unruly student, and talked to the bear."

"What did she say?" I demanded.

"She explained a bar was no place for a bear and that if he stayed, he might get shot." He threw his head back and chuckled at the memory. "She eventually convinced it to leave and asked the bartender to call the bear relocation squad, then turned back to me and continued to drink her bottle of Molson Canadian, cool as a cucumber."

I inwardly groaned. To imagine I had talked down to her. I was such a fool.

"I knew I had to further my acquaintance with her," he continued. "Imagine my shock when I saw her studying set-up in her private cabin and learned just how deeply she'd delved into medieval literature. She was devoted to her studies—there was plenty of time for it where she lived. In her mind, there was nothing at all incompatible with a life of talking to bears and analyzing Chaucer. It was the most extraordinary thing." He shook his head, clearly still in awe.

"That's ... brilliant," I murmured. I didn't need to worry about my growing attraction to Cedar, I realized then. Someone as extraordinary as her would never be interested in the likes of me.

"You cannot even begin to imagine how formidable she is," Cavendish-Percy was clearly on a roll now. "She saved my life countless times with bears, and once with a particularly aggressive male cougar who was underfed and hungry. She could go right from shooting and butchering a moose to studying the original text of Tristan and Iseult in Old French."

"Heavens," the Warden said, faintly.

"Cedar, quite frankly, was the reason I came up with this scheme in the first place," he continued. "I knew I had to put a spin on it to appeal to the King and, long story short, the Commonwealth excuse fit the bill."

I was fast developing a whole new respect for Lord Cavendish-Percy.

"Cedar knows everything about surviving, no, *thriving* in the wildest place you could ever imagine," he continued. "She can set a bone, build a log cabin by herself, run a trap-line, and keep herself busy with the entire works of Aristotle for a week when she's snowed in. I had to get her here, of course."

"What were her parents like?" the Warden asked, still stuck to the back of her chair by the centrifugal force of Cavendish-Percy's storytelling. "They must have been rather odd to live so isolated from the world."

Cavendish-Percy frowned down at his hands in his lap. "They were completely devoted to their bear research—it is brilliant and important research, without a doubt. Still ... they'd been leaving Cedar to fend for herself since she was young. I suppose there was a bit of camaraderie between them and Cedar, but they seemed far more connected to the bears than to her. I didn't feel welcome or unwelcome by them—they were just indifferent to anything that didn't concern the bears."

"Including Cedar?" The question flew out of my mouth before I could stop it.

"Especially Cedar," William said. Our eyes met. He felt protective of her, and dammit—I did too, yet I couldn't afford to feel anything towards her at all.

"I have three more students lined up to come so far—one will be arriving each term. Cedar should be able to help the next students who arrive, you know, show them the ropes, but it's been troubling me that Cedar has no-one to do that for her."

"That's why we brought you here today." The Warden's bright blue gaze sharpened on my face. "When William asked me if I could suggest somebody to act as a mentor and a guide, I thought immediately of you."

Of course I wanted to, but introducing Cedar into my life more than she was already there was like setting a series of undetonated explosives for myself.

"Thank you for thinking of me," I said, as smooth as possible. "But I'm afraid it would be a conflict of interest as her thesis advisor."

Judging by their expressions, the Warden and Cavendish-Percy remained undeterred.

"That's not a conflict of interest." The Warden shook her head, her white coiffure not daring to move by a strand. "On the contrary, it would be a tremendous benefit for Cedar to be mentored by someone who has such a complete understanding of her field of study."

"But—" I was thinking as fast as I could but thinking on my feet had never been one of my strengths. When my father did pay attention to me on extremely rare occasions, it was often to mock me for my need to think things through before acting.

"This is not without a benefit to you, you realize," Mr. Cavendish-Percy added. "I would be very grateful. You might find funding for your particular areas of research may ... flourish, shall we say?"

I knew Cavendish-Percy's astounding wealth had ample funds to back up such a promise.

"But—" I began again, my mind spinning.

"I owe Cedar for what she taught me, and I feel very protective of these students I'm sending over here," Cavendish-Percy interrupted. "I'm not a careless person, despite what people may assume. If I was, I'd be long dead by now given my propensity for putting myself in extreme situations. Cedar's world is so completely different from Oxford, but she's a brilliant girl. She deserves this opportunity. I know she'll adapt quickly and win people over, but I would sleep better at night if she had someone to help her."

I made a silent plea to the portrait of a man with an elaborate white wig and very thin lips above the fireplace. I wasn't strong enough to do what they were asking.

"There's another reason I thought of you." The Warden turned her eyes on me, and I suddenly had the impression of being five years old again, that time my nanny caught me feeding my haggis to my dog Oswald under the table. "Cedar is an attractive girl, and perhaps innocent in the ways of the world. I need someone who I can implicitly trust to not overstep the line with her. Seeing as you say you are such a stickler for keeping a certain ... shall we say ... professional distance with your students, I know I can trust you."

"Of course," I said. An external barrier between me and Cedar. This should be good news, so why did it feel like the opposite? "But—"

"I know you will be a gentleman with Cedar. Also, wouldn't this be an excellent opportunity to prove yourself to be," She cleared her throat, "not a typical branch of the family tree, if you understand what I mean?"

I did. She'd seen the photos and knew that safekeeping my reputation was more important than ever. They wouldn't promote me within the college if the Warden or Professor Harris suspected I possessed an atom of my father's recklessness.

Cementing my spot at Beaufort and Oxford, might mean that any little encounter with my father or the paparazzi wouldn't threaten to destroy the safety net I'd been weaving for myself for the past five years. I had to accept.

"I'll do it."

Lord Cavendish-Percy and the Warden both beamed at me. "You won't regret it," the Warden said.

Of that, I wasn't convinced.

THIRD WEEK

CHAPTER SIXTEEN

Cedar

I had half an hour to kill before my tutorial with Alfie. He'd scheduled it for early morning this time. As I sat on the edge of my bed, worrying about which Alfie I was going to find, there was a knock on my door. My Scout, Josie.

"Come on in," I called. Honestly, the idea of having someone come into my room every morning just to empty my trash can and tidy up struck me as just plain absurd, even three weeks into term.

Josie stuck her head in my door. "Nothing to clean up, as usual?" she asked, taking a quick scan of my space.

"Nope," I said. "Sorry."

"You should buy some pretty things for your room," she said. "Make it a little cozier, luv."

I looked around. There were a few books on my desk and my notebook. I'd put my clothes in the drawers. What else did I need? After Willy had taken me out for lunch during his brief visit, I took him up and showed him my room. He'd suggested posters, but when I asked, 'posters of what?' he didn't have a good answer.

"I'm really sorry I don't have more things for you to tidy up," I apologized.

She waved her hand. "No worries there, luv. Your stairwell mates give me plenty to do. I might stop coming to bother you though. Will you let me know if you need me?"

I smiled at her. "Will do. Thanks Josie."

She shut the door. I collected my things and made my way down my stairwell to check my pidge. Since Matriculation I'd vowed to become more conscientious about that.

I'd been hoping to see Alfie before our tutorial, but he seemed to have vaporized, just when I thought that after Matriculation ... well, I didn't know exactly what to think.

I couldn't deny being drawn to him, but it was just so ridiculous. Alfie and I had nothing in common. The three other men I'd been with had been outdoor types like me, contented with a quick, mutual release with no strings attached.

I walked along the pathways of the main quad towards the Lodge, deep in thought.

There hadn't been much conversation with those other men, and certainly no romance. My body was merely being rebellious when I was around Alfie, the same way my feet itched to run all over the pristine, off-limits grass I walked beside now.

The whole skirt ripping thing gave me reason to believe the real Alfie was far more human, and lively, than I'd ever imagined. Then again, I hadn't had the chance to talk to him since that day. Maybe the tutorial would clear up some of my confusion, although I didn't know if I could bear him treating me like a stranger after those precious moments of camaraderie.

I spotted Robbie behind the booth in the Lodge, and he beckoned me to come over.

There was something about seeing him—something steadying. I waited as he finished reprimanding a freshman for asking him a stupid question.

When the freshman escaped, Robbie turned to me with a beatific smile. "Cedar! How are you? I took a few days off, but I've been wondering how you'd been getting along."

It hadn't been easy, to be honest. I had no idea what the university was looking for in an MPhil thesis. Besides getting my head screwed on right about Alfie, I planned to ask him more specifics on the parameters of that during our tutorial.

Surely my research would get easier once my research topic was approved, but for the moment, I was still disoriented. I hated feeling lost. In the forest it meant possible death, and that engrained trigger was hard to break, even here.

However, I didn't want to burden Robbie with any of this. "Great!" I said, infusing my voice with as much cheerfulness as possible. Once I figured out how things worked—and I would—I could relish the satisfaction of knowing I didn't ask anyone for help. I'd already been doing that far too often for my liking since arriving.

Robbie frowned, clearly not buying it. "I'm not sure I believe you. In any case, Alfie put a note for you in your pidge earlier today. He told me to remind you to check if you forgot. I heard about Matriculation." He waggled his eyebrows.

"Yeah, it was a bit of a nightmare, but I learned my lesson about checking my pidge," I said ruefully.

"Glad to hear it." His attention was claimed by a college fellow who'd lost the keys to his study.

Along with a bunch of strips of paper I shoved in my bag to read later, my mail slot contained the note from Alfie. I expected it, but my heart tripped all the same as I read his messy scrawl. For someone so controlled, his handwriting was surprisingly chaotic.

Cedar. Please come to the tutorial fifteen minutes before the planned start time. Regards, Alfred.

My heart felt heavier, weighed down with disappointment. *Regards.* He'd ripped my skirt and clipped up my hair and all he could say was *regards*? Was what happened at Matriculation just another bit of that British unpleasantness, as he'd explained at The Bear, that shouldn't be mentioned?

Anyway, why on earth did he want to talk to me now, after he'd been avoiding me?

I was still mulling this over when I reached the door of Professor Harris's study. It was open.

I took a steadying breath and walked in. Alfie was leaning against the windowsill in such a way I found myself wondering if he hadn't fine-tuned that nonchalant pose for several minutes before my arrival. There was a tension in his long, lean body that struck me as anything but casual.

"Hey stranger." I tossed out the words with deliberate carelessness.

The casement window behind him was open wide despite the chilly late October air. "Hello Cedar," he said, his eyes catching mine, and staying there. "I'll shut the window in a bit," he said, finally. "I just needed some fresh air."

His short hair had grown just enough since the beginning of term that one rebellious curl had started to form just underneath his left ear. I smiled to myself. Nobody could control or plan for everything, not even Alfie.

Alfie dug his hands further in the pockets of his jeans. "If I didn't know better, I would say something about me is making you laugh."

Now he mentioned it, I didn't know how to hide my fleeting

thoughts and emotions. How could I? My parents never paid attention to what my face was doing, and there wasn't anyone else to hide them from. "Nothing important." I shook my head.

His face took on that forbidding mask he donned when he was determined for people to take him seriously. I wondered what had happened in his life that his default assumption was that people would not.

"Don't try that high and mighty look on me," I said. "It won't work." I remained standing, just a few feet away from him. It felt like sitting down would be a capitulation.

"What look?" he asked, yet there was a flicker of something in his eyes—panic maybe?

I'd just ignore his haughtiness and pretend like he was still acting normally. That would serve him right. I picked up one of those weird hangy-offy bits on my black academic robe and did a twirl. "What are you so ticked off about? I'm wearing my robe. See?"

He frowned. "That reminds me, how much do I owe Binita for her skirt?"

I waved my hand. "No worries. I bought her a new one, and she thought the whole thing was hysterical."

His eyes flew open wide. "You told her I ripped it?"

"Come on," I chided. "I had to tell her something. Besides, I know I can trust her not to blab it around. There was nothing damning in it for you. On the contrary, Alfie—"

"Alfred in this context," he corrected me.

How could this be the same man that clipped up my hair with those fingertips? Yet, for him to be daunting, I had to be daunted. *Nope*. I would no longer play that game.

I rolled my eyes. "Fine. Anyway, you acted heroically, *Alfred*. Without you doing that I don't think I would have made it to

Matriculation."

His brows pulled together. I could tell he was feeling thwarted by my refusal to be cowed. "That's not true."

It was entertaining getting a rise out of him when he was determined to be aloof. "It is! I could only waddle like a penguin in that skirt and those heels. Honestly, I don't know how Binita does it."

Alfie's mouth pressed together, but in such a way that revealed a crease low on his right cheek. *Ah.* "You *were* having a terrible time. I couldn't let that go on."

Was he thawing, or was that just wishful thinking? "No true gentleman could," I quipped in my best attempt at a British accent. It was laughingly bad.

He smiled at me then, a real Alfie smile. Relief filled me with a whoosh. *There* he was. "Your robe looks very nice," he admitted.

Now I could sit down on the leather couch. I grabbed the two extra streamers that hung off the back of the robe. "Seriously though, what are these bits for?" I asked. "It's been keeping me awake."

"We can't have that." Alfie's eyes had taken on a playful sparkle. "What's your guess?"

"To attach a sled to them so I can drag my books behind me?"

"Why not?" His lips twitched. "Or to tie up in a decorative bow?"

I studied the little pleats sewn into the main strips. "To carry extra ammunition for impromptu gunfights?"

"Or encounters with bears? Did you know Lord Byron brought a live one as a pet when he studied at Cambridge?" His face was alive now.

"A bear? Honestly, Byron always sounded to me like a complete tool. His poetry is reductive too."

"Yes, from what I've gathered he was a right prat and, agreed, his poetry is unrelentingly self-indulgent."

"Why on earth would he bring a bear to college?" Also, where did Byron find a bear in the first place in England?

"It was a protest against the fact he wasn't able to bring his pet dog along to Cambridge."

"Keep a bear in captivity is just cruel. It confirms he was a selfish A-hole."

Alfie tilted his head, grinning now. That smile made everything about his face just click in a way that made my breath catch. "Well done. We have thoroughly torn Byron's reputation to shreds."

"What happened to the bear in the end?"

"I believe he was shot."

"Shooting bears is actually a last resort and should only be done if you need the meat or to save your own or someone else's life."

Enjoyment lit up Alfie's face. "So you're teaching *me* rules now?"

A need to make him smile like that more often beat in my chest. "I think we both have things we could teach each other. I don't appreciate you treating me like the village idiot, you know," I said. "And it's hurtful, especially after sharing ... friendly... times together." Friendly was definitely not the word for what his touch had done to me, but it would have to do.

He studied my face with a focus that I'd never had aimed at me before in my life. Finally, he swore under his breath. "I'm sorry, Cedar," he said. "It's wrong of me, I know. It *feels* wrong, but honestly, I don't know how to act around you. You're fascinating, yet I have to keep a certain distance between us. You make that hard."

Fascinating? That was just ridiculous. Still, it was the last part that intrigued me the most. "I do?"

"Yes, I try to and you just ... you just don't let me. The only other people in my life who do that are Lachlan and Robbie."

"I would bet that's probably good for you."

He frowned. "I don't know. It's complicated. The thing is you're my student too and you're ..." he trailed off, still frowning in thought.

"I'm what?"

"Extraordinary."

"No way," I said. I might be a novelty at Oxford, but my parents' disinterest was proof enough that I was painfully ordinary.

Alfie snorted and shook his head at me. "You may be many things, Cedar, but unremarkable is not one of them."

Our eyes locked, but neither of us spoke. The quality of air in the study changed—the dust motes seemed to speed up in the beam of autumn sun coming in the window.

He sat down on the couch beside me. He covered my hand with his and a jolt of heat coursed up my arm, directly feeding into my heart. I wanted to move closer to him to shorten that invisible thread between us.

He tightened his grip. His fingertips wrapped around my hand, pressing into my palm. Just that felt so good. I wanted to lean in to feel more.

"You terrify me, Cedar." His voice was low. The line of his throat convulsed as he swallowed. "You're unpredictable and I purposely keep things I can't understand and control out of my life for good reason. But you ... I can't keep you out, can I?" His eyes searched mine.

"Do you want to?"

He shook his head. "No."

There was a noise in the hallway. He let go of my hand go as if it had just burst into flames and leapt off the couch. He began pacing back and forth in front of the desk. His hand shook as he raked his hair. "You see?" he said, his voice strained. "I crossed a line there."

I leaned back against the couch, joy and confusion throbbing behind my sternum.

He retreated to the safety of the chair behind the desk and checked his watch. "The others are going to be here soon, and we've strayed far off-topic." He sent me a wry smile. "That tends to happen to me around you. I haven't even told you why I summoned you here early."

"What?" I arched my eyebrows in mock surprise. "It wasn't to tell me how unpredictable and scary I am?"

The crease in his right cheek reappeared. "Well, you *are*."

"Only if you're easily frightened."

"Perhaps I am," he said. "In any case, I called you here early because I was recently convocated to a meeting with the Warden and William Cavendish-Percy."

"Really?" I said. "I went out for lunch with Willy when he was here. It was great to catch up with him, but what did they want you for?"

"The crux of the discussion was that Lord Cavendish-Percy—"

"Just call him Willy."

Alfie rolled his eyes. "I don't stand on such terms with Lord Cavendish-Percy to be able to do that. In any case, he and the Warden asked for me to be your guide at Oxford. You know, someone to come to if you had any problems or questions."

I frowned, unsure what to do with this piece of information. Just when I was making headway, would it make Alfie more stilted towards me or less? "But you're already my junior advisor."

"Yes, but you can ask me any kind of question, not just about academics."

"Like what?"

"Anything to do with your welfare or navigating the college or the university."

"Or the thingies hanging off my robe."

"Or the thingies hanging off your robe." He gave me a roguish smile, despite his starchy tone. Playful Alfie made those tiny hairs on the back of my neck stand on end. "I neglected to answer that, didn't I?"

"An unacceptable oversight." I crossed one leg over the other and did my best impression of being prim.

He chuckled. "I will do my best to rectify that Ms. Wild. The exact origins of the streamers with the folds is lost in the mists of time, but it is assumed they are the remnants of the original closed sleeves of the commoner gowns."

I cocked a skeptical eyebrow. "Seriously?" That didn't seem a good enough reason.

His lips quirked again. "Oxford likes to hang on to old things, in case you hadn't noticed."

"Like Professor Wilcox?" I asked. The grizzled scholar who shuffled around Beaufort like a ghost had to be approximately three hundred years old.

He covered his mouth with his hand, the crease in his cheek deeper than I'd ever seen it. "I never said that the rules and customs of Oxford make any sense. I just said that abiding by them makes life here infinitely smoother."

"Hm," I said, non-committal. "And as my guide, you're supposed to teach me those rules and customs?"

"Yes."

I wasn't brought up to follow rules I didn't understand or agree with. That was why my parents lived in the woods in the first place—to escape the arbitrary control of society. Indeed, when they got going in the evening in front of the fire, my parents loved nothing more than a good rant about how they could only access true freedom living off-grid. "Good luck," I said. "I suspect you'll need it."

"I'm afraid you're correct. Besides being available to help you, I think it's expected that I show you around Oxford a bit too."

"Forget about expected. Do you *want* to show me around?"

He didn't answer right away. Our eyes connected and the air around us snapped. "I do," he said in a rough voice. "More than anything."

"And you complain *I'm* unpredictable."

CHAPTER SEVENTEEN

Alfie

I ran through places around Oxford I could show Cedar on my way to have a casual rugby toss-about with Lachlan after his team practice.

When I'd been on the Oxford Blues team during my undergrad, the practices had taken up a good chunk of my time, but Professor Harris had approved of being a Blues rugby player. He always said that students who showed the discipline it took to be a Blues athlete tended to apply that to the rest of their lives and go far. Despite my confusion around Cedar, I still yearned for Professor Harris's version of "going far".

What would he think about me guiding Cedar around Oxford?

On the one hand, he'd made his dislike of her and the whole Commonwealth Scheme clear. On the other, the Warden had personally requested me to act as a guide and mentor. Professor Harris respected nothing as much as the complicated hierarchy of the college.

As I made my way up Iffley Road I sorted through my random

ideas, an anticipation I couldn't quash bubbling through me. I definitely had to introduce her to The Turf Tavern to make up for the night she'd missed it because of me.

The Ashmolean Museum was a sure thing. Their collection of medieval archeology, like Saint Thomas Becket's reliquary casket, would fascinate her. The Botanical gardens ... would she find that pathetic compared to the forest she was used to? I'd have to ask. Carfax Tower? Perhaps a stroll across Port Meadow and a pint at the Trout? That thought warmed me from the inside out.

The Cherwell was parallel to where I walked up the noisy, exhaust-filled Iffley Road. Why did people need to constantly honk when they drove? I should have taken the river footpath instead. Punting! Cedar's experience at Oxford wouldn't be complete unless I took her on a punt.

The memory of her hand underneath mine and the sizzle in the air of Professor Harris's study roared back. On second thought ... no punting. We would be close together in a boat—it was a wildly romantic thing to do, and I could not put myself in that position again. She could surely resist me, but I wasn't convinced if I could resist her. I crossed out punting on my mental list.

The incessant honking was drowned out by the screaming siren of an ambulance driving at full speed up the road. In no time, its flashing lights came into view, and I covered my ears.

I sent out a hope that whoever it was racing towards was going to be fine. By the time I reached the turnoff to the Oxford University Rugby Football Club, two more ambulances had passed me.

As I made my way towards the clubhouse where I planned to meet Lachlan, I heard a rabble of voices coming from the parking area. I went around the corner and saw the three ambulances parked there.

The entire team and all the coaches and assistants were huddled around a player—I could tell from the cleats I saw at the end of the stretcher being loaded into the back of one of the ambulances. The rest of the injured rugby player was hard to make out. He was wearing what looked like a neck brace and had tubes everywhere and an apparatus over his mouth and nose.

My heart in my throat, I reasoned with myself that those weren't Lachlan's neon orange cleats. It wasn't him.

I kept my distance until the ambulances shut their doors and roared away.

The players remained, some sitting, some standing on the pavement of the parking lot. My stomach sank. Whatever happened, it must have been serious. I searched the crowd for Lachlan and finally spotted him, his massive back turned towards me as he sat with his head in his hands on the edge of the parking lot.

I made my way over and sat down beside him on the curb. "Lachlan. What happened? Are you all right?"

When he raised his face to answer, I jerked back at the tears flowing from his bloodshot eyes and the distress written across every familiar feature.

"Oh no," I murmured.

"He's dead," he said, shoulders heaving. "The paramedics did everything they were supposed to do, but he was dead, Alfie."

"Who?" I asked gently.

"That brand new lad from Wales. He was at your college. Angus tackled him and he fell. There was a terrible snapping noise. At first, we just thought it was a bone or his knee or something. We thought maybe he'd just been knocked out for a bit, but then I knelt down and ..." Lachlan shook his head. "He was turning so white, Alfie. I felt his neck for a pulse. Nothing. I felt his chest for a heartbeat. Nothing. I yelled for help. The medical staff came running, and I was pushed aside, but it was too late."

I searched wildly for words of comfort. "You can't know that Lachlan. It must have been horrible for you—for all the players on the field—but they can do amazing things these days, you know."

He pressed his thumbs into his eyes. "No," he said, his voice catching. "He was gone."

From what Lachlan said, it sounded as though his assessment was probably correct. My job here wasn't to cheer up my friend with false optimism, but rather to just ... be there.

"What's next?" I asked, rubbing his back.

He sighed a long, shaky sigh. "Wait for a phone call from the hospital. Coach followed the ambulance there."

"I imagine everyone else will stay here and wait together."

Lachlan nodded.

What did they need? *Tea*. It wasn't much, but it was something.

"I'm going to make you some tea." I said to Lachlan. "And your teammates too." *And I was also going to put a hefty shot of whisky in it to steady their nerves.*

"That'd be braw," Lachlan said, still consumed by his shock.

I patted his back and went into the clubhouse to heat up the kettle. Luckily, the clubhouse liquor cabinet remained just as well-stocked as when I'd been a Blue. I added generous glugs of whisky into each cup and took them to the parking lot. When they finished, I made more. Each trip gave me a chance to check in with Lachlan. Slowly ... painfully, Lachlan and his teammates began to move inside and onto the couches and chairs in the clubhouse. I made sure their cups were never empty.

Barely anybody spoke, and every spare thought I had that wasn't centered on Lachlan was for that Welsh boy, and for a miracle to happen. I was heating up yet another kettle of water when the assistant coach's phone rang, and the news came through.

Lachlan had been right. The boy was dead on arrival. A broken neck. Instantaneous. My eyes went immediately to Lachlan's face, which was paler than I'd ever seen it before. It was going to be a long night.

***

Two days later, I was sitting at the High Table for the dinner service, squeezed between a monastically silent physics DPhil candidate and the college Chaplain—a repressed sort with bushy eyebrows and a prodigious collection of nose hairs.

I wondered briefly if icicles would grow on them in Canada and wanted to share this vision with Cedar. No, I couldn't do that. Besides, I'd been so busy with Lachlan and the team I'd barely seen her since our last tutorial.

I hadn't known the boy who died—never even met him, actually—but I could still help my friend. Now I looked out to see if I could spot Cedar amongst the jam-packed tables full of robed students. She must be out there, dammit, but almost everyone's heads were bent over their plates. Surely I could recognize her wild hair anywhere.

I had to get back to planning some outings with her. I told myself it was to make the Warden happy, but in fact ... I flashed back yet again to that moment when I'd sat down on the couch and put my hand over hers and time seemed to stop. It had taken every fiber in my being not to lean in and explore her lips with mine. I shook my head at my plate. The stiffness between my legs was indisputable proof that the High Table was *not* the time or the place to be thinking about Cedar.

The Chaplain was in a talkative mood, unfortunately. I had been placed beside him at High Table enough times to know he rarely opened his mouth without something offensive coming out.

Nevertheless, it was considered a great honor to be invited to High Table. I'd already partaken in the traditional pre-dinner sherry in the Senior Common Room. Usually, I quite enjoyed the pomp and the honor of being invited, but that evening I couldn't help but see it through Cedar's eyes. It was ripe with tradition and history, of course, but it was also, well, pretentious.

"—and that is why rugby is the only manly sport left at Oxford, don't you agree, boy?" The Chaplain nudged me.

My face flushed red. I'd been caught out daydreaming, which was a social solecism for the Junior Fellows invited to High Table. Best be vague. "Rowing is a fine sport too," I said.

"Bah!" A few chewed bits of the stewed beef in claret sauce we were eating flew out of his mouth. Good God, what an unpalatable man. He smelled like overripe Stilton.

The view from High Table, at least, never disappointed—the vaulted oak ceilings, medieval stone walls, and long wooden tables and benches set with that elegant line of lamps. I adored looking down and watching the rows of black-robed students eating—so many brilliant minds mixing and bouncing off each other, the way they'd done in this spot for centuries.

There! I caught sight of Cedar, who was mostly hidden by the hulking form of Raphael. Frustrating. No wonder I hadn't been able to spot her before.

She was sitting with Shaun and Binita and a handsome friend of Binita's who I knew was a full Blue in fencing. The beef stew that I'd been enjoying until then congealed into a lump in my stomach. Binita's friend was laughing at something Cedar said, completely entranced. Of course he was. I couldn't be jealous, but my jaw ached. How long had I been clenching it?

"Are you listening to me, boy?" the Chaplain demanded.

Bollocks. I'd let my attention wander again. Despite the fact that the Chaplain smelled like moldy cheese and spat his food, he'd been at the college forever, and had the ear of many of the older dons.

The physics student beside me could very well be a genius, but he would never get anywhere at Beaufort College. His silence marked him as an ungrateful guest, and the dons liked nothing better than a show of slavish gratitude from their invitees at the High Table.

The reality was there was no better place to best establish and strengthen connections with the higher-ups in college who decided my academic future. Professor Harris was down at the far end of the table, beside the Warden. He had a true gift for mealtime influencing, and the nod he'd given me before we sat down was confirmation that he expected me to be an impeccable guest and use my time wisely.

Just don't look at Cedar. "What do you think of the beef stew?" I asked the Chaplain. Discussing the food was a sure bet, as was asking for the dons' opinions on things.

He grunted while shoveling down great forkfuls of it. Did the man even chew or did the food just go straight down his gullet like the seagulls I used to chase as a boy in Scotland? Lachlan and I would feed them chicken bones just to watch them swallow the whole things in one go. The Chaplain was every bit as impressive on that front.

"Passable," he said finally. "But why did they ruin a perfectly good stew by throwing vegetables in there?"

I didn't, of course, start talking about the benefits of Vitamin A, but murmured something in agreement. "Decent claret though," I commented.

"Capital!" he exclaimed with an enthusiasm that had me wondering just how much of the Communion wine was used for his own personal consumption. “Say, did you hear about that Welsh rugby lad who died?”

“Yes, it was tragic,” I said. I thought about mentioning I was there just afterwards, but I couldn’t stand the thought of the Chaplain using that for gossip fodder. “I cannot even imagine what his poor family is enduring.” It was enough to see how Lachlan and his teammates were still deep in grief and self-recrimination, even though the doctors had insisted it had just been a freak, unfortunate accident.

“Snapped his neck.” The Chaplain sucked back his glass of wine. “Death was instant.” He snapped his fingers at the waiter to bring more, then buried himself in his stew again.

He spoke with a complete lack of empathy that chilled me through.

My gaze moved inexorably back to Cedar. Binita was saying something to make her laugh. Her eyes were crinkled in the corners and sparkled with mirth. I wanted to be the one making her look that way, but ... no, I was on probation, and I had promised the Warden to be a gentleman, and besides, we had nothing in common besides a love for obscure medieval texts.

Yet, if that were the case, how did I explain away what happened when I’d covered her hand with mine and even when I watched her now? How could I make sense of that bolt of something I couldn’t name—and had never felt before—which electrified every one of my cells?

No-one could know that I possessed a side to me that was every bit as extravagant and undisciplined as my father. I had to keep it on the tightest leash—a leash that Cedar made me reflexively want to drop.

Indulging in these inexplicable feelings for her would destroy the life I had worked so diligently to build. She disoriented me, and I could not afford to be disoriented. So why couldn't I look away from her then?

At that instant, she turned her head in my direction as if she could feel my eyes on her. My breath caught. She held my eyes with hers, unflinching.

The chatter of voices and clatter of cutlery and frowning portraits of old men adorning the walls faded away. It was just us. The left corner of her lips twitched up. She winked at me.

Joy rushed through every one of my cells. Foolish as I was, I winked back, trying not to grin. We stayed like that until the Chaplain gave me an elbow to the ribs.

"What do you say to that?" he demanded.

I tore my gaze away from hers. "What?" I demanded, too annoyed by my link with Cedar being broken to respond with my usual deferential tone.

"What is wrong with you, boy?" His cheeks puffed up in indignation. "Do I need to talk to the Dons about you?"

"No." I shook my head, my mind grasping for excuses. "I was just pondering a recent Chaucer translation I came across." An academic excuse was always the most acceptable.

"Hmph," he said. "Well, you're proving to be a tedious dining companion."

I cursed myself. More than negative peer reviews for a publication or stepping on the quad grass, that was by far the most damning reputation to have in college. If I wanted proof that Cedar had the potential to be disastrous for me, here it was. "My apologies."

"I was talking about that rugby lad from Wales. The dead one."

This was the person in college whose role was providing spiritual comfort?

"Of course," I said, all ears now. "I have some friends who still play on the Blues squad and they're gutted. To say it was a shock is an understatement. It's difficult to understand why such things happen."

Instead of saying something philosophical, the Chaplain just snorted. "Well, everything happens for a reason, et cetera, et cetera. What I was *saying* to you when you weren't listening to me was the lad was from Wales, so now I have to organize a funeral service here in the College Chapel."

"That's an excellent notion—that way his family can meet his rugby teammates and college friends and they can grieve together."

He frowned at me. "It's a dashed lot of extra work for me is what it is. To make it even worse, these parents of his want to speak at the funeral service."

"Well ..." I was confused. "That's good, isn't it? It will personalize the service and perhaps mean less work for you? I admire his parents for having the courage to do so. I cannot even imagine—"

"You understand nothing, my boy," the Chaplain said. "I don't want them speaking at my service. I am a stickler for running only High Church of England services. A weepy speech from the parents is just so unbearably undignified."

The man's utter lack of compassion struck me to silence. I'd been so dead set on ingratiating myself to the Dons of Beaufort College, I'd never paused to consider that it may also require some moral murkiness on my part.

"If a speech is the parents' way of achieving closure," I began recklessly. "And helps them, even one iota, cope with the loss of their child, then I believe they should be allowed to do it."

The Chaplain eyed me with disfavor. "I suppose I shall be obliged to acquiesce," he sighed. "But I don't like it. It's all very irregular."

"I'm sure that is nothing compared to the loss of a beloved son."

"You simply do not understand," he said, his face turning an alarming shade of crimson.

With that, he began regaling the poor Maths Don on his other side with the same story. I looked out to Cedar again, but she was busy talking to Binita's fencing friend, her brows drawn together in concentration as she listened to every word in that focused way she did.

Why had I spoken up like that? In the past I might have just smiled and nodded. Had she changed me already, without me noticing?

CHAPTER EIGHTEEN

Cedar

I'd never been to a funeral before. When one of my dogs died, I would carry it and leave it deep in the forest where it would be eaten and what was left would return to the earth.

Binita had told me that everyone in college was expected to attend the rugby boy's funeral, and I didn't want to be the odd one out. It was incredibly sad, even though I had never met the student. He'd surely come to Oxford with some of the same hopes and dreams as I had—full of new experiences and new friends. All that ended in an instant for him.

I hadn't set foot in the College Chapel yet, even though I'd been fully intending to. I'd read that it was a historical treasure, just like the Hall, and likewise dated back to the thirteen hundreds. The thing was that even though of course I was well researched in religion and churches—especially as they pertained to life in the Middle Ages—I'd never actually stepped foot in one.

As I joined the flow of students heading inside, the sensation that I didn't belong throbbed through me.

I didn't believe in God—at least not this kind of God with Saints and Jesus and all that. The only kind of Church I knew was the feeling of being a part of something bigger when I was underneath the biggest, oldest trees in the forest. I couldn't explain it, but they felt as sentient as I was. Life and death were just a normal, everyday part of life. The idea of sticking the band-aid of religion on it, especially in this day and age, seemed so very odd.

The chapel was filling up and, as the crowd thickened, the people filing in started to press up against me. We were all wearing our gowns, so there was a lot of fabric everywhere. Being short, I couldn't seem to get a good breath of air.

Panic stirred under my breastbone. Yes, I'd come to Oxford to be closer to people, but not *this* close. I pushed my way over to the edge of the main aisle and took a moment to catch my breath.

Worn stone carvings of saints were everywhere I looked. While I knew I should be interested in them from a historical perspective, I felt they were all judging me. I was an imposter. I had no idea what to do or how to be in a church. My breath came in ragged jags that grated like gravel in my throat. I needed to get back outside.

A hand emerged from the pew behind me and grabbed my wrist. I spun around. *Alfie*. Relief poured through me.

"Are you quite well?" Alfie asked, peering into my face.

I shook my head. "I've never been in a church before," I said. "It's creepy, and all these people. I can't breathe."

He pulled me into the pew where he stood, away from the river of students. "I should have realized … I imagine you're not used to crowds."

I thought of the endless swaths of untouched forest that splayed out around my cabin. "You could say that."

"Will you come sit with me? I need to go closer to the front and sit beside my friend Lachlan. He's on the rugby team. Do you mind?"

Of course I didn't. "I would appreciate that, but do we have to go back in there?" I nodded to the flow of people that was scarier than any rapids I'd ever navigated.

He shook his head, his eyes warm with understanding. "I know a better way. Trust me."

And the strangest thing was that, despite his past behavior, I did. "Let's go."

He led me over to the opposite side of pews where, I realized now, there was almost nobody at all.

"Why don't other people use this way?" I asked him as he led me forward.

"Us British are fairly used to being in crowds. Sometimes, I wonder if we find it comforting."

"Comforting?" I could not even imagine.

"I'm sorry I haven't had the opportunity to show you around in the past few days. I've been spending time with Lachlan—"

"Of course you have," I said. "The entire team must be devastated."

He nodded. "They are." He found a pew and began leading me down it. "Lachlan's just in front of us here with the rest of the team.

Curiosity rushed through me. What would this friend of Alfie's be like? Aristocratic and cold, or warm and down-to-earth? Anticipation beat against my ribs like the wings of a trapped bird. It shouldn't matter to me this much, yet it did.

Alfie gestured at me to sit down beside him.

Once we were settled, he tapped on the shoulder of a massive man sitting directly in front of us. The man turned around and gave a watery smile to Alfie, then his kind blue eyes travelled over to me. His smile widened. *Nope. Nothing cold about him.* Relief washed over me.

"Lachlan," Alfie said. "I'd like you to meet one of my students, Cedar Wild. Cedar, this is my friend Lachlan MacGregor. We grew up together in Scotland."

I reached my hand forward and the feeling of his massive paw clasping mine left me almost wanting to laugh. That was frowned upon at funerals, wasn't it? "Nice to meet you," I said. "And I'm so sorry. The last few days must have been terrible for you guys."

He nodded. "Thank you. They have been, but Alfie's been helping out, not just me but other members of the team too."

He spoke with an accent. I was still trying to figure my way around British accents, but whatever his was, it sounded very different from the way Alfie pronounced words. He studied my face. I met his eyes and studied him back. From the tilt of his mouth, I could tell he was amused by my blatant scrutiny.

Finally, he gave me a wink and turned back around to murmur something to his teammate. Lachlan and the rest of the team were wearing their team jerseys instead of academic robes like the rest of us.

"Sorry about the staring," Alfie said. "I'll give him hell for that once this is over."

I shook my head. "No need. I just hope I didn't scare him by staring back."

The corner of Alfie's mouth twitched. "He's not easily intimidated."

"Neither am I." I tried but failed to keep a poker face. Alfie chuckled deep in his chest—a sound that resonated deep inside me. "He seems like a good guy," I added.

"The best."

The organ music, which had been in the background until then, began booming so loudly I could actually feel my eardrums vibrate. A white-robed man walked slowly down the aisle, swinging a metal thing that emitted a stinky, cloying smoke.

"Incense," Alfie whispered down at me.

I wrinkled my nose. "Ugh."

"Agreed."

I just couldn't wrap my mind around this religion thing. Nobody around me look confused or surprised. How could they all be going along with it? Didn't it feel silly, like it did to me? It was all make believe, like how I used to pretend sticks in the forest were fairies.

"What is it?" Alfie asked me in a low whisper.

I shook my head, trying to make sense of it. "I understand religion in the context of the medieval world. Most people weren't literate, after all, but I didn't think people still took it seriously."

Alfie's eyes went wide. "I never considered it like that. I suppose we all just accept it as part of our lives. A shared tradition even if we don't believe. Don't you think it's important to have rituals?"

I'd never thought of that. It was true when I was younger, I'd longed for things like Christmas and Easter and birthday parties like I read about in stories, but if I did choose to initiate one or two rituals for myself in the future, they definitely wouldn't include organs and incense.

The smell of it had wafted over to us by that point, and it clogged my throat. I coughed. "That stuff is rancid."

Alfie smothered a laugh. "That's definitely something they could get rid of." I tilted my head down so I could get a deep whiff of Alfie's clean scent of soap and cologne. *Ah.* Better.

The parents of the deceased rugby player made a moving speech through tears, and I marveled at what it must be like to have parents who loved so whole-heartedly. They had clearly given their whole hearts to their child, whose life had snatched away from them so suddenly. For a moment, I could almost understand my parents' disinclination to integrate me into their sentiments any more than necessary. Loving was such a risk.

Lachlan's shoulders shook during the parents' speech. Alfie reached out and placed a hand on his back and kept it there until the speech ended. That small gesture of solidarity hollowed out my stomach.

The chapel was historically awe-inspiring with its intricate stain glass windows and soaring stone arches. Still, I couldn't shake the feeling of being a trespasser. We had to get up and down several times during the final stretch of the service. At first, I was always a few beats behind everyone else.

Alfie must have noticed, because he began to cup my elbow with his hand to give me advanced warning of when I would need to stand and sit again. I cast him a look of gratitude.

It finally occurred to me that maybe Church was just a place where everyone felt free to support one another through hard things. No one had ever done that for me in my life, and now that I had felt it, sadness weighted me down. Now I knew what I'd been missing.

CHAPTER NINETEEN

Cedar

Afterwards, Alfie left with Lachlan and his rugby mates for a pint. My elbow still burned with the memory of Alfie's light, thoughtful touch. Solidarity. That was what he had shown me, just like he'd shown Lachlan. But I'd noticed there was a soft glow in his eyes when he looked at me compared to when he looked at his friend. Was it more than solidarity?

The sky was spitting a frigid rain, and my legs itched, restless.

Maybe if I went to the library, the hallowed surroundings would give me some measure of peace. I needed to check an original French manuscript of the Le Roman de la Rose for a side idea I had for my thesis, comparing it to Tristan and Iseult. Before I even brought it up with Alfie, I wanted to ensure I knew the material backwards and forwards and had thought it through thoroughly.

At the library, I tried to concentrate on translating the old French from the earliest Roman de la Rose manuscript at one of the big oak tables. No matter how hard I tried to focus, my mind kept ricocheting back to the warm solidity of Alfie beside me in the pew, and the hot prickle on the back of my neck when he was close like that.

I arched back in my chair to stretch—these desk chairs may be ornate and historic, but they sure as heck weren't comfortable. I spotted Raphael studying at the next table. When had he come in? Why hadn't he said hello? He was what we would call a 'squatch' back home, short for sasquatch—a mythical, big-foot-esque creature in our forests. Like the sasquatch, Raphael was reclusive, massive, and hairy.

There was an empty seat beside his, so I collected my photocopies and notebook and moved over to say hello. Work was not going to be a possibility until I blew off some steam.

"Raphael," I whispered. The librarians ruled Beaufort's library with an iron fist—loud voices were not tolerated. An idea popped into my head. I knew what I had to do, and company would be nice.

He jerked and peered up at me. His pale skin looked clammy and waxy, and there were dark circles under his eyes. Still, he was a strapping man—the kind of man I ran in to on every street corner in Stewart. The difference was those men back home spent much of their time outside, cutting logs or reeling in fish on a boat or rappelling off frozen waterfalls, whereas Raphael seemed to spend his hours hunched over books. There was nothing wrong with that, of course, and the few things he'd said in tutorial showed he had an impressive intellect, but surely there was a middle ground.

"Oh ... hi," he said finally, then ducked his head again.

I was nothing if not persistent. "How long have you been here for?"

"Since the funeral," he said.

"Heart-breaking, eh?"

He pressed his lips together and nodded.

"Are you feeling restless like I am?"

His eyebrows drew together over his nose. When I finally got a glimpse of his face, I saw he could be ruggedly handsome, if he cut his hair and maybe shaved once in a blue moon.

He frowned down at the manuscript he was studying. "I don't know ... I suppose I always feel restless."

That was understandable, seeing I never saw him doing anything more active than pulling library books off the shelf. "Have you ever played any sports?"

He shook his head. "There was never any money for that."

"We never had much money either, but we lived in the middle of the forest, so I spent a good chunk of every day moving around outside. I find that being under the trees helps my restlessness, or what we call cabin fever back home. Do you want to come outside with me this afternoon?"

"Why?" His face was a picture of confusion.

I shrugged. "To get rid of the cobwebs. This morning was sad, and I can't study and think properly if I don't get fresh air. I'd bet you're the same."

He looked towards the arched, stained-glass windows where the rain pattered against the panes. "But it's raining." His voice was bewildered, as though I'd asked him to go on a space mission to Mars during a meteor storm.

"It'll be even more refreshing that way," I said. "Come on. I'd love the company."

His brows drew together. "With *me*?"

"Why not? If we start and you want to come back to college, no problem," I said. "It's just a walk to get out in nature for a bit."

He smiled at me then—quite a lovely smile. "All right," he said. "All right," he repeated it, as if to convince himself.

"Great," I said. "Let's go back to our rooms and get changed. Do you have a pair of jogging pants or something?"

"I don't know," he said. "But I can look."

"Just throw on what you can find," I said. "Meet you at the Lodge in half an hour?"

He nodded. "Okay ... I think."

***

Raphael arrived at the Lodge dressed in ancient, stained jogging pants that looked like they dated from the Second World War, a pair of battered running shoes with huge holes in them, a far too tight gray T-shirt, and a wool sweater around his shoulders.

There was nothing in the vicinity of Oxford that resembled nature in the sense that I knew it, but I figured anything was better than nothing. Before we started, I checked on Raphael's phone (I hadn't got mine going yet) and found a bunch of hiking trails. One was titled a "nature loop" which seemed a grandiose thing to call a stroll on what was described as a chip path, but things were different here, I reminded myself. There wasn't too much elevation change and the trail started at the edge of town. Perfect for Raphael.

"What are we doing?" he demanded, sweat already beading on his forehead. "Where are we going?"

I shrugged. "Just a walk. I wish I could take you on a proper hike up a mountain where I'm from. I think you might like that, but in the meantime, a walk will have to do."

He went clammy looking again. "I've never—"

"I'd never been on an airplane that wasn't a float plane before coming to England." I shrugged. "Trying new things helps us figure out what we want to keep in our lives, and what we don't. If we don't try, we don't know."

"I suppose you have a point." His words weren't exactly enthused, but good enough.

"Don't worry about speed," I said. "I'm just happy to be out in the fresh air with a friend."

We'd begun to walk towards the doors to New College Lane, but now he stood stock still. "We're friends?"

"Sure," I said.

"Goodness. That's new for me."

We set off at an easy stroll, and it was Raphael, rather than me, who picked up the pace as we left the city behind and got into the forest.

Some of the trees were already bare, and some stayed green all year, but there was an occasional splash of fading yellow or crimson along our route.

The horns and cars faded in the distance. Leaves rustling overhead and the chirps of birds in the bushes were the only sounds that accompanied our breathing and the soft thumps of our feet hitting the earth. It was certainly nothing that I would consider true wilderness in my book, but it wasn't town either. That was something.

I filled my lungs with fresh air. Come to think of it, I hadn't been able to do that properly since arriving in Oxford. My tangle of thoughts about Alfie started to loosen. We were becoming friendly, weren't we? Maybe that was enough.

I glanced over at Raphael. His face glowed with exertion, and he had a beatific smile stretched from ear to ear.

"How you doing?" I asked.

"I ..." He gasped, but it was a happy gasp, one of disbelief. "I never knew."

"I know." I laughed. "Feels good to be in the woods, doesn't it? There's just something about trees, no matter how small they are."

When we looped back around into town we stopped under the Bridge of Sighs. Raphael's hands were on his hips, and he was breathing deep, like he was tasting oxygen for the first time in his life. He hadn't really changed physically, but there was a new light shining in him.

"When can we do that again?" he asked.

I shrugged. "Tomorrow if you want, although I eventually would like to find some outings with more elevations and forests, but there may be none of those close by. I guess we'll just make do. You can go out by yourself too, you know. Nature is always there, for all of us. I'm realizing how easy it can be to forget sometimes when we're surrounded by all this stone."

"Thank you, Cedar," he said. "Thank you so much."

I caught the sight of two familiar figures walking towards us on New College Lane. Alfie and Lachlan. I pressed my palm against my chest as my heart did a flip.

Alfie stopped short when he saw us. "Raphael." He nodded in his direction, then focused in on me with such intentness that I wondered if I had some dirt on my face. "What have you two been up to?"

"Cedar took me for a walk!" Raphael exclaimed with a whole new enthusiasm in his voice. Alfie's eyes widened, no doubt surprised at the change in him. "In the woods!"

Alfie dug his hands deep in the pockets of his wool jacket. "How lovely," he said, but something in his words struck me as insincere.

I had no idea why, but my fingers twitched with the desire to unwind the college scarf from around his neck.

"We're headed out for another pint at The Turf right now,"

Lachlan said. "Do you want to join?" His eyes shifted to Raphael. "That includes you too, of course."

Raphael's face lit up, but then he shook his head. "It's very kind, but I'm all sweaty."

Lachlan's eyes were still red, and his cheeks showed the salt tracks of tears—he needed more time alone with his best friend. "Thanks so much for the invite," I said. "But can I take a rain check? I need to shower too."

Alfie was frowning.

"When can we meet tomorrow?" Raphael asked me.

"Same time, same place?" I suggested.

"I'll be there," he said. "What can I do to repay you, Cedar? This has been a revelation."

Alfie's head went back and forth between me and Raphael like a ping pong ball.

"Don't mention it. Truly. It was my pleasure."

"But what can I do for you in return?" Raphael asked.

My eyes flicked to Alfie, remembering the end of our conversation at The Bear. "I didn't do it to get anything in return."

Raphael, however, shook his head. "There has to be something."

He wasn't going to let this go. My brand-new printer, laptop, and phone popped into my head.

"Are you good with computers?" I asked Raphael.

"I'm *brilliant* with computers," he said. That was something I never could have imagined him revealing even a few hours earlier. "Why?"

"Before he left, Willy bought me a printer and a laptop and a phone. There all still in boxes. I'd love some help setting them up."

Raphael grinned. "Perfect. I'll come to your room tonight—"

"I'll do it," Alfie interrupted. "I'm supposed to be helping Cedar with this sort of thing."

"Are you sure?" Raphael asked. "I'd be more than happy to—"

"Certain," said Alfie, in that imperious way that reminded us all that he technically was an actual Lord.

Raphael shrugged. "I'm not about to argue with one of my research advisors, but don't worry, Cedar. We'll find something else." With a jaunty wave that was completely unlike his pre-walk self, he bounced off.

I tilted my head at Alfie. "I didn't know you were good at that kind of thing."

"Oh ... yes."

Lachlan snorted and Alfie kicked him in the shin.

Wait. He wasn't? Why else would he insist on it then? "Okay," I said, cautious. "I'll see you tonight?"

"How about we meet up in Hall?" He smiled at me.

"Perfect."

I didn't miss the amused yet delighted look on Lachlan's face at his exchange. At least we'd cheered him up for a few seconds.

CHAPTER TWENTY

Alfie

I'd been invited to dine at the High Table again that night, and it was starting to feel like a punishment rather than an honor. I could see Cedar, Binita, Shaun, and Raphael at one of the far tables, laughing and smiling. How I wanted to be with them. More specifically, with her, sitting shoulder to shoulder like we'd done in the chapel.

After the meal was finished, the High Table descended from the dais and began the traditional procession out of the Hall. All the students, including Cedar and her friends, had to stand up as a mark of respect.

As I passed her, I felt like a pompous ass instead of a proud academic. She was changing me, and I had to put a stop to it. Tonight, in her room, I would set things straight once and for all. But what had she really done? It felt impossible to pinpoint. She had moved the target I was aiming for without me noticing.

I tried to escape early from the Senior Common Room where all the dons and senior fellows gathered for after-dinner coffee and port, but before I reached the door, Professor Harris appeared before me.

"Ah, Alfred!" he exclaimed. "Just the man I was looking for. It's a pity you weren't placed beside me at the High Table, as I have news of a possibly authentic addendum that has been discovered in London, believed to be written by Margery Kempe. I thought immediately of you, of course, and how it could benefit your research."

"How wonderful!" I struggled to sound enthusiastic.

I tried to pay attention as he regaled me with the details. Before Cedar, I would have been honored that he stopped to talk with me, but tonight all I could think about was getting to her room.

"Are you listening to me, Alfred?" Professor Harris straightened his spine.

"Of course I am, sir. My mind is merely running away with all the possibilities if this addendum is authenticated."

It was the perfect answer, but it was also a total lie. I'd been fretting that Cedar would think I had opted out of helping her—or worse yet, forgotten.

Professor Harris smiled and went on to enumerate the authentication process that was already underway. What was wrong with me? Normally, I found this sort of topic fascinating.

"Do you have any idea how I can view it?" I asked, finally, to Professor Harris, playing my part.

"I was thinking that we could make a day trip up to London when it's ready. What do you think?"

A day trip to London with Professor Harris? Even through my distraction, I knew that would be an entirely new level of collaboration with him. "Wonderful," I said. "Just let me know when. I'll jump at the chance."

"Smashing," he said. "Care to wager on its authenticity?" His eyes narrowed.

I laughed. "I never bet on such uncertainties. We all know what the authentication process is like."

Disappointment flashed in his eyes, but he quickly regrouped. He hadn't been serious, had he?

"I should get home," he said. "But quickly, how is it going with your ragtag group of MPhil students?"

I was obsessed with one, jealous of another. Unbelievably, Shaun was turning out to be the easiest to handle. "Torture," I said honestly.

Luckily, this was exactly the sort of beleaguered comment the dons enjoyed making about their students. Professor Harris snickered, something I didn't think I'd ever seen him do before.

"That sounds about right," he said. "Especially with that peasant in your class."

Peasant? Did he mean Cedar? My fists clenched.

He patted me on the shoulder. "Don't look so worried, Alfred," he said. "I promised you I'm working on getting rid of her and that whole nonsensical Commonwealth rubbish. Never fear."

And with that, he left me seething with anger as he walked out of the room, whistling.

I was frozen to the spot for several seconds before I left too.

Professor Harris had called Cedar a peasant. *How dare he*. He couldn't get rid of her—she didn't deserve that. Besides, the Warden was in complete support of Lord Cavendish-Percy's scheme. She had more power at college than anyone, so perhaps I could safely put that fear out of my mind.

Peasant. It was a horrible thing to say, but he didn't know Cedar like I did, and many of the assumptions he had clearly made about her were the same things I had assumed before getting to know her. He would soften about her in time ... surely?

I checked my watch. *Dammit.* I was extremely late.

I had set off at a walk, but I started running towards my rooms. I couldn't have Cedar thinking I'd forgot about her. I knew I had to hold strong and not go beyond the bounds of gentlemanly behavior with her, but I couldn't have her thinking I'd forgotten.

Surely I had more than enough self-restraint to control my baser instincts with her, no matter what kind of effect she had on me. After all, it was my problem, not hers. Being in her bedroom, helping her, was an excellent opportunity to strengthen a muscle that had been weakening of late.

The one thing I hadn't told Cedar, and that she couldn't find out, was that I was hopeless at computers and had never set one up before. Printers were a whole new world for me. Whenever I needed tech help, I called Lachlan and in exchange I edited all his essays before he turned them in.

It was so ridiculous that I'd offered to set the thing up for her, but I'd been overpowered with the need to be the one to help Cedar, not Raphael.

After laughing at me, Lachlan finally sent me a few websites with clear instructions. I'd spent the two hours before Hall studying the steps so I could be of actual use to her. I had also printed wads of instructions I planned on taking with me, so I needed to fetch them before heading to Cedar's room.

Besides, I had to feed Norris. The ways Robbie and I had smuggled dog food into college bordered on slapstick comedy. Norris was the reason why I never allowed anybody but Robbie, Annabelle, and Lachlan into my room. I also reminded myself to check that his stairs to the toilet were pushed up against it and that the lid was up.

I took the stairs two by two and was out of breath by the time

I got to the top where my room was tucked away under the eaves by the clock-tower. I was forever grateful for its privacy—an ideal location for keeping Norris a secret.

I looked up at the door and froze when I saw Cedar leaning against it. My lungs seized and I couldn't catch a breath. *No.* She wasn't supposed to be here.

"There you are," she said, no trace of annoyance in that arresting face of hers. "I figured you must have been waylaid somewhere."

How was I going to stop her from coming into my rooms now? She couldn't see my dog, or just as disastrous, the prep work I'd been doing to pretend like my computer knowledge was actually up to snuff.

"Apologies," I stalled. "Professor Harris decided he needed to urgently discuss something with me."

"Oh? What?"

"A recently unearthed addendum that they think, or hope, was written by Margery Kempe."

Her flecked brown eyes went wide. "Margery Kempe, as in everyone's favorite English Christian Mystic?"

Despite the stress of having Cedar at my doorstep, I couldn't help but grin at her quick medieval lit repartee. "The very same."

"Is it autobiographical, like The Book of Margery Kempe?"

"Possibly, yes."

She chewed on her lower lip, deep in thought. Her right incisor slightly overlapped her next tooth. They both tugged gently at her pillowy lower lip. The wild part of me growled with desire, fully awake now.

"That's exciting," she said, finally. "Can I see it when you get a copy?"

I nodded. "Of course. I'll be sharing it with all of you." How was I going to get her back to her room and away from my door?

"I'm curious," I stalled. "How did you know which room was mine?" This was not information I shared if I could help it.

"I asked Robbie," she said.

Robbie knew exactly why not to send people to my room. He'd foisted Norris on me in the first place. Why had he told her?

I gestured at my door. "How about you go ahead to your room, and I'll be there in a minute or two? I just need to grab a few things."

A pucker appeared between her eyebrows. "You're not going to invite me in?"

The look in her eyes was killing me. "That would be inappropriate—"

"You know what? I think I'll go find Raphael and ask if he can help me instead."

Panic was like a flapping bird in my chest. "What? Why?"

"If it's inappropriate for me to be in your room, it's inappropriate for you to be in my room."

Bugger. I'd forgotten how clever she was for a split-second. I had two choices. One, let Raphael help her, or two, let her in on my secret and trust her. I should pick the former, for so many reasons.

She turned and walked towards the stairs. She placed her hand on the worn wooden banister.

"Don't go!" I said in a choked voice.

"Why not?" She turned, her bright eyes missing nothing.

"Can you keep a secret?"

"I'm a vault."

"Fine." I blew out a lungful of air and fished my key from the pocket of my jeans. "Just ... you might be surprised."

"I like surprises. At least, I haven't had very many of them, but I think I do, as long as they don't involve animals stalking me."

Norris wouldn't stalk her, but he would attack her with affection. "Hold that thought."

She stood behind me as I unlocked my door. I could smell the fresh scent of pine in her hair—headier than any perfume. I swung my door open and Norris, as usual, was waiting for me on the other side, his stubby little tail twitching wildly and his tongue hanging out of his mouth. He began yipping in excitement. Luckily, his yips were always on the quiet side, as if he knew he couldn't be discovered.

I ushered Cedar in, then shut and locked the door firmly behind us. "May I present Norris? Nobody can know about him," I said. "It's strictly against college regulations to have a pet."

Every feature on her face glowed with delight. I watched her, hypnotized.

"Hello Norris." She bent down to pick Norris up in her arms and carried him over to the couch. Holding him in her lap, she scratched his belly. He wriggled with pleasure. I could hardly blame him. I stood there like an idiot, entranced as her hand skillfully found those spots that were like nirvana for Norris—under his collar, behind his ears, his lower back ...

"You're probably wondering..." I began, after watching her for who knows how long.

"What I want to know," she interrupted me, "Is why a stickler for the rules like you would take a risk like this. Except of course, dogs are the best, especially this little guy."

Norris whined with delight.

"It's a long story."

She lifted an eyebrow. "Summarize."

"I've always loved animals. I had a dog when I was little."

"What was his name?"

"Oswald."

"Oswald? That's almost as good as Norris."

I smiled, remembering him. "Besides Lachlan, he was my best friend. One day Robbie called me down late at night and said he'd gone to the shelter with his granddaughter to choose a cat for her. While he was there, he fell in love with this mutt." I pointed at Norris, who was looking up at Cedar with slavish devotion. "The staff at the animal shelter told him Norris was going to be euthanized the next day. Robbie took him, but then when he brought Norris home his wife couldn't breathe for allergies."

"Oh no."

I nodded. "He brought him to my rooms with a bag of dog food and begged me to keep him for a night or two until he found another solution."

"How long ago was that?"

"About ten months ago." I looked down at my feet. I wasn't proud of taking such a risk, but then I couldn't bear the idea of letting down Robbie and having Norris harmed in any way either. It was a daily tug-of-war between my heart and my head.

She chuckled. "And to think you gave me such a hard time for not wearing a robe to my first tutorial. You're the biggest rule-breaker of all."

Remorse struck me square in the chest. "Yes, that was wrong of me, but I'm not—"

She waved her hand. "It's awesome. I love the fact you're hiding a contraband dog. Wait. How does he go to the bathroom?"

There was no way to admit it without sounding like someone whose pastime was doing cross-stitches of sayings like "a dog blesses this home" to decorate the walls. Still, I could see no other way. "I had to train him to use the toilet."

Her eyes went wider than I'd ever seen them before. I imagined her dogs in the forest were not quite as spoiled. "How does he even get up there?" she asked, finally.

I cleared my throat. "Er ... I built him a set of stairs."

She just stared at me, her eyebrows almost up to her hairline. "I have to see this."

"No ... really ..." I protested, but she was already across the room with Norris in her arms.

She got up and let out a delighted laugh when she peered inside the washroom. "That's impressive," she said. "Although a miter saw would have come in handy. Your angles are pretty rough."

I collapsed against the back of the couch, thoroughly humiliated. I shut my eyes. After a minute or so, I felt her sit down beside me again.

"You've just changed my opinion of you," she said. "Again."

I highly doubted it was for the better.

When I finally opened my eyes, she was scratching at the scruff of Norris's neck. Her nimble, clever fingers slipped skillfully under his collar. Norris was making tiny grunts of bliss. I was jealous of my *dog*.

Automatically, I reached out to scratch Norris's ears like I always did. My hand met with Cedar's. The current between us gave me that shock I craved. I immediately wanted to feel it again, to feel it all the time.

"I didn't realize until now how much I've been missing my dogs," she said in a voice that sounded a bit flustered too. "In the forest with nobody around and my parents always working, they were my only friends. You must really love Norris if you break the rules for him."

"I like to look at it as doing a favor for Robbie, but you're right. I am breaking the rules. He's grown on me," I admitted.

"I'm relieved to hear that," she said. "I was coming to the conclusion that nothing was as important to you as the Oxford Code of Conduct."

I sighed. "I know I must seem like such a prig to you, but there are reasons for that."

"Oh?"

"Yes," I said, not elaborating further. She knew about my father, of course, but part of me wanted to tell her everything—how I was desperately trying to find a safe shore where I could build a little shack for myself, and not have it blown over again and again.

"Whatever your reasons, I'm happy to see that sometimes you put your moral compass above the rules." Her brown eyes sparkled then, revealing amber flecks like flakes of gold.

How could Cedar Wild be here in my room, on my couch, sending my dog into paroxysms of delight? This should feel dangerous, but instead it felt ... right. "Moral compass?" I asked.

She nodded. Norris's tongue was hanging out of his mouth now, bliss incarnate. "Uh huh. There are the rules and what people tell me to do." She sliced the air with her hand in front of my chest. "And then there is my own moral compass." She touched her breastbone, then sliced the air above her head. "It's trial and error, for sure, but no rule stands a chance if my moral compass says otherwise. It trumps everything else."

It was a revolutionary idea. It would never work for me, of course, aside from Norris. What Cedar didn't understand was that, because of my father's scandal-ridden existence, I had no scope for error. Still, it helped me understand Cedar better.

"I still feel guilty about Norris and live in terror of being caught," I admitted, not wanting to give her the mistaken impression that I was some sort of rebel.

"If I can help you with Norris, let me know. I think I'd make a very good accomplice."

I chuckled. "I doubt I've seen even the tip of the iceberg of the things you can do." Once it was out of my mouth, the double meaning occurred to me, and I wasn't able to hide my consternation.

She raised her eyebrows. "You'd be amazed." I should have known she wasn't one for playing coy. Her boldness should terrify me. Instead, I found it utterly captivating.

Alarmed by the flush of warmth that was spreading outward from my groin, I hopped up from the couch and went over and poured some dog food into Norris's bowl. He didn't budge from her arms, not that I could blame him. How I ached for her fingers to run through *my* hair. "Remember, I'm supposed to help you tonight. We should be on our way."

"Can we bring him with us?" Cedar asked. "I can smuggle him under my robe. Huh! I guess they can be handy for that too."

I shook my head. "We can't take risks like that, for Norris's safety."

"That's true." She sighed, and reluctantly placed him on the floor, where he made a beeline for his food.

"I'm sorry, Norris," she said, with genuine regret. "But I promise I'll come visit you again soon and give you many, many pats."

I grabbed the wad of papers I'd printed out from my desk and opened the bedroom door for her. She reached out and squeezed my arm as she went out. It felt like a brand, even through my sweater.

She glanced up, and our eyes met. Time seemed to stop. "Even if I forced your hand," she said. "Thank you for sharing your secret with me." Her brown eyes flicked back to Norris, who was already snorting as he gobbled his kibble. "I'm glad we're friends."

I should be happy, yet that last word was a rapier to my heart.

She yawned.

"Are you too tired to do this tonight?" I asked, hating to put it off, but at the same time needing a bit of a reprieve to marshal all my wild thoughts and get them securely back under lock and key.

She rubbed her eyes. "How long do you think it will take?"

Given my inexperience, it could take very long indeed. "Several hours," I said. "If I come over tomorrow night after Hall, would that work better for you?"

She frowned, but then finally nodded. "I think the funeral took it out of everyone today."

It had, and I looked forward to a fresh, and far more rational, start with her the next night. "Tomorrow night then?"

"Tomorrow night." She bit her lip again, and I clutched on to the door I held open, trying to stop myself from pressing my mouth against hers, and tasting her lips for myself. I pulled my gown around me or else I was going to embarrass myself. Yes ... a breather between us was necessary.

She paused for a few beats on the landing. I was torn between wanting her to go before I did something rash and for her to never leave. I wanted to drag her back into my room. Hell, into my bed.

Then she nodded once—short and sharp. "Sleep tight, Alfie." She went down the stairs, then she was gone before I realized I'd been too stunned to wish her goodnight as well.

FOURTH WEEK

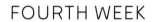

CHAPTER TWENTY-ONE

Cedar

In my room after Hall I sat at my desk, trying to busy myself with reading a few texts I'd borrowed from the college library while I waited for Alfie to arrive to set up my computer and stuff. The sexual tension between us the night before, when I met Norris, was undeniable—at least for me. I had my suspicions, but he remained inscrutable.

I slammed the books shut. Who was I kidding? I couldn't concentrate on anything, knowing Alfie was imminently going to be spending at least a couple of hours in my room. Maybe we just needed to have sex to get it out of our systems as I'd done with the three men I'd been with before. A physical need met. No more, no less.

The problem was that everything with Alfie felt complicated. No, it *was* complicated. I couldn't just stop seeing him. He was my Junior Advisor.

I stared at the computer, printer, and iPhone boxes piled up in front of me. I was right that there was more to Alfie than the image he tried so hard to project to the world. Norris was confirmation of that. That also made meaningless sex a tricky business.

Yes, I loved Alfie's intellect, but the repressed English scholar didn't intrigue me. I was drawn to the man who rescued a dog that would otherwise be euthanized, built him a set of stairs to the toilet, had a bag of liver treats on his windowsill, and a knitted dog sweater drying on the cast iron radiator in his room.

I shook my head. *I was getting way ahead of myself. One step at a time, Cedar.*

A knock on the door.

I leapt off my chair and opened it with a flourish. Instead of coming in, Alfie stayed on the threshold, staring down at my door handle. "Your door wasn't locked?" he asked.

Of the things I'd been anticipating about his arrival, it wasn't that. Were locked doors one of the rules about Oxford that I didn't know about? "No."

"Do you ever lock it?"

What a bizarre question. "Surely with everyone in college there's no need—"

"There *is* a need," he said, shaking his head. How did we get back here again, to rule-following Alfie, just when I thought we'd made so much progress? "There is a ton of theft in Oxford, even within college walls."

Theft? I had a hard time believing that. From what I could see, everyone in college had everything they needed.

"Come in." I waved him in the door. He kept flexing his fingers. Was he nervous?

I shut the door behind us, then locked it. It felt wrong, as though I was locking myself in rather than locking others out. It gave me the itchy sensation of being trapped.

He took a deep breath and walked inside my room, his eyes

growing wide with alarm as he surveyed it. Why? It was just a room, and not much different from the day I'd moved in.

"Where are your sheets, Cedar?" He pointed down at my bed and my sleeping bag that lay on top of the bare mattress.

"I don't need sheets," I said. "I rolled out my sleeping bag my first night here. Why would I need anything else?"

Back home, we all slept in sleeping bags. I'd never questioned it.

"To make your room a little cozier," he said. "You know, homey."

I hiccupped a laugh. "My Scout said the same thing. What is it with the Brits and coziness?"

Now I thought about it, Alfie's rooms had looked lived in, with pillows and blankets and a nice, soft looking dog bed for Norris on the floor. I didn't even know where to begin with such things.

I looked around my room through Alfie's eyes.

Besides my suitcase on the floor, the laptop and printer box on my desk, and a photo frame and book beside my bed, my room was empty.

Alfie's eyes roved around the space, and the shock etched on his features made me shift my weight from one leg to the other and back again. "It's a bit ... austere. I'm sorry. I should have taken time to come and check out how you settled into your room before now."

"It's fine," I said. "I mean, it's fine for me. This is what I'm used to."

The insides of our cabins back home were simple and pragmatic—rifles, a wood stove, warm clothes, computer, satellite internet. "I wouldn't even know where to begin with buying sheets. I mean, I guess I could research it, but—"

"I can help you," he said. "I should have done it some time ago."

"Skookum," I said. "What do you think I should add to make it ... homey?" That was a concept I was going to have to research as well.

"Before considering throw pillows and fairy lights," he said, his face serious. "You should lock your door." Alfie was proving to be like a dog with a bone about certain things.

I couldn't help but roll my eyes. "Right. The stealing thing."

"Not just that." His green-blue eyes went darker, like a stormy sea. "There could be intruders—men, specifically, who might stumble in here after drinking and try ... well, try to take advantage of you."

It was sweet, really, but laughter burst out of me all the same.

"What?" He jerked back, clearly affronted by my amusement.

I waved him to sit down on my mattress, then sat down beside him. "The only thing I would worry about in that sort of situation is that I might injure the guy. I wrestled a cougar once, you know, with only a big branch for defense. You've never seen me truly fierce—"

"I beg to differ. The night we met, you growled at the paparazzi."

"That was just a feint, trust me. The real thing—well, you might as well know—I've been told I can be scary."

Alfie studied my face with an intensity that no person had ever contemplated me with before. My skin tingled everywhere. He was trying, really trying, to figure me out.

"You're an enigma, Cedar Wild," he said, a quiet reverence in his voice. "Cougars. Sleeping bag. An interest in Tristan and Iseult."

My throat thickened, and I couldn't think of any way to answer him. My eyes kept straying to that thinner lower lip that he'd been biting, and the lush, full upper lip above. His face shouldn't make sense, but somehow it did—so much so that my lungs were full of static, making it hard to take a deep breath. My heart thrummed fast in my chest although I was sitting still.

"It's not easy to take care of you," he said in a rough, low voice.

"I don't need taking care of," I answered, but softly, almost a whisper.

He reached across the increasingly small space that separated us and caught my chin between his thumb and forefinger. The feel of his fingertips against my skin sent sparks up my spine. I'd never felt like this before. This was uncharted land.

"This is a very stubborn chin," he said. "How can I make you understand everyone needs to be taken care of?"

The concept was so foreign to me that my mouth dropped open as my mind whirred. My parents had, from my earliest memories, instilled in me they were not there to "mollycoddle" me, as they put it.

The idea someone would *want* to take care of me—I had honestly never considered that before, and as much as it kindled a bonfire of warmth inside me, it also made me prickle with shame. I shouldn't want taking care of—I shouldn't need it. Yet here I was, wanting and needing.

Alfie hadn't let go of my chin, and his touch became the epicenter of my consciousness. His body swayed towards mine. I leaned in, mirroring him. His lips were mere inches away—

Abruptly, Alfie let go of my chin as though it had caught on fire. He tried to cover it up by giving me an awkward, hasty hug before leaping off my bed. "I'd better get going with this computer," he said, his voice strained. "It's getting late."

What just happened? We'd been just about to kiss. I was sure of it. I couldn't be reading him that inaccurately, could I? Had I done something wrong—broken one of those many, many rules I didn't even suspect existed?

Alfie tore into my laptop and printer boxes with his back turned to me.

An unwelcome memory came flashing back. I'd ran up to the cabin to beg my parents to come and see a fish trap I'd built in the lake. I was bursting with pride at how I'd researched fish trapping techniques off the internet and then improvised and built my own. Somehow, my accomplishment wouldn't feel complete unless I shared it with them.

For once, they'd agreed, and made their way down the path to the lake after me, when suddenly both of them stopped short.

I turned around. "Come on! I bet there's already fish in there."

"Do you see that?" My mother grabbed my father's arm.

My father nodded. "I've never seen him before. Different markings."

A gamey, overripe stench floated through the trees. Not again. A bear.

"We have to get the DNA kit," my mother hissed. "What an opportunity!"

"But you were coming to see my trap," I protested. "You promised."

My parents just made violent hushing motions with their hands. "Not now, Cedar," my father hissed. "This bear … this is *interesting*."

I shouldn't have been surprised or sad, because they'd already proved to me time and time again that the bears were more important to them than me. I would not let Alfie prove again I wasn't worth holding anyone's attention.

"I'm going to get ready for bed," I said. I needed to put a bit of distance between us to figure out what just happened.

Alfie just nodded without turning around. "Jolly good."

Jolly good? What the hell was I supposed to do with that? I went into the bathroom and rage-yanked on my plaid pajama bottoms and "Prince Rupert—Home of the King Salmon" T-shirt.

I wore a variation of this to bed every night, but after leaping away from me like I was radioactive, at least Alfie wouldn't think I was dressing up for him or cared about whatever had just happened on the bed between us.

I took the elastic out of my hair and ran my fingers through it while deciding that my best course of action was to act like nothing had happened. Nothing *had* happened, so why did it feel like it had?

When I emerged from the bathroom, Alfie had ensconced himself in my desk chair and entering commands into the new laptop while checking the stack of papers he'd brought with him.

He must have heard me close the bathroom door behind me, because he turned around and froze, that intent look in his eyes again. After a few tense seconds of this, and me putting my hands on my hips and frowning at him, he gave himself a shake.

"Is it really?" he asked, his voice hoarse.

"What?" If I hadn't been completely confused before, I was now.

"Prince Rupert. I imagine named after Prince Rupert of the Rhine, Duke of Cumberland. Is it truly the home of King Salmon?"

"Yes," I said, with some asperity. "They swim around with tiny, bejeweled crowns on their heads."

He burst out laughing at that and, all of a sudden, the atmosphere in the room felt normal again. It was a relief, like the ice cracking on the lake in the late spring.

"No, really, Cedar," he said, after he stopped chuckling. "Tell me. I'm truly curious."

"They're called King Salmon not because they belong to the royal family, but because they're huge. Some get up to seventy pounds."

His eyes went wide. "You're joking?"

I shook my head. "No. We'd go there in the summers sometimes because my parents also study the white spirit bears, which they refer to as *ursus americanus kermodei.* They only live in the Great Bear Rainforest around Prince Rupert. The First Nations view them as sacred and call them *moskgm'ol.*"

Alfie stared at me, riveted. "You've seen one before?"

I looked away then. One experience in particular had marred my memories of spirit bears, but I tried to push that out of my head. "Just stop dwelling on it," my parents had instructed when I kept having nightmares afterwards.

"Many," I said. "I've also caught a sixty-five-pound King Salmon once, but that's my record so far."

I'd also slept with the fisherman who'd taken me out on his boat—in the cabin under the bow on a blanket that smelled vaguely of fish and had iridescent salmon scales clinging to it—but I didn't mention this to Alfie. That fisherman certainly hadn't held my chin between his fingers or considered me as someone who needed taking care of. With Alfie, everything was so different. So much less straight-forward. I didn't think I was equipped to handle any of it.

"What does skookum mean?" Alfie asked, his eyes still intent on me, and especially the front of my T-shirt. I'd taken my bra off in the bathroom, I realized belatedly. "You said it when I mentioned helping you with the sheet situation."

"Skookum?" I said. "You know, it means good, great, awesome."

He shook his head. "I've never heard it before, and I'm doing a doctorate in English."

I shrugged and climbed into my sleeping bag. "It's from the word skookumchuck. It's one of the words from Chinook wawa, the old trading language used between the First Nations and the settlers. I'll look up the etymology, but everyone uses it where

I'm from."

"Fascinating." The shine in his eyes made me wish that word was for me, rather than etymology.

I nodded towards the computer. "How's it going?"

"Fine." He spun back around and pressed a few more keys. "I'll be out of your way soon."

"No rush," I said. "And thank you again for doing this." I picked up my book.

"You're most welcome," he said, and turned around again to look at me. "What are you reading?"

"Tristan et Iseult again, how Marie de France treats it in the Lai du Chèvrefeuille. I'm thinking of bringing it into my thesis too."

Alfie opened his mouth to say something, but no words came out.

"You'd better get back to it," I said, nodding at the laptop. "What do you British say? Chop chop."

CHAPTER TWENTY-TWO

Alfie

The set-up was hellish, and of course I had grossly underestimated the time I would need.

The college clock-tower chimed two o'clock before I finished. Even then 'finished' was a relative concept. Things seemed to be more or less up and running, but I suspected that I'd missed steps, and that Cedar might have some issues.

I would be there to figure out how to fix them for her, of course, but as I rubbed my eyes, I knew I would only mess things up further if I tried to do anything more without some sleep.

Cedar had read for about half an hour and then murmured to me she was going to sleep. She flicked off her college-issued bedside table lamp and within a few minutes had begun to breathe more deeply.

I tried not to turn around and stare at her like some sort of deviant, but how could I concentrate on anything else while she was in the room?

I'd come so close to leaning forward and kissing her before, on the bed. Wildness had possessed me and obliterated all my noblest intentions towards her. I'd been sporting a raging hard-on. Leaping up and turning my back to her so suddenly was a necessity.

But she'd been leaning in towards me as well, hadn't she? She must think me a madman.

What was I going to do with my attraction to her? My willpower was hanging on by a thread, and when she emerged from the bathroom in her T-shirt and pajamas, I couldn't look away. I was fairly certain she was wearing what she wore to bed every night, but she was the most gorgeous woman I'd ever seen.

Her thick, dark hair flowed over her shoulders, wavy and wild. Her eyes flashed, probably with well-warranted anger at me, and she'd quite obviously taken her bra off in the bathroom and ... well ... there was no way I couldn't look at that spectacular sight.

I lost control around her. Fear locked in my chest. She slept with her door unlocked. She was guided by her own moral compass, not rules. She was content sleeping in a sleeping bag, for heaven's sake. She was everything that was dangerous and unpredictable. How could I keep my heart safe with someone like her?

I got up to leave with the sheaf of papers in my hand. The computer screen emitted a ghostly blue light, and I didn't know how to turn it off. Hopefully it would just go into hibernation eventually.

She'd dropped her book on the floor beside her bed, so I went over and picked it up, trying not to linger on the long lashes resting on her cheek, and her hand curled up under her chin, and the little breath of air she exhaled.

When I stood up again and rested her book on her bedside table, her hand flew out of the sleeping bag and grabbed my wrist. I jumped, my heart pounding in my chest. Her instincts were fast, even half asleep.

"It's just me, Alfie," I whispered. "Your book fell on the floor, so I was putting it back on your night table before leaving. Go back to sleep, Cedar."

She cracked an eye open. "Sit down for a second," she said, letting go of my wrist.

"I shouldn't," I said, even though all I wanted to do was strip off my clothes and jump into that sleeping bag to feel her against me. "I should let you sleep."

"Just for a moment," Cedar murmured. "I have something to ask you."

It was impossible to resist that sleepy request. "Yes?" I asked and sat down as gingerly as I could on the edge of her mattress, angled for the best view of her face.

"Why didn't you kiss me earlier?"

I would have believed the blood in my veins flash-froze in that instant, if my heart wasn't galloping so wildly in my chest. "Surely—" I attempted to sound surprised.

She placed her warm hand that had been tucked under her chin on my forearm. Goosebumps rippled all the way to my shoulder. Her eyes seemed huge in the dim light. "Was I imagining the whole thing?"

How could I answer this and still retain the last shreds of my self-control?

"Please don't lie to me," she said. "I'm confused and I hate that feeling. You can say no, that it was all in my head, but be straight with me. Please. I need to know what happened there, and the other times. I need to make sense of it. Of us."

She blinked, her face open and vulnerable in a way that disintegrated the last few bricks of that wall between us I'd been so feverishly trying to build.

"I was trying to be a gentleman," I murmured, remembering the Warden's words.

"A gentleman wouldn't have left me like that," she whispered back. "Wondering ..."

She was right. I couldn't find the words to make amends, so I did what my instincts had been screaming at me to do for the past three weeks. I leaned down, cupped the delicate line of her jaw and cheekbone in my hand—her skin did feel like silk—and brushed my lips over hers.

A small gasp escaped her, severing my last thread of willpower. Her mouth drove me mad. I couldn't get enough of the fullness of her lips, or the small, sensual movements of her tongue darting in my mouth. She tasted like mint toothpaste and fresh air and freedom.

"Oh," she murmured after several minutes of exploring the miracle of kissing each other—changing up angles, licking, lightly sucking. I was inside that supercharged field of magic between Cedar and me, and I wanted to live within it forever.

My stiffness was becoming painful, impossible to ignore. She pulled me against her, so I stretched down, horizontal to where she lay.

Our bodies melded together with only our clothes and the nylon and down of her sleeping bag between us. I gasped at the press of her breasts and clutched the curve of her hip under the slippery fabric like an anchor.

We kept going like that for a while, both frantic, until she murmured a soft curse word and unzipped her bag in one swift movement.

"You can unzip it from the inside?" I let out a little puff of wonder, helping her out of it.

"Oh yes." She grinned in the blue computer light.

"Thank God," I groaned, and kicked the sleeping bag to the floor.

She hooked her leg over my hip, and I ground into her, driven by instinct.

She kissed me long and hard, taking and giving in equal measure. I had never experienced anything this glorious before. All other women I'd been with—and there hadn't been that many—were tepid shadows compared to this live flame in my arms.

"I wasn't wrong?" she gasped.

I shook my head, and relieved laughter bubbled up in my throat. "You were imagining nothing. I've been longing to do this with you for some time now. I wasn't hiding it that well, was I?"

She took my hips in her palms and drew me even tighter against her. I let out a strangled sound that didn't sound human. She flicked her tongue against my neck, and I let out a ferocious roar of desire. No, I hadn't been fooling anyone, except, perhaps, myself.

"Not so much." She kissed me again, then pulled away. I was desperate to close the space between us immediately, but she resisted when I tried to pull her against me again. She was *strong*. "I need to know why you fought us—this—so much. Was it about the college finding out?"

My need for her was so blinding that I could scarcely marshal a coherent sentence. Fear whooshed in again when I realized just how completely she had already crashed through all the safety measures I'd constructed around my heart.

I wanted to slip inside her, feel her everywhere, show her just how extraordinary and perfect she was to me, but just kissing her was cracking my soul wide open. I adored her, I adored this, but her question reminded me nothing had changed about our circumstances. This way led to ruin for me—the loss of the life I'd planned for myself—and possibly for her as well if Professor Harris got wind of what was going on between us.

"You're so far away all of a sudden." She put a few more inches of space between us.

I would not lie to her—not again. "The truth is I don't know if I can handle you, Cedar." I waved a hand over both of us. "I don't know if I can handle this."

She sat up, scooting herself over to the far side of the mattress. "Now you're telling me you're not sure? Are you kidding me?"

"I'm ...". I pushed my hand through my hair. How could I explain that while I was sure I wanted to be with her, the consequences could be disastrous—for both of us? We needed to talk more about all that before we did what I was aching to do.

"You've lost interest." She nodded. "I get it. Usually guys wait until after sex for that, but I suppose I shouldn't be surprised."

"What?" I stared up at her, and her eyes were so full of anguish that I had to look away again. "How could you think that?"

"I know it when I see it," she said, her voice a sharp-edged blade now. "Get out of my room. Now."

"Cedar," I said. "We just need to talk. That's all."

She shook her head, her face as cold as the blue light from the computer screen. "There's nothing to talk about. I'm not someone who lives in half-measures, Alfie. I can't be with someone who isn't sure. Thanks for the computer help. Now get out."

"But—"

"Leave," she just said, cutting me off as abruptly as she'd let me in.

I slunk out the door, shattered, yet still wishing I could convince her to lock it behind me.

FIFTH WEEK

CHAPTER TWENTY-THREE

Cedar

That was every bit as hellish as I'd expected. I stood up from the couch at the end of my first tutorial with Alfie since that night. I rushed out of Professor Harris's study even though Alfie was calling after me.

If Alfie wanted a life as hushed and weighed down as the spotless carpet covering the old, beaten-up wooden floors of his idol's study, then he could damn well have it without me.

Since I kicked him out, he'd tried to call and text me with the new phone he'd set up for me until I blocked his number. We were wild for each other one moment, then my question had stopped everything. Well, not so much my question as his answer. It was clear he was still undecided about me, and I was done with feeling like I didn't know where I stood with him.

I flew down the stairs and out into the quad, where I gulped at the fresh air like a freshly caught rock cod. Being shut in an airless room with Alfie for an hour and a half, catching whiffs of his cologne, and being acutely aware of how he was trying to catch my eye with his gaze had been a nightmare.

I'd been rejected enough by my parents. I just couldn't do it again, not with him. *He didn't know if he could handle me.* He'd used up his last chance, and I shouldn't have really given him any chances at all.

I stalked to the Lodge to check my pidge. Normally the bustle and the scent of Earl Grey tea that Robbie was constantly brewing or drinking was a dose of comfort, but Robbie eyed me with a frown as he dealt with a don who was trying to place an international call to a university in China.

I appreciated his concern, but I didn't need Robbie's inquisition while I was in such a foul temper.

I pulled out the wad of slips and papers. On the top was one for a black-tie dinner in college for all students and their guests on the last day of Michaelmas term.

Black-tie dinner? I'd have to ask Binita and Shaun about that. My walks with Raphael had quickly evolved into Raphael running, and me doing the same so we could chat, but he wasn't the person to ask. I suspected Raphael would be just as clueless about black-tie dinners as me.

I tucked the notices in my bag and turned to head towards the Bodleian for a bit of time in one of the manuscript rooms there.

"Cedar." That voice. I wish I could shake it out of my head. Alfie was following me towards the door out to the street. "Please. Just spare me a moment. We need to talk." His familiar face was unusually pale, and he had dark circles under those extraordinary eyes of his.

My heart thumped oddly. *Don't you dare feel sorry for him.*

"We don't," I said. "Go away."

He darted in front of me, blocking my route out to the street. He pinched the bridge of that crooked nose of his. "That tutorial was the worst thing I've ever lived through. Just please give me an opportunity to—"

"You're either interested or you're not, and if you think I'm such a destructive force in your life, you're clearly not," I said, unyielding. "There's no middle ground."

His face went rigid, and a throb of remorse beat in my chest until I realized Alfie wasn't staring at me, but at something over my left shoulder. I spun around, where a man in a light-brown suit and a fedora so low on his head you couldn't see his eyes was waving at him.

A woman fluttering on the man's arm was wearing a sort of silk headscarf around her hair and tied under her chin. The largest pair of sunglasses I'd ever seen, heavily encrusted with jewels, hid her eyes. They looked recently salvaged from a costume party gone wrong, or maybe some sort of play?

"Imagine my luck!" the man in the fedora cried out. "Salutations, prodigal son! It's me, your dear old dad."

Alfie's eyes narrowed, sparking with anger in a way I'd never seen them do before. "What are you doing here?" he demanded. Even at our worst moments, I'd never heard him speak in such a glacial voice. His eyes shifted to the woman, who was giggling behind her hand.

"I walked right behind you," the man said, unintimidated. "But you two seemed too preoccupied with your little tiff to even notice." He leered at us, then waggled his eyebrows.

So this was Alfie's notorious father? An unwelcome surge of sympathy for Alfie tugged at my heart, despite the fact I was done with him.

"You!" Alfie turned to the woman.

"You're supposed to call me your Royal Highness," she simpered, drawing stares from the students flowing in and out of the college doors.

"I'm assuming from that headscarf you're trying to be incognito, am I incorrect?" Alfie said with asperity.

"Clever boy," his father guffawed. "Although there's no reason for you to be so starched up. Aren't you glad we're paying you a visit?"

"No," Alfie answered, his voice like flint. "I certainly am not. The paparazzi have just started leaving me alone again, after a concerted effort to be extremely boring so they'd lose interest. I imagine you coming here will bring them to my door yet again. Honestly Father, you have no—"

But his father buffeted Alfie's back with a few hearty slaps. "I can never comprehend why you let a few paps bother you. So they get a few photos? So what?"

"Unlike you, I cherish my privacy."

"Privacy? Poo."

"Why do I even bother?" Alfie grimaced. "You must understand that it reflects negatively on my reputation in college."

"Malcolm," the lady—who I had to assume was the princess, although I didn't find her anywhere near as impressive as I expected royalty to be, given all the hullabaloo they generated in Britain—said, "It is inconceivable to me how you managed to sire such a tedious son."

Alfie turned a fierce gaze to her. "I never asked you to come here or invited you to comment on me or my life."

"I'm a Royal Highness. I'm honoring you with my notice," she said with a lift of her chin.

Ugh. She was awful. For the first time in my life, it dawned on me that attention could be a negative thing. Even though Alfie had mentioned his dislike of unwanted attention, that concept had never sunk in until this very moment.

"Highly debatable," Alfie said. "I'll remind you that you are the farthest thing from my mother, who happens to be in the Caribbean taking refuge from the repeated scandals my father here brews up."

"Now, now, Son," Malcolm said. His mouth pulled into a frown. "I'm certain your mother has a string of young, bare-chested lovers on St. Barts by now—pearl divers or basket weavers or some such thing. Never fear for her. Aren't you going to introduce us to this lovely young lady here? Is she one of your conquests? Do tell me she is."

"Don't you ever talk about a woman like that in front of me," Alfie leaned forward, menacing.

I was suddenly aware that Alfie was at least four inches taller than his father, and far broader in the shoulders, not to mention full of those coiled rugby muscles underneath his master's robes that I'd felt against me. "This is one of my students, and you owe her an apology for speaking of her like she wasn't standing right here." There was no fear in Alfie now, just fierceness. It was mesmerizing. My mouth went dry.

"I'm so terribly sorry," Malcolm said, and stuck out his hand to me. "My stickler of a son is quite right. My manners definitely left something to be desired."

I didn't want to shake it, so didn't. *Manners be damned.*

I began to wonder if maybe in my black or white mind I hadn't judged Alfie's wariness about new things, and new people like me, a bit too quickly. I couldn't even imagine what it was like to grow up with *this* for a father.

Malcolm finally dropped his hand. "Wait! Aren't you the girl that hauled my son off the cobblestones that night which was in all the papers?"

Before I could answer, he lifted the brim of his fedora so I could finally see his eyes. They were the same brilliant green blue as Alfie's, but they held none of the intelligence or kindness that Alfie's did.

Robbie burst out of the Lodge then, a murderous scowl on his face.

"Are these people bothering you, Lord Invernay?" he demanded. He nodded to me, a question in his eyes.

Was I all right? I gave him a brief nod. I should leave them all alone with this. It had nothing to do with me anymore, but for some inexplicable reason I shared Robbie's protectiveness towards Alfie.

"This is none of your business," Malcolm snapped at him.

"You," Robbie hissed. His black eyes gleamed like obsidian and his fists clenched. "Haven't you plagued your son enough?"

"Who are you?" Alfie's father looked down his nose at Robbie with complete dismissal and disdain, the same way the fishing guide I'd slept with looked at an undersized fish on the line.

"I'm the Porter," Robbie said.

"How dare you speak to me like that? I'm a Duke!"

Robbie's nostrils flared. "All I see is a father who doesn't care if he makes his son's life a downright misery."

"I could have you hanged for that!" said the princess.

Alfie turned to her, his eyes vicious. "Don't be ridiculous."

Robbie didn't back down. "Thanks to the two of you," he said to Malcolm and the princess. "The paparazzi have been giving Lord Invernay a terrible time, which he's done nothing to deserve."

"Ah, Alfie," Malcolm looked at Alfie with mock pride. "I'm so pleased you have inspired such loyalty in the servants. It's heart-warming, you know."

A muscle in Alfie's jaw twitched. I could see in his eyes and the tension of his arm and fist that he was a hair's breadth away from hauling off and punching his father. If he did, I would cheer him on.

A crowd of students and other dons had stopped and were staring, peering at the princess in particular, whispering to each other.

"Let's take this outside the college." Alfie's voice was forged in steel.

"Willingly," Malcolm said.

Robbie and I exchanged a look and followed them. I couldn't completely understand myself, but I wanted Alfie to know that even if we were finished as a potential couple, he wasn't alone. I suspected Robbie wanted him to feel supported as well.

We stepped out the door onto New College Lane which was, thank God, deserted.

Alfie turned on his father. "I insist you apologize to Robbie." His eyes flashed.

"Who on God's green earth is Robbie?" His father smiled a supercilious smile, but his eyes—unnervingly like Alfie's yet, at the same time, nothing like them—darted around.

Alfie gestured towards Robbie. "This is Robbie, a longtime Porter at the Beaufort College Lodge and a good friend of mine. Apologize to him."

"Why? You're friends with a porter? How very irregular." He reached up and scratched his brow. "You're becoming rather eccentric in your old age, my boy."

"You should never speak of anyone the way you just did about Robbie and Cedar. Apologize."

Malcolm lifted his eyes to the heaven, as if supplicating them for patience, and then said, "I'm very sorry, because my son apparently thinks I have something to be sorry for. Is that good enough?"

"No," said Alfie. "Not nearly. But I'm already bored with you, so could you please tell me why you are here?"

"To see you, of course!" Malcolm exclaimed. "Of all the ridiculous questions. You're my only son, and I've missed you."

Alfie snorted. "Is that so?"

"Of course. We've been up in Scotland, you know—"

"Oh, I know," Alfie said. "The entire United Kingdom knows thanks to your complete lack of discretion."

"It wasn't our fault!" the princess cried out. "They have the longest lenses now."

"Can I remind you that you're both married?" Alfie crossed his arms across his chest. "To other people? I swear, life would be so much easier for everyone around you two if you just followed the rules of civilized society for once."

"Poo." The princess tossed her scarved head. "You were brought up in the same world we live in. Since when has a marriage contract stopped anyone from having affairs?"

Alfie glowered. Had the princess inadvertently scored a point?

He took a deep, steadying breath. "I've accepted by now you have no scruples," he said to his father. "But you." He turned his iron gaze back to the princess. "Your husband is in line for the throne. Doesn't it bother your conscience at all to cuckold him? What about the dignity of the Royal Family?"

Her eyes flashed in a way that had me quickly revising my previous assumption that she had nothing to her besides flightiness.

"What about it?" she hissed. "My husband is having an affair too—make that 'affairs' plural. Also, he's having them with *men*. Apparently, everyone knew he was gay except me. I would wish him all the best if it wasn't for the fact that he and his family knowingly tricked and sacrificed me. I'll be damned if I'll listen to a further word about damaging the institution."

I hadn't been expecting that, and from the shocked look on Alfie's face, he hadn't either. Even Robbie looked shell-shocked. No wonder she was flaunting herself with Alfie's father.

"I ... I didn't know that, and I'm very sorry," Alfie said, with a note of sympathy in his voice that hadn't been there before. "If that's true, that's a terrible thing they did to you. I'm also sorry we have a Royal Family in Britain who is so unacceptably antiquated that it hasn't dawned on them that hardly anybody would take issue with a homosexual prince."

"The King is a miserable old bigot and homophobe." The princess blinked. Was she going to cry? "If I wasn't so angry at my husband for using me as a front, I would pity him. That's the truth."

Alfie nodded, regrouping. "I'm truly sorry for that, and what you have suffered at their hands," he said. "I had no idea, but if that's the case, wouldn't it just be better for both of you to get divorced?"

She rolled her eyes. "They would never let me do that."

"Surely they can't stop you," Alfie said. "They can't lock you up in the Tower of London anymore."

"No, but they can take all my money and jewels away. I'm in a prison, you see? Your father has the magic ability to make me feel as though I'm free."

Malcolm was looking at her with indulgence.

Alfie grimaced. "Seeing as I can't change your minds about your relationship, could you at least attempt to be more discreet?"

"Why should we?" Malcolm demanded.

"Always thinking of others, aren't you?" Alfie arched a brow. "You must understand, I want a life of my own, not one that is constantly hijacked by your scandals. When the Press gets a tantalizing glimpse of the two of you but then can't follow up because you disappear again behind the royal fortress, they come after *me*."

I waited for his father's reaction to this, unsure what it would be.

"I'm sorry, Son," said Malcolm, and rested his hand on Alfie's shoulder. "That was inconsiderate of me."

Alfie's mouth dropped open and his eyes glazed over with shock. "You're ... apologizing?" he asked.

From the little I'd learned about his father, it was strangely out-of-character. Still, something about Malcolm's *mea culpa* made my throat thicken. I couldn't ever imagine my parents apologizing to me. As far as they were concerned, they had raised me—or rather let me raise myself—right. I wasn't sure they were entirely wrong. It was just now that I was away from them, I was starting to wonder about certain things.

"Don't sound so astonished!" Malcolm laughed. "I'm not an ogre. Most people adore me."

Alfie blinked. "You're not going to tell me I'm a crashing bore?"

His father smiled—a charming, sympathetic smile that made me realize all at once how he could be considered a charismatic person. "I'm realizing that I haven't been trying hard enough to understand you. We're very different."

Alfie's face became almost childlike with eagerness—I got caught a glimpse of the lonely, eager boy he must have been. How long had he been waiting to hear these words from his father?

It was then that something hidden deep in my instincts sounded an alarm.

What triggered it? Was it the slightly slower way Malcolm was talking now, or how the princess kept glancing between her diamond encrusted wristwatch and the bend in New College Lane, shifting her weight from foot to foot?

Was there something not quite *sincere* about Malcolm's apology? My adrenaline started flowing in the same way it did when I realized I was being stalked by a bear or cougar. I pulled on Robbie's sleeve. "Something's wrong," I whispered.

He too was looking moved by Malcolm's change of heart, much to my surprise. I would have thought him as suspicious as me.

"What is it?" he mouthed back at me, his brows lowering.

That's when I saw them, the vertical line of telephoto lenses sneaking around the stone wall in the bend in New College Lane. I grabbed Alfie's arm and pointed at them. "Photographers!"

He went as still as a deer in the forest. Malcolm and the princess shared a knowing, satisfied smile that filled me with molten rage. They had set Alfie up. To think I'd felt a stab of sympathy for the princess. Malcolm's apology had been to stall Alfie long enough for the paparazzi to get a photo of Malcolm, the princess, and the prodigal son together.

"Shit," I whispered to myself.

"What have you done?" Alfie asked Malcolm, his voice breaking on that last word.

What a complete betrayal. My arms ached to wrap around Alfie, to let him know not everyone was as terrible, but then, I hadn't listened to him either, had I?

The photographers let up a collective cry and stampeded.

"Cedar," Alfie shouted at me. "You and Robbie, get back inside."

"You too!" I yelled over the noise of the paps, knowing how much he would hate having these photos in the papers, although it was probably already too late.

"Go!" He pushed me towards Robbie, who swept me back inside the college again, closing the huge medieval wooden door behind us with a resonating bang.

"We can't just leave him out there!" I protested.

"It's what he asked me to do, and it's what he wants," Robbie said, his palms still pressed against the shut door.

"We have to get him."

Robbie shook his head. "He can't have you—or I, for that matter—photographed rescuing him again. It would be disastrous."

"But—"

"Cedar," Robbie said, looking me in the eye. "If you want to help Alfie, you need to go back up to your rooms or into the Lodge or go and study at the college library. Make yourself scarce and just pray that the paps didn't get a good photo of you before escaping inside."

"I don't care if they get a hundred photos of me." I was worried about Alfie, not about me possibly appearing in the tabloids again.

"I'm aware of that," Robbie said. "But Alfie does. He's trying to protect you, so don't make it hard for him. Please. He knows—he's known for a long time that the paps would find you far too interesting, which would make things one hundred times more difficult for both of you."

"But—"

"You have to trust me on this, lass."

"Fine," I said. "Before I leave though—when Alfie's dad was doing that big apology to him were you buying it?"

Robbie stared down at his polished brogues. "I'm afraid I did ... for a few seconds anyway."

"I'm surprised."

He grimaced. "I suppose I was swayed because I wanted it to be true for Alfie—I want things to get better for him, but his father makes everything so very—"

"Complicated," I said, thinking about his attempts to talk with me over the past few days. Alfie would surely adore not having to think through the consequences of every one of his actions, but he didn't have that luxury, I realized now. I had kicked him out of my room, my bed, so quickly, without even giving him a chance to explain himself. The weight of that landed in my stomach.

"How did you see the photographers so quickly?" Robbie asked.

I shrugged. "Something just wasn't right. The back of my neck prickled."

Robbie tilted his head. "Alfie is lucky to have you and your instincts."

I didn't deserve such a compliment. I'd been as all or nothing with Alfie as my parents had been with me and well … the wider world. Black or white. That was the only way I'd ever learned to view things. I'd seen now that Alfie's life was mostly, through no doing of his own, a lot of indeterminate gray.

"I'm the last person Alfie needs." I understood now, after meeting his father, why he needed a woman who was reserved and polite and unchallenging—the complete opposite of me. He might not even mind being bored.

"Don't delude yourself, Cedar," Robbie said. "Now, be off with you. Make yourself scarce for a few hours."

With my head full of contradictions, I did.

CHAPTER TWENTY-FOUR

Alfie

I should stop for a moment and admire my surroundings. They were remarkable, after all. With the cloisters' arched oak-rafted roof, flagstone floor, and vertical windows carved out of golden Cotswold stone, this was one of the places in Oxford where I felt transported to the way things were in medieval times.

Two days after the fiasco with my father, I was still reassuring myself that I'd done what damage control I could. Exhaustion made me feel like I had concrete blocks attached to my feet. I hadn't been sleeping very well, or very much at all.

I sat down on one of the stone benches carved into the outer wall. I leaned my head back and tried to catch my breath, something I'd felt incapable of doing since my father's ambush ... actually, that wasn't accurate. It had started when Cedar had kicked me out of her bed. Since then, I'd been running away from something I couldn't name.

It was Saturday morning, and I had a whole day to get through before I could go to bed with Norris wrapped around my head, not to sleep, but to toss and turn and wonder how my heart had become so snarled.

I'd been so shamefully stupid with both Cedar and my father. How had I not seen my father's sincerity and apology as the manipulation it was? And Cedar ... I must have sounded so lamentably wishy-washy to her, expressing doubts while I was entwined with her on her bed ... or her mattress, anyway. I closed my eyes and gently banged the back of my skull against the stone arch behind me. Robbie was right. I *was* a daft pillock.

Why had Cedar stayed when I was arguing with my father? It tortured me she'd witnessed my gullibility and my father's perfidy and the wreckage of my life, no matter how hard I tried to set things on a saner course. She no doubt was thanking her lucky stars that she was rid of me but, even then, I couldn't make heads or tails of her support that day.

I'd only seen her from afar since then—across the quad or at another table with her friends in Hall.

The paps had indeed gotten photos of her, but luckily I was blocking the line of sight between her and the zoom lenses, so they were all blurry and partial. At least her privacy was still more or less intact. That, at least, was a tiny solace.

Footsteps echoed on the flagstones, but maybe if I didn't look up, I wouldn't have to speak to whoever it was. I was hardly in the mood for conversation.

A relieved sigh accompanied slower steps. "Alfie. It's you," Cedar said. "We haven't had a chance to talk in private since the other day."

Trust Cedar to come out and address the awkward thing head on. I was starting to adore her for that, but which catastrophe was she referring to? I honestly didn't know anymore. I looked up, and despite everything, her face gave me a fleeting sense of peace.

"Cedar," I said. "How are you?" I couldn't stop myself from drinking her in—that broad, natural smile of hers, the smudge of blue pen high on her right cheekbone. Good God, I'd missed her.

She sat down beside me, holding a pile of books in her lap. The feel of her warmth so close was exquisite torture.

"You look like death warmed over," she said, appraising me.

This got a laugh out of me. "Flattering, yet probably true. You know how it is." My words were as disjointed as the thoughts whirring in my head.

She shifted the books in her arms. "Actually, I don't know, and I've been wanting to ask you."

I honestly didn't know if I could bear to go down this road again—not with her. I'd already made such a mess of things. I nodded down at the books in her lap, trying to distract her. "What have you got there?" I read the spines. "Ah. Essays on Chaucer, and Guillaume de Dole, and Chretien de Troyes—the usual suspects I see—"

Cedar put her hand on my arm, stopping my flow of inconsequential nothings. My shoulders dropped and I had the strangest sensation of my body unknotting. Everything became so hushed that I could hear the few remaining leaves rustle on the ancient oak tree in the middle of the small quad at the center of the cloisters.

"Please don't do that," she said.

"What?"

"Talk to me like we've barely met before. What happened with your father?"

"You truly want to know?"

She nodded. "I realized maybe I shouldn't have been so hasty the other night when we ... when I booted you out, and I've been worried about you since the thing with your father. Can we talk?"

I hated to be confronted with my own stupidity as much as any man, but if it meant that Cedar could become a part of my life again—even a small one—the indignity was surely worth it. "We can talk, although it's all a mess in my head. By the way, how is your computer working?"

Lord help me. There I went again, avoiding uncomfortable topics like a true Brit.

She looked at me, that quirk at the corner of her lips that I had kissed. "It wasn't," she admitted. "The printer wasn't either, but Raphael came and fixed it all."

I dropped my head in my hands. "I'm such a git."

She reached over and gave my back a lovely rub that didn't last nearly long enough. That electricity in every cell of her body—I craved it. "You tried," she said. "That's what matters. Anyway, about your father. Has he ever tried a stunt like that before?"

I shook my head. "Many other outrageous things, but no, never that precise maneuver." Thinking back to how stunned and pleased I'd been when he apologized, I felt like I wanted to crawl out of my skin. "The second I saw the paparazzi, I realized he must have tipped them off."

She tilted her head, revealing even more of that gorgeous neck. "You're sure it was him?"

I ground my teeth together. "Yes, or more likely both he and the princess."

"I've made a lot of guesses on my own, but what I want to hear from you is why you thought he would set you up like that?"

Why indeed? I had a fairly good notion, but I still couldn't digest the twisted morality of it all. "My father's need for attention is as deep as the Mariana Trench," I tried to explain. "He wouldn't hesitate for a second to use me to attract it. As for the princess, I imagine she has a burning desire for the prince—the entire Royal Family, in fact—to get their comeuppance. My father and I are just weapons in her battle."

"I can sort of understand her motivations," Cedar said. "But your father is willing. You're not. Why bring you into it? Wouldn't it have been easy for them to attract attention all on their own?"

"Yes but having photos of the three of us together makes it seem as though their relationship is much more serious than it actually is. My father never stays with any of his conquests for long. Besides, I didn't detect any real love there, just a common interest and ruthlessness about using any means available."

She shook her head. "But you—"

"I'm just collateral damage."

She clicked her tongue after a while. "You know, my parents always told me that humankind is disappointing. They think I failed them by breaking away from their beliefs and coming here to find out answers for myself. More than anything, I want to prove them wrong about people, but when I came across your dad …". She bit that bottom lip of hers that I had gripped between my teeth. "I'm forced to admit there might be some justification for living like hermits. I hate that."

"I'm sorry," I said, feeling like it wasn't enough.

"It's not just your dad," she continued, her eyes darker than usual. "It's everything. I love Binita, but why would she wear clothes so tight and uncomfortable? They're torture devices. And Shaun, why does he think everything I say is so hilarious and freakish? Why was Robbie so grumpy with me when we first met? You with all your contradictions. I just don't understand people, Alfie, and I'm starting to doubt that I ever will."

My hands itched to touch her, and I squeezed them tightly in my lap. It was excruciating to know I had let her down the worst of all, inadvertently proving her parents' theories. "I hate that we're so inconsistent," I said. "Especially me."

She sighed and leaned back against the wall beside me. "I'm starting to think maybe it's me that has to change, or my expectations anyway. By the way, what did you do about the paparazzi when Robbie and I went inside?"

"You didn't read the papers?" I asked, astonished. It never occurred to me she wouldn't go and find out for herself.

"Unlike everyone else in Britain, it seems, I'm not in the habit of reading newspapers. Unless I trained ravens to deliver the mail back home, I don't know how I would have accessed them even if I wanted to."

"Ah. Right. Not even on the internet?"

"Our internet was a precious resource. It was strictly used for my parents' research and my academics. Anyway, almost no news ever affected us."

I nodded. How different her life had been from mine. It was extraordinary that we'd been able to connect at all. "Right, of course. That makes complete sense."

"So, what did you do?"

I shrugged. "I knew from past experience that the only thing to do was to act in the least scandalous way possible, so I herded my father and the princess to The Old Parsonage for high tea. I acted as jovial and relaxed as possible, as if it was merely a planned visit with my dear father and a long-standing family friend. I even offered to pose for photos for the photographers and took some questions, describing the outing as exactly that, and referred to the princess as my "dear Aunt Tabitha".

Cedar exploded in mirth, and my heart soared.

"I told them she is a cherished old friend of my mother's and that I'd been brought up calling her aunt."

She clapped her hands together, her eyes dancing. "So *devious*."

Pleasure radiated through every cell in my body at the evidence that I had impressed her.

"I'll bet they were mad," she added with a gleeful grin.

"Furious." I chuckled as the memories of their thwarted expressions came back to me. "They thought they could manipulate me into a photo op I didn't want, but I turned the tables. My father was vibrating with frustration by the end of the afternoon, and the princess kept pinching him under the tea table."

She made a sound—a mischievous, low hum of amusement that made me want to press my mouth to hers, to feel that vibrancy against me.

"Skookum," she murmured, watching me with a glow in her eyes. "See, there's a perfect example of how to use it. Your revenge was skookum."

God, she was irresistible. "How did you see the photographers before the rest of us?" I had to keep talking, or I was going to ravish her right in the middle of these cloisters. Even though she had perhaps moderated her opinion of me, I doubted it was as much as I hoped.

"Wild woman intuition." She winked at me.

"Oh *really*?"

She nodded. "I don't know if I can explain it exactly, but in the forest, I had to be very aware of my surroundings all the time. Those of us who do that day in and day out develop an instinct for sensing an ambush just before it happens. There was something in your father's voice, and the princess's shiftiness that put me on the alert, even before I saw the lenses come around the corner."

She was the most astounding person I'd ever met. My whole body burned with the desire to show her exactly how she made me feel. "That's a handy skill."

She nodded. "It's saved my life more times than I can count, and definitely helped me to save Willy on three or four occasions while he was staying with us."

The belltower rang out just then, twelve bells for noon. Time for Hall.

"So." I had no idea how to conclude this gift of a conversation, but I knew I certainly didn't want to. "There you have it—all the skeletons in the Invernay closet. I think we've established now that I had a very odd upbringing, and my parents were all but absent, but I suppose in the end part of me was thankful for that. Thank God they sent me to boarding school when I was thirteen."

"They did?"

"Of course. Eton. Family tradition and all that. I imagine your upbringing was the complete opposite. How could it not be, living with your parents, all alone in a small cabin?"

"I built my own cabin when I was old enough," she reminded me.

"How old?"

"Thirteen, same age as you when you went to Eton. I researched and did the whole thing myself. I made a *ton* of mistakes."

I could picture this, but surely ... her parents lived right there. "Your parents helped?"

She squeezed her eyes shut for a moment. "No. They made a point of not helping, like with everything else. According to them, it was the only way I could build my own skills and self-reliance, but as I got older, I wondered if it was more because they just couldn't be bothered. They live and breathe bear DNA research, both of them. They observe them, take notes about them, theorize with each other over the bears' behavior day and night. It doesn't leave a lot of time for much else." A shadow passed over Cedar's face.

I'd never considered the matter before, but maybe neglect could happen even in the context of physical presence.

Her gaze slowly raised to meet mine. I hated to see that some of that usual warmth in her eyes had dimmed. "It was pretty clear they found me boring."

My mouth dropped open at this. "But that's impossible. I can think of many, many words to describe you and boring is not one of them." How I longed to reach out and show her. "Cedar, you're the most fascinating person I've ever met."

"You mean aggravating," she said, with a quirk of her lips that didn't reach her eyes. "Like when I wouldn't listen to you when you were trying to tell me something and booted you out of my room. About that—"

"No," I said. She was wearing her hair in one thick French braid, and maybe I could just touch that? I tugged the end of it to underline my point, a silky, thick rope. "I mean fascinating." I wanted more, so I reached over and squeezed her hand. "I reacted the way I did because I didn't know what to do with someone so extraordinary."

She frowned. "And I reacted just like my parents would have. I've seen now how complicated your life is Alfie. I get it, or I'm starting to."

"My timing was lamentable." I weaved my fingers between hers. How right her palm felt pressed up against mine. "Same goes for my habit of speaking my thoughts out loud when my guard is down."

The shadow on her face stayed, stubborn, although I could tell from the stillness of her shoulders she had been listening. It didn't matter that I could hardly be called religious—the golden Cotswold stone and timeless echo of the cloisters made every word we exchanged feel sacred.

"You could *never* be boring, Cedar." The mere idea was ludicrous.

"That's really, really nice of you to say," she said. "But with my parents, I couldn't help but think ... well, I still can't help but think that maybe if I was a different person, more like them, they would have been more interested in me."

She didn't shed a single tear, but I felt every iota of the grief and confusion that radiated off her in waves. I thought of how my reservations must have sounded to her—indistinguishable from yet another rejection.

Then, even the cloisters seemed to melt away, as did the noise of some people roughhousing nearby. I wasn't aware of anything but the need to show Cedar just how compelling and sublime she was. Words weren't enough—they could never be enough.

I pulled her into the circle of my arms. "Don't think that." I reached up behind her hair and ran my fingers down the nape of her neck. She shuddered and I was instantly rigid. "You *can't* think that. I won't allow it."

Just then Shaun came screeching around the corner of the cloisters, with Binita hot on his heels. Clairvoyant, and fast-moving as always, Cedar scrambled back to her spot beside me just in time.

"Time to nosh!" Shaun declared. "Oh hullo there," he said to me. "Care to join us?"

I remembered then, an invitation to sit with a visiting English prof from the Sorbonne. "I would love to," I said with feeling. "But I've already said I'd dine at High Table."

"Oh well!" Shaun shrugged. "Your loss, being with a bunch of poncy tossers instead of us."

I exchanged a searching look with Cedar. It was my loss indeed.

SIXTH WEEK

CHAPTER TWENTY-FIVE

Alfie

When I arrived at The Turf, I was thrilled to see that Lachlan had snagged the Holy Grail—our very own bench beside one of their outdoor bonfires. Probably being a prop on the University rugby team hadn't hurt in that endeavor.

I gave him a hug and a back slap and sat down on the bench beside him. "You've already bought two bags of chestnuts?" I rubbed my hands together. I loved roasted chestnuts. "Brilliant."

"I'm not just the brawn." Lachlan put the chestnuts on the grill over the flames. "Although that did help." They smelled toasty and warm.

It was a frosty day, so chestnuts and a roaring outdoor firepit were the perfect accompaniments to the pints of bitter he'd ordered us. We'd both spent our formative years in Scotland, so we weren't about to shrink from the weather being "a wee bit oorlich" as Lachlan put it in his broad highland accent.

"What's the news?" Lachlan asked once we'd both taken several sips of our beers.

I poured my heart out to my friend about my being kicked out of Cedar's room, and my father's trap, and my conversation with Cedar in the cloisters the day before.

Lachlan listened without interrupting until at a certain point he held up his huge hand like a stop sign. "Yes, yes, but how *was* the snogging with Cedar?" he demanded.

It felt like an inadequate word for what had happened between us. Even now, I could conjure up her heady scent of pine trees, and the feel of that vexatious, captivating chin between my fingers. She tasted even better than she smelled—like wild honey and fresh air. My wanting her had been so fierce. I knew now that if I ever was lucky enough to get a second chance with Cedar, my wilder, baser instincts would win. I still didn't know if I could live with that, but at the same time I seemed unable to live without her.

"Yer not answerin'."

I poked the chestnuts with one of the metal skewers that lay beside the fire. "It was so incredible that I know if I start again, I won't be able to stop."

"Like that, is it?" Lachlan considered me over the fire. "You never talked like this about, who was that lass you were seeing on and off last year? I forgot her name again."

I rolled my eyes at his pointed amnesia concerning my ex-girlfriend's name. "Imogen?"

"That's it. You can hardly blame me for not remembering. She *was* forgettable."

Lachlan wasn't wrong. She'd been the sort of aristocratic debutante who felt it was somehow below her station in life to enjoy sex—or maybe, I reflected, I had just been really shit at it. Still, until I'd opened my wretched mouth, Cedar seemed as enthusiastic as I was.

Imogen and I had drifted apart, and I wasn't sure my memory

could conjure up her face even if I wanted to. "Imogen had excellent manners," I said, feeling guilty at bad-mouthing her.

"She was a crashing bore, you mean." Lachlan rolled his eyes.

I cracked open a chestnut of my own and popped it in my mouth, enjoying the piping hot, mealy texture. "Maybe," I said. "But people probably say the same of me."

"Only because you want them to think that," Lachlan said. "Especially the paps, which I suppose is understandable. I know that's not who you really are though."

Lachlan knew me better than almost anyone, yet he had never understood why my father's chaos had driven me to seek the exact opposite. I knew he found the taciturn image I went to great lengths to project out into the world annoying, but he put up with it.

"Maybe not," I said. "But it's who I need to be."

"This Cedar lass had thrown you into a tizzy. I know I've only chatted with her twice—and only briefly both times, but she seems different somehow. Real."

I groaned. "She's everything I want but can't have."

Just at that moment, I heard Shaun's voice. "Good Lord, it's the Lord!"

I turned to see Shaun approaching—the only person at Oxford with the sheer audacity to address his Junior Advisor as simply "Lord".

With a backward flourish of his hand, Shaun said. "Your students have come to humble themselves before you. Actually, that's a lie. This is just a coincidence. We were gagging for a pint."

Beside him was Raphael, who was already looking like a different person now that Cedar had shoehorned him out of the library and got him outside. Binita was sporting a new, vibrant shade of blue in her hair. But all of them were forgotten, as completely as

Imogen, when I saw Cedar. My eyes couldn't take in anything but the sight of her.

She was wearing her usual outfit of brown boots, worn jeans, and a fleece top, but I'd never seen anything more ravishing. Her eyes were slightly guarded, but her lips twitched up in a smile that—was it just in my imagination?—seemed meant for me. To think I'd kissed those perfect freckles over the bridge of her nose. I wanted more than this fragile truce of friendship with her. When she was in front of me like this, I wanted everything.

"Please." Lachlan beckoned them to the benches that surrounded our fire. "Join us for a pint."

Shaun frowned down at the wooden surface. His lip curled in disgust. "It's icy."

Cedar patted his back. "A little cold never hurt anyone."

"It's true," Raphael said, completely sincere. "Cedar and I ran a new trail the other day and we were caught in ice rain, but we didn't turn back. It was the most exhilarating thing I'd ever experienced in my life."

Shaun slanted him a look. "My poor, naïve boy," he said. "We'll have to work on that."

Raphael grinned back at Shaun. He'd pulled his long hair back in a bun, and it completely changed his face, or was it the way he carried himself now?

A possibility struck me. Was Shaun gay, and was he possibly interested in Raphael, who was revealing himself to be someone completely different from the first impressions he'd given us? Since when had my tutorial become such a magnet for romance? It was supposed to be about medieval literature. Then again, medieval literature was all about matters of the heart too. In many ways, people hadn't changed all that much since the thirteenth century.

Cedar sat down beside me on the bench and my heart skipped

a beat. Binita ended up beside Lachlan, and I saw something unexpected.

"Is Binita blushing?" I whispered to Cedar.

Cedar narrowed her eyes at her friend's face. "Holy cow. I think she is. She's so confident, I didn't even know her face could *do* that."

"That's some braw hair you have there," Lachlan said to Binita.

Binita turned an even deeper shade of crimson. "Are you mocking me?"

"I'll translate," I said. "That's a compliment in Scotland. It means fantastic."

"Oh." She blinked. "Yes, I just changed it to the blue. I had my doubts, but I've decided I'm going to love it."

Lachlan smiled down at her—he was well over a head taller—like some sort of friendly giant. "It's brilliant," he said, and the smile on Binita's face told its own story.

"Introductions I suppose?" I asked. Everyone nodded.

I did the rounds and ended with Cedar, who Lachlan had so briefly met before. With her warm body so close to mine, I had to resist the urge to reach out and intertwine our fingers, then softly rub the palm of her hand with my thumb—a secret message communicating what I really wanted to do with her instead of this friendly chit chat.

"It's nice to see you again, Cedar." Lachlan smiled at her.

She gave him one of her heart-stopping smiles. "It is. We didn't get much time to talk last time."

Shaun made shushing motions with his hands. "Enough of this meaningless prattle. Lachlan, you must know that Lord Invernay here is as inscrutable as they come. We need you to give us some dirt on him."

"Pardon me?" I demanded. "What about privacy?"

Cedar made a *phhst* sound between her teeth. "Overrated."

Lachlan's eyes lit up with delight. One of the things he'd complained about in regards to Imogen was that she never challenged me or put me in my place. "I'll do my best."

I cast him a look of mock betrayal.

"So what were you two up to?" Shaun asked.

"Just sharing a wee pint and a whinge." Lachlan shrugged.

Cedar vibrated with giggles, her hand over her mouth.

I turned to her and the gleam in her eyes ensnared me. "What?" I asked, laughter in my voice too. It was contagious, even though I didn't know what she'd found funny.

"I love that word 'whinge'. We never use that in Canada. Shaun also said another hilarious word earlier. What was it again Shaun? It started with an 's'."

"Stroppy," Shaun supplied.

"That's it! Fantastic."

"Snogging is another good word that starts with an 's'," Lachlan said, full of mischief.

I shot him a warning glance.

"What does it mean?" Cedar asked.

"Kissing!" everyone answered as though we were a chorus.

I could lean over and kiss her right now. How I wanted to ... but I would never do anything with this lot as an audience. "So where are you all off to after your pint?" I had to divert the conversation.

She shot me a speculative look. I had the oddest feeling she saw straight into my thoughts. "My friends have graciously offered to help me with a bit of a problem," Cedar said.

"What problem?" Why hadn't she come to me? I was being daft—of course she hadn't. I was not turning out to be much of a guide.

"It's tragic." Shaun shook his head in sorrow. "The poor girl has nothing to wear to her first ever black-tie dinner. Cedar is basically Cinderella, and you're looking at her fairy godmothers."

I'd received an invitation for that as well in my pidge, although I tended not to go to such things. This time, however ...

Cedar nodded. "They corralled me into it."

"Wait," Lachlan said. "Can I be a fairy godmother too and tag along?" He smiled at Binita as he asked this.

"The more, the merrier!" Binita declared. "How about you?" she asked me. "Do you fancy being a fairy godmother or does it go against your rules?" She said this with an arch look that made me wonder if Cedar had discussed me with Binita.

"Not at all," I said smoothly. "I just need to don my wings."

CHAPTER TWENTY-SIX

Alfie

It was Binita, not Shaun, despite his push to take control of the shopping expedition, who led us to a frock shop on the High Street.

The windows were full of an intimidating selection of encrusted jewel-toned cocktail dresses and full ballgowns with sweeping trains—things that looked suitable for a party at Buckingham Palace.

Actually, I'd been to a few of those in my formative years—my father had always enjoyed hob-knobbing with the royals. Despite the cornea-burning jewels and finery, the royal parties were known to be tedious affairs. As my father succinctly put it, "everyone is always on their best behavior, which means nobody is any fun at all."

Cedar held back, frozen in front of the window, as the rest of her friends and Lachlan barreled through the heavy brass and plate glass doors.

I waited for her. Everything about this chance of redeeming myself in her eyes had to go well. Her usual high color had drained from her cheeks.

A fantasy of me freeing Cedar from one of those monstrous frocks—much in the manner of a heroic superhero rescuing a heroine from a burning building—lodged itself in my brain. My body quickly called me to order. *No. You can't imagine her like that when in public.*

"I'm sure there are simpler styles," I reassured her. "Binita probably knows what she's doing."

"Remember the penguin skirt I borrowed from her at Matriculation?" Cedar reminded me.

How could I have forgotten that? Mainly, I remembered that rush of satisfaction when I tore the back seam so she could move her legs. Decidedly, I was developing an unhealthy fetish for freeing Cedar from clothes.

"Right," I said. "Don't forget you have final say, no matter how invested Binita and Shaun are. It's your body, and if you walk out without buying anything, that's fine too."

"I can't exactly show up to the black-tie dinner dressed like this." She waved down at her clothes.

She looked perfect to me, but she had a point. "That's true, but I'm sure we can find a happy medium. Have faith."

She took a gulp of air. "I'll try," she said. "Shaun and Binita are getting quite competitive over this. Don't leave me alone with them." She turned beseeching eyes to me. "Please?"

My chest filled with hope at Cedar asking me to help her, even in this minor capacity. "You can count on me."

She turned to me then, a sphinxlike expression in her eyes. "Can I?"

Before I could answer, Binita came to find us and yanked us inside the store—a hushed world of plush carpeting and sparkling chandeliers. The overpowering scent of lavender potpourri seemed to suck all the breathable air out of the space.

"It stinks as bad as the chapel," Cedar said to me, *sotto voce*.

Before I could agree, Shaun snatched Cedar away from Binita and led her to a dressing room where they had already compiled an alarmingly large number of dresses. The elegant saleswoman was trying to intervene, but it was patently clear that she had lost control of the proceedings.

Shaun pushed her into the changing room, but before she could pull the tasteful fawn-shaded velvet curtain across her cabin, Cedar grabbed my arm like a life buoy.

"Stay nearby," she pleaded, panic in her eyes. "Promise?"

Maybe this was the way back to her—small, quiet things I could do to build up her trust again.

"I'm not going anywhere." I gestured towards the Louis XIV style settee across from the changing room. "I'll just be over there."

She nodded and shut the curtain.

I sat down. This settee was rock hard. No wonder Louis XIV was in such a foul mood all the time.

No one paid much attention to me. Lachlan was following Binita around, making her laugh thanks to his comments which illustrated his complete lack of knowledge about women's frocks. Shaun commandeered Raphael into following him around to hold the dresses that Shaun plucked off the racks and flung at him.

Cedar emerged in the first dress, a lurid, pink tulle monstrosity. When she looked at her reflection in the three-way mirror set up at the end of the row of changing rooms, she almost collapsed with laughter. The saleswomen looked at her askance, but I joined in.

"Jesus Murphy." Cedar wiped tears from her eyes. "Which one

of you is to blame for this?"

"Whoever it was," I said. "They have much to atone for. That's an absolute travesty of a dress. Was it a joke?"

"It was me," Shaun said, placing his chin in his hand as he contemplated her with critical eyes. "But she can't carry it off."

"Oh please. A Pretty Pony on their period couldn't carry that monstrosity off," Binita said, a glow of triumph in her eyes. Cedar was right—this had turned into a cutthroat competition.

Lachlan exploded with laughter. "That's one howlin' color, I'll give you that."

"All right, all right. That's enough chaff, thank you very much." Shaun held out his palms to quiet us. "We learned something. No tulle, and *definitely* no pink. Take it off, Cedar!"

Cedar was still laughing as Binita came over armed with an elastic and bobby pins she'd whipped magically out of somewhere and pinned Cedar's hair up.

My amusement died as I took in the lovely curve of her neck. I hadn't kissed there. How had I missed that spot?

She disappeared into the changing room and proceeded to come out in a series of dresses, each slightly better than the previous one. It was a long process, but Shaun and Binita, via their rivalry, seemed to be getting somewhere.

Cedar emerged in a royal blue strapless floor length gown, beautiful in its simple design.

I paid little attention to the frock though, as nice as it was. I was wholly consumed with how it revealed her shoulders and her straight collarbones with the intriguing indents just above. That would be a perfect place to kiss as well. It filled me with longing and regret. I had missed that too. How? Same with the notch at the base of her throat, and the sweet line of her vertebrae that emerged from the low silk back of the dress, and her shoulder blades … good god, her shoulder blades … Heat rushed through every inch of my body when I considered how I could spend a day on those alone.

"Alfie!" Lachlan's voice came from the other side of the store. "Binita's just found the perfect wedding veil for my Scottish complexion. You have to come and see! It even has fake pearls."

But I was in no state to be standing up. Besides, I had promised Cedar not to stray far. "In a bit!" I shouted back.

A minute or two later, after Cedar had disappeared back into the changing room and just when I had somehow managed to get a handle on my imagination, she whispered through the curtain, urgently. "Alfie? Are you still there?"

"Of course I am." I launched myself off the settee to go to her. "I promised, remember?"

"Thank God, because I'm stuck."

"Stuck?"

"I couldn't reach around and get the zipper completely undone. I tried to pull the dress over my head but now my shoulders are jammed." She blew out a whoosh of air. "*What the hell*?" she muttered, and then, "You might as well come see for yourself. I don't see how else I'm going to get out of this without help."

I could barely control myself on the couch on the other side of the curtain. How was I going to exercise restraint when I was inside that small, private space with her in a state of undress? I wanted to ravish her and take off her dress inch by inch, kissing a path on her exposed skin …

"Alfie?"

I couldn't leave her stuck, either. Anyway, even though I was struggling with my need for her, the fact she'd invited me in for help was confirmation that she only considered me a friend. My chest hurt as that sunk in. *Gentleman*, I reminded myself.

I opened up the curtain as quietly as possible and slid in. I tried to take the sight in indifferently. Oh dear. That was impossible.

Cedar stood in the middle of the changing room, facing the mirror. One of her arms stuck straight over her head and the other one was bent at a ninety-degree angle. Her elbow was jammed in the narrow waist section of the dress. I tried not to look at her shapely legs that were now visible, but I didn't entirely succeed.

"You really *are* stuck," I murmured.

"Don't just stand there! Help me," she pleaded. "Turns out I'm a little claustrophobic about being stuck in ball gowns. Who knew?"

"Understandable." I was going to touch her soon. *Calm Alfie .... calm*. I managed to locate the tag of the flippy bit of the zipper under her left arm. Her skin felt warm and soft. Memories came rushing back so fast and powerful that I lurched towards her for a second before catching myself. I caught it and zipped it down all the way.

The dress fell from her. She tried to grab the bodice, but the silky fabric slipped out of her grasp and slid down around her waist. If I was a gentleman, I would look away from her reflection in the mirror, but ... well ... I wasn't much of a gentleman, as it turned out.

There was the curve of her waist and the absolute glory of her breasts and ... what were those?

Huge, shiny scars tracked across her torso, from under her right breast all the way around her side and across her back, finishing near her spine.

She snatched the material up to her front, but I took a step towards her and traced one of the thick scars on her back, anger and regret obliterating everything else.

She shivered and pulled away. "I know they're ugly." She

wouldn't meet my eyes in the mirror.

"No." My voice was low and rough, and my heart lurched at the evidence something had hurt her so badly. I couldn't even imagine what could have caused something that deep and painful. I couldn't stand that she'd been in pain, even before I'd met her.

"It's nothing." She shook her head.

"Cedar." I moved closer to her. "It's not nothing. I can see it for myself, and I can hear it in your voice."

"It was my fault."

"I can't see how that could be true."

"A bear swiped me," she muttered.

The way I sucked in my breath made her eyes jump to mine. *Had her parents made her think it was her fault?*

"You remember those Kermode bears I was telling you about on the islands off of Prince Rupert?"

I nodded, still not trusting myself enough to speak.

"I was about ten and I strayed too far from camp one day. I wanted to look for the little crabs I played with on the beach. A female bear was nearby, and either she believed I was a threat, or she was hungry. I was talking to myself, which was stupid because my parents had told me that children talk in a high pitch that attracts predators—"

"Cedar." I turned her around and backed her up until her back was pressed against the mirror. I splayed my hands on either side of her head. The need to cover her with my body—protect her retroactively—obliterated all caution. "No."

"I shouldn't have left camp on my own." Her voice was so quiet now. "But the beach was only a two-minute walk away, and there was so much to see down there. I was bored of all the bear talk between my parents and their fellow researchers. Anyway, it was a stupid mistake and I paid for it."

I shook my head, rejecting every word of her reasoning. "It was *not* your fault. You were a child."

"I should have known better."

"Oh Cedar," I said. "No."

And just like that, I forgot about all those places I wanted to kiss Cedar. I just needed to shield her from anything that could hurt her ever again.

I wrapped my arms around her and held her tight against me. At first her fists were against my chest as she held the bodice of the dress up between us, and then, suddenly, she released it and wrapped her arms around my torso and held on to me like an anchor. My breath hitched. Nothing had ever felt this good.

Her head fit perfectly against my chest, and I slid one hand up the back of her hair and pulled her even tighter against me. My breath fogged up the mirror behind her head. I was only vaguely aware of a pool of blue silk dropping to the changing room floor at our feet.

"Alfie?" she questioned, but I cut her off with a fierce kiss that was, in itself, an answer. It went on and on, stormy and wanting.

Shaun and Binita were calling my name. *Dammit.* I pressed a final kiss against her lips like a brand. Forget everything else—Cedar was mine to protect now.

She was still pressed against the mirror, her cheeks flushed and her lips red and slightly open. She nodded, her eyes glowing, that tether between us vibrating with unspoken words and unfulfilled desires.

"They're going to catch us," she whispered.

A sense of rightness like nothing I'd ever experienced hummed through me. I could handle this. I could handle loving her. She was worth everything.

"I'm just helping her get unstuck from a dress," I called out, impressed by how my voice sounded somewhat normal.

"I'll bet you are," Shaun retorted in a taunting voice.

"Cedar, are you all right?" Binita called, as if I was some sort of lecherous Don Juan. Come to think of it ...

"Now that Alfie has gotten this stupid zipper unstuck, I'm fine," she said.

I helped her pick up the dress off the floor and gathered it around her once again, dropping a final kiss, like a promise, on her shoulder. She cast me a wide-eyed look.

Binita yanked back the curtain, and Lachlan brought in a new armful of dresses, with a questioning arch of his brow directed at me. How could I explain what I was feeling to him? I knew now—I didn't just watch and notice and want Cedar. This wasn't just lust. I had fallen for her with every part of my being.

CHAPTER TWENTY-SEVEN

Cedar

After dinner, I went to the library.

I sat down in one of the creaky wooden chairs and pulled out two texts about Margery Kempe and the authentication process for the various writings attributed to her. If Alfie was going to see that new addendum, I needed to know more.

It was a fascinating topic with very few definitive answers, and a lot of murky gray areas, but my eyes kept wandering off the page to the murals painted above the bookshelves. I shifted in my chair. My body filled with the restlessness of crucial things left unfinished.

The way Alfie had tried to protect me with his body from something that happened to me twelve years ago and those *kisses*. The message had felt clear to me ... *to be continued*.

Yet he and Lachlan had left us when Binita decided I needed to get shoes as well, and he hadn't been at Hall for dinner. Where *was* he?

I shook my head and stared at the medieval rendering of the

moon up on the murals—yellow and benevolent. Ha! Not as benevolent as the people in the Middle Ages liked to think. Was I mooning over Alfie? Yes. I had to stop. I hunted moose. I analyzed medieval texts. I tracked cougars. I didn't *moon*.

The library was quiet as it tended to be when it wasn't close to exam time. I chewed the end of my pen. How many other students had been coming here over the centuries, tortured by longing?

I flicked on one of the little lights that lined the center of the tables and tried to turn my mind back to the murky world of medieval manuscript authentication.

I eventually began to lose track of time as the few remaining students studying packed up their things and left. That heaviness of sleep hadn't stolen over me yet—who was I kidding? With the memory of Alfie's impassioned kisses, it was shaping up to be a night of tossing and turning in bed. There was no rush. I'd stay until closing time.

A few minutes later, the wooden door to the library squeaked open and I could hear somebody walking down the center aisle towards my table. The footsteps drew closer until the very person who had been filling all my thoughts came around the corner. "Cedar!" he said, his eyes glowing. "Finally. I've found you."

A thrill raced through me as I remembered his body covered mine, his fingers tangled in my hair.

"Here I am," I said, smiling like an idiot.

He pulled out the chair beside me and sat down. "Thank God." He rubbed his thumb over my left cheekbone. "You have a smudge of ink." My eyes flew to his.

His hand dropped and his eyes scanned the room, stopping on Professor Wilcox hunched over a pile of texts—probably the only other person left in the library. Why hadn't Alfie been at dinner? He would have known he could find me there.

We stared at each other. A million words were on the tip of my tongue, but I couldn't decide on the right ones to start with.

"You weren't at dinner," I said, at last.

"No." A shadow slid over Alfie's face. "My mother popped by for one of her unannounced, impromptu visits. She comes to London a few times a year to buy new clothes."

"That's nice." My voice sounded weirdly high-pitched.

He sighed. "Debatable, but her visits are always extremely brief. Drinks and dinner at Le Manoir aux Quat'Saisons—her favorite restaurant in Oxfordshire." His eyes shifted over to the Professor Wilcox in the corner, and I hoped he was thinking the same as me—*please leave, you ancient relic.*

"I bought a ticket to the black-tie dinner," he said. He scanned my face intently. "I couldn't miss it now. I have to see the dress you picked."

Binita had barged into the dressing room as I was trying on a sage green dress that she had declared "the one". She wouldn't let anyone in to see it, promising me I would relish surprising everyone with a grand entrance.

I think she momentarily forgot that grand entrances were her thing, not mine, but I was so stunned from Alfie's ardor that I'd agreed.

"Binita is *very* excited," I said drily.

"I'm sure," he said, and that crease in his right cheek appeared. His eyes drank me in.

What was I waiting for? The uncertainty hollowed out my stomach, and I inhaled deep. "I'm not going to act British and pretend what happened in the changing room didn't happen."

The crease deepened. "Neither am I."

"What *was* that?"

He glanced over at Professor Wilcox again who had closed his eyes—either thinking, sleeping, or dead. He was *very* old.

"My feelings for you have won, Cedar." His voice was low and even, just for me. The words were so preternaturally calm that he could have been discussing Chaucer and not how he'd plastered me against the dressing room mirror.

Won? Won what? "You ravished me," I said, also careful to keep any emotion out of my voice. Professor Wilcox might pick up on that and start listening to the words—if he could still actually hear, that was.

"I did indeed. It was amazing, but a large problem remains."

My heart pounded in my ears. "What?" I demanded. Was Alfie going to withdraw from me yet again? My voice must have been louder, because the Professor's eyes flew open. Not deaf then. *Damn*. "I mean, what problem?" I said in a more moderated tone. The professor closed his eyes again.

Alfie's hand landed on my thigh, underneath the table, and he leaned so close that I could feel the warmth of his breath, and the smell of wine and—was that the scent of a wood fire?

"Were you near a bonfire?" I asked.

"Fireplace," he said. "They have them all over the restaurant. It's very luxurious. All I could think about when I was eating my Cornish sea-bass in an anis sauce was how I wanted to take you there."

"Oh," I said, silenced for a few moments by the thought of going on a date with Alfie—a true romantic date. I'd never been on one of those.

"We're getting off topic," Alfie said with mock sternness. "The problem this afternoon was I couldn't finish what I started." The hunger in his eyes made my breath hitch. "And I very much want to."

He waited then, for me to make the next move.

"What else would you have done?" I said, my vocal cords straining with anticipation. He leaned even farther forward, and his lips brushed my left earlobe. "I would have kissed you more—a lot more. Not just on your mouth either. I would have taken my time and worked my way down to the nape of your neck—I could spend hours there. Don't even get me started on what I would do with my mouth and your breasts. But don't think my hands would be idle while I'm doing all that."

I swallowed. "They wouldn't?"

"No, I would use them to anchor your hips first."

"And?" My voice was a mere thread.

"Then I would slide them down and run my fingers along your legs. I would pull one leg up, ever so gently, and wrap it around my hip so you could feel how much I want you."

Alfie was certainly avoiding nothing now, and his directness made a hot rush of lust run up my spine. I'd never done this with any other man before—drawn things out first—it was frustrating, but exquisitely so.

He opened a particularly large medieval bestiary text in front of us to shield us from Professor Wilcox's line of sight.

"What are you doing?" I asked, my heart pounding so powerfully I briefly wondered if my ribs could contain it.

"This." He leaned forward and gave me an achingly slow kiss behind the book.

My legs shook with desire. I gasped with it.

"Would you like to come to my room?" he broke away and asked, his chest rising and falling like he'd just run a marathon.

"Yes," I said, fervent. "I would."

He smiled one of his real Alfie smiles and was sliding one of my books in my bag when the college belltower rang twelve times for midnight. The Professor jerked awake and packed up and left with surprising alacrity. I never knew he could move that fast.

We were alone. The air crackled around us.

"Let's go," I said, but when I looked at Alfie again, his forehead wrinkled.

A surge of combined lust and frustration made my hands shake. "Are you having second thoughts *again*? I thought that—"

Alfie stood up then and, in one fluid movement, hoisted me so I was sitting on the edge of the oak library table. "I was just thinking that now we're alone, I don't know if I can wait to get to my room."

His urgency took my breath away for a few seconds. "But the library is closed now." I wasn't used to paying attention to things like that, but I knew Alfie did.

"I don't care."

I gasped. "You're breaking the *rules*, Lord Invernay? I'm shocked."

"There are some things worth breaking the rules for." He silenced me with a crushing kiss. His eyes were blue and wild, like the hottest part of a flame. "Besides, if we go to my room Norris will stare at us the whole time."

I chuckled but fell quiet again as he closed the gap between us so that he was standing between my legs. One hand rested on my lower back, supporting me, and the other scraped up the back of my neck, anchoring into my hair. Our breath mingled together.

I slid my arms around his neck and brushed my lips against his. "As much as I love dogs, I'm not really into canine voyeurism," I murmured.

He smiled against my mouth. "Unfortunately, if this goes well, you may have to get used to it."

"If what goes well?" I chuckled.

"This." His lips fell onto mine, commanding and hot. I flicked the tip of my tongue against his lower lip, and he *growled*—a sound that reverberated down my spine and pooled between my legs.

He was everywhere all at once, his evening stubble rubbing against my cheekbones, his lips on my closed eyelids, his hand snaking underneath my fleece, then whipping it off over my head.

"You're perfect," he said, fierce. "I never want you to forget that." He pressed reverent kisses on my freckles, somehow communicating to me just how captivating he found each and every one.

I pressed my fingertips against the back of his head, pulling him closer. His hair felt as silky as it looked. I yanked off his soft cashmere sweater and then the white T-shirt underneath. His muscles were sleek and well-developed, his skin rippled with goosebumps where my nails scraped it. "This chest," I murmured, flicking it with my tongue. "I can't believe you've been hiding this under all your academic robes." I was fast developing a whole new appreciation for rugby.

He groaned and claimed my mouth again, his fingers busily undoing the clasp of my bra. He was magnificent unrestrained like this.

My hands dropped down to the shape of him, hard and ready under the denim of his jeans. I whimpered and he sucked in a breath as he fished a condom out of his pocket. "Jesus Christ, Cedar. My knees are going to give way."

He turned his attention to my breasts. If it wasn't for his hands on my waist, anchoring me, exactly as he'd promised, I would've collapsed backwards on the stack of books teetering on the table behind me.

Our breathing was equally jagged now, in perfect sync. How was it that of all the men so far in my life, I ached for this aristocratic academic more than any mountain man? I couldn't explain it, but when he plunged into me—and finally it was not just him and me, but us together—it was more ferocious than anything I'd ever experienced.

I didn't know how or why life had made us crash together, but as I felt an incandescent current snap up my spine, I cried out his name. Not even a second later, he growled mine. We were both equally helpless against this thing we were together, and equally astounded by it too.

SEVENTH WEEK

CHAPTER TWENTY-EIGHT

Alfie

I woke up when the belltower rang six o'clock. Before I even remembered who I was, or what I'd done the night before, I was aware of a heavy-limbed joy that pervaded through every part of me.

I turned over on my side, and there she was—the source of that feeling.

Her fist was curled mulishly under her chin like it had been in her bedroom. Her mouth was relaxed, and her hair strewn all over the pillow ... my pillow. Norris snuffled around my head, as he usually did, but thankfully it wasn't interrupting her sleep at all.

It was still dark outside. These early December days boasted very few hours of actual daylight, but the yellow lights in the quad cast a warm amber glow through my thin curtain. Thank God it was at the weekend so Annabelle would not be barreling in the door at any moment and discovering this extraordinary creature in my bed.

Cedar's long lashes rested on her cheek, freckles danced over her nose, her almond eyes slanted at the corners. She'd cracked my soul open, and I didn't think it would ever be whole again without her.

Her eyelids flew open. I smiled down at her from where I'd propped my head up on my hand and reached over to smooth her hair. Norris crawled over and snuffled around her head.

I was so moved by her, naked under my duvet with me, that I was at a loss for words.

"Please don't tell me you regret what happened," she said.

I shook my head. Part of me wondered how she could possibly think that after what we'd done—three times, no less. "Never. You?"

She blinked. "You weren't saying anything, not even 'good morning'." She said those last two words in that terrible fake British accent I adored.

I smiled. "Looking at you ..." Those full lips that had done all manner of staggering things to my body, that brain of hers that never ceased to astound me—my heart stuttered even now as she studied me. "You're going to think I'm a tragic, maudlin case, but I was robbed of words."

Her eyes sparkled. "You're not feeling remorse about being in the library after hours?"

I shook my head, grinning now as I remembered.

"But we had *sex* in there!" She lowered her voice to a scandalized whisper for this, and I couldn't resist leaning down and giving her a kiss.

"Even the *sex*," I copied her whisper. "As a matter of fact, I remember particularly enjoying the *sex* part." For once, I had let myself be driven by instinct and the freedom had been glorious.

She laughed. "That's a relief, because I know how you love rules. I hate the idea of you regretting breaking the rules with me last night."

I gave her a wolfish smile. "You make me forget all the rules."

Norris hopped down off the bed and moved over to his favorite spot on the couch.

"Good." She reached over and traced the line of my jaw, her touch waking up that instinctive part of me I worked so hard to ignore most of the time.

I ducked my head under the duvet and reverently pressed my lips against the silvery scars wrapping around her torso. She needed to know I found them as breathtaking as the rest of her. When my head popped up again, she was blinking at me, her eyes full of surprise.

I stared at her in disbelief. How could I be poleaxed with need for her again so soon? I suspected there would be a before and an after in my life, and last night marked the delineation.

She reached over me and plucked up one of the unopened condom packages off my bedside table. The night before, in our haste, I'd spilled them while fumbling at the box that had been in my bedside table drawer I'd bought in an unwarranted fit of optimism when I started seeing Imogen.

I was achingly ready, but when I tried to take the condom away from her, she leaned forward and said, 'let me', then gently bit my earlobe.

"But ..." This was new. Putting on the condom was always a rather shameful, businesslike activity that I took care of with my back turned to my bedmate. "Are you sure?" I said, my voice strained by the unbridled need to plunge inside her again.

Instead of answering, she lifted the package to her mouth and ripped it gently with those white, slightly uneven teeth of hers. My entire body froze as I watched her, my erection throbbing.

"That is the sexiest thing I've ever seen," I breathed.

"Come closer," she breathed softly, and when I did, she wrapped her capable hand around my cock. It was almost too much when she stroked me up and down as she eased the condom on. Once she finished the job, she pushed me back against the pillows and straddled me, using that clever hand of hers to guide me into her.

Instead of my usual considerate restraint, I plunged into her to the root. "That's it," she murmured. "That's perfect."

"No holding back," I groaned, whether to herself or me I wasn't sure.

"I don't even know how," she gasped.

***

It was so astonishing that we had to lie there afterwards, not speaking or moving, just catching our breath.

When the black sky paled to dark gray, Cedar slipped out from under my arm and padded over to pick up her clothes. I'd torn them off the night before and had dropped them willy-nilly all over the floor.

I sat up now. "You're leaving? What's wrong?"

She pulled on her jeans and smiled at me over her shoulder. "Nothing," she said. "In fact, you did many, many things right, but don't get me started listing them, because then I might never leave."

I flushed with male pride at this, but still ... "Where are you going then?"

She slipped her fleece over her head and bunched her bra and underwear and shoved them in her jean pockets. *She was naked under her clothes.* "Don't worry. I'm sneaking out while it's still early so nobody sees me. If this is really as frowned upon as you say, better to be discreet."

I was just on the verge of assuring her she didn't need to worry about that, but then shut my mouth. The mirage of having both Cedar and my fellowship shimmered in the distance, enticing but still a delusion. Professor Harris had made it clear he disapproved of her, and the Warden had specifically asked me to remain a gentleman with Cedar. There was nothing *remotely* gentlemanly about what we'd done in the library or in my bed.

"I wasn't going to ask you to keep this ... us," I pointed at her and then back at me, "... a secret." That felt ingenuous, yet it was the truth. As short-sighted as it was, I hadn't thought of it at all since the dressing room at the frock shop.

She came over to the bed, took my head in her hands and leaned it against her stomach. Her fingers ran up my scalp. God, how could I be ready for her again? Yet I was. "You didn't ask me, but I care about you, and you care about your position here, so I guess we can keep this secret for a while."

I sighed against her. She was heaven. "I hate to—"

"It's fine." She dropped a kiss on my head and then turned towards the door. She gave me a complicitous wink. "I'll see you at breakfast."

I nodded, but I knew seeing her in Hall wouldn't be enough. I wanted to spend more time together—just the two of us. It was Sunday, after all. "Do you have any plans today?"

She shook her head.

"Take a day off studying," I urged.

She lifted her eyebrows. "Would my Junior Advisor approve?"

"Wholeheartedly."

"Well, if that's the case, I can't refuse."

"We'll leave after breakfast and get away from college. I want to take you somewhere."

"Aren't you a bad influence for a thesis advisor?" she tutted.

I grinned. "The worst."

"Look at you, breaking the rules." She gave me a final wink and shut the door behind her.

I flopped back in bed, already wishing that she was still with me. "Only for you, Cedar," I said to the ceiling, and then Norris whined to get back up on the bed and I lifted him up. "Oh, and you too Norris. Don't fret. I didn't forget about you."

CHAPTER TWENTY-NINE

Cedar

An hour and a half after breakfast, I was trouping through a muddy field with Alfie. Luckily, my boots were waterproof.

"I didn't realize it would be so boggy," he grimaced.

We'd been holding hands since we left Great Clarendon Street and started on the footpath beside the river. I'd never actually held hands with anyone before, and it felt strange and wonderful all at the same time. Alfie's hand was larger than mine, and nicely toasty. Our fingers somehow wove together naturally.

I was still reeling from the newness of it all. What had happened between Alfie and me last night was completely different from anything I'd experienced before with any other man. I still wasn't sure exactly what to do with that.

When I'd woken up to see him staring at me, biting his lip, fear gripped my throat. Was he having second thoughts? I understood then, in a way I never did before, the direct correlation between how much you let a person into your heart and how much they could hurt you if they let you down.

With the three other men I'd been with, my heart hadn't been involved in the slightest. But with Alfie, the connection between us filled that aching vacuum in my soul. This was uncharted terrain.

"Boggy?" I scoffed. "You should see the conditions I had to tramp through every day at the cabin. Besides, check out my boots." I stopped and lifted a foot to show him. "Indestructible."

He'd stopped too and took my other hand.

We stood face to face in the middle of the squelchy field. The low mist clinging to the grass gave everything an eerie, suspended air. Alfie glanced around. We were alone.

He hadn't needed to tell me he cared about keeping us a secret. I knew he did, so I offered before he even had to ask. I didn't like it, and if breakfast was any indication, I didn't think I would find treating him like a mere acquaintance at college easy, but I didn't want to make his life more difficult. I'd seen for myself how his father did a fine job of that all on his own.

Alfie's hands left mine and then his fingertips reached up behind my ears, holding my jawbone in the palms of his hands, cradling my face in a way that made me believe he could never let me down.

"I'm going to kiss you," he said, that crease in his cheek flashing. "Speak now or forever hold your peace."

"Peace?" I chuckled. "You have met me, haven't you?"

His lips met mine, perfect and firm—that tether between us tightening until it quivered with tension. My hands reached up under his wool pea coat, pulling him even closer. Wonder rushed through me at how we fit together, how as soon as I finished kissing him, I wanted to do it again.

His cashmere sweater was soft against me. That wonderful Alfie smell was trapped in the wool—ink and books and his cologne.

We might never have stopped making out in the center of that field if it wasn't for a sharp whistle piercing the still air.

We broke apart just in time to see a man dressed in a tweed jacket and matching knee-length pants. What a bizarre outfit. What were those, jodhpurs or something? There was no horse in sight, but he walked briskly with a wooden cane, preceded by four dogs who frolicked through the mud with their tongues hanging out of their mouths.

Alfie sighed. "What is that man doing here? How dare he?"

"I know. To think! The sheer gall of him, walking through a public field."

Alfie clicked his tongue. "Although ... perhaps he did us a favor. If he hadn't interrupted us, I might have had my way with you in the mud." Our eyes met, his sparkling with humor. "A tad brutish, perhaps."

"You say that like it's a bad thing."

He caressed the palm of my hand with his thumb—a secret message just for me. "You're rapidly showing me it's not. You're perfect."

We started walking again.

Many epithets had been applied to me—clever, excellent shot, tough, blunt—but perfect was not one of them. As much as it warmed me up by several degrees, it also made me uncomfortable, like Binita's pencil skirt. "I'm really not."

He dropped a kiss on my temple. "You're perfect to *me*. With you I can just ... be."

How things had changed. "You certainly didn't think that at our first tutorial."

He groaned. "I was an idiot."

"I forgive you—you're making up for it now."

His eyebrows drew together. "Are you sure the discretion thing doesn't bother you? I've been feeling terribly guilty about it." He squeezed my hand for emphasis.

"I offered," I pointed out.

"Yes, but I hate to impose that on you when you're so deliciously free. I envy that, you know."

I wasn't sure it was something to envy. It dawned on me that part of the reason I was so free, as he said, was that few people besides him and Willy had ever bothered much with me before.

I shook my head. "You have enough to bear with your father right now, and his not caring about what he projects out in the world."

Alfie's light eyes went a few shades darker. "That's not it exactly. My father cares *too* much what people think of him. It's just that he wants to be seen as scandalous and daring. In his mind, the worst possible thing he could be in other people's eyes is forgotten."

That made sense. "Like you try to be."

"Exactly. The more outrageous he gets, the more boring I become. It drives him mad."

"I can see how that could be satisfying." Still, Alfie was condemning himself to a very hemmed-in life in reaction to his father. It seemed uncharacteristically short-sighted of him.

"It's hard, putting up with weird parents when you don't have siblings to share the load," I said.

He let out a puff of exasperation. "Cheers to that."

Fine rain began to fall as we crossed the most picturesque stone bridge—the kind I would never have believed actually existed outside of fairy tales.

Alfie pointed out a stone pub built right on the riverbank. "There it is. The Trout—one of my favorite pubs and well worth the walk, I promise. I hope you're hungry."

***

"Are you all right to sit outside?" Alfie came back to where I stood by the river's edge, watching the water from the Thames rush angrily through what Alfie told me was a lock. I'd never seen one before and I was still trying to wrap my mind around the concept of trying to domesticate a river. "There are no tables left inside. I should have made a reservation, but what can I say? My brain has been a bit preoccupied by other things." He gave me a wolfish grin and I grinned back, his co-conspirator.

"No problem," I said. "I love watching rivers when they run high like this."

"Are you sure you won't be cold?"

I stared him down long enough for him to realize the absurdity of his question. It was a mild ten degrees. In our forest, it sometimes went down to minus forty.

He gave a little bark of laughter. "Right. Sorry! And here I was hoping to cuddle you and keep you warm."

"You can still do that," I said. "I'd love that, but are you sure it's—" My eyes darted around. We hadn't really gone into the details of our situation. "Safe?"

He took my hand and led me to a table right beside the river. The roaring of the water was so loud we had to lean our heads together to talk, which was perfect.

"It's fine," he said. "There's nobody who knows me inside. I did a quick reconnaissance mission on my way to the loo."

Something sunk inside me, despite the fact that I was the one who had offered discretion.

"Are you hungry?" he asked.

"Always," I said, and he pulled me close to his side, and began telling me all about the best things on the menu.

By the time the sticky toffee puddings were brought to the table, all full of warm, runny caramel and spiced cake, we had ditched prudence and were eating and kissing as the mood struck us. We whispered and laughed together and always had one hand touching each other under the table.

Everything was perfect—this gorgeous old stone pub on the river, the sumptuous Sunday roast meal with perfectly puffed things Alfie said were called Yorkshire puddings, this improbable yet amazing man beside me.

I took my second bite of the warm toffee pudding and my eyes rolled back in my head at the sheer amount of pleasure warming me from inside out. "Ohmygodthisissoamazing," I moaned, letting my head drop back.

When I collected myself and looked over at Alfie again, he was staring at me, his fork hovering chin-level and his pupils dilated. "If you do that again," he warned in a strained voice. "I'm going to take you right here on the pub table. Fair warning."

I dissolved into giggles. I felt much more intoxicated than the pint of beer I'd drunk warranted.

"My new goal is to make you say, 'ohmygodthisisamazing' when I'm inside you," he added, conversationally.

I swallowed my sticky toffee pudding, this image now pushing everything else aside in my brain.

He peeked up at me, his eyes full of mischief. How I adored him like this, playful and open. "Are you up for the challenge?"

I nodded, my brain unable to string any coherent thoughts together except Alfie and I together in his big bed.

"You have some toffee on your lips, Cedar," he said. "I think I need to attend to that."

He gathered me against him and kissed me thoroughly, his tongue gently tracing my lips. "You taste delicious," he murmured.

Pleasure melted away all my hard edges. "It's the toffee."

"No, it's not."

A waitress caught the corner of my eye, and we broke apart. "Are you done with those?" She nodded down at the puddings. I thrust my hands over mine, protectively. "No! I'm not done."

Her eyebrows rose, and her eyes darted between Alfie and me. A pleat of consternation appeared between her brows. "Fine," she said, and walked off to the next table.

I took another bite. I was going to finish every speck of this thing. "Why did she look at us like that?" I asked.

"Like what?"

"Confused."

"Did she? She probably just wants the table to seat another group. Sundays are always popular here. Anyway, I'm ready to whisk you away back to my rooms ... when you've finished your pudding, of course."

I applied myself to it in earnest, and we talked and laughed, and Alfie had his arm wrapped around my waist and we sat, glued together, taking up only a small edge of the round table.

He was encouraging me with plans of all the things we were going to do when we got back to his bed as I scraped the last bits of toffee and cake off my plate, our heads low and close together.

Somebody cleared their throat above us, and my first thought was that it was the waitress again, trying to hurry us along.

Alfie's arm dropped from my waist in an instant and he slid over, putting several inches between us. I looked up into the disapproving face of Professor Harris.

I glanced over at Alfie, and the person I'd just been with had vanished. He was now replaced with a cold, pale clone. My lungs felt like they were filling with concrete.

"What am I seeing here?" Professor Harris demanded.

His accusatory tone made my spine prickle with the need to tell him off, but the haunted look in Alfie's eyes held me back. Sure, this guy was a professor and Alfie's mentor, but what gave him the right to talk to us as though we were children and he, our parent?

Surely, Alfie would have to tell him now. Maybe it was best to just bite the bullet and go public with us and let the chips fall where they may. Relief filled me at the thought. I wasn't good at pretending.

Alfie blinked. "Ah. Good afternoon, Professor Harris. The Warden has tasked me, at Lord Cavendish-Percy's request, to guide Cedar around the college and Oxford. I thought a Sunday roast at The Trout would fit the bill."

My heart dropped. Alfie was going along with the charade that nothing had happened between us. I should have expected it, but still ...

"Why are you sitting so close?" How long had Professor Harris been watching us anyway? I didn't think Alfie's chances of convincing Professor Harris that he was just acting as my guide were very high. Besides, surely Alfie wouldn't answer such an inappropriate question.

"There was no other way for us to hear each other over the river," Alfie said. "It's calmed down over the last few minutes now they've narrowed the door of the lock."

Oh ... he would. The pudding congealed into a lump in my stomach.

"Is that so?" Professor Harris raised a brow, disdainful. He looked at me with not just dislike in his eyes, but loathing. Why did Alfie's mentor loathe me? I'd only met him three times and only long enough to exchange pleasantries.

Alfie chuckled as if to say that the mere idea of us being anything more than student and advisor was laughable. How could he be capable of such duplicity? "Of course, why would you think otherwise?" he asked, all emotion wiped from his voice. A chill encased my heart. The Alfie I knew had vanished. Again.

Unease spread its tentacles down my back. My parents could do that too. When I asked them for help, or just for a chat, they always said—completely without emotion—to leave them alone, that they were busy, that I should figure it out myself.

But once, when two interviewers came from National Geographic magazine, I had been walking in the cabin to stack freshly cut wood beside the woodstove. While talking to the journalists, my mother pulled me over to her side and introduced me to them in a honey-edged, affectionate tone I'd longed to hear my whole life.

She lifted me onto her lap and kissed the top of my head while I swung my legs, soaking up every minute of it. I remember thinking that everything had changed in that moment. My mom had finally realized she loved me. I was finally worthy of her attention. Maybe if she did, my father would too?

When the journalists left, I was bursting with joy and the need to talk to my parents about all the thoughts and feelings that had been trapped inside me for so long. Finally!

Mom sat back down after closing the door while my father accompanied them out to the trail. I started to crawl back onto her lap, eager for another cuddle.

She pushed me away, as unreachable as Alfie was now. "What are you doing?" she demanded.

My little heart quivered but hope still burned in me. "But ... before when the men were here ..." I pointed to the door.

She just frowned at me, and I had the familiar impression she was looking right through me again. "I'm busy right now, Cedar. They've put me behind with my work. How about you start dinner?"

I thought about arguing, but my heart was far too broken for that. It was worse to have hope and have it destroyed, than having no hope that people would change in the first place.

"I'd like to meet with you first thing tomorrow morning," Professor Harris said to Alfie. "Eight o'clock. My study."

"I'll be there." Alfie waved goodbye as Professor Harris shot us one final damning look and stalked off towards the bridge.

"Alfie?" I reached for him, needing reassurance.

"Not yet." Alfie pressed a stilling hand against my arm.

"He's gone," I said.

"We can't be too careful."

I pushed my dessert plate away from me. As much as I loved being with Alfie, I didn't know how long my heart could withstand the emotional whiplash.

CHAPTER THIRTY

Alfie

On the walk back to town, it was as though the light inside Cedar had been dialed down. I knew I was responsible. I held her hand as we crossed the Port Meadow again. Going along with my mood, the magical mist of the morning had burned off, and the sky had filled with low, forbidding clouds. Icy raindrops fell.

How could holding hands with Cedar feel different than before? Even though we were connected by touch, she felt a million miles away. Still, I didn't want to get into our disastrous meeting with Professor Harris until I smuggled her back to the privacy of my rooms.

I had to drop her hand when we got to Little Clarendon Street, and it felt like a betrayal.

It was stupid really. I thought we were safe at The Trout, and look where that had gotten me? I wanted to shout my love of Cedar to the rooftops, but I had to hide it and, worse still, make her hide it. I hated myself, but even more, I hated my father for backing me into this corner. If there was a way out, I would have taken it, but I didn't see one.

When we arrived back in college, we passed the Lodge with tacit agreement not to go in. If Robbie was working, there was no chance he wouldn't pick up on the strange energy between us.

We reached the foot of Cedar's staircase and Cedar stopped—so did my breath for a moment.

"I'm going to go up to my room," she said, and wrapped her arms around her torso.

I still wanted to shield her from any pain like I had in the dressing room. The certainty that what she needed protecting from right now was me made me want to vomit.

Dread weighed me down when I thought of my meeting with Professor Harris the next morning ... but I couldn't think of that now. I couldn't think of anything until Cedar and I had worked through this misunderstanding.

"Please," I pleaded. "I know that was horrible. Can you come up to my room and we can talk?"

"You were just so different." She shook her head. "It was like someone waved a hand in front of your face and you became someone else entirely ... you became the same person you were at the beginning of my first tutorial with you. I need some time to get my head around that."

My heart throbbed sickeningly. "Trust me," I begged. "The real person is the one who kept you awake all last night, loving you." I scanned the quad. A flock of black-caped dons were heading down the quad path in our direction.

"Just give me five minutes," I urged. "I need to check on Norris too."

I hadn't mentioned Norris with any ulterior motive, but that seemed to decide her. "OK," she conceded. "Five minutes."

I raced up the stairs to my rooms and she kept up. I fumbled with my key and opened the door. Norris wiggled with happiness at our return. He made far more of a fuss frolicking around Cedar's legs than mine, and when she picked him up, he gave soft yips of delight.

"Such a Lothario," I grinned at Cedar but the smile she gave me back was half-hearted.

I beckoned her towards the bed, but she shook her head. "I don't trust us to actually talk on the bed." She nodded towards my beat-up couch. "How about there?"

"Sure," I agreed easily, although my mind whirred. If I was this easily disconcerted when Cedar tried to put distance between us, I couldn't even imagine her shock when I treated her like a quasi-stranger in front of Professor Harris.

She sat down, still holding tight to Norris.

"First," I said. "Can I make you a cup of tea?"

She made a gagging sound. "No, thank you."

Right. She drank coffee. I made a mental note to run out and buy a coffee maker and the best quality coffee I could find.

"Five minutes," she reminded me. "I came up here to talk about what just happened, so let's get to it."

I sat down, as always shocked yet impressed by her directness. "First, let me apologize," I said. "I was completely caught off-guard when Professor Harris came up to us. My mind spun off as I wondered how much he'd seen and how long he'd been there for."

She nodded. Norris's eyes were half closed in bliss. How I envied him. "I wondered that too."

"There was no way of knowing, really, so I just fell back on what I knew ... I acted the way I know he expects from me. I was trying to allay his suspicions, protect our privacy. I know it must have been bewildering for me to change in a snap like that. I apologize."

She blinked and I flinched at the confusion I saw in her gold-flecked eyes. "It was scary to see how fast you can go from Alfie to Alfred, Lord Invernay, who treats me like an annoying gnat."

I dropped my head and cursed my father and the tabloids once again. If only I could just be myself. I'd never actually been given the room in my life to explore who I was, deep down. I was certain of one thing though—I was my real self when I was alone with Cedar.

"The person I am with you—that's the real me. You have to believe that."

"Do I?" she asked. "Because when Professor Harris was there you made a pretty convincing case otherwise."

"I thought you wanted to keep this a secret, at least for a little while. Did I misunderstand you?"

Her lips twisted and her eyebrows drew together. "I guess not. I did say something to that effect, but I'm fast discovering saying it and experiencing it are very different."

I sighed. "I'm sorry it's so complicated right now. I promise I'm going to figure things out, but I've always been someone who needs to think before acting. Nothing has changed about my feelings for you." I reached over and tucked back a stray lock of hair that had fallen in front of her left eye. "If you could see into my heart, you'd see yourself. I adore you Cedar—wildly and recklessly."

A smile grew on her face—the most luminous smile I'd ever seen. My bones melted with relief. I couldn't lose her.

***

Cedar slept in my bed that night, and I did everything in my power to make her see how, without my understanding it, she had become the beat of my soul. As a result, we only slept in snatches.

Now, as I walked across the quad to Professor Harris's office, I wondered if being with Cedar and staying at Beaufort was even possible. It was such a tightly tangled knot I couldn't even find the end.

I dug my hands deep in my jeans pockets and bowed my head as I made my way through the windy December morning. Cedar would be in Hall by now. How I longed to be sitting beside her rather than facing what was surely going to be a hellish conversation.

I'd been so intoxicated with her that I hadn't really taken a moment to consider how exactly I was going to fulfill my promise to Cedar and figure a way to keep the college happy and go public with our relationship.

I hated having to go and see Professor Harris without having landed on a solution. The frequent ambushes by the paps and my father made me dread feeling unprepared. The only choice left to me was to try and discern exactly what Professor Harris had seen, then decide if I could maintain the status quo ... at least until I figured out what else to do. If he'd seen us kissing, I didn't see how I could salvage anything.

Robbie was crossing the quad in the other direction, and he lifted his arm to hail me. I checked my watch. Ten to eight. My shoulders dropped at seeing his familiar face.

He gave me a friendly nod. "Good morning M'Lord." He doffed his bowler hat.

"No chaff from you this morning, Robbie."

"Where are you off to, with your gown billowing behind you like that?"

"Is it?" I turned and looked behind me. "Yes, well, that does happen when it gets windy, you know."

"How's Cedar?" he asked. From the dreamy smile when she woke up, I had good reason to believe she was very well indeed, but I couldn't tell Robbie that.

"She's settling in nicely," I said.

"Have you two made up?" Robbie asked. How on earth did Robbie know she hadn't been talking to me before my father's arrival? I really shouldn't ask myself such questions anymore, and just accept that he always knew ... oh no, did he know *everything*? No, I couldn't go on that assumption with Robbie either.

"Yes." I tried to keep my voice as neutral as possible, which was difficult as flashes of just how thoroughly and how many times we'd made up overtook my mind.

"What was that look?" Robbie narrowed his eyes and leaned in to inspect my face closer.

"There's no look."

"Oh yes there was. What's going on with you and Cedar?"

How was I supposed to play this? I couldn't tell anybody, even Robbie, until I figured out how I needed to handle the situation. I gasped, pretending I was affronted. "How could you think that of me? I'm her tutor, not to mention that the Warden asked me to be her guide and remain a gentleman with her."

Robbie frowned, not even attempting to hide his disappointment. "Pity," he said. "As much as you like to pretend otherwise, you're flesh and blood just like any human being. She's just the firecracker you need."

"Are you a *romantic,* Robbie?"

He pursed his lips and rocked back on his heels. "I suppose I am. You have to stop living like one of those Early Christian Martyrs you study, Alfie. It isn't healthy."

This was well-trod territory between us—Robbie thinking I was repressing myself too much, and me feeling like I didn't repress my baser instincts nearly enough. I certainly hadn't in the end when it came to Cedar. My stomach lurched with that familiar fear of being unable to avoid my father's excesses.

"I would love to bicker with you a little longer," I said, "But I'm due for a meeting with Professor Harris in five minutes."

Robbie made a sound of disgust so guttural that must have brought up some phlegm. "That lady's blouse? It's a shame you have a mentor who encourages your worst traits."

I merely shook my head. "Not now, Robbie. Have a good day," I said over my shoulder as I walked off.

"Ta," he grunted back and watched me go.

***

I knocked on the closed door of Professor Harris's office, an iron band of stress tightening around my torso. What had he seen? Was this already over for me, before this meeting had even begun?

"Come in," he said in his measured voice. Usually it calmed me, but now it just yanked that piece of metal even tighter.

I opened the door. The normally comforting smells of wood polish and old books didn't feel like valium, as they usually did. Instead, they reminded me I might be on the verge of being cast out of this peaceful sanctuary, walled away from my father and his antics. All my dreams of a safe, interesting life would be obliterated.

If Professor Harris and the rest of the college found out about me and Cedar, there would be a scandal. Scandals made me feel like the whole world as I knew it was slipping and sliding under my feet.

I was crazy about Cedar, but I had to admit there was nothing safe about her, or the way she lived. That wasn't going to change.

How precisely was I expecting this was going to work long term?

"Good morning," I said. "I trust you enjoyed your lunch at The Trout?" What other choice did I have besides brazening it out?

"I did," he said. "Thank you, although I must say my digestion was disturbed."

"I'm sorry to hear that."

"It was seeing you and Cedar together. My stomach was upset from worrying about you, Alfred."

"Oh?" I had to remain as vague as possible until I knew more.

"Yes. I've been disconcerted ever since I saw you and that girl cuddling up like a pair of lovebirds. Perhaps I didn't understand the context properly. I thought I would give you a chance to provide me an explanation."

My whole body went weak with relief. *Cuddling*. That meant he hadn't seen the rest of it.

Before I could formulate what I was going to say, Professor Harris smiled. "I just wanted to put you on your guard, of course. You two looked far closer than anything I should ever witness between a student and an advisor. Imagine if you had bumped into anyone else in college besides me! The gossip mill would be churning."

His mood was also far more magnanimous than I'd hoped for. "Thank you for your discretion, sir," I said. I did indeed feel grateful that he was giving me a chance to explain or ... truth be told ... to lie.

On the naked facts though, I couldn't argue with Professor Harris's concern. I had thought the same thing myself until Cedar had broken through my defenses. "Like I said, the Warden and Lord Cavendish-Percy asked me to be her guide, and the river was loud."

Professor Harris looked at me for a long time, with a slight upward curve to the edges of his mouth. At first it seemed to be a smile, but the longer he held it, the more it seemed a sort of rictus of the face. "There was nothing else between you two that I should know about?"

"No."

For a split second, Professor Harris's eyes narrowed into slits, making me think incongruously of a snake. No, that was just my guilt making my mind play tricks on me.

He shuffled some papers on his desk. "You know I'm here to help you at Oxford. I've invested a great deal of time and effort in you, and I think you have a very promising academic career here."

This gratified me of course, but it just made what I stood to lose seem even more devastating. "Thank you, sir."

"But you know," he continued. "Consorting with a student is very unwise. I want to protect you, Alfred, but I cannot if you go down such a disastrous path. Anything beyond an academic relationship with one of your students is damning enough, but surely you realize Cedar is ... well, a curiosity here at Oxford. She is not at all the sort of girl who could advance your career here, although she would be easily capable of dashing your hopes if she led you into any ... indiscretion."

That got my back up, despite his caring tone. "I admit I was prejudiced at the start too, but I was wrong. Cedar is a brilliant student. Oxford is lucky to have her."

His eyes did that strange thing again. Did he know I was lying?

But the expression vanished almost as fast as it appeared. Professor Harris chuckled. "I'm sure she is but let us agree to disagree. I still believe her and her like are not quite Oxford material."

I couldn't let him think such a thing about Cedar. "I think when you see her proposed thesis, you'll think differently."

He nodded. "Perhaps I will. That is all, Alfred. Don't let me down."

CHAPTER THIRTY-ONE

Cedar

My hands were warmed by the cup of spiced cider I'd bought for myself while I waited for Alfie to arrive and join me at the covered market.

He'd texted me while I was in the manuscript room in the Bodleian to say that he wanted to meet up and tell me about his meeting with Professor Harris. So, here I was, in front of the butcher shop Alfie had specified.

To distract my mind from imagining what Alfie was going to say, I concentrated on the strange surroundings. They'd festooned the market with red and green holiday decorations and trees. It seemed like Christmas had vomited indiscriminately over the multitude of food shops and boutiques.

We didn't celebrate Christmas in the cabin, or birthdays, or Easter, or anything like that. My parents didn't believe in traditions imposed by society. The only time the subject was addressed was during fireside rants about capitalism. No wonder this all looked garish to my eyes. Had nobody ever noticed that the colors red and green didn't go all that well together?

I sipped the mulled cider. Hmmm ... now this was something I could get behind. The warm cider spiced with cinnamon and cloves warmed my throat. I could feel my face heating up as I took a second sip. This wouldn't have gone amiss in the forest. I would like to drink this with Alfie, under a warm duvet, and then taste it on his lips, but what if Professor Harris—

No. No good would come from going there until I knew what happened.

My attention was caught by the dead pig that took up the whole window of the butcher shop. At first, I assumed it was yet another plastic decoration like the monstrous plastic reindeer I'd passed earlier, spray-painted in gold.

When I looked closer, though, I saw the poor pig was real. To add insult to injury it had a polished apple stuck in its mouth. I knew most people bought their meat rather than hunted it here in England, but still ... it disturbed me to see a dead animal hoisted up as a festive decoration.

At least the pig was taking my mind off things. I had been kicking myself for offering to keep my relationship with Alfie a secret ever since The Trout. Getting a taste of Alfie going cold and distant with me—even if he was pretending—was like a tub of glacier water poured over my head. It had *definitely* woken me up.

Someone tugged my ponytail from behind. I whipped around and met Alfie's eyes. Like whenever we were alone, they shone with love and desire and everything honest.

He smiled but dug his hands into his pockets.

Right. We couldn't hold hands here. Too public. My throat thickened. That small gesture told me everything about his meeting with Professor Harris before he'd even said a word.

He leaned over and whispered to me. "I want to, but this place is always packed with students and fellows. I usually see someone I know."

"Right." I had never realized how much I loathed the feeling of being hidden away like a shameful secret.

He tilted his head towards the pig in the butcher's window. "Making new friends?"

This managed to get a weak smile out of me. *He was trying.* "Yes, his name's Percival, and he's super pissed off about that apple they jammed in his mouth. He thinks it's undignified."

Alfie glanced at the pig appraisingly. "Poor Percival the Pig. I supposed it's a waxed apple too—looks far too shiny to be organic."

It was easier to joke about Percival than dive right into the obstacles in front of us. Jesus Murphy, was I turning into a Brit? "Will people actually eat him, or is he just ... festooning the shop?"

"Percival was brought into this world for a dual purpose I believe—to decorate and to be eaten. Poor sod. Not much of an existence, is it?"

"No." I shook my head. "I think the animals I hunt in the forest have it better. They get shot—and I'm an excellent aim. I don't torture them with a bullet through their gut or anything like that. Then, I butcher them in the bush. It's a lot more dignified."

Alfie's eyes sparkled with delight. "Sometimes I forget who I'm dealing with when it comes to you, and I love nothing better than when you remind me. Tell me, why no stomach shots?"

"Takes too long to die," I said. "Agonizing for the animal. Plus, it spoils the meat more often than not." I pointed at the space between my two eyebrows. "Right between the eyes, that's the most humane shot. Instant death."

"Remarkable," he breathed.

"It's not like there are any grocery stores nearby." I drank the last bit of my mulled cider and gathered every ounce of courage I could find within myself. Enough beating around the bush. "Now, tell me what happened with Professor Harris today."

Alfie smiled down at me, and all of a sudden the tacky Christmas decorations made sense, as did the Christmas music that was being piped in the tinny speakers overhead. This season could be quite lovely with someone like Alfie to cozy up with. "Of course, but first, I'd like to get one of those mulled ciders like you're having."

"Had." I threw my cup in a garbage can that was unbelievably decorated with green and red metallic baubles. They even decorated the garbage cans? "I think I might need another."

"Your wish is my command," he said.

With our fresh mugs of steaming cider firmly in hand, we strolled past the market stalls. It was the most incongruous place—there was a handbag store beside a fruit and vegetable stand, which was beside a store that served nothing but bottled tripe.

"Out with it," I said, finally.

He sighed. "Sorry. I'm just enjoying being with you so much so that I'm procrastinating bringing it up, but that's not going to help, is it?"

"Nope."

He pressed his lips together. "I don't know why I'm so hesitant. To be honest, I was expecting far worse. Professor Harris was far kinder about it than I expected. He didn't see us kissing either, so thank god for that."

That sunk inside me with an odd beat of my heart. Did I actually wish us to be found out? No, that could be disastrous for Alfie, and I cared for him too much to want that. "So what did he say?"

"He said he was just trying to protect me and warned me of the consequences if any relationship between us beyond friendship was discovered."

The lump in my throat was back. "Are those consequences just as bad as you thought they would be?"

Alfie nodded. "Every bit as disastrous as I suspected. He made it clear he was trying to protect me, but he was worried."

I knew how much Alfie liked and respected Professor Harris, but I still couldn't figure out why. The man struck me, from the way he preened and fawned at High Table as he looked down triumphantly at the lower tables, as someone who got off on having dominance over others. There was something wrong in his eyes too—something far too calculating, but of course I couldn't say any of this to Alfie.

"I've been running through my options," he said. "I've been considering moving colleges."

What? Knowing Alfie and his devotion to Beaufort, that was a huge deal. "Is that easy?"

"No. It usually only happens when you need to be matched up with a fellow who is specialized in your studies, and it requires several gushing letters of recommendation from the college you are leaving."

"Let me guess. Professor Harris is the most qualified professor for your little corner of medieval literature?"

He nodded.

We passed a cheese store that smelled like dirty socks. "So that's not going to be an option," I surmised.

Alfie grimaced. "Maybe I could apply to Cambridge, even though that move is tantamount to an act of treason here. I doubt I'd ever be able to come back to Oxford."

"If we're doing this to be together, I'll still be here," I reminded him. "Willy isn't sending anyone to Cambridge on this Commonwealth Scheme. He's a Beaufort College man, remember?"

"Bollocks," Alfie murmured. "I've been mulling this over since I left that meeting this morning, grasping for solutions …".

"And?"

"I haven't found one yet."

"So, in the meantime, secrecy?" Why did I bother asking? I already knew the answer.

He bit his lip and nodded. "I'm so sorry," he said after a while. "I hate this, and I know you do too."

I wasn't going to deny it. I hated feeling like a problem that needed solving, especially after a lifetime of my parents treating me that way. I honestly didn't know how long I could do it for.

I was trying to find the words to explain this to Alfie when he was tackled from behind by Lachlan.

"Alfie!" Lachlan buffeted him with a hearty blow on the shoulder. "Good to see you. You haven't been answering my texts. What are you on about?"

Before Alfie could answer, Lachlan turned to me. "Cedar!" he exclaimed. "I dinnae see you there. It's lovely to see you again. I just left the pub after a pint with Binita."

"Oh?" I exchanged glances with Alfie. This was interesting enough to hit pause on our conversation for a few minutes.

"Aye, she's a bonnie lass. Do you know what she talked me into doing?"

I shook my head. Honestly, Binita was so brilliant she could probably get people to do pretty much whatever she wanted them to do.

"She talked me into coming to the Beaufort black-tie dinner. Please tell me you'll be going?"

We both nodded and Lachlan grinned. "Excellent."

Was it though? Alfie and I would have to hide the fact we were together all night. There would be no handholding, no sly kisses, no referring to ourselves as a couple. It would be one long exercise in frustration to have Alfie act as though I was an afterthought in front of everyone else. My heart contracted.

I'd been so wrapped up in my own thoughts that I only noticed Lachlan's silence after Alfie nudged me gently. Lachlan's eyes were moving back and forth between Alfie and me with a knowing look in them.

"You shagged," he said. There was nothing resembling a question in his words. "Are you together?"

I should have felt alarmed, but instead I felt light with relief. But wait, was Alfie going to deny it, deny *us* to his best friend? His beautiful eyes widened momentarily, then his mouth curved in a wry smile. He nodded.

My heart soared. Somehow, sharing it with someone else—even if it was only Lachlan—made this thing between us feel one hundred times more real.

"You know me too well." Alfie grinned.

"Of course I do, ya wee bawbag." Lachlan leapt forward and grabbed each of us in his tree-trunk arms and pulled us against his chest, more a headlock than a hug. "I'm so happy. You've finally done something sensible, Alfie."

Alfie and I laughed with the same shakiness. This all was so new, but it also felt so right.

Lachlan finally let us go.

"Just for the record, I make sensible choices all the time," Alfie said.

"Not nearly as sensible as you think," Lachlan scoffed. "Take Imogen, for example."

Alfie flushed red. "Let's not."

Lachlan waved his hand. "Fine. Anyway, I don't feel like arguing with you. This is something to celebrate!" He looked down at our hands, his brows snapping together. "Why aren't you holding hands?" he demanded. "That's no way to treat a lass."

Alfie lunged forward and covered Lachlan's mouth with his hand. "Shhhhhh. We have to keep it a secret for the moment."

Lachlan frowned. "Why?"

Alfie rolled his eyes. "Think about it. I'm Cedar's advisor. Professor Harris would disapprove, as well as the Warden, who told me specifically to act gentlemanly towards Cedar."

"She *what*?" I demanded. Of all the misogynistic, patronizing things to say. How *dare* she? I wanted to storm in there and say how much I objected but of course, I couldn't. Not yet anyway.

"I know, it was wrong of her." Alfie turned to me. "But the fact of the matter is that Oxford can be a painfully antiquated place."

"No shit," I breathed, anger beating at me from the inside, demanding to be let out.

"But how long can you keep it a secret for?" Lachlan asked, as if reading my mind. "You'll be found out eventually."

"We know," Alfie said. "This is new, and we're just trying to figure that out now. It's a work-in-progress."

Lachlan's frown made it clear Alfie's explanation didn't satisfy him. "That doesn't seem fair to either of you."

"No," Alfie said. "But it's something we have to work through in our own time."

Lachlan just pursed his lips and raised his brows questioningly at me.

I shrugged. It felt impossible, but somehow now that Lachlan knew, a little bit less impossible than it had before. Maybe it would happen like that, in small increments. I would have to exercise something I was sometimes not sure I possessed—patience.

EIGHTH WEEK

CHAPTER THIRTY-TWO

Alfie

The next few days were bliss, except for the tortuous moments when I had to pretend I wasn't madly enamored with Cedar.

As an unspoken thank you for putting up with the secrecy we needed to maintain, I'd planned a Sunday surprise—a punting excursion. There was no more idyllic or iconic way to enjoy Oxford than from a punt, and I yearned to be the one to introduce her to the tradition.

Besides, I loved watching her reactions, not just to the new places I took her—I'd been right about her adoring the medieval collections of the Ashmolean—but when I kissed her under her jawbone or slid my hand between her legs. Everything.

She sat beside me in Lachlan's Mini, as I drove us down to the boathouse.

"It was nice of Lachlan to lend you his car," she said, watching my hand with curiosity as I shifted gears. "I never learned to drive."

"No roads?"

"You guessed it. I can drive a boat though—how different can it be?"

"Er ... quite different. Do you want me to teach you?"

"That would be fantastic. I hate not knowing how to do things. When?"

I chuckled at her enthusiasm. "Maybe you could come up to Scotland with me at Christmas? We have loads of vehicles up there and plenty of space."

Her hand moved over to my thigh, burning through the denim of my jeans. "Really?"

She sounded so stunned that I darted a glance at her. "Of course."

She leaned over and kissed my ear, and I almost swerved off the road. "You can't do that!" I protested, laughing. "You're far too distracting."

She smiled. "Okay. Okay. I'll behave. Or at least I'll *try*. So where are we going?"

"Like I said, it's a surprise."

"The suspense is killing me," she said, her hand squeezing my leg harder.

Heaven help me. "Good things come to those who wait."

"I've never believed that."

"Prepare yourself to be proven wrong." I pulled into the parking lot behind the brick boathouse on the Cherwell. "Here we are."

She looked around. "Where exactly is *here*?"

I merely ushered her out of the car and pulled my duffle bag of supplies from the boot.

"It has something to do with the river," she guessed, as we walked around the beautiful building that housed all the rowing skulls for the Oxford regattas.

I wanted to hold her hand more than anything, but for the

moment I just guided her with subtle touches towards the dock. "Such deduction skills," I teased. "You really are Oxford material."

She chuckled. "Shut up, you unbearable snob."

I led her down to the cluster of punts tied off the dock and paid the man at the rental booth. When I rejoined her, she was staring at the punts, a crease between her brows. I knew that expression now. Her brain was trying to figure out this new experience.

"Ready to go for a punt?" I threw the duffle bag into the nearest one.

"Is that what we're doing?"

"Yes." I was assailed by a moment of doubt. "Is that alright?"

"It's awesome, but I was just looking at these—they're such an odd shape for a boat. Flat bottoms, squared off ends—not very efficient for speed, are they?"

I took her hand then and gestured at her to step in. It was the gentlemanly thing to do, after all. "Precisely. Punts are designed to slow us down."

She took her seat. "I never considered that. I saw some of these on the brochures and websites about Oxford, but I didn't really understand what all the fuss was about."

"I'm going to show you." I hopped onto the stern platform and picked up the punting pole. "All you need to do is sit back and relax. I'm going to take us somewhere a bit more private."

I didn't miss the mischievous sparkle in her eyes. "That sounds promising."

As I punted down the river, Cedar's eyes drank everything in: the suck and splash of the water against the bank, the overhanging trees—now bare for the winter—the clouds in the sky turning an orange hue to signal the early December dusk.

My pole dug into the mud again and again as I propelled us around the river bend. After a while, I was aware of Cedar's gaze on me.

"This *is* nice," she said.

Warmth spread across my chest. "Yet another one of my schemes to get you alone."

It wasn't as though we didn't spend every night together—we did. It was always in my rooms. Even though I had gone down to her room and put on the sheets I'd bought for her (Egyptian cotton; it was time she tasted a bit of luxury), I had the bigger bed and the discreet tucked-away location.

I'd talked to Annabelle and told her I had a new lady-friend and that for the moment we needed a bit of privacy. She'd been thrilled and assured me she wouldn't dream of interrupting our idyll. If people were paying attention, they would see that Cedar and I sported matching dark circles under our eyes—we explored and loved each other all night long between snatches of sleep.

One would think my need for her would be satisfied, but it was dawning on me that perhaps there was no quenching this. Even now every cell of my body was electrified by her closeness. She would only have to do the smallest thing—a questioning look, lifting up her hair to expose the nape of her neck, a stretch of her legs, and I would be instantly hard.

It was getting almost impossible to be around her at college. The more time I spent with her, the more anything about her tapped into my central nervous system and made me want to haul her to bed.

Once I'd taken us a fair way down the river, I punted us over to the bank, lay down my pole, and set up the second part of my plan: blankets and piping hot mulled wine. There was a sharp winter chill in the air but no rain. Perfect.

In five minutes, she half-sat, half-lay, snuggled up against me in the punt's bow under the thick wool blankets I'd packed in my duffle bag.

"I love the mulled wine," she said. "Excellent idea."

"I remembered how much you liked the mulled cider at the market."

She kissed me, slow and lingering. As much as I knew I was taking stupid risks, I couldn't resist the warm, sweet spice of her lips.

Being outside of college together was always a gamble, but things had been quiet with my father and princess up in Scotland, and I hadn't seen any photographers skulking around for some time. Being boring always worked sooner or later. Pity the effect never lasted.

The trees rustled and we drifted along, slower now, like a leaf in the current.

I ran my fingers over the thick, silky braid of Cedar's hair, musing that I'd love nothing better than just float along in my relationship with Cedar, and not have to worry about Professor Harris, or the Warden, or William Cavendish-Percy. I still wasn't any closer to a solution for us.

Cedar sipped her hot wine. I'd bought us each a new thermos just for this. "It's so strange," she said. "In my forest I never could have imagined this ... or you." She brushed a hand along my jawline, and I was instantly ready for her. *Not here, you savage.*

"What did we ever do for fate to throw us together like this?" I said, struck anew by wonder of it. "How lucky are we?"

"I think about that often," she said. "What were the chances?"

"Not high," I said. "Or perhaps we were meant to be, depending how you perceive life. What do you think?"

She took another sip of her thermos and nestled a bit further into me. "I guess I haven't decided that yet."

"Me neither." I moved even closer to her. "I'm certain of one thing though—"

"What?"

I dropped a kiss on the tip of her nose, pink from the cold. "I'm the luckiest bastard who ever lived."

She sat up just enough so our mouths met and she melted into me, her mouth warm with hot wine and spices. No, I didn't think I would ever be able to get enough.

I lost track of the minutes passing, and under the blankets we got as fevered, entwined, and close as we could without taking our clothes off. She broke away suddenly and scanned around us. Except for the scratching of the branches above us and the lapping of the water on the riverbank, it was so quiet we could have been on our own planet. "Have you ever?" She raised a brow.

"Made love in a punt?" I asked, incredulous. No, I hadn't. I was far too rule-abiding for that. Trust Cedar to entertain the idea.

"Yes," she said, reaching down to the proof that my body had definitely been considering it, even if my brain hadn't dared go there.

"We can't!" I laughed. "Anyone could see us. Besides, with our mutual enthusiasm I'm sure we'd both end up in the Cherwell."

"There's nobody around and, besides, we're under three blankets."

"You terrify me," I said, honestly. It wasn't her so much as the fact that the more time I spent with her, the more I wanted to just chuck everything rational and be as free as she was.

"Terrify, shmerrify," she said.

"Now there's a well-constructed argument." I kissed her again. How could I resist with those freckles, those sparkling eyes, and that wry curve to her lips?

"Isn't it? I thought so. C'mon, I think we could manage it."

Could I manage it? Could I manage her? The more time we spent together the more I longed to keep us safe, to protect this special thing that was growing between us, yet her bravery, independence, and daring were some of the things I admired most in her. I couldn't have it both ways.

When I didn't answer, she pressed her hips against mine, and I clutched her deliciously round bottom reflexively, bringing her even closer still. My breath hitched with need.

"I think I scare you in the right way," she murmured in my ear, triggering a shiver of desire down my spine.

"I love you," I sighed, because it was the only thing I knew for certain.

Cedar sat up like a jack-in-the-box. Even though the punt was flat-bottomed, the sudden movement made it tip vertiginously. She ignored it. "What did you say?"

I looked her directly in the eye. "I love you." I took advantage of her surprise and eased her back down next to me again and pulled her on top of me. I brushed a strand of hair that had fallen loose from her braid behind her ear. "What are you going to do about that?" I widened my eyes at her, daring her to take a risk too.

"Love you back." I knew what that gleam in her eyes meant. She unzipped my jeans, and her clever hand was wrapping around me.

"But Cedar ..." I gasped. "We're in public, and everyone has a smart phone."

"Just ignore me," she said. "Pay no attention." She slithered below the blanket and my breath started to come in gasps. She was everywhere—under my jumper and behind my earlobe. I made a choking noise. "My God, Cedar," I said in a strangled voice. "Are you having your way with me?"

Her head poked out from under the covers, her left eyebrow cocked. "Do you want me to stop?"

My body cried out for those hands and lips. Under no circumstances could she stop. "Carry on, my wild thing," I groaned.

She laughed and disappeared again, teasing, torturing, until she wrapped her lips around me, and I threw my head back, gasping a broken expletive. *Caution be damned.* She fished a condom out of my pocket. These days I was always prepared.

At one point I thought I heard a rustle in the branches, but I was past the point of caring. We could be loving each other in the middle of the college quad, and I still wouldn't be able to stop.

Just as I was close to climax, I couldn't stand it any longer. I pushed down her jeans. She slipped on the condom. The need to feel her as close as she could be beat like a caged animal in my chest and my cock fit her perfectly. Caught in the reeds under a tent of tree branches, I couldn't care about anything but how her body took me in, making me safer than I'd ever been even when she put me in danger.

She'd said it was good for me to take risks, and the silky heat of her convinced me she was right.

We drove each other to the same sparkling, timeless place where nothing existed except us. *Caution, schmaution* as Cedar would say.

CHAPTER THIRTY-THREE

Alfie

The wind howled as I made my way across the quad to teach my tutorial. The sky was so gray it was almost black, and the bare tree branches banged against each other. I knew I was grinning goofily as I walked along, but I just couldn't stop. Happiness lit me up from the inside like a one-thousand-watt lightbulb.

"Hello!" I greeted two second year English students passing in the other direction. "Good morning!"

They stared at me in round-eyed shock, muttered something, and scuttered away.

Oh dear. Had I frightened them?

I couldn't help it. I'd made love to Cedar in the punt three days ago. It had been glorious, and nothing bad had happened. Maybe I could loosen the reins a bit.

I'd just left her warm and tousled in my bed and would be seeing her again in a matter of minutes. More than just the lovemaking, I adored chatting and laughing with Cedar—sharing secrets and random thoughts under the duvet. How had I become the luckiest sod on earth? I had no idea where such blind optimism came from—perhaps from being in love—but I knew everything would turn out fine.

My phone in my back jean pocket buzzed when I was halfway up the stone stairs of the Fitzjames building.

"Hello," I answered. Most of the world barely used phone calls anymore to communicate, but in Oxford, many of the staff and administration had yet to receive the memo.

"Alfred Invernay?" The synthesized voice made me stop in the middle of the staircase. A computer voice? This had to be some sort of mass marketing or a phone scam. I thought of hanging up, but curiosity won out.

"Yes."

"I'm in possession of some ... interesting photos." I froze, and my thoughts immediately flew to the punt.

"Is this a tabloid?" I demanded.

An unpleasant computerized chuckle. "No. A stranger. However, I do have an excellent quality zoom lens. Did you perhaps go on a punting trip with your girlfriend recently?" The word 'girlfriend' was said with a nastiness that even the synthesized voice couldn't conceal. Bile rose in my throat.

"Seeing as I've struck you to silence, I shall answer that for you. You two engaged in some rather public acts of indecency when you thought you were alone on the river."

"What do you want?" I demanded through clenched teeth. My whole body throbbed with rage at the audacity of someone trying to cheapen what had been a momentous, private moment.

"Money, or else I'll go to the tabloids with my pictures ... and I have a full collection. Admirable definition."

"How much?" I demanded. The staircase felt like it was falling away underneath my feet.

"Half a million pounds."

My mind spun. *He had to be joking.* "Don't be ridiculous," I said tersely.

"Now, now. Don't be like that. I know the coffers of the Inver-nay Estate are far from empty."

Rage made all my retorts tangle up in my throat.

After a while, the voice clucked. "I thought you might react this way, and I'm going to give you a little food for thought. Your girlfriend? That Cedar Wild girl? I know about her and where she comes from. Don't you think her background would fascinate the tabloids? She might garner so much negative publicity about having sex with her advisor that she'll be forced out of Oxford. I'm just picturing the headlines," the voice mused, obvious plea-sure coming through the synthetic tones. "Son of Princess-Lover Seduces Savage from the Wild."

"You bastard," I hissed.

"Just think! It would be like Tarzan and Jane, but in reverse—wouldn't the tabloids pounce on that?"

My fists clenched. If this man—and somehow, I was certain it was a man—was in front of me ... I finally understood what Cedar meant about feeling capable of seriously hurting someone else. "Leave her alone."

He tutted five times to lay it on thick. "Now. Don't be like that. She might enjoy memories of her brief flash of fame when she is moldering back in her cabin in Canada. Now, I'm sure this has all come as a bit of a surprise to you, so I'm going to give you some time to mull it over. I'll call back tomorrow afternoon at four o'clock. Money or tabloids ... it's as simple as that. Goodbye."

The phone clicked, and I sagged against the chilly stone wall of the medieval staircase. The man could throw me to the dogs for all I cared, but I had to protect Cedar. She wouldn't be in danger of losing her chance at Oxford if it wasn't for me, or more specifically, my father's infamy. I couldn't let the blackmailer threaten her. This was up to me to fix.

In shock, I fell back on my habit of going through the motions and trudged upstairs to Professor Harris's study to meet with Cedar, Shaun, and Raphael.

I thought briefly of going to my mentor for help but dismissed that thought as soon as it arose. He disapproved of Cedar, and had warned me in his calm, kind way that any relationship between us would probably spell the end of my future at Oxford. Besides, he wanted to get rid of the Commonwealth Scheme too because he was trying to protect the sanctity of the Oxford application process. I didn't agree with him, but I understood his reasoning.

Could I call my father? For a moment, I was tempted, but no. He wouldn't help. On the contrary, he would tell me to allow the man to send all his compromising photos to the papers, then regard me as a freak because I didn't relish the subsequent notoriety.

I staggered into Professor Harris's study and the heads of my three students—ha! Who was I to be teaching anybody?—swiveled in my direction.

Cedar's expression sharpened as she took me in. "What's wrong?" she demanded.

"You look like hell," Shaun said.

"Cedar," I said, my voice coming out oddly. "Can I speak to you in the hall for a moment?"

She nodded and followed me out. I shut the door behind us.

CHAPTER THIRTY-FOUR

Cedar

My body was incandescent with rage after Alfie filled me in on the phone call. His face was paler than I'd ever seen it, and there was genuine fear in his eyes. I wasn't scared. I was livid.

When he mentioned there were photos of us in the punt, a wave of guilt crashed over me. I had been the one to push to make love, and it had felt like a perfect moment we'd managed to catch forever. I'd been so naïve. Maybe, it hit me with full force for the first time, Alfie had a solid basis for his constant caution.

"We have to think," I said when he was finished. My brain felt on fire, all logic consumed by rage. "What are we going to do?"

He shook his head. "I have to deal with this alone, Cedar. I've already dragged you too far into my sordid life."

I wouldn't let him take the blame for this. "Isn't it more that I'm like a bomb that has exploded your life into smithereens?" I hated that my recklessness had pitchforked Alfie's life into crisis, yet again. It was the last thing I wanted for this man I now loved.

"No!" he answered vehemently. "Never, but I can't let you deal with this."

I clenched my jaw, feeling sidelined like I'd been with my parents my whole life. This involved me. "I am going to be a part of this whether or not you like it," I said. "There are two of us in this relationship, and in those photos. My whole life I've been shunted aside like some bit player. I'm not doing that anymore. We are going to fight this together, Alfie."

His head jerked back. Was he that unused to the idea of someone not abandoning him in a time of crisis? "But you can't. I need to protect you."

I shook my head. "We need to protect each other."

He stared at me for a moment. "I won't be able to convince you out of this, will I?"

I shook my head. "How dare they invade your private life, and mine? How dare they try to blackmail you? Even if the worst happens, I would rather face it with you than leave you on your own."

He raked his fingers through his hair, deep in thought. Suddenly, he reached out, grabbed me by the shoulders, and gave me a desperate kiss. We were still kissing when the study door opened.

"What have we here?" Shaun exclaimed with delight.

"I thought so," Raphael rumbled behind him.

I pushed Alfie back in the study and shut the door firmly behind us.

"We can't tell them," he hissed to me.

I waved over at Shaun and Raphael who were now standing there, expectantly. "Do you think they haven't figured it out? Give them some credit, Alfie. Besides, they can help us." Both Alfie and I were used to coping with everything on our own—maybe it was time to change our habits.

"But—"

"Look, I'm starting to think that our stubbornness about not letting others help is weakness, not strength. We can trust them."

Alfie's eyes darted over to Shaun.

"I know I have a reputation as a gossip." Shaun winced. "But not when things matter—like this."

I pulled the desk chair around the desk and placed it where it faced the couch.

"Sit here," I said to Alfie. I sat down on the wingback chair beside him and gestured at Shaun and Raphael to sit across from us on the couch. They did so without argument.

"If I tell you something, can you both promise it will not leave this room?" I asked them.

Shaun turned to Raphael and telegraphed a question to him. Raphael nodded, then they turned back to us.

"You can trust us," Raphael said, with a quiet confidence that was a total reversal from how he'd been at the beginning of term. That time in nature had done him more good than I ever could have imagined.

Alfie was still looking shell-shocked. "Cedar," he began. "We can't—"

"We can," I said. "And we're going to."

"Cedar, I understand what you're trying to do, but I can handle this."

"Tell them, or I will," I said, gently. I understood how this went against everything he'd learned of life so far.

I was relieved when he began talking, but very quickly my ears pounded with rage again at the audacity of the man on the phone and how he was trying to extort half a million pounds from Alfie.

When Alfie finished, he threw his palms in the air and slumped back in his chair. "There you have it."

"The bastard." Shaun shook his head. "Let me just say, though, I think the two of you make a divine couple in that opposites-attract sort of way."

"Not the time, Shaun." Raphael nudged Shaun's knee with his.

"Sorry." Shaun winced. I'd never seen him this compliant.

"Who do you think it could be?" Raphael asked. "Your father?"

My mind hadn't gone there yet, but it wasn't beyond the realm of belief given his history.

Alfie frowned down at his hands. "I hadn't thought of that... he does love keeping himself in the tabloids, but would that extend to me? Also, why would he ask for money if it would come from his own bank accounts?"

"Yeah, that makes no sense," I said. "Still—"

"We can't completely rule him out," Alfie said, bitterly reading my thoughts. "I know. He's that perverse."

"Sorry."

Alfie shook his head. "It's the way it's always been with him."

"The blackmailer is a bully," Raphael said, cracking his knuckles thoughtfully. Shaun watched with apparent interest. "I've been bullied for a good part of my life. It's about time I started standing up to them."

"But this person isn't bullying *you*," Alfie protested. "This isn't your fight."

"Does that really matter?" Raphael said, and all of our eyebrows shot up, impressed. "Now, you said this person is calling you back in twenty-four hours?"

Alfie nodded, grim faced. "Yes."

"I might be able to figure out a way to record their call and trace it."

Alfie's mouth dropped open. "Really?"

"I can't make any guarantees," Raphael said. "It's a tricky business, and I don't know if I'll be able to get the equipment I'll need here in time—"

"I can take care of that," Shaun said. "With my name, it isn't hard to get my hands on pretty much anything at lightning speed." He crossed his hands over his knee, smug. "I may not be a technological wizard like Raphael, but I have plenty of other uses. Trust me, I can get shit done."

I believed him.

"Is there anyone else we need to bring in?" I asked. "While keeping it on the down low of course?"

"Lachlan," Alfie said. "I don't know what he can do, but he always manages to find some way to make himself useful. Besides, he already knows about us." He reached over then and took my hand in his.

"Awwwwww." Shaun put his hand on his heart.

"Binita," I said.

"This is getting to be a lot of people ..." Alfie chewed on his fingernail.

Shaun scoffed. "With Binita's brain, you're hardly in a position to say no."

Raphael nodded. "I know I'd have a better chance of success with the phone tracing if she helped me. Technology is all about numbers, and there's no-one as brilliant with numbers as Binita."

"All right," Alfie agreed, warming up to things a bit. "So just the four of you then?"

Shaun and Raphael nodded.

"And you promise to keep it a secret?" Alfie asked again. He kept clenching and unclenching his jaw.

"Yes," Raphael and Shaun answered in the same exasperated tones.

"But ... why are you helping us?" Alfie asked.

"Because we're your friends," Raphael said. "It's what friends do."

***

That night in bed we made love in a frantic attempt to connect and push the blackmail out of our consciousness for a while. As I lay cradled in the nook of his shoulder afterwards, he stroked my arm.

"How did Binita react?" Alfie asked me.

"Surprised, then angry for you," I said. "She's completely on board and has already been conferring with Raphael and Shaun about the equipment they'll need."

Alfie squeezed my shoulder.

"How about Lachlan?" I asked.

"Same," he said. "If we're able to find the blackmailer, Lachlan will definitely up the intimidation factor in a confrontation."

I nodded against him. "Yup."

"This is so new to me," he said. "Letting people help. On one hand, it's a relief. On the other it makes me feel as though everything is slipping out of my control."

I ran my fingers across his chest, and he made a small sigh of pleasure. "It's the same for me. I feel like I'm betraying my religion of being self-reliant. I was brought up with that being the main tenet of my life."

"It's hard changing," he said. "And there's no guarantee of a happy ending, you know."

I was painfully conscious of that. "I'm a realist. Living in the forest, I don't think you can be any other way and survive. It's just that what this person is trying to do is so wrong. If there's an off-chance we can stop him, I would hate not to try. We've both been doing this 'do everything ourselves' thing for our entire lives. Maybe it's time to try doing something different."

He reached up and held my chin between his thumb and forefinger, caressing it gently. "This obstinate chin of yours gives me strength."

"Like a talisman?" I chuckled.

"Precisely."

I sighed. "One thing I know, I don't want a life like my parents, isolated and alone."

Even the lovemaking and the shared humor couldn't quite conquer the dread that had taken up residence in my chest. To have this all blow up on us would feel like a stem snipped off just before the flower was about to bloom.

"I don't know who I would be anymore without Oxford," Alfie murmured in the dark. Norris snuffled in his sleep.

I wanted to argue that we would still be ourselves, wouldn't we? We would still have each other. Did Alfie not think the same thing?

"I have confidence we would figure it out," I said. "Still, I understand how upsetting it would be to give up all the work you've put into building a life here."

He didn't answer right away, just kept stroking my arm, staring up at the ceiling. "I could lie to you," he said finally. "But I want there to be honesty between us. I've loved it here at Beaufort College since the moment I stepped foot in the place. I adore the idea of a place that is devoted entirely to learning. I love medieval literature and could happily devote my whole life to that without ever getting bored. I feel like I'll never get to the end of all the things I want to study. I just ... fit."

But which Alfie fitted? Was it the Alfie who was holding me and stroking my arm now?

"I knew it would be complicated, but I never thought we'd find ourselves here," he said, chewing his lip. "There's a lot to lose."

I frowned at this. He felt far away suddenly. "There's a lot to fight for as well."

CHAPTER THIRTY-FIVE

Alfie

The next day, I was in my room with Lachlan and Cedar, bursting with frustration. I started pacing back and forth across my floor.

Cedar lay on her stomach on my bed, her chin in her hands, deep in thought. Lachlan was sitting on the couch, punching his fist into his hand meditatively.

My skin itched as my panic increased. It wasn't easy to keep the threats the blackmailer had made regarding Cedar a secret, but I couldn't worry her about that. I would save her spot at Oxford, even if it meant sacrificing myself. No matter what she said about fighting this together, that truth resonated deep within me. If I hadn't been damaged goods to begin with, she never would be faced with such a threat. By giving in to my feelings for her, I'd infected her too, and her future.

If we failed to record the phone call, I was dragging all these other people into my failure as well. This was all so new to me, and the responsibility pressed down like cinder blocks on my shoulders. Had it been a mistake to let people in?

There was a knock on the door. Perfect timing. Lachlan was there in a flash, looking through the peephole. He was my self-appointed security detail, it appeared. I'd known he would make himself useful.

Raphael and Shaun came in, their arms full of what looked like listening and recording equipment. They both boggled at Norris yipping and squirming around their feet.

Shaun's face distorted with disgust. "What is that ungodly thing?"

The secret of Norris seemed so minor compared to the photos of Cedar and me in the punt that I'd completely forgotten about it.

"His name is Norris," I said, not interrupting my pacing. "And he's a secret too."

Norris didn't share my reservations about teamwork. He was wagging his tail so enthusiastically I worried his bottom half would fall off.

Shaun whistled. "A dog ... or whatever that thing is? You are a dark horse, Lord Invernay."

I rolled my eyes. How I would adore being anything but. "Please shut the door, we don't want anyone to stumble in by accident."

Binita pushed through them then and shut the door firmly behind her. She flashed a radiant smile at Lachlan, and he flushed bright red. A wave of envy slammed me. How lucky they were to conduct a normal, private relationship without photographers and tabloids and the eyes of the world. Cedar deserved that, not this mess.

Binita clapped her hands together. "Let's get to it," she said. "We don't know how long this is going to take us. The man said four o'clock this afternoon, right, Alfie?"

"Right." I nodded.

Within minutes, Shaun, Binita, and Raphael were setting up the equipment on my desk. Shaun was being more serious than I'd ever seen him.

After a half hour of waiting, Lachlan's stomach grumbled ominously. "How about I get food for all of us? Jacket potatoes all round?" Lachlan asked. "We can't do his if we're perishing from hunger."

Lachlan took our orders—just cheese on Cedar's, no beans, whereas Shaun, Raphael, and Binita got the works. I shook my head. "I'm too nervous to eat," I admitted.

"Your appetite will come when you see the rest of us eatin'," Lachlan said. "I'm getting you one anyway."

There seemed no point in arguing.

I felt relatively useless as Binita and Raphael, with Shaun's help, continued to work on the equipment.

"Can I help?" I asked.

Raphael raised his brows. "I saw how you set up Cedar's laptop and printer. No offense, but I think we'll be better off without it."

I sat on the bed beside Cedar instead and held her hand like an anchor. She gave my palm a kiss. "I'm not going to try and cheer your up," she said. "There's no way this couldn't be stressful."

"No," I said. "Same for you."

"Not as much as for you." She shrugged.

My only small bit of solace was that she still thought her risk was small, proof I'd done something right in all this mess.

I sat beside her, nibbling the jacket potato that Lachlan had brought back for me, hating that I couldn't do much more except to wait. Cedar squirmed uncomfortably on the bed too—I knew it wasn't easy for her to wait idly either, but we would just be in their way if we tried to help.

When it was twenty to four, Raphael and Binita declared the

setup was complete.

"When he calls," Raphael instructed, "The name of the game is to keep him on the line for as long as possible. Can you do that?"

Cedar pressed the middle of my palm with her thumb—a vote of confidence. "Of course I can," I said. "I'm relieved to do *something* at last." My shoulders dropped a bit.

Twenty tortuous and eerily quiet minutes of waiting later, my phone rang.

Raphael did something on the control board Shaun had carried in and nodded at me to pick up.

"Hello," I answered. Even with that one word, it was hard to keep the rage brewing inside me out of my voice.

"Hello, Alfred," the synthesized voice said. It came right through the speaker Raphael had set up, filling my room. Shaun's eyebrows flew up and he mouthed, *what's with the voice*? Raphael put a hand on Shaun's leg to quiet him.

"I hope you've been thinking a lot since yesterday," the blackmailer said. "What is it going to be? Money or scandal?"

I looked over at Raphael and Binita who were both wearing big headsets. They both gave me an encouraging smile and a thumbs up. *They've done their part now Alfie, don't bugger this up.*

How did this stranger know to choose the word 'scandal' that triggered a visceral repulsion in me like nothing else? "I need time to get the money together," I said, hating to concede anything to this man, even if it was a necessary part of the trap we were trying to set.

"I'm happy to see you're coming to your senses. It would be such a shame to see those photos in the tabloids, wouldn't it? Your feral girlfriend would be so publicly soiled, wouldn't she?"

My eyes met Cedar's and hers were sharp and merciless. Her index finger twitched, as though she were firing an imaginary trigger.

I understood her completely. My hands itched to crash through the phone and strangle this vile human being on the other end of the line. I had to keep him talking, but anger built up in my throat, blocking it. Binita made air circles with her finger to signal *keep going.*

"Stop talking about Cedar," I said. "This has nothing to do with her."

"My dear boy," he said. "The photos I took tell quite a different story."

I gritted my teeth. "So ... like I said I need to get the money together. It could take some time. There are trusts and—"

"Nonsense, my boy. I think if you talk to your father, you'll find he is quite used to paying hush money. I'm quite certain he could help you out."

"Let's keep my father out of this," I said.

"He'll be in it sooner or later if you don't pay me off. He'll see the tabloids and read about it himself. Might be satisfying to turn the tables on him after all these years, wouldn't it? On second thoughts, I think it might be best for you if I publish those photos after all ... it might be the full circle moment you and your father need."

Every word he said pushed the horrible possibility that my father could be the blackmailer further from my mind ... at the same time, this whole thing stunk of him. Could the blackmailer be one of my father's many enemies getting revenge on him through me? After all, the money would ultimately come from the family's bank account. It would be far from the first time I'd paid the reckoning for my father's sins.

Cedar came over and took hold of my hand that wasn't clutching onto my phone. Shame prevented me from looking at her—to have her involved in the sordid reality of my life.

"How do you plan to collect the money?" I asked.

Raphael nodded at me to keep going.

"I've set up an anonymous account in Switzerland. You can transfer the money there." The voice chuckled, a repulsive sound. "Just like in a James Bond film, if you are partial to such horrible drivel. I would hope better taste of you."

"What's the account number?" I asked.

Raphael's eyes lit up and he mouthed, "Got them!" Binita did a silent cheer.

The blackmailer read out the account number to me, and I wrote it down. "How can I contact you when I've assembled the funds?"

He clucked again, five times like before. "Not so fast, my boy. I will set the timeline, not you. You have until eight o'clock Friday evening."

"But—" Friday was the very next day.

"I quite have my heart set on my photography appearing in the Saturday Daily Mail, you know. It's long been one of my aspirations." He laughed at this, a bitter, condescending laugh. Whoever this person was, he was a snob. From his speech patterns, he was also well-spoken and educated.

"Is that so?" I said.

"Absolutely. Good afternoon." With that, he hung up. I stood with my phone, which was connected to a multitude of tiny wires and cables, in my hand.

"Where is he?" Lachlan demanded of Raphael and Binita. "Tell me where and I'll go kill him with my bare hands."

"Then you would end up in prison," Binita said; a voice of reason. "Not helpful, although I share your sentiments entirely."

All of us turned to Raphael who was frowning at his computer screen. The air thickened with tension. "Did you get it?" I asked.

He grimaced. "Sort of."

"What do you mean, sort of?" Shaun demanded.

"It's come down to a switchboard. From there, I can't locate the exact number."

"A switchboard where?" Cedar asked.

"Here," Raphael said, looking up at us with round eyes. "Within the college. The caller is calling from Beaufort."

"Are you sure?" I asked. What enemies did my father possibly have within my college? I couldn't forget that he'd gone through Beaufort himself—stories were still told about his antics. The idea the betrayal had come from within the one place I'd thought I'd found safety made my stomach churn.

Binita fiddled with the headset she'd taken off. "Certain," she said.

"Are you surprised?" Raphael asked me.

"Shocked," I said, but now I thought about it, I'd figured out already that even the computerized voice couldn't hide the upper-class intonations and sentence structure of the blackmailer. Why not Oxford? "You know, when I think back, the blackmailer seemed to know a lot about me. I never thought—" Bile rose in my throat.

"If it's someone in the college, we have to bring in Robbie," Cedar said.

I nodded. "He's working today, I saw him this morning." At least that was something I could do, besides be a passive victim of a criminal. "I'll go get him," I said, and rushed out of the room, my head spinning and desperate for a gulp of fresh air.

I rushed down the stairs, still trying to wrap my mind around the idea that someone in college had it in for me. It had to be an enemy of my father's. I made a concerted effort to be boring enough that I couldn't imagine why anyone would want to target me directly. Maybe I wasn't the most personable fellow, but I was generally civil, and kept to myself and my books.

I thought of my full room upstairs. How had Cedar managed to change all that? I wasn't sure exactly how or when it happened, but she had turned my world on its head. My social life no longer consisted only of Lachlan. I was with Cedar and her friends. I wavered between feeling relieved about the extra support and camaraderie, and anxious about the extra exposure. I was too used to relying on privacy as self-protection.

"Alfred!" I stopped and looked up. *Damn*. I'd been so deep in my ruminations I'd walked right by Professor Harris.

"Sorry sir." I lifted my head, desperately trying to marshal my thoughts and appear somewhat normal. "I was thinking."

He dug his hands in his pockets and tilted his head. "Ah, well, I suppose that's a good thing. I'm just coming out of a tutorial for freshers. Ghastly essay writing technique." He looked unruffled and serene in his usual tweed blazer and tie. How I longed for the tidiness of his life, now more than ever. "Excited for our trip tomorrow?"

"Er ... excuse me?" I asked. What trip?"

"Surely you haven't forgotten! To London, to see the possible Margery Kempe addendum."

It went without saying that it had slipped my mind entirely. What was the point, seeing as my whole life at Oxford was about to implode anyway. "I'm not sure—"

His head jerked. "Alfred! Is it possible you are not as serious about medieval literature as I thought? This is a once-in-a-lifetime opportunity."

In this moment where I felt like I was letting down Cedar so badly, I couldn't bear letting down Professor Harris as well. That sickening feeling of the ground dropping away underneath my feet made me desperate to grab on to something solid. He'd always been that sturdy touchpoint for me since I arrived at Oxford.

I was growing increasingly certain the blackmailer was an enemy of my father's from within Beaufort College. If Raphael couldn't pinpoint the exact phone number, it dawned on me that Professor Harris was my best chance. He had a way of knowing everyone's business in college, especially as it pertained to me. The train ride would allow me to ask about my father's potential enemies, possibly without even revealing the blackmail. He was my best chance at extracting Cedar, and perhaps me too, out of the crisis.

"What time are we leaving?" I asked.

"Ha! That's better! Seven-thirty train to London and then we'll catch the four o'clock back here."

That would leave me some time before the eight o'clock deadline. Good God, tomorrow was the black-tie dinner as well.

"Where shall we meet?" I asked.

"Seven at the Lodge? I'll order a taxi."

"Perfect," I said, and went to get Robbie, feeling far steadier on my feet.

CHAPTER THIRTY-SIX

Cedar

Alfie came back up to the room with Robbie in tow, both of them wearing similar haunted expressions.

"Terrible business," Robbie said in way of greeting, and picked up Norris. He distractedly greeted him like an old friend, his black eyes churning in thought. "The call came from within college? You're certain?" he asked Raphael and Binita.

They nodded. "We're sure," Binita said.

"We've been coming up with a list of suspects." Lachlan waved the piece of paper in his hands. We'd been working on it since Alfie left, but the list was short. None of us could think of any specific person, but at the same time, Alfie's chilly front meant that it could also be anyone. "But first, Robbie, does anyone pop into your mind?"

Robbie slowly shook his head. "Not off the top of my head, no. I need to think. Who has it in for Alfie to the point they would follow him and Cedar? Hello lass," He lifted his head to me. "Didn't I say you were just what Alfie needed? More people should listen to me."

I sighed. "But look how that turned out."

"It's not like you to give up," Robbie chastised, and I straightened, realizing he was right. Alfie and I and our friends would fight this and fight it together.

"I'm not giving up," I said. "We'll figure this out."

Alfie cast me a look I couldn't quite interpret.

"Was anyone else in competition for your fellowship?" Lachlan asked Alfie. "You never mentioned it."

He thought for a second. "There were two others, also DPhil students, but I don't see them around college very much anymore. Their names are Josh Campion and Emily Matheson."

Robbie nodded. "I'll look into them."

"What about staff?" I asked. "It might not be a student."

"Professor Harris," Lachlan burst out, and I looked at him in surprise.

I didn't like Professor Harris any more than Lachlan seemed to, but I knew what an important role he played in Alfie's life. Besides, Alfie said he'd been kind and understanding about seeing us at The Turf. What motivation could Professor Harris have for such a thing? I watched Alfie carefully.

Alfie rolled his eyes. "Ridiculous. Don't you agree, Robbie?"

Robbie rubbed his chin.

"You're not taking that seriously, I hope?" Alfie's eyes snapped. "Professor Harris would never do that."

"You sure?" Lachlan said. "I've never liked the control he has on you, and perhaps if he suspects anything between you and Cedar, he's scared of losing that."

"No," Alfie said. "It's not him. I just met him on the quad, and he was teaching a freshers' tutorial when the blackmailer was calling us. He has an alibi complete with witnesses."

Robbie grimaced, his hands behind his back. "I would think it unlikely too," he said. "Still … Lachlan has a point. There is something not quite right about that man."

"We're headed down the wrong path," Alfie said. "I've been thinking, and the only person it could be is an enemy of my father within Beaufort. I don't have any enemies here. I'm far too boring for that, but my father … from the stories I sometimes hear … he made plenty. Once we figure out who that person is, we can catch our man."

It had come down to Alfie's father. Again? Unbelievable. My instincts told me that maybe Alfie was ruling out other possibilities too fast, but then I didn't know Malcolm's history at Beaufort.

Robbie pursed his lips. "He did indeed make some mortal enemies. He seduced more than one don's wife, I can tell you that."

"Exactly!" Alfie said, triumphant. "As a matter of fact, I was thinking that perhaps Professor Harris could *help* us."

"Excuse me?" Lachlan demanded, incredulous.

Alfie sighed and crossed his arms across his torso. "You may as well put that ridiculous suspicion of yours out of your mind, Lachlan."

Lachlan didn't bother to try and hide his disappointment. "Something is off about Harris. I stand by it," he said, shaking his head.

"I need to get back to the Lodge," Robbie said. "But I promise I'll leave no stone unturned on my end. Malcolm's enemies within college … it does make sense, you know."

Raphael nodded. "I'll take this equipment back to my room and see if I can localize anything further."

"I'd come help," Binita said. "But I have to teach a tutorial in twenty minutes."

"I'll come," Shaun said. "Make you tea and massage your shoulders while you're slaving away."

"I'd like that," Raphael said.

Something was definitely going on between those two.

"I have to be off too," Lachlan said. "Rugby practice. Anyway, I think maybe it's best if you two brainstorm on your own for a little bit. Who knows?"

I exchanged glances with Alfie, but again I couldn't read his expression. Something niggled at me. Something not right.

"Thank you guys so much," I said. "Let's start a text group to exchange information, then we can meet again tomorrow morning, say eight o'clock?"

"Um ..." Alfie appeared to take great interest in his shoes. "I'm going to London with Professor Harris tomorrow."

We all stared at him, eyes boggling.

"The Margery Kempe manuscript," he said, looking at me. "More importantly, if anyone can pinpoint some dons who hate my father enough to target me, it's him."

How could he possibly think of going to London at such a time, and following Professor Harris even now, when we were about to lose everything? Alfie had a confidence in the man that the rest of us lacked. We weren't a team in Alfie's mind. Maybe we'd never been.

The familiar ache of abandonment filled every cell, despite the fact that I was surrounded by friends.

"We'll talk later," I said to everyone, as they made their hasty way out. As for Alfie, we were going to talk now.

By the time we were finally alone in the room, the air had filled with the tension.

"I don't understand," I said.

"I know how it must look at first glance." He made a pleading gesture with his hands.

"It looks bad. Quizzing Professor Harris is just a pretext for continuing to play it safe, Alfie. It's a long shot at best. Don't you see we're stronger if we work together? I'm sure we can figure it out. You're abandoning us."

"I'm not! I'll be working on the problem too, just separately. Divide and conquer." Something unsure in Alfie's eyes made me doubt the sincerity of his reasoning.

In that moment, I felt like I didn't know Alfie at all. "Divide is the key word there," I said. "I'm here to help, as are our friends. You don't need Professor Harris. This theory you have about your father's enemies—it feels to me like just another excuse for isolating yourself. Aren't we beyond that?"

"This could work, Cedar."

"How much of your decision to go to London has to do with not letting down Professor Harris?" I couldn't help but feel that he was choosing Professor Harris over me. This involved both of us, so weren't we supposed to be dealing with this as a couple too? Maybe I'd been deluding myself. Maybe when it came right down to it, I'd been alone all this time.

Alfie's head dropped. "Some," he admitted. "The thing is, Cedar, we haven't actually seen those photos. We were under a mound of blankets, if you remember—"

"Oh, I remember." It felt like a different lifetime though, with a different Alfie than the one who stood across from me now.

"I was thinking ... maybe the photos don't have the destructive power the blackmailer wants us to think they do. If they can be explained away, and I can stay on Professor Harris's good side and say they were misinterpreted ... I could say we may have strayed too far but that we've broken it off, and we won't do it again ..." His words came out in staccato bursts, feverishly trying to smooth over the past ... to smooth over *me*.

I sucked in air loudly enough to stop Alfie. "I do not want to be explained away."

"That's not what I meant—"

I knew now that the highs of love were matched by lows that were like nothing I'd ever felt before. The knife of betrayal twisted in my gut. "If you fail at getting useable information from Professor Harris, your plan is to double down on denial, and then the whole secrecy and respectability thing to try and save ourselves?"

"Well ... yes, but my main motivation is to find the bastard who is turning the screw."

"But, if you don't, us as a couple would go back into hiding?"

"We'd still be together, but perhaps we could be circumspect for a while, then eventually manage—"

How could he possibly want to go *backwards*? "I'm not something to be managed," I said in a throbbing voice. "*We're* not something to be managed."

"That's not what I meant," he said. His eyes remained hooded, and his face stormy. "You're deliberately putting the worst possible spin on my words—"

"Because I cannot believe they're coming out of your mouth. Who are you, Alfie?" I simply did not understand.

"I'm just trying to salvage something for us ... for both of us. It's a long shot, but if we can't identify the caller, it may be all we have. This disaster, well ... we were foolish, and now we have to try to be wiser."

Grief swept through every cell. Alfie hadn't changed. He was still two very different and irreconcilable people. The one I loved was only half of a whole I couldn't accept.

"And what?" I demanded. "Spend the rest of our days behind closed doors, never able to hold hands in public or sit side by side at a black-tie dinner? Hiding that I love you, hiding from the photographers and blackmail, hiding my background, hiding behind rules and regulations and expectations of others? How can you even ask that of me, Alfie? I did not come all the way to Oxford to live just a different version of being hidden away from life."

Exhaustion weighed down his features. "Look Cedar ... can't you try to understand?"

I shook my head. Had he heard anything I'd just said? "The problem is there is no end date to our hiding, is there? Not when you're determined to spend the rest of your life playing it safe."

"But Cedar, it's so silly not to try and at least salvage something from this mess."

"This mess?" I pointed at him and then back at me. "You mean us?"

He froze. I'm not sure if that's what he meant, but he'd said it.

My pulse raced in my neck. I was sickeningly reminded of my parents, who retreated to the woods rather than being let down by people. Had they been right? "You know what is the most dangerous thing of all? A life with no risks. That isn't a life, Alfie, it's not living at all—at least not the way I want to live."

He raked his hands through his hair. "Do you know what it is to love you?" he demanded. "You don't lock your door and you attack paparazzi. I could be responsible for your whole life exploding because of your association with me and my wretched family. I'm scared *all the time* because of you, Cedar."

Did he think loving someone as risk averse as him was *easy*? "You talk like you want to cage me up like a wild animal so I'm a danger to nobody. Life *is* risk. Think of that Welsh boy who was just playing a rugby game. You can do everything right and still get sick or get tackled the wrong way or get hit by a car."

His silence was so heavy it seemed to weigh down on me and everything in his room.

"Why are you even with me?" I asked.

He collapsed on the couch. "Because I love you, Cedar," he said. "I'm madly in love with you, but that doesn't make this easy."

I couldn't do this. My chest ached as my heart fractured into a million pieces. "I'll be sleeping in my room tonight," I said.

"Cedar ..." he pleaded. "Please."

"No." I walked towards the door, then turned at the last minute. "You know what? I think you're drifting, anchorless. Who are you really? The Alfie I love, or the Alfie who plays it safe?"

"Can't I be both?"

I shook my head. "I'm realizing that's impossible. Besides, I only love the first one. I'm growing to despise the second."

"Despise?" He lifted his shiny eyes to mine.

"Yes. The first one was the only one who didn't make me feel like that lonely, rejected child all over again."

He made a choking sound.

I opened the door. "You need to repair that moral compass, Alfie. It's broken in case you hadn't noticed."

"I'm just trying to protect you!" he burst out, his face a mask of struggle.

"I can protect myself."

"You don't understand."

"I do, all too well. Before you can be anything to me you need to figure out which Alfie you are."

"Don't leave," he begged.

"You stay safe," I said, opening the door to leave. "I know you're good at that."

CHAPTER THIRTY-SEVEN

Alfie

Professor Harris and I were on the train on our way back from London's Paddington Station, and it had made an unscheduled stop at Slough. Adrenaline ran through my body, making me feel jittery and nauseous.

The entire day had been hellish, and as much as I hated to admit it, Cedar and Lachlan had been right to be skeptical. I hadn't been able to extract any useful information from Professor Harris whatsoever. He was happy to talk of my father's perfidy but remained vague when I asked about potential enemies. I'd never noticed how closely he played his cards to his chest. To make matters even worse our train was already over three hours late because of an impromptu rail strike.

"The strikes are atrocious," Professor Harris said, over the top of his copy of The Telegraph. "Margaret Thatcher would have quashed it in a trice."

Why was I even here? The night before I had entertained the fantasy of fixing the blackmail problem and eliminating the threat against Cedar, but now I was face to face with the ugly fact that I'd been a coward, and I'd failed. This trip had been no help whatsoever.

I'd sent at least one hundred texts to Cedar, but she wasn't answering. I couldn't even blame her.

We were due to arrive in Oxford, barring any further delays, at around seven thirty, just half an hour before the blackmailer's deadline and the beginning of the black-tie dinner, although I had no idea where that stood. Of course I didn't—I hadn't been there to work with Cedar and our friends.

The only text I received was from Lachlan, who updated me that they were still working on locating the two students who had been in the running for the fellowship, and also trying to narrow down the phone location. He also castigated me for being a 'right bawbag' for abandoning them all, especially Cedar. It was a completely accurate assessment.

The wheels screeched on the tracks. Finally, we were moving. The odor of stale crisps and coffee pervaded the carriage. My mind kept going back to Cedar's accusation that I was two different people and I needed to choose one.

I wanted to choose the me I was with Cedar—the free, uninhibited person, but I was also terrified that if I went down that road, such indulgence would quickly devolve into behavior like my father's. More than that, I didn't know how to be the person I was with Cedar in private in public at Oxford. Was it even possible to merge those two parts of myself?

Cedar deserved more than this wretched split personality she had been putting up with. No wonder she had put her foot down. The knowledge I had let her down twisted in my gut. The thought of life without her made the entire world shift to black and white.

"Daydreaming again?" Professor Harris asked. "You didn't answer my question."

"Sorry ... yes?"

"Goodness, you are proving distractible lately. I asked if you had put the proper distance between you and Cedar Wild."

I reached up and rubbed my sternum where my heart ached. I had, but only because I was an absolute coward, and had flown back to my old habits as soon as things got stressful. I'd realized, there in the bedroom, that I wasn't worthy of her. Oh, but how I wanted to be.

There was no better time to start than the present. "Why do you dislike her so much?" I asked.

His eyes narrowed. "I beg your pardon?"

"Why do you have it in for her? I thought you'd barely spent any time with her."

"She's entirely unsuited to Oxford." He was a bit flummoxed I noticed with no small amount of satisfaction. "We've discussed this, Alfred. Besides, it's not just my opinion. Many share it."

"Is that so?"

"Yes. Why? Do you like her?"

I wasn't going to hide so much of myself anymore. My stomach dropped with terror, but this had gone on too long.

"I do," I said. "Very much."

He clicked his tongue five times at me in disapproval. "Mark my words—you are heading for a fall, Alfred."

He didn't click his tongue two times like most people, but five for extra emphasis. A tinge of suspicion vibrated through me, and then ... the final piece of the puzzle clicked into place. The blackmailer had clicked his tongue five times as well.

The truth reverberated through my body, but still ... it so completely overturned everything I had believed until that moment that my mind had a hard time assimilating. Could it be possible that Lachlan had been right, and I had been wrong—about everything.

I pinched the top of my hand to keep myself from hauling off and punching Professor Harris right then and there. Everything pointed to him being the blackmailer.

Cedar was right about my moral compass needing serious repair—the pieces I needed had been there all along. Lachlan, Robbie, and Cedar. How could I have been so stupid? Still, there was the matter of his freshers' tutorial alibi.

"Say, your tutorial with the freshers the other day," I said. "How did you deal with their poor essay writing skills? It might serve me in the future."

He hesitated—just for a split second, but enough to give me the confirmation I needed. "I cover their papers with red," he said. "And give them deltas. That usually gets their attention." His smile was cold and superior. How had I never seen that Professor Harris's calm was the sort of unfeeling sort—that of a person who had fun sticking tacks in caterpillars?

"What was the essay topic?" I asked.

Again, that split second of hesitation. "Chaucer, of course. Wife of Bath."

"Of course," I answered blandly. I thought of asking him the names of the students in that tutorial, but I didn't want to raise his suspicion any further, so I started chatting about the perfidy of rail strikes again. Slowly, he lowered his guard.

I excused myself to the bathroom, and in the tiny metal cubicle, sent off a hasty text to the group telling them they had been right, and it had been Professor Harris all along.

I waited for a few seconds longer, but nobody texted back. Had they even received it? The internet on British trains was notoriously spotty. I slipped my phone back in my pocket. I had to go back. I had to trap Professor Harris, and to do this, I couldn't arouse his suspicion.

I went back to my seat, determined to fill the time left on our trip with inconsequential nothings. It was torture, but I somehow managed to appear as blasé as him.

"Say, are you going to the black-tie dinner tonight?" I asked Professor Harris as the train pulled into the Oxford station. I couldn't believe I had been able to act so normal given every fiber of my body had wanted to lunge at him and pummel him to a pulp with my fists. *How dare he*?

I would stop him, and I didn't care if I exposed myself in doing so. My past meant I would probably always be a relatively careful person, but I couldn't let that prevent me from doing what was right—not anymore.

"Of course," he smiled blandly at me. "I never miss any of those, and neither should you."

While I'd been keeping up the conversation, my mind had been whirring with the details of my plan to catch him in the act of blackmail. I would need the Warden. I needed proof—just the number of clicks of his tongue wasn't enough evidence. As things stood now there was no witness, so it was my word against his. I checked my phone quickly. Nothing from Lachlan or any of them. I hit "resend".

I grabbed my bag and checked my watch. Good God. Seven thirty-five. I was rapidly running out of time.

"I'll be there without fail," I said to Professor Harris with a smile as duplicitous as his. The race was on.

***

It was quarter to eight when I arrived back at college. Professor Harris caught a separate taxi, much to my relief, saying he needed to pop home and change into his tuxedo.

In the taxi I checked my texts. Nothing. Not even from Robbie or Lachlan. What was going on?

I raced to my rooms, keeping an eye out for my friends, but they appeared to have vanished.? Once there, I threw on the tuxedo in record time. My father had bought it for me when I started Oxford. I dashed across the quad to the Senior Common Room. The Warden would surely be there right now, socializing as the head of college with the dons and the new students as they had the traditional pre-dinner drinks.

I felt the blood drain from my face when I scanned the room and realized she wasn't there. Where could she be? She never missed putting in an appearance at such events. My mind recalculated quickly, and I checked my phone—a major faux pas at this sort of college event. Still nothing.

I had to go on the assumption that I was the only one who knew it was Professor Harris. I would have to deal with this alone. There was a sort of poetic justice in that.

I slid out the door of the Senior Common Room, back across the quad, through the cloisters, and then crept quietly up the stairs in the Fitzjames building, armed with my plan to sneak into Professor Harris's study before he came back to college.

He would be calling from the privacy of his office—I was sure of it—and he would call soon. I knew if I didn't answer he wouldn't hang up. Oh no, he'd still need to tighten the screws by leaving a long, tormenting message. Above all, Professor Harris loved to hear himself speak.

I would hide behind his couch and record a video, capturing him and his voice—the irrefutable proof I needed.

My heart pounded. If I messed this up ... well ... I wouldn't let anything happen to Cedar. Maybe she didn't want to be protected, but that didn't change the fact I loved her. If she wanted to stay at Oxford, I would sacrifice myself to make that happen.

I snuck up to the study door. *Dammit.* Closed. I rested my ear against it. No sounds inside, so I twisted the doorknob slowly, carefully. I knew if I turned it too fast it tended to squeak, something that drove Professor Harris crazy and that no member of the maintenance crew had ever been able to fix.

I pushed it open a tiny bit and peered inside the study. Empty. I stuck one toe inside, but the sound of running water coming from the attached bathroom and the tap and clink of something against the sink made my heart contract.

He was changing here. He'd lied. There was no other explanation than he hadn't gone home at all. He must have ordered the taxi to one of the side entrances to the college that he could access with his staff key and snuck in to change in his office and make the phone call to me, his erstwhile victim.

My pulse raced. What if I could get behind the couch before he came out of the bathroom? I opened the door another little bit, but then the bathroom door of Professor Harris's study creaked open and he stalked across the carpet towards me. I leapt silently to the other side of the door and plastered my body against the wall. I held my breath.

He shut the door firmly. *Goddammit.* How was I going to trap him now? I would have to burst in while he was on the phone. It wasn't ideal – I wouldn't get a good recording, but I had to confront him. I had to do *something*. I could not let him get away with this.

I held my phone up in front of me and waited. At eight o'clock on the dot it vibrated. "Hello," I said, in a whisper. Luckily, I knew the door to Professor Harris's study was solid seventeenth century oak.

"Lord Invernay." That synthesized voice again, but now that I knew it was Professor Harris, it seemed obvious. Who else would want to destroy Cedar as well as me? Why hadn't I put the pieces together before? Me and my stupid tunnel vision—I would have to work on that. "I just checked my Swiss account and I'm dismayed to see no funds have been transferred."

"No," I answered. I needed to talk more, keep the conversation going until I could burst in on him and catch him in the act. I would video that, as much of it as I could get. How quickly would he hang up?

"Does this mean you're not going to come to your senses?" he asked.

"Before I decide, I'd like you to tell me exactly what you're planning on doing if I don't pay you?"

"You need a refresher? And I heard you were not entirely a dullard." What an awful man.

"Five hundred thousand pounds is a lot of money," I pointed out.

"So it is, but if you don't pay it, I'll send my entire gallery of photos of you and Cedar Wild shagging like wild animals on a punt on the River Cherwell to the Daily Mail." He clucked his usual five times. "Really, dear boy, such behavior is not at all the thing."

How had I fallen for his loathsome superiority when he was in reality such a worm? The knowledge that I'd considered him as a role model for so long made my entire body twitch in disgust.

"Wild animals?"

"Yes. Cedar Wild is no better than one to begin with, and instead of taming her she has turned you into no better than a savage yourself. Disgraceful." My fingers itched to wrap around his neck.

"Why do you hate her so much?" I crept in front of the door, whispering now.

"She is a disgrace to the Oxford name. Uneducated. Uncultured. Rebellious. When I see what she's done to you ... it makes me sick. Oxford needs to be rid of her and her kind. She has soiled you beyond repair, so you need to go as well."

The poison. Suddenly, my father didn't seem quite so bad in comparison. "Why do you care about the sanctity of Oxford so much?" I demanded. "Do you know me?"

"Don't be ridiculous."

I flicked my video on to record, turned the knob, and burst through. Professor Harris sat there behind his desk, his phone in one hand with a little black device—the voice synthesizer no doubt—beside him. Keeping my phone low and hidden from his line of sight, I made sure to get that in my video.

"How dare you?" I seethed. "You're a disgusting human being."

He hung up the phone carefully and sat back in his chair. From the calculating look in his eyes, the truth of what Lachlan said rung through—here was a person who needed to control everyone around him. He could not bear to feel like he didn't have the upper hand.

"You pompous snob," I hissed.

"Now, Alfred," he said, weaving his fingers together in front of him. "Be reasonable. Until that horrendous Cedar arrived here, you were endeavoring to be just like me, were you not?"

"Yes," I said. "And I've never been so ashamed of anything in my life. To think I had such role-models as Robbie and Lachlan, and I chose *you*."

His lips pressed together, and he gathered his wits about him. "It was rather clever of you to figure out it was me," he said, finally. "You can tell me how at a later date."

"I doubt it."

"Why is that?"

"Because you'll be in jail."

He chuckled then, and my breath came in ragged bursts of rage. "Don't be silly, dear boy. You have no proof. I would wager you have a video of me *hanging up my phone.* It will come down to your word against mine. Who will believe you, especially when I have the photos? They are excellent motivation for someone as foolish as you are to try to discredit me, aren't they?"

As much as I hated to admit it, he had a point. It might come to my word against his and he was a well-respected don. I was, well ... the son of my father. Still, he didn't know I'd been videotaping. I hoped to God I had pressed the right button, but I could hardly check now.

"I don't care what happens to me," I said. "I'll leave Oxford for good. The only thing I ask is that you leave Cedar out of this. I didn't tell her about your threat to get her removed from Oxford, and there's no reason she needs to worry about that."

"Oh ... but haven't you understood yet? My primary goal from the beginning was to get rid of her."

Under no circumstances would I allow that to happen. "I will do anything ... pay anything ... take any hit, but Cedar deserves this chance. She's brilliant and fascinating and capable. Cedar deserves to be at Oxford more than anyone here. If my father didn't exist, nobody would be interested in us at all. Make me suffer as much as you like, but not her."

"How very selfless, Lord Invernay." He arched a brow at me.

I pounded his desk and had the satisfaction of seeing him jump. I was a lot bigger than him, I realized suddenly. "If you expose one single thing about Cedar, I will make you pay. Trust me, it wouldn't be pretty."

He blinked, shocked. I'd never shown him this brutish side of me before, but I was not holding back now. "You wouldn't," he said, but with a slight quiver in his voice.

"Oh, but I would," I rested my knuckles menacingly on his desk, leaning in towards him. "You think you know me, but you don't. You don't know me. You think who I've pretended to be is reality, but that isn't the true me at all. I will not sleep until you have received your punishment, whether it be via my fists or some other means. Don't worry that I won't find a way, or that I'll be limited by the restraints of civilized behavior."

Professor Harris's eyes darted back and forth. Ha. He wouldn't look directly at me.

Before I could drive my threats home, a voice came from the doorway of the study I must have left open. "I don't think that will be quite necessary, Lord Invernay," the Warden said.

Cedar, Lachlan, Robbie, Shaun, Raphael, and Binita stood around her, their mouths open.

With a slight movement of the Warden's index finger, two uniformed police officers pushed through the crowd at the door and went over to the desk to clip a pair of handcuffs on Professor Harris.

"You are under arrest for blackmail, contrary to Section Twenty-One, Subsection One of the Theft Act of 1968," one of them said, as they hauled him away. "You do not have to say anything. But it may harm your defense ..." They left the room, leaving me to blink at my audience. *What had just happened*?

Before I could figure it out, my eyes found Cedar, wearing a sage-green, knee-length silk dress and looking as magnificent as she looked furious. How could I have been so stupid as to lose her?

CHAPTER THIRTY-EIGHT

Cedar

Alfie stood in the middle of Professor Harris's study, blinking at us after the police officers hauled Professor Harris away.

Professor Harris had made a threat against me, and Alfie had kept it a secret? I'd heard Alfie extolling my virtues, but that didn't change that he'd sidelined me again. Relief and confusion and anger warred inside me.

He'd made it clear that he was willing to sacrifice himself to keep me from suffering. That, of course, was touching, but how could he still not understand that it wasn't at all what I needed from him?

He'd kept me in the dark, removing my ability to participate in decisions that included me as much as him. How could he not understand that the only thing I wanted from him was honesty and that without it, nothing else mattered?

I pressed the heel of my hand against my sternum. God, it hurt.

"Please explain what just happened here," Alfie said, his hand shaking as he raked it through his hair. Part of me wanted to rush to his side, but I couldn't let myself do that with someone I didn't trust. "I don't—"

"We need to return to the dinner," the Warden announced regally. "By the way, there will not be a whisper of scandal about this. I will deal with the press if they intrude. I will tell them Professor Harris has resigned his fellowship for mental health reasons."

"Not entirely untrue," Binita said, crossing her arms in front of her.

The Warden sent her an appreciative glance. "Perceptive as always, Ms. Kapoor."

"But—" Alfie began.

"Come to the Hall with us, Alfred," the Warden said. "I'm sure your friends will fill you in on the way. Obviously, your text set this in motion."

"How much do you know, ma'am?" Alfie asked the Warden.

He glanced at me, telegraphing something I didn't understand.

I opened my mouth to tell Alfie that the Warden knew everything about us—there was no way I could tell her about the photos without giving her a bit of background—but before I could say anything, Alfie said, "You should know Cedar and I are together. I love her."

Are? Love? Why was he speaking in present tense?

The Warden held up her hand. "I know all of it."

Once we'd received the text from Alfie, we didn't have a second to lose. We took the information to Robbie. Robbie pointed out the Warden needed to be brought in for a sting to work. She was the one who could call law enforcement on behalf of the college, and she was our irrefutable witness. He'd assured us that we could trust her, that 'she was a right one, sharp as a tack.'

"So—" Alfie blinked, assimilating this information.

"Neither you nor Cedar are going to have any issues with the college or the university. From Beaufort College's point of view, your relationship is far from ideal, but you are both adults and these things happen. I happen to like both of you. I would hope you won't be spending a lot more time in punts, however."

Everyone grinned except Alfie and me. We exchanged haunted glances instead. Was he asking himself the same question as me—would we be spending any time together at all in the future? Or were we over?

"But why did Professor Harris do it?" Binita frowned, her need to understand every aspect of a situation on full display.

"Gambling debts," the Warden said. "His wife left him two months ago, you know. Also, he is an insecure control addict. He must have sensed he could never get Cedar under his thumb, and when he started to feel that Alfred was slipping away ... well, I never much liked him. He tried to convince me to get rid of the Commonwealth Scheme, but I rebuffed him."

"That's why he kept offering to bet me on things!" Alfie said, more to himself than the rest of us. "I always assumed it was a joke." He pinched the bridge of his nose and looked up at the coffered ceiling. "I've been such a fool," Alfie began. "I apologize to—"

"Yes, yes, you can do that on the way," the Warden said. She turned to walk back down the hall, and the rest of us followed. Out of the corner of my eye I saw Alfie shut the study door behind him and follow us.

Raphael started filling him in behind me—how we'd worked all morning to try and localize the number, but how we had been losing hope until we received his text. He explained how we'd spun into action. With Robbie's help (and his access to the keys) Raphael and Shaun had snuck into Professor Harris's study and bugged his phone while I'd gone to the Warden and filled her in on everything.

I stayed with her while she arranged for Professor Harris's arrest and made sure everything was handled as discreetly as possible. She'd been amazing.

"So how did you figure it out?" Raphael asked Alfie.

I held my breath, waiting to hear Alfie's answer.

"When Professor Harris clucks his tongue in disapproval, which he does far too frequently, he does it five times instead of the usual two, just like the voice on the phone," Alfie said. "I'm so sorry ... I was wrong about everything."

"But it ended up working out," Raphael said, forever kind. "And that's all that matters." Was it though, if Alfie's discovery was a mere fluke?

"Why didn't any of you text me back?" Alfie asked.

"We were far too busy," Raphael explained. "Once we received it, we were racing until we arrived at Professor Harris's study."

"I know you found the answer, but you still should have stayed with us," I said quietly to Alfie as we made our way down the stairs and into the cloisters. I needed to talk to him—alone.

Moonlight filtered through the arches of the cloisters, turning the golden stone to silver. The oak tree in the middle rustled in the night breeze.

"You're right," Alfie said, his blue eyes dark in the dim light as he studied me. "I've been blind in so many ways. Cedar and I need to talk," Alfie said. "We'll catch up. I cannot thank you all enough."

"I understand," the Warden said. "Come on, let's leave these two." With a majestic wave of her arm, she led them away.

Part of me wanted to go with them, and the other part of me knew that this confrontation had to happen. I reminded myself I didn't back down from a fight, yet my heart hurt at the knowledge that Alfie had kept things from me again. Did stopping Professor Harris change anything at all?

Alfie's phone vibrated and he held up his index finger. "Just a second. It's a text from my father."

I nodded and started to pace back and forth. I'd never felt like this before, like my body and soul were being held together by flimsy elastics, and they were about to snap.

Alfie rolled his eyes as he read the text.

"What is it?" I asked, then reminded myself I was no longer in a position to ask such things.

He took a deep breath. "My father. Just a warning to tell me the paparazzi might be descending on me again. He was caught on camera with the princess's hand up his kilt. Honestly, that man ..." But the way Alfie said it was different than usual. Instead of bitterness, his voice held a kind of exasperated affection.

His eyes met mine again, and he shrugged his left shoulder. "Compared to Professor Harris's brand of evil, my father's antics seem rather quaint in comparison."

Did this mean Alfie was going to stop living his whole life in reaction to Malcolm? If so, there was something good that had come from this ordeal.

Our friends' voices were finally swallowed up by the night.

I swallowed the lump in my throat. There might be improvement, but nothing changed the fact that Alfie had kept a critical secret from me. It would no doubt happen again. I couldn't accept that ... could I?

Alfie dug his hands deep into his tuxedo pockets. Surely, he could hear my heart pounding. He looked gorgeous in his tuxedo. He wore black-tie as easily as I wore my fleece and boots. A rush of heat beat through my limbs. I wanted to take it off him, piece by piece. How could I still want him so much when he'd let me down? I just didn't know what to do with all the contradictory pieces of information bombarding my brain.

He took a deep breath. I braced myself for an apology—one I didn't think I could accept.

"Cedar." His eyes crinkled in the corners. "Before anything, I just want to say you look stunning." His eyes were warm, but he kept flexing his fingers.

I hadn't been expecting that. I tugged at my dress, self-conscious.

"Binita came through," he added, with a quirk of his lips.

She had. It was sage-green silk with a tight middle part (what had Binita called that? A bodice?) and a flowy skirt that hit just above my knees. It looked good, even if I still wasn't convinced it looked like *me*. Binita had scoffed and said that humans were meant to constantly evolve. Maybe she was right—it would probably do me some good to expand my horizons. I studied Alfie. I'd never dreamed, though, that the process could be so painful when it came to the people we loved.

"Thank you," I said. "But my dress isn't what we need to talk about."

Alfie's shoulders dropped. "I know, but I had to say it. I know I messed up and let you and our friends down. Even though my trip inadvertently helped us, I should have stayed with you."

I looked down at my hands. "You abandoned me, Alfie. I thought we were a team, but you didn't even tell me about the threats Professor Harris made against me. It's ... humiliating and hurtful."

"I know." He bit his lip. "I cannot begin to explain how ..." His voice broke, but he managed to collect himself. "How sorry I am. I hated that being with me could cause you harm. I felt like it was my job to fix it."

"I am fine with that risk," I said. "Which you would have known if you'd bothered to ask me."

He nodded. "I know. I suppose part of me was also grasping for something solid to hold on to in the crisis. I grabbed on Professor Harris—an old habit that's now broken."

But who was to say that someone else wouldn't arrive in Alfie's life to take the now vacant spot of his former mentor?

"I realized too late that the solid thing in my life was you, Cedar." His eyes were imploring now, begging me to say something.

How could I not be moved by that? Still, it wasn't enough. "It should be you too," I said. "It can't just be other people in your life. You need to be your own anchor."

He stared at me, arrested. "You're absolutely right," he said, at last. "I think I began doing that today on the train, even before I realized about Professor Harris's guilt."

Waves of restless need swept through me. I wanted to fall into Alfie's arms and forget everything, but he probably would let me down again. Could I live with that? The old Cedar would have set 'no' in a heartbeat, but now ... the need to run away from all of this filled my body.

"Can we keep walking?" I asked. "I don't care where—I just need to move. I need to *think*."

Alfie's eyes went dark with concern. "Of course."

I began to walk out of the cloisters, towards the college exit.

"How much of my conversation with Professor Harris did you hear?" Alfie asked.

"Almost all of it, I think," I said.

"You mean ..." We headed out the college doors into New College Lane. Thank goodness everyone seemed to be at dinner. The lane was deserted. The yellow light of the streetlamps bounced off the damp cobblestones, and the air was filled with mist.

"Yes, I heard the part about you willing to sacrifice yourself for me. Why didn't you tell me about the threats towards me, Alfie?" I slowed down the pace now, trying to make sense of it.

"I was wrong. What I should have done was to tell you so that we could have dealt with it together."

"That's what I wanted. That's all I've ever wanted."

"I know. The thing is, Cedar, I'm only human. I feel like I made massive strides today in becoming more the person I am when I'm with you. He's who I want to become, but you must understand—I will make mistakes. Caution has been hard-wired into me and will probably always be a part of my nature. I want to learn, and change, but if I'm honest, I know I'll never be as fearless or unheeding of conventions as you. Can you accept that?"

I saw his truthfulness for the gift it was, yet ... "I don't know," I said, feeling as though I was being torn in two. I wanted to give him another chance, but he was saying he was probably going to let me down again. "You just abandoned me—left me alone and went off by yourself. It hurt ..." I swallowed hard. "More than I ever thought anything could hurt me."

"And proved your parents right about people." Alfie scrubbed his face with his hands.

"Yes. I'm furious about that." I hated that Alfie's actions had turned up the volume of that nagging voice in the back of my mind—maybe people were just a disappointment.

"Cedar, I'm so sorry, but you know, people aren't perfect."

"What do you mean?" I sucked in the chilly night air.

"We're all just trying our best, but most of us come into adulthood damaged in some way. We can heal each other, but that's a process of trial and error. Sometimes we let each other down before understanding how to do better. Usually over and over again."

"But how can I trust you?" I demanded.

"I don't know the answer to that, but you *can* believe I'm trying my best to change. Life is hard, and our pasts—yours and mine—haven't always been easy. We were both abandoned in our own way. It's going to take some trial and error before we get this right."

I clutched the bodice of my dress. "I don't know if my heart can handle that."

"Have you ever considered that expecting people to be perfect, then cutting them out when they're not, is its own form of cowardice?"

I blinked. How had I never seen things from that angle before? Was it because I'd never been exposed to a compassionate approach to my fellow humans? Alfie was right. I'd fallen back into that black or white thinking I grew up with again. "Point taken," I admitted.

"Do you want this evolving yet imperfect me?" he asked gently. "It's a package deal, I'm afraid."

"I—"

"Take into account that I'll probably always enjoy learning and academic gowns and old stone buildings and wearing a tuxedo from time to time. Part of me is pretty tame, Cedar ... not wild at all."

I could do that. In fact, I could see myself growing to love those things too. They were what made him Alfie, after all.

"But all of me loves you," he added.

I reached out and took his hand in mine. His hand trembled slightly, but his palm was warm and fit perfectly against mine. I was just about to tell him I loved him back when I happened to glance up. "Hey," I said. "Look where we are."

That now familiar Bridge of Sighs arched over our heads. The alley to The Turf was mere steps away from us. "This is where I found you that first night."

He smiled at me, his eyes luminous. "You turned my life upside down, Cedar Wild. Somehow, from the moment we first met, I knew you would. It terrified me. Now though, no matter what happens between us I'm so, so grateful."

He was letting me choose, without pressure or an ounce of dishonesty. He was being brave and laying himself bare.

I took a step closer to him, my breath ragged. If there was a moment in life to be fearless, it was now. His eyes opened a bit wider, and something sparked there.

"If we're going to do this for real," I said. "You have to promise me something."

"Cedar." He put his hand to his chest. "Believe me, anything."

"I guess I can handle you still being tame on the outside. It's probably an excellent complement to me—but I can only accept it on one condition."

"What's that?" He pulled me closer. I could make out his cologne and feel the heat of him coming through his tuxedo. Was that the beat of his heart, or mine? Every cell in my body longed to close the distance between us.

"Promise to save your wild for me."

His beautiful face changed completely, his eyes lighting up and his mouth curving into a slow smile that took my breath away. He stepped forward and gathered me in his arms. The feel of him surrounding me made my breath catch on a sob. It had been a hard twenty-four hours and, somehow, Alfie had become home.

"I'll be so wild for you, Cedar," he murmured in my hair, rubbing soothing circles on my back. "So wild I don't even know if you'll be able to handle it."

"Never underestimate what I can hande," I whispered. Our lips met in a kiss that felt as enduring as the Bridge of Sighs above us.

CHAPTER THIRTY-NINE

Alfie

I would have kissed Cedar forever except for the photographers shouting my name.

"Lord Invernay! What are your thoughts on wearing knickers under your kilt?"

"And the fact that your father does not?"

"Who are you kissing? What's your name, lass? Are you Lord Invernay's girlfriend?"

"When are you getting married?"

Cedar and I reluctantly broke apart, but instead of fleeing, I rested my forehead against hers. "We have visitors," I sighed.

"Really?" The corner of her mouth twitched up. "I hadn't noticed."

"Did you just get engaged?" another shouted.

The paps were getting ahead of themselves as usual. Nevertheless, Cedar and I had both taken a giant leap forward, although I certainly wasn't going to inform *them* about it. She was in my arms now, her silky bodice pressed against my torso and her hair brushing like silk against my jawbone. That was all that mattered.

"Tell us your name, lassie!" a deep-voiced pap shouted.

"Do you want me to roar like a bear again?" Cedar asked, low enough so her question was just for me. "I really enjoyed that last time."

I considered her question but, without me noticing an exact time or place in the past twenty-four hours, something had shifted inside me. Sure, there would probably be photos of us in the tabs tomorrow, all because my ridiculous father had been caught with the princess grabbing his manhood underneath his kilt. I could continue to torture myself about his behavior or I could laugh. Honestly, laughter was already bubbling up in my throat—laughter I wanted to share with Cedar.

I chuckled. "Maybe not tonight. It's been quite a day."

"It has," she agreed. "So, how do you want to handle them?"

"We'll make our way calmly back into college, but first ..."

"First what?"

"Do you want to do a twirl in front of them in your beautiful dress? Trust me, it deserves all the camera flashes and more."

Cedar grimaced. "I don't think so."

I threw my head back and laughed, ignoring the paps's continuing barrage of questions.

Tilting her head towards them, she raised her eyebrows at me. "You don't care about them anymore?"

I shook my head. "You were right about needing to be my own anchor. So they write stories and post photos of me, so what? I'm no longer going to give them the power to stop me from living my life." I leaned down and gave her one last kiss—a promise for later, after the dinner, when we would finally be alone.

She still had her arms around me and gave my bottom a little squeeze that the paps couldn't see. She'd understood the message. "All of a sudden, you seem lighter."

"I feel lighter. No matter what they say or do, the only opinions I care about from now are yours and Robbie's and our friends ... and my own, of course."

Her sparkling eyes widened. "That's pretty huge, Alfie."

"I know, and if you keep running your hands over me like that when I can just peer straight down your bodice, something else is going to be pretty huge."

Her shoulders vibrated with amusement. "I've heard some people say patience is a virtue, but I'm not sure I buy that. Maybe you could teach me."

A whole new range of possibilities unfolded in my imagination. "It would be my absolute *pleasure*."

When we were good and ready, I put my arm around her shoulders, and we walked back to the college door together. We simply ignored the photographers who continued to snap photos and hurl questions at us—questions I felt no compunction to answer.

She reached up and took my hand. "I know it's only been a day, but I missed you, Alfie. I thought I knew loneliness before, but it was nothing compared to the last twenty-four hours. Before, I didn't have a concrete idea of what I was missing. Today your absence was all too real."

"I'm sorry," I said, and dipped my head to kiss her temple. "Like I said, I will no doubt make more mistakes. Lots more."

Cedar grimaced. "I will too. I'm not perfect, so it's kind of ridiculous for me to expect others to be, isn't it?"

"It is." I squeezed her hand. We still had a lot to learn but now, I believed, we were finally able to give each other space and time to do that. "I missed you too. I realized what a fool I was the minute I boarded that train. I was wretched the whole day with the idea of losing you."

I opened the college door and shut it again after us, against the photographers.

"We'll make it up tonight," she said, her slanted eyes gleaming with mischief. My life would be a barren wasteland without that look in it.

"Deal." I leaned down and gave her a firm kiss to seal the promise.

"Will you do something with me on our way to the Hall?" she asked when she finally pulled away.

I grinned down at the expression on her face. My first instinct was to ask for more details, but it was time to start taking more leaps of faith. I tucked a loose strand of hair behind her ear. "What, my little rogue?"

"Run across the grass with me."

"Do we dare?" I raised my left eyebrow.

"Yes."

It wasn't exactly climbing up the Radcliffe Camera stark naked, but it was a start. "Let's go."

Her fingers weaved between mine. We were off.

CHAPTER FORTY

Cedar

The Dining Hall in its black-tie magnificence took my breath away almost as much as Alfie in his tuxedo running hand-in-hand with me across the quad grass. Almost, but not quite.

The lights were dim, the rustle of silk and satin was in the air, and everything felt touched with magic. Part of me still couldn't believe this was my life now—friends grinning at us from a table halfway down the Hall, and this dashing aristocrat with his arm still wrapped around my shoulder.

We stopped just inside the door. I was still reaching up and holding his hand and I gave his palm a brush with my thumb. "Are you ready for this, Lord Invernay?"

He smiled, then leaned down and planted a reverent kiss against my lips in front of the entire Hall. It was so urgent and ardent I worried my dress was going to singe right off my body. That was one of the things I loved about him—he kissed like a sailor arriving on shore leave.

I heard a few wolf-whistles and some applause in the distance, but if we didn't care about the paparazzi, we certainly weren't going to be distracted by any other audience. We took our time and then some.

When we finally parted, he sighed with relief. "I've waited too long to do that."

I shrugged, my face on fire. "Don't worry, we can make up for lost time."

"I'll be holding you to that."

Hand in hand, we joined our friends at their table.

"Just in time." Raphael winked at me. His hair was tied back in a low bun, and he looked completely different from the person I'd met eight weeks before. He was well on his way to appearing like some sort of rugged, Viking warrior-type. "You just missed all the prayers and speeches in Latin."

Lachlan couldn't wipe the grin off his face as he looked up at us. "Secret's out?"

"If it wasn't before, it certainly is now," Binita laughed.

"It took me far too long," Alfie took my hand under the table. "I owe you all a sincere apology for acting like a—"

"Daft pillock," Lachlan completed Alfie's sentence.

"Precisely." Alfie nodded. "Thank you all for everything you did for me."

"And for Cedar," Shaun said. "It wasn't just for you."

"For us," Alfie corrected himself.

"You guys were awesome," I added.

The first course of a silky parsnip soup, smelling sumptuous enough to temporarily halt our conversation, was brought to the table by an army of uniformed waiters. I examined my china soup bowl and the wine glass being filled for me more closely. They all bore the Crest of Beaufort College. How could I actually be living all this? Yet here I was, proof that anything was possible.

According to the individual menu propped in front of my place setting, still to come were a leek and chicken pudding, a raspberry syllabub trifle, a second dessert, then another dessert consisting of platters of cheese featuring Stilton and farmhouse cheddar with dried fruit and nuts, as well as chocolate truffles, with a choice of port or Sauternes.

"Have you looked at this *menu*?" I demanded. "Is it like this for every black-tie dinner?"

"Pretty much, but it's better seeing it through your eyes." Alfie watched me, his eyes sparkling in the dim light. "Everything is—it makes the whole world more interesting."

I thought of the not stepping on the grass rule, sub fusc, the names of our degrees, and our grades in Greek. "Or weird."

The crease in his cheek flashed. "That too."

"Two more students are coming from Canada in January on the Commonwealth Program. I wonder if they'll be as confounded as me?"

Shaun rubbed his hands together. "Goody. I can't wait to see what they're wearing."

"Be nice," I chided.

"Never," he grinned. "But I'm *always* charming."

"Cedar," Binita said, as we dug into our soups. "You'll have to take Alfie to the forest some time."

Everyone except Alfie roared with laughter.

"What?" Alfie demanded. "I'd do just fine. I played four years of Blues rugby and grew up in the Scottish Highlands."

"You probably would," I conceded. "But just in case I'd be there to take care of you."

"I would pay to see it." Lachlan chortled to himself.

"Dream on, my friend." Alfie pointed his soup spoon at Lachlan. "Even though I'm not as fussed about an audience anymore, some experiences are just for Cedar and me." Alfie stroked the curve of my waist as a reminder.

"No fair," Shaun grumbled. "You're going to deprive us of the chance to see you come to fisticuffs with a bear?"

"I am," Alfie said, remorseless.

"I wouldn't let that happen." On second thought, not everything in the forest was controllable ... and people were not that all that different I was fast discovering. "We look after each other or ... we're hoping to."

Alfie squeezed me close against his side. I could feel the long, firm muscle that ran down his torso. Later, I would take his tuxedo off piece by piece and kiss my way down his exposed skin. "The fact we're radically different actually makes us stronger."

"A force to be reckoned with." I gave a triumphant nod. Together, the possibilities felt infinite.

"That's actually a smart idea," Binita mused. "Looking after each other."

Raphael exchanged a look with Shaun. "It is," he said, his voice gruff.

Was Shaun actually *blushing*?

"We haven't mastered it yet," I said. "But we're eager to learn."

Alfie leaned down and whispered in my ear, "And we're going to be *very* devoted students."

I met his gaze, that current between us an endless loop of discovery. "You can bet on that."

Finis

THE BONUS EPILOGUE

Would you like to read the bonus epilogue for Oxford Wild featuring a Christmas camping trip in Scotland where the tables are turned? This time it's Cedar, not Alfie, in her comfort zone.

Just go to **mailchi.mp/laurabradbury.com/oxfordwildepilogue** to get yours!

THE GRAPEVINE

Interested in receiving Laura's recipes, sneak peeks at her new work, as well as exclusive contests and giveaways, insider news, plus countless other goodies? Sign up for Laura's Grapevine newsletter and join our fantastique community.

Just go to **www.bit.ly/LauraBradburyNewsletter**

Merci

I have many people to thank for Oxford Wild, as I do for all my books. First of all, a massive thank you to all my readers who have been with me through thick and thin (including several trans-Atlantic moves and a liver transplant!). I couldn't and wouldn't do this without you.

For Oxford Wild, my team was a truly international effort. Thank you to Jolene Perry in the US for her amazing developmental editing, as well as her tips from someone who grew up in the remote North. Sian Phillips in Wales squeezed me in for a copy edit, which I so appreciated. Enni Amanda in New Zealand at Yummy Book Covers created the bon-bon book cover of my dreams.

My fantastic beta readers Deb Maddox, Lucy Spence, Nicole, Kathy Meuller, and Julia Brickell (if I forgot you, I'm very, very sorry. I read every email and incorporated all the changes) improved the book so much and their eagle eyes helped me get rid of those nefarious typos.

The lovely Jennie Goutet, Julie Christianson, and Karen (KC) Dyer performed magic on my blurb and tagline. My fellow writers are seriously the best.

Thank you always to Trish Preston for being the most amazing unicorn of an assistant.

As always, thanks to my husband and my daughters for not

caring at all about my writing, and for constantly getting me away from my laptop. Life is never boring with the four of you.

Thank you to Nyssa for giving me life with her courageous decision to give me a large chunk of her liver almost five years ago. I never take one second of my bonus time for granted.

Thanks for Pepper, our rescue dog, for keeping me company on the couch as I wrote this.

And lastly, thanks to my disdainful law tutor at Oxford who said after I read one of my first property law essays out loud, "Your writing is quite engaging, even though your legal arguments are complete rubbish."

About Laura

Laura Bradbury is the author of the bestselling Grape Series, the award-winning cookbook Bisous and Brioche, and the Winemakers Series of Contemporary Romance novels.

She earned a law degree from Keble College, Oxford (with a respectable Upper Second thankyouverymuch) but Laura's true love was always writing. She married a Frenchman and ran off to France after graduation so she would have something to write about. Sign up for her beloved monthly Grapevine at www.bit.ly/LauraBradburyNewsletter or find her on IG at https://www.instagram.com/laurabradburywriter or on her website at www.laurabradbury.com

Author's Note

Writing Oxford Wild has been a lovely stroll down memory lane at a time when the world felt like it was in limbo between the COVID and post-COVID world. I wanted to write some pure romance candy (the kind I love) for a much-needed swoony escape. My inspiration for this book came from several different and weird places.

First off was my two years reading for a law degree (called a Bachelor of Jurisprudence because Oxford has its own words for everything) at Keble College, Oxford.

I spent a lot of time in the Bodleian Library while my Frenchman fiancé (you can read all about that in my Grape Series of memoirs) worked as a society photographer for Moet et Chandon champagne. I studied and went to pubs while Franck flitted over to Paris via Eurostar once or twice a month to take photos of Gerard Dépardieu quaffing champagne at a soirée at Versailles. I was jealous at the time, but when I look back on my Oxford years, I shouldn't have been. It was awe-inspiring to study in such a Kubla Khan of academia and history.

When studying at Oxford, I overlapped with Tom Parker-Bowles who was a student at Worcester College, on my bike route home to our flat. This was at the height of the affair between Charles and Camilla, and I remember the paparazzi camped out in front of the college gates and haunting the pubs and clubs he frequented, all because of his mother.

Unlike Alfie in my story, he had the reputation of being a party animal (he also chalked up a cocaine charge from that era). Still, I couldn't help but feel sorry for him.

I would have *loved* to study medieval literature at Oxford instead of law. My undergrad was in English and French Literature, and I spent my third year at the Sorbonne studying old French texts with the professor who did the definitive translation of Tristan et Iseult from old French to modern French. A sense to do something "practical" with my Literature degree let me to law, but I never practiced and now I'm a happy full-time writer. LOL.

I had a tutor at Oxford who was not dissimilar from Professor Harris (except for the gambling and blackmail). He taught me well, but we quickly developed an aversion to each other. He was a priggish Brit, whereas I was a bumpkin from the colonies who laughed too loud and didn't pronounce words the proper way.

Cedar is an extreme version of the Canadian student at Oxford. I grew up in a small city, but by age twelve I could gut a fish, hand fish crab, and shoot a deer. Even after living in Paris, Oxford was a complete culture shock.

The idea for the Bear research done by Cedar's parents is inspired by real-life work that recently blew my mind. Just go here: https://www.genomebc.ca/blog/link-between-grizzly-bear-dna-and-indigenous-languages-found . Fascinating.

FIND LAURA ONLINE

THE GRAPEVINE NEWSLETTER

bit.ly/LauraBradburyNewsletter

INSTAGRAM

instagram.com/laurabradburywriter

TWITTER

twitter.com/Author_LB

BOOKBUB

bookbub.com/authors/laura-bradbury

FACEBOOK

facebook.com/laurabradburywriter

BOOKS BY LAURA BRADBURY

GRAPE SERIES

My Grape Year

My Grape Québec

My Grape Christmas

My Grape Paris

My Grape Wedding

My Grape Escape

My Grape Village

My Grape Cellar

THE COOKBOOK BASED ON THE GRAPE SERIES MEMOIRS THAT READERS HAVE BEEN ASKING FOR!

Bisous & Brioche: Classic French Recipes and Family Favorites from a Life in France

by Laura Bradbury and Rebecca Wellman

THE WINEMAKERS TRILOGY

A Vineyard for Two

Love in the Vineyards

Return to the Vineyards

Made in the USA
Las Vegas, NV
03 May 2022

48384659R00210